From the moment he met her on shipboard, he had thought of nothing else but her strange, haunting beauty. But Eric Andersen finally told himself that the likes of Sophia Hill were not for him.

And then, one night, she appeared in the doorway of his room.

He walked toward her, gently took her in his arms and began to kiss her.

She pulled away from him. There was a wild, new look in her eyes.

"Is that the best you can do, Eric?"

FROM THE REVIEWS

EDISON MARSHALL

PRINCESS SOPHIA

POPULAR LIBRARY • NEW YORK

POPULAR LIBRARY EDITION
Published in January, 1960

Copyright © 1958 by Edison Marshall
Library of Congress Catalog Card Number: 58-8103

Published by arrangement with Doubleday & Company, Inc.
Doubleday & Company edition published in August, 1958
First printing: April, 1958
Second printing: September, 1958

Published in England by Frederick Muller Ltd. in April, 1959

DEDICATION:

*To four true physicians, of the staff
of the Medical College of Georgia, in
order of seniority,*

VIRGIL PRESTON SYDENSTRICKER

JOSEPH DEWEY GRAY

WALTER EUGENE MATTHEWS

ROBERT BENJAMIN GREENBLATT

whose art has sustained my unwearied pen.

AUTHOR'S NOTE

The main characters in this novel are fictitious and are not intended to resemble any real person living or dead.

The story of the S.S. *Princess Sophia* embraced in this book is true in the main. I have used the real name of her captain, L. P. Locke, and depicted him according to the description given me by one of his fellow ship captains. The scene of his naming of the vessel after Sophia Hill is fictitious. His thoughts and remarks related here are fictitious, although in keeping with my concept of his character. The real names of some of his officers and of the captains of other vessels concerned with the story of the *Sophia* are given. The behavior of her passengers and crew during the crisis is described according to my concept of the Alaskan.

I am deeply indebted to Captain Lloyd Bayers of Juneau for access to his records of known events at Vanderbilt Reef between 2 A.M., October 24, 1918, and 8 A M , October 26, 1918. All conjecture beyond what is known is the author's own.

BOOK ONE

1. The Strange Girlhood of Sophia Hill

The big house of plantation style where Sophia Hill was born stood in the town of Beaufort, on the South Carolina shore, once the summer resort of the rice aristocracy, whose broad lands fronted the rivers Tulafinney and Combahee. It compared favorably in size and dignity with most southern plantation houses and had somewhat more grandeur, although it fell far short of a few baronial halls near Charleston and Richmond, some millionaire's mansions in the North, or certain country seats in Europe.

It was of frame, painted white, with long verandas where sitters in the evening could catch the breeze. From the front entrance to the stairs ran a wide hall on which opened four spacious, high-ceilinged rooms, the seaside and the landside parlors, the dining room, and the library. Behind the stairway stood two other rooms, one a pantry and laundry with passage to the separately built kitchen, and a sewing room, which was once the nursery. Four large and airy bedrooms lay overhead, one pair quite fine, the other comfortable; in the rear was an immense bathroom, a linen room, a storeroom, and the narrow stairway leading to the attic. Each of the eight main rooms had a fireplace with a decorative mantel. The main stairs boasted mahogany banisters. The furniture was heavy and rather pompous, fashioned in the last or the next to the last decade before the Civil War, when the rice fields prospered well.

The fact remained that the interior of the big house, throughout its lifetime until now, was never as attractive as its exterior. No doubt the main cause was its setting, a wooded point of land thrust into the bay facing Ladies Island. The high tides of the full moon—"pow'ful tides," as Sarah Sams described them—rose without sound or foam to the top of its sea wall, and in the mossy gloom of the live oaks the mockingbirds sang almost as sweetly as Keats's nightingale in her leafy bowers.

In the days when its owners, the Sams family, stood among the foremost of the planter aristocracy, its white paint was spotless and its shutters bright green. Yet even then its effect upon the mind was dimly sad. At close range you could not see its whole: it looked partly overwhelmed, about to be crushed by the moss-hung limbs of the giant trees. Then in those three troubled decades following the Civil War, when the Samses were going to seed, like most of the rest of the rice-planting families, and the paint flaked off in ugly patches and the faded shutters hung awry, it became a study in melancholy. Yet strangely it appeared to possess more real beauty than ever before.

About the year 1888 it began to attract the attention of a few excursionists making their way from northern cities to Charleston, Key West, and newly founded Palm Beach. Already the Old South was becoming legendary, a dream of romance was weaving in the American mind, and when a tourist stopped and gazed at the old mansion he was often compelled to question a venerable Negro, himself born a slave, who cut the lawn and milked the cow and mulched the rose garden. The answer, stripped of its almost incomprehensible Gullah dialect, was of this order:

"Suh, dis hee is de old Sam place. I done took kay of it long befo' ol' massa die. But nobody of 'at name live hee now. De las' was Miss Julia Sam, and she marry de professa 'at come from Bossen. Maybe you hea o' him? He name Professa Hill, and he 'pointed presi*dent* of de colud school on Lady Island.

"Yessuh, de rich people up no'th who found Fairbank School for de colud, dey 'point Miss Julia's husband—befo' dey marry—de presi*dent*. Pitty soon she die of de cough, but de professa live hee yet, wif de little girl, she eight yee old now, what Miss Julia bornded.

"Her name Miss Sophy. 'At as good as I can say it. But her las' name Hill, and so dey ain't no Sam live hee no more, 'scusin' Sarah and me, and her pa and me took 'at name when Abe Linkum set us free."

2

Sophia's name came from the Greek word meaning wisdom. Most people, white and colored, mispronounced it *Soph*-ia, but the correct pronunciation was So-*phi*-a, the middle syllable rhyming with pie. She lived up to her name, at least in being remarkably quick to learn, and at eight she had picked up and stored away far more knowledge than the house girl, Sarah, could quite realize. For instance, she knew the inward lives of both Sarah and the old gardener,

8

Phineas, better than did her father, whose card read "Stanley Hill, Ph.D.," but whose real name, in all that really mattered to her yet, was "Dear Papa." She understood perfectly their Gullah speech. Their words were short and apt, used and reused, although with many picturesque and fanciful connotations. Their occasional attempts to tell secrets in her presence almost always failed; these were so poorly disguised and she was so practiced at listening to Dear Papa, whose learned speech was one long riddle at whose meaning she must grope and guess.

She knew the old house well, from its landside parlor where she sometimes sat, playing grown-up lady, to the recesses of the attic. This she had begun to explore when she could barely toddle up the narrow stairs, and it was still a source of unending fascination. Here were stored, along with much summer heat, such things as broken furniture, chipped china, and cracked glass; a baby carriage, the splendid like of which had not been seen on the Beaufort footpaths these fifty years; bassets covered with leather or pieces of carpet in varied patterns; mahogany sewing boxes with angular tops; albums of pictures of men in uniforms and ladies in satin brocade; a children's landau that a strong slave or a small pony could draw; dolls that looked good as new except for dust, some of them more beautiful than Sophia's own best-beloved doll; children's books with carved wooden covers, and big lithographs and paintings in gilded frames.

Among the dressmakers' forms, neatly covered in black jersey, stood one at which Sophia would stand and stare with a fast-drumming heart. It was taller and much more slender than the others. It was the most shapely, too, a beautiful young woman's shape; still, she wished it was not here, that she could go out in the night and dig a hole and bury it in the ground. She knew too well whose body it *imitated*—this last a Negro term for any likeness. Over the high mantel in the seaside parlor, the best parlor, where Sophia almost never went, hung a portrait of a girl of about fourteen, fresh as in life, whose young body held the promise of this very beauty. And among the big leather trunks, overflowing with mementos of the great days of the Samses, was one as strongly locked as Bluebeard's room. A long time ago she had asked Sarah what it contained. Sarah had told her, along with the injunction never to meddle with it, never touch it. Well, Sophia had no wish to touch it, let alone

9

open it. She wished she could dig a hole and bury it in the ground.

Sarah never went to the attic with her and sometimes tried to keep her from going, then pretended not to know that she had gone. Sarah was afraid of meeting someone, who walked lightly in silence on the narrow stairs, or seeing that same one, dimly beautiful as a fading sunset, bending over the locked trunk.

The space, the place, the strange deep hollow that she searched most carefully of all was a gilt-framed looking glass, with its ornate base and scroll standing twelve feet tall in the front seaside bedchamber. The face that she found there was not very pretty—yet. In fact, she thought, grown-up people would call it plain. It appeared too broad for its length, the eyes too long and narrow and deep-set, the nose a curved bump like every child's, the mouth wide and thin, and the chin strong. She knew all that would change—she would make it change. Her skin was not as white as people expected in a girl of such pale gold hair. If it would look better to be whiter, a better match for her fair hair and light-colored eyes, she would make it grow so. Her clothes were not very becoming. Dear Papa did not have much money, so Sarah, who could not sew very well, made her everyday clothes and the second-best child's dressmaker in town made her Sunday clothes. That did not matter, since Dear Papa liked them, and anyway all that would be different when she grew older. Meanwhile no clothes could be as important as what she saw in the mirror when she wore none at all.

The occasions were not frequent. She was afraid of being caught making this close scrutiny, and it made her flush with guilty excitement, as when Dear Papa bathed her in the big, porcelain-lined, mahogany bathtub. Even so, her main sensation was sharp pleasure. At other times she could not remember, or at least quite believe, that her young body could be so beautiful.

It looked just as it should look, she felt. She would never have to change it, only let it grow in the present pattern. Her legs were already long and rounded, her waist distinct, her shoulders pretty as a picture, her neck long and slim, and—what no boy could boast of—already there was the shadow of a promise, more surmised than seen, of what Sarah called "de fine bus' of a lady." When the slow years passed, and the live oaks grew thicker of trunk and wider

10

of branch, the dressmaker's form that would be made for fitting her long dresses would be just like the beautiful one in the attic. Perhaps it would be even more beautiful, she thought quickly. Then all the stars that twinkled in the warm sky would wake and shine.

When she stood sideways to the mirror, looking over her shoulder, she saw that she stuck out boldly behind and slightly in front. Well, that was all right. Dear Papa had spoken of it once, half in fun, then had told her gravely that it should be so, and she must never be ashamed of any part of the lovely body that nature meant to give all little girls. Then he had said something else, more to himself than to her, which her quick ear caught and her quick mind captured and remembered word for word, although the meaning she did not know.

"There is nothing in the wide world as beautiful to the sight as the human form. To male eyes, the female. To female, the male. Many other visible beauties are its reflections."

And as for her plain face, she would make it beautiful. She would think and think, and wish and wish, and, perhaps the most powerful magic, dream and dream. All this she must do and, cross her heart and hope to die, she would do, to please Dear Papa.

3

It was Sophia's way to wake up at six every morning, make her face shiny bright with soap and water, comb and brush her hair until it shimmered in the mirror, put on a clean dress, then go down to the dining room to wait for Dear Papa. He appeared on the stroke of seven, clean-shaven, hungry, noisy, beautifully dressed, more tall than she had dreamed last night, his bony scholar's face with its great forehead as gay as his vibrant voice. As soon as he had kissed her he would begin shouting to Sarah to bring breakfast—lots of eggs, country sausage, grits with gravy, and pancakes with maple syrup shipped from his own cold North. He had always time to talk with her awhile—the subject ranging from cockroaches to constellations—before, at ten minutes to eight, he ran to catch the ferry to Ladies Island. From then until about five she moved in a kind of dimness. This brightened a little when she sewed or shelled peas or strung beans with Sarah or when she tagged after old Phineas about the garden, looking at birds' nests

11

and bugs and little green snakes, but it thickened and became strange and almost frightening when she roamed the big silent rooms alone.

At five in the afternoon she took her seat on the veranda. Her heart would be waiting almost still, like a dog in a doorway, then suddenly it would bound up. Into the walled yard would come Dear Papa, in his bouncing stride. Then began the good time, the time of wishes coming true, when the hard times that had come "a-knockin' at de do'" in the song Dear Papa loved to sing were as far away and unthinkable as the ice and snow of which she sometimes dreamed in a deep, sinking dream in the full black tide of night.

Dear Papa gave her lessons, but these were not work, only a thrilling game, which, by hard listening and strong storing away and quick thinking, she almost always won. Reading and writing came first, these were the most important; unless she mastered these the wonderful gates of the golden cities would not open, and all the roads she could ever travel came to dead ends. There was always geography and history—so she could know where she stood in space and time—and some arithmetic to teach her precision. Best of all, there was always one story—usually of gods and heroes who lived long ago, or great adventurers in the West, or of a battle where tall young men hurled themselves against the guns and died—or always one long poem which Dear Papa read aloud, or a short one she must learn by heart. Dear Papa said that poetry was meat for the imagination, and that she must gorge on it because beautiful witches were hard put to it to do their job of enchanting unless they had been fed on poetry when very young.

Sophia knew what enchant meant. Morgan le Fay had enchanted the great hero, Roland. "But I never want to enchant any man but Dear Papa," she thought, with a glowing heart.

At eight o'clock school was out, and Dear Papa had emptied a tall glass, misty with coolness, of whisky and water. Between then and half-past eight he had another, while both of them ate the good things Sarah had left in the icebox—fried ma'sh hen, ham smelling of the smokehouse, and sometimes the small sweet oysters that Phineas gathered in his bateau, not a stone's throw beyond the sea wall, or clams from the beach, or even deviled sea gulls' eggs, and, in season, sliced duck shot in the abandoned rice fields.

And then there came the last act of the day—of the play, she might say, because Dear Papa had already read to her parts of *Midsummer Night's Dream* and taken her to see *Beauty and the Beast* performed in Charleston, and life with him was somehow like a play.

She did not say even to herself that it was the best part of her day. She thought it sometimes, flushing a little, then quickly turned her attention to some other matter. What happened was only a nice warm bath with plenty of soap. When she had undressed and got in the tub Dear Papa would come in, laughing and joking, take off his coat, roll up his sleeves, and make sure she was as clean as a whistle. She did not know why, in that little wait before he came, her heart beat so fast. Sometimes she could hardly follow his gay talk, her attention became so fixed on his strong, silk-smooth hands. Sometimes, though, his words died away and a different look came into his face, and she lay perfectly still in the tub, with her gaze on the ceiling.

The faculty of Fairbanks College usually met on Saturday, when there were no classes, although about once a month he sent word by a colored messenger for Sarah to stay and give Sophia her supper and her bath and sit up in the Big House until he returned, for he would be out late. Every so often he came home, bathed, changed, and went out to dinner to the home of a friend. On such nights Sophia had a good time with Sarah, making clothes for her doll, or hearing stories of Sarah's childhood on Ladies Island, or talking about hants. But when Sophia went to bed she slept not at all or very lightly with strange, wandering dreams until she heard Dear Papa's light, quick step on the stairs.

Spring had come again to the Low Country, and the ashes in the big hearth were cold, and the gray moss greened, and the sand fiddlers scuttled wildly in the tide runnels when this lovely order began to change. The first sign of the oncoming crisis was like a pale-colored thunderhead a long way off in the sunny sky, looking hardly bigger than her hand. When she looked again it had become incredibly more tall and broad, and almost before she knew it, it had spread heaven-wide and blotted out the sun and the lightning zigzagged to the ground in furious darts and the thunder crashed and the dark rain roared.

More and more frequently Dear Papa sent word of a late homecoming. He spoke of work piling up at the college: no doubt that was the reason. But instead of getting better, it got worse, until it came about that he stayed away from Sophia two or three evenings every week, and all of Sunday afternoon. Almost nine now, her nipples itching as they swelled, she would not speak of it for all the world, least of all to Dear Papa himself, and Sarah pretended not to notice it. Even when he stayed at home he acted differently, gazing at Sophia with a troubled gaze.

On a sunny Sunday afternoon, when lonesomeness had driven her out of the echoing house onto the lawn, a neighbor boy named Lucas Elliot came running lightly through the gate, bouncing and catching a ball. She was quite sure that she did not like Lucas—in the first place he presumed too much on his being a year and some months her senior, and she found him disturbing in other ways. While indubitably graceful, brunette and tall and handsome like so many of the best boys of the Carolina Low Country, he was self-assured to the point of arrogance, and when he pulled her hair it was not to tease but to hurt. Still, today she found herself welcoming his visit.

"Your pop isn't home today, so I reckon you won't mind my dropping by to see you."

"No, he's not here. His name is Dr. Hill, not my pop. But you're welcome as long as you mind your manners."

"Where is he, by the way?"

"That's his business, not yours."

"You always start spittin' fire as soon as I mention him. But I didn't have to ask you where he is. I already know."

"Then you can talk of something else."

"All Beaufort knows where he is. He's spending the afternoon with Miss Howard, the young, pretty teacher from Baltimore who took Mr. Thompson's place when he got sick at Christmas. Her first name is Juliette, somethin' like your mamma's first name, Julia. He must think quite a lot of her to be with her two or three nights every week and every Sunday afternoon."

He had said all this while he bounced his ball, every movement lithe and precise. It was a great stock of ammunition to fire in one burst, but how great he did not know. That he must never know. She did not answer at once; as when Dear Papa put a hard problem to her, she must take her time and think with all her might and main. Lucas liked to hurt her. She did not run after him as did some of the

14

other girls at children's parties and she knew so many things of which he was ignorant. The fact remained he had somehow guessed a little part of her secret. It took all the strength of her mind and heart not to reveal that he had hurt her more than pulling out one hair at a time till she was bald.

Still this did not mean that he had spoken the truth. That part she could not yet deal with—whether or not he was lying. The immediate emergency was to save her pride.

"I guess you're too ig'rant to know why he and Miss Howard spend a good deal of time together," she answered, pretending to look for a four-leaf clover.

"Well, I can guess."

"Are you sure?"

"Everybody says they're fixing to get married." His tone was not now so confident.

"That would be lovely if it turns out so. He says that she's the smartest young woman anywhere around here. Well, since you don't know, I'll tell you. At present they're writing a book together."

"A book?"

"One that you wouldn't be able to read. It's going to be published in Boston and sent all over the world. It's to be named *Negro Folkways in America, and Their Origin in the Dark Continent*."

She did not know that she had passed the hardest examination ever given to her; anyway it hardly mattered beyond this moment, for nothing in the world that she could say could set at naught what he had said.

Lucas was plainly beaten for the time being. He stopped bouncing his ball and put it under his arm and gave her an uneasy glance.

"I never said they weren't writing a book. If they wrote it together, that would make it all the more likely they'd get married. And you've turned mighty white about something, Sophia."

"Why should I turn white? You're seeing things."

"Anyway, lots of people say that he ought to marry again, if only so you could have a mother. Every girl needs a mother. They say he ought to send you to public school instead of being your whole family and your schoolteacher besides. One lady said it was unhealthy—somethin' like that—for you and Professor Hill to live all alone in this big

15

house. You might turn out the smartest girl in Beaufort but you still need a woman's care—a nice stepmother or an old white woman for a housekeeper."

"I'll leave it to Dear Papa to say what I need."

"Well, all right, Sophia, are you invited to Janie Lou Simmons' birthday party next Thursday at Port Royal?"

"Yes——"

"If you want me to, I'll have Moses drive by in our carriage and pick you up. He's going to drive me anyway and it won't be any trouble."

"Why, that would be very nice."

4

Sophia came quietly into the house. Her head was empty; she made it so. Her heart was empty, too, it seemed, or numbed like her arm when she had lain on it in bed; the only thing she could think of to do now was to look at the clock. A tall clock that one of Dear Papa's family had shipped to him from Boston stood in a back downstairs room. It was tall and lean and severe-looking, with no decoration and a very plain face, out of keeping with Low Country parlors; still, that was the proper appearance for a clock, she thought. It was on no frivolous business on the earth, it meant exactly what it said; the hour was so-and-so and all the king's horses and men could not change it one iota; a certain point had been reached in everyone's life and there was no retreat.

It said five forty-five. She had thought it was later than that. About six hours and a quarter from now she could expect to hear Dear Papa's step on the stairs; until then she did not know what to do. She wished she could sleep, but, even so, she would dream, gray dreams, weaving slowly and sorrowfully. She wished she could die until then. God was too strict not to let His children die when they liked, stay dead until a wind changed, or a tide went out, or the trouble that they saw had passed away, then come back to life. But once dead, perhaps they would not want to come back, everything was so dark and quiet, and in that case His will would not be done.

When she heard Dear Papa come in she would get up and open the door and ask him to go down with her to the best seaside parlor and light the chandelier. Then with that beautiful young girl looking down at her from the picture, she would ask Dear Papa to speak truth.

16

Beyond that her thoughts refused to move. Now she walked slowly upstairs, shut the door of her room, took off her pretty Sunday dress, and lay down on her bed. When Sarah would come to tell her that supper was ready—Sarah fixed her nice hot suppers on these days of Dear Papa's absence—Sophia would tell her that she had taken a headache from looking too long at the sunlit bay.

Not much more than an hour had passed, the sun was barely down and the windows glimmered, when she heard someone running up the stairs. Her door burst open and there stood Sarah, her eyes big.

"Miss Sophy! I couldn't find you nowhay. Why for you go get in de bed? Now you gotta get up and put on yo' pitty dress, for dey company come and waitin' for you in de bes' room."

"What company——?"

"De boss done bring a lady and he say for you to come down and make her 'quaintance."

When Sophia began dizzily to put on her dress Sarah helped her, then poured water in the bowl in which to dampen a cloth and wipe her face, then gave her hair a quick brush.

"You look mighty pitty now," Sarah told her in her rich voice, "and don't my Possum be skay, and no matta what yo' papa tell you, don't you cry!"

No, she was not scared—she was past all that—and she would never cry in the lady's hearing. That much was settled.

In a moment more she had entered the seaside parlor, tall as she could walk, a smile on her face. Dear Papa and the visitor had been sitting on the small, high-backed sofa, but both rose, smiling. Dear Papa's smile looked strained and perhaps his face was not as ruddy as usual, although he was never more handsome or stood so tall and proud. The lady's smile was sweet. Sophia had not expected her to be so young —not more than twenty-five while Dear Papa was nearly forty. Sophia did expect her to be this beautiful. She had seen her before, as Lucas was talking about her, in a kind of daydream. She looked quite tall, even when standing beside Dear Papa, and was slender and shapely. Her hair was almost raven black and her eyes were a startling blue, yet the bad daydream that Sophia had dreamed had come true. She had a dim but sure resemblance to someone always in this room, who lived here in some strange way, the reality

17

of the image in the lifelike portrait over the fireplace. And that, Sophia thought, with a wave of darkness in her brain, was why Dear Papa loved her.

"Juliette, I wish to present my daughter, Sophia," Dear Papa was saying in his jubilant voice. "Sweet, this is Miss Juliette Howard, from Baltimore. Now let's all three sit down, for we have something serious to talk about."

He smiled at Miss Juliette, and she returned the smile, and then he remembered to give a big smile to Sophia. When they were seated, Sophia's feet side by side as she had been taught, he spoke on.

"We'll come straight to it. It is too important to—well —beat about the bush. Sophia, as you probably know, Juliette and I have been seeing a good deal of each other. We have reached the point now that we must make a decision. It concerns you very deeply. The way you feel about it will determine whether she and I shall go on or turn back. We have agreed on that."

"Perhaps you could state it a little more simply for her," Juliette suggested, her eyes big and bright.

"I understand perfectly well," Sophia said.

"Juliette and I are not engaged to be married," Dear Papa went on. "No matter how much I care for her, I couldn't ask her to marry me until I got your permission. Some people would think that was a strange thing—and a strange way to put it. I don't think so and neither does she. The question of your happiness comes first. Both she and I are already happy in our work and lives. We both think we could have a happy, successful marriage, provided you'd be happy too. If not—and although there's no hurry about your deciding, I feel that you will soon know perfectly well —she and I are not so much in love that we can't part. If you want our lives to go on as they are, we will part."

"I don't think this is quite fair, Stanley," Juliette broke in, "although I don't know why. Listen, Sophia, I had a stepmother and it didn't work out very well. But I remembered my own mother, and you don't remember yours, and so this might be different—and better. I think I could love you very much, Sophia. Now tell your papa and me whether you think you could love me."

"I'm sure I could, Miss Juliette," Sophia answered in a firm voice.

"Do you mean it, darling?" Dear Papa demanded.

"Of course I do. She's pretty and sweet as my own

18

mamma was, I feel sure. You've every right to get married. I'll be getting married someday—to someone like Lucas Elliot—and I wouldn't want you to be alone with no one to love you."

"Stanley——" But Miss Juliette stopped and her lips closed tight.

"What is it, my dear? You'd better say what you're thinking. This is a critical moment. We'd better not leave any stone unturned."

"It's incredible—the way she talks! Stanley, you had no right to let this child be so old for her years. She doesn't even cry—her eyes are bright as jewels! I feel that there's something wrong——"

"There's nothing wrong at all, Miss Juliette. Papa had to have someone to talk to, so he talked to me. I know lots of big words, but that doesn't change me."

"Will you kiss me, Sophia?"

"I'd love to kiss you."

Sophia got up, leaned down a little, and kissed Juliette's cheek.

"She meant that, Juliette," Dear Papa said.

"I believe it now. Her lips were so soft."

"Then we can consider it settled?"

"Yes," Sophia answered, "and if you please, I'm going up to my room for a little while. This has been a big surprise—and I want to lie down."

"Certainly you may, my sweet. No one will disturb you, but if you'll come down and have a little icebox supper with Juliette and me, we'll be greatly pleased."

It had not been a big surprise, Sophia thought, as she climbed the stairs. That was a fib, but she had to tell it in order to explain the rest of her sentence, which was true. She wanted to lie down and never get up again. She wanted to go to sleep and never wake. She wanted to be done with Sophia forever, to fix Sophia so she wasn't any more. She thought of the big knives, long, bright, sharp knives, that would cut open a big beef roast, let alone a soft little girl like her, but these were in the kitchen, out of her reach. She thought of Dear Papa's guns, a revolver and a shotgun, but either one would make a big noise, and she did not want that; she wanted everything to be very quiet. By the time she had got into her room, a back seaside room almost always cool, breezy in a southeast wind, she saw her way perfectly clearly.

In her deep tall closet lay a wooden box containing many of her summer clothes. With some difficulty, because her hands were shaking and her muscles feeble, she untied the hard knots of the quarter-inch rope with which the box was fastened and pulled it free. Then she tied a noose in it, neat as could be, with a slipknot such as Phineas fixed on his mooring line, and by pulling aside the hangers where hung some of her prettiest dresses she bared three feet of a lead pipe running across the closet from wall to wall. She fumbled and almost fell when, standing on the box, she fastened the end of the rope to the pipe, the noose hanging two feet below and well over four feet above the floor. Her final act of preparation was to push the chest well to one side and stand it on end.

But this last labor spent her strength, and in trying to breathe she sobbed. Running to her bed she fell upon it, shaken with uncontrollable sobbing. She had wanted quietness and still tried to get it by stifling the sound in a pillow. The spell began to pass. Strength was coming back to get up and do what she must do, a last act of love for Dear Papa and of escape and, in some way, of penance for some great sin. It was a hard chore and harsh punishment, although she need not fear the pain. She would jump hard and her pretty little neck would break to check her fall.

And she had started her first movement, slow and weak, to rise from the bed when she heard Dear Papa's feet drumming fast and loud upon the stairs.

She could not lock her bedroom door because it had no lock. All she could do, in what little time remained, was to slam her closet door. When Dear Papa burst into the room she was standing by her bed, her arms rigid at her sides, her fingers spread and quivering, and her heart fainting.

"Sophia! You've been crying."

"I couldn't help but cry a little——"

"That's not all. What else has happened? Why are you so pale? What door was that that slammed?"

"I shut the room door——"

"No, it was your closet door." He started toward it.

"Please don't open it! I beg you, Dear Papa. If you love me even a little——"

"A little. God knows I love you more than anyone in the world. I always have. I always will. I knew it as soon as you went out, and I told Juliette. She and I are not going to be

20

married. We've broken off for good, and she is as glad as I am. Now tell me what's in the closet that you don't want me to see. If you don't, I'll have to open it. I'm your father. You're in my care."

"Don't open it. It's all done with now. I thought—I don't know what I thought."

"Were you going to run away?"

"I wanted to go away. But I never will, as long as you stay with me. And I'm so happy!"

"Then I won't open it. And all will be the same as it was before."

Her tears ran down her face although she did not make a sound. Dear Papa came up to her and bent down and kissed her in a way that was their secret, his lips lying motionless against hers for a long time. Then he went quietly out of the room.

Within five minutes the box of clothes was again bound with the rope, the knots were retied, and everything else was in place. Anyone could look in the closet and never imagine the evil dream that had almost come true among the pretty dresses hanging on the bar.

5

All was the same as before in the big house among the live oaks, as Dear Papa had promised. The little change that came a few months after Sophia's tenth birthday did not count. At least she told herself so, and set her mind not to think about it or hardly notice it. The fact that she dreamed about it, the dream getting stronger or weaker as it wove, like music heard far off, she did not attempt to explain.

It started with Sarah remarking that Possum had been growing like a beanstalk. Possum was her pet name for Sophia, given to her because of her large-pupiled pale-colored eyes that Sarah said could see like a possum—better than a wil'cat—in the dark. Then she went on, for Dear Papa's notice.

"She done grow out of all her dresses and dey can't be let out no mo' cause dey let out all de way."

A moment or two later Dear Papa took Sophia's hand and they walked together to the sea wall. They looked at the busy fiddlers and the long green ma'sh and heard a ma'sh hen holler as the tide turned back, and then he took both her hands.

21

"It's quite true you're growing very fast," he told her gravely. "And I'm afraid it means I have to stop doing something I like to do."

Sophia looked into his eyes and said, "Well?"

"Giving you your bath. I love to, because your body is so beautiful. But I'm supposed not to look at it any more."

"Why can't you look at it as long as you think it's beautiful? Isn't that in keeping with what you've taught me?"

"I think it is. But different philosophies of life, all with truth in them, are in conflict with one another. Do you understand what I mean?"

"I think so."

"We must never have secrets from each other. I want you to answer a question—it will help me in this and in future matters. Do you or do you not understand why I must stop giving you your bath?"

Her face flushed, but she continued to gaze at him in profound earnestness.

"I understand why you think you must. Because you take too long."

"Yes, I take too long. I can't help it. Now let's run like hell to where Phineas is cutting hedge. I 'spec' he'll show us a toad-frog."

They ran, and the incident dropped into the past.

The seasons crept by, the sweet, gently changing seasons of the Carolina Low Country, and they added up to years. Occasionally Dear Papa talked of her going to the public school, or even to a seminary in the cold North, but he'd be damned if he'd send her to one of the finishing schools in Charleston or Baltimore. Actually he did none of these things, but continued to tutor her, and the fact remained that at thirteen she knew more poetry, mythology, and astronomy, and more about the English language, and was better oriented in geography and history than most college freshmen. She had not caught up with herself in mathematics, physics, chemistry, and languages, but there was plenty of time for these. Meanwhile her body was swiftly losing its childish look and her face was changing wonderfully, as though by a fairy's gift.

Soon after this, trouble set in again, not heavy trouble nor continuous, not knockin' on de do', only lightly rapping. One evidence of it was a minister's calling late in the afternoon and speaking for nearly an hour in an austere voice to Dear Papa. The latter had been able to make only

22

brief sallies in reply, and none at all when, at the doorway, the clergyman shook a solemn finger at him and fired a parting blast.

"You, sir, are an agnostic! See that you don't raise your beautiful little daughter to be the same!"

When Sophia joined Dear Papa he was sitting in the landside parlor, his feet sprawled and a rueful look upon his face.

"Darling," he burst out, "I've done wrong in not sending you to church. The minister says so—and he had every right to say so, reminding me that he was Julia's minister before you were born. The vestrymen all say so, and I suppose the whole town. I explained that you knew more about the Bible than nine out of ten of his parishioners. 'Perhaps so,' he replied, with great severity, 'if she has read it like a novel, instead of the Word of God!' Well, I would have liked to send you to a colored church on Ladies Island if the white people would have stood for it. One to whom God is Ol' Massa, one without any organ, with only those roof-rocking voices in harmonies beyond harmony, one where they sing 'How Dey Done My Lawd!' instead of 'Beautiful City of Light.' I told him I had encouraged your religious instincts by having you learn by heart the great *Elegy*, and by reading about the martyrs and such novels as *Ben-Hur* and *The Christmas Carol*. He answered me, 'Novels, pew! What are they compared to a good, righteous sermon!' Then I made the mistake of telling him you had read *Uncle Tom's Cabin*. Nothing I could say after that assuaged his ire."

"Well, I'll go to church if you think best."

"Do you think best, Sophia?"

"Yes."

So she did go regularly and listened to the sermons and joined in the singing and the prayers, but the light the preacher promised never shone upon her, and instead a ghost came in and sat beside her and its name was Loneliness.

Then there was the difficulty about children's parties. She played the guessing games and won most of them, and rather enjoyed kissing games, although, it seemed, in a way different and more secretive than the other girls—a less natural way that made her feel guilty. The boys were attracted to her, she was so patently the prettiest in the bevy, but this might not be the main of her attraction, since they be-

23

haved so badly. The other girls united against her and by little undercover acts managed to ostracize her. So it came about that when the invitation to a party was given directly to her she did not tell Dear Papa and did not attend. Before long almost all the party givers ceased to invite her.

She was going on fourteen and had almost got there, and she had already grown into as startling personal beauty as this ancient seagirt breeding ground of beauty could remember, when the Fates, the Three Sisters of Dear Papa's lore, moved strongly for or against her, which she could not know.

The time was late summer of the year 1894. It happened that a schoolfellow of Dear Papa, later a medical student under Dr. Havelock Ellis at St. Thomas's Hospital in London, and for the last few years engaged in psychological research in Vienna, touched Charleston on his homeward journey; and, in spite of the pressures of time, took the boat to Beaufort to dine with his old friend. Dear Papa called him Emil and introduced him as Dr. Linden. He was a short man, prematurely bald, with a quiet manner and deep-set eyes. He seemed quite startled by Sophia's appearance and after he and Dear Papa had had a drink together on the veranda, meanwhile talking in low tones, he seemed particularly attentive to all of her remarks at dinner and noted her smallest actions.

Sophia was allowed to remain at table while the two old schoolmates sipped brandy and coffee. Once, as they were talking away at a great rate, she was given a chance to score.

"Emil, what was the name of the witch who enchanted Ulysses in the sea cave on the island of Ogygia?" Dear Papa had asked. "It slips my mind."

"Circe," the doctor replied.

"Hell, no. Circe was the hag that turned his sailors into hogs. Sophia, do you remember?"

"Of course I do. Her name was Calypso, and she kept him captive seven years, until Zeus sent Hermes to rescue him."

"*Touché!*" the doctor said, with a faint smile, while Dear Papa's eyes shone and her heart glowed.

But something quite disturbing happened a few minutes later. Dear Papa became grave and spoke in what Sarah called "he big boss voice," which he employed when he expected immediate obedience.

"Now run along to bed, my sweet. The doctor and I are going to have a long talk in the library."

Sophia offered her grave good nights, kissing Dear Papa, shaking hands with the doctor; then she ran along—but not to bed. She walked upstairs, letting her high heels click on the steps, tiptoed down again, and slipped into the landside back room, once a nursery, now a sewing room. It happened that there had been a passage cut through a closet between this room and the library. In it were stored old schoolbooks, biographies of men renowned in their day but now forgotten, outworn histories, sets of sentimental novels no longer readable, and stacks of dusty periodicals. Curtains so rarely opened that they hung in long-fixed folds shut off the closet from the sewing room. To all intents and purposes the opening into the library had been closed by a tall, massive, old-fashioned secretary, but actually it did not stand flush with the wall, and the gaps made an easy passageway for any sound above a whisper.

Perfectly certain that the subject of Dear Papa's and Dr. Linden's talk would be herself, and strangely frightened, Sophia slipped between the curtains, blew away the dust from a pile of magazines, and sat down with her ear close to a crack.

She had not long to wait. When the two men entered the library Dr. Linden admired the mellowed leather of the books, then they took chairs, and the sound of matches striking and the pleasant smell of tobacco told her they were lighting pipes or cigars. Then Dear Papa said in an agitated voice.

"Emil, we might as well come to it. What do you think?"

"I don't think. I know. Sophia is terribly in love with you."

"She loves me too much, I know, but she's not *in love* with me."

"I meant exactly what I said."

"Emil, that's incredible. Whatever it is, it began when she was four—even before that. It hasn't changed since then——"

"That's the trouble. It should have died away—taken another form—when she reached four. Stanley, I have the advantage of you because I've just come from the most dynamic, the most significant psychological laboratory in Europe. I had a chance to read the manuscript of a forthcoming book, *Studien uber Hysterie*, by a Jewish neuropathologist you've never heard of. I was so impressed by his work that I asked to call, and in the upshot I was invited to have a small part in his studies. Actually his thinking had gone far beyond that book. It had to do with the conflict between the conscious and the unconscious mind. He finds that a great deal of that conflict arises from infantile sexuality, and especially the physical love of a male child for its mother and the female for its father. Mind you, this is perfectly natural and almost universal. Only when it lingers on into later childhood, repressed or denied, perhaps out of shame or guilt or God knows what, it can damage the personality."

"Do you think Sophia's personality has been damaged? By God, I don't. Speak plainly."

"No, I don't think it has. But the seeds of tragedy are there; whether they grow or melt away in the good earth remains to be seen. I want her to stop listening to you as though you were a god. I don't want to see her face reveal emotion when you give her a smile—like Alice in the song."

"Well, what am I going to do? You've diagnosed the ailment—I don't question it—now what's the cure?"

"Before I can suggest any I'd like to have a better idea of what caused it. Now it's your turn to speak plain."

Dear Papa waited long seconds—while Sophia's breath stopped and her skin prickled—then he answered quietly, "I will."

"Love has a terrifying power to beget love," the doctor said. "You lost your beautiful wife when Sophia was two years old. In time didn't Sophia take her place in what was once called 'the wanderings of desire'?"

"I deny that. Or it was so submerged in what you call the unconscious mind that I didn't know it."

"You'll know this much. This is a hard question but I want an answer. This is a medical matter. Did you in dreams—the dreams of sleep I mean—ever . . ." But Dr. Linden's voice dropped very low and Sophia could not hear.

"It's a hard answer for me to make, old friend. Remember I am of Puritan upbringing. I broke away, but some of the old stricture remains. No, I never dreamed that. I dreamed I did everything short of that, and when it occurred with anyone else—a woman I could never identify—Sophia was always somewhere about."

"That means that she was the subject of those dreams,

26

too. The conscious mind was not quite inert and it changed the images conjured up in the unconscious. Stanley, you need tell me nothing more. Now I'm going to prescribe. Sophia must escape from the most—the worst—of your influence. She must find an outlet for her tension in normal ways. I propose that you send her to the local high school for at least one year. She won't learn anything much and she'll be lonely as the devil but she'll shine in her classes and, a little at a time, begin to take some interest in young people's affairs. You can send her to college at sixteen."

"Where, for God's sake? I realize the need is great but the risks are great too."

"I know the very place. While in Charleston I heard a great deal about the college there, founded before the Revolutionary War. It's small—all to the good—and has a remarkable faculty and standards. Since a boat makes the round trip daily, she can come home on Friday and go back Sunday afternoon. Thus the rupture wouldn't be too severe."

"I don't know. Still, I'll follow that course. I have some good friends there——"

Sophia heard no more because she was stealing away, out of the closet, through the sewing room, up the stairs to her bedroom. She had been cold with fright, but now her skin was glowing and in her mind was a rush and tumult of feeling which she could not yet resolve. As the door closed and she gazed upon her familiar surroundings, the truth broke upon her—the lovely, the irrefutable truth.

What did it matter where she went to school, how far off, how long she stayed, how rarely she came home? When she grew lonely and longing she had only to remember that Dear Papa was the same—that he loved her best in the world, always, and in all the ways that she loved him.

6

The early spring of the year 1898 was stormy, with southeast winds and unusually high tides. Tree moss waved day and night, and shutters rattled, and two fishermen from Ladies Island whom Sarah knew well were drowned off Edisto Island. The Charleston paper, which Sarah could read quite well, told and retold of Uncle Sam's big boat being blown up in Cuba, and how a big war, maybe as big as the war Abe Linkum fought to set her daddy free, was just about to break. Sarah went often to her church and there

27

she sang with great fervor the troubled song her people learned and remembered from long ago, "Ain't Goin' To Study Wa' No Mo'."

Since her mind was bent on signs and wonders, she heard more often than before light steps on the attic stairs and across the creaking floor to a corner where stood a locked trunk. So it came about on a Friday night in March, when Sophia was home from college, and the rain beat against the windows and the live oaks groaned in the blast, she was in a mood to grant a request that her darling had made many times before.

"If you knowed how it hurt my head to tell fortunes, you wouldn't ask me," Sarah said sorrowfully.

"Just one time, Sarah."

"It feel like my head goin' bust open, and de sweat run off me, and my arm and leg get stiff. And when de spell pass I get so sleepy I can't keep my eyes open. But it a good night to tell it if I ever goin' to. You and me all alone till de boss come home from facklemeetin'. 'Pears like any fortune I tell tonight will sho' enough come true."

Sophia shivered a little, deep inside of her. This year she was going on eighteen, her application to enter Radcliffe College in September had been accepted, yet she felt what seemed a distinct warning against hearing Sarah's prophecies. But she put it by, took refuge in fatalism, and when Sarah brought to the sewing room a big well-illustrated Bible, her most prized possession left to her by Ol' Mass' Sam, she opened it at random as Sarah instructed her.

"Now run yo' finger down de left-hand page and let it stop when you feel a little jump inside yo' head."

Sophia's finger stopped only a few lines from the top. She had felt nothing inside her head, but there could be no doubt of the sudden, sharp prickling sensation at the back of her neck.

"What do it say, Possum?" Sarah asked, her face drawn and her eyes rounding.

"It's the eleventh verse of the thirty-third chapter of Numbers. And it reads—it reads—'And they removed from the Red Sea, and encamped in the wilderness of Sin.'"

"Oh Lawd!"

"What does it mean, Sarah?"

"They's an ol' plantation nee Watertown what dey call Mount Sinai. I reckon us goin' move away from de bay—it plenty red someday when de sun goin' down—and yo' papa buy 'at old plantation and us live there. It way in de country and mighty wild, wif piney wood and swamp and wil'cats and coons and rattlesnakes."

"I don't think it means that. I don't know what it means. Now I'll open the Bible at another place." For she knew the ritual, having seen Sarah tell Phineas' fortune.

"I tell you what, Possum. Us won't finish the fortune-tellin' now. Yo' papa like to come home any minute now, and I got to mend 'em socks he gave me befo' he come, and after 'at I'll sew a while on yo' pitty new dress." Sarah used a wheedling tone Sophia had heard before.

"We will go on with it. What are you afraid of, Sarah? I'll open here, and run my finger down the right-hand page——"

It appeared to stop of itself about halfway down the page. The letters seemed to leap out of it, as though they were printed in blacker type. Sarah was staring at her with wild eyes.

"It's the Book of Ruth, Chapter Four, thirteenth verse," Sophia said. "And it reads, 'So Boaz took Ruth, and she was his wife: and when he went in unto her, the Lord gave her conception, and she bare a son.' "

" 'At's a good fortune. I hee de story befo'. Ruf came from a long way off, and Boaz, he was a mighty man, wif plenty money. She done lay down beside him when he was asleep, after he been drinking, on a heap o' co'n in de co'n field, and natuh did de res'. 'At mean you goin' marry de massa o' a big plantation makin' plenty co'n and cotton too."

"Sarah, did you ever go and lie down beside a man sleeping on a pile of corn?"

"I sho' ain't, but one time a boy come and lie down beside me when I was sleepin' on a bale o' cotton. And 'at de way it should be, Possum, not like Ruf done."

"How old were you, Sarah?"

"I reckon I was thu'teen."

"Good heavens, I'm nearly eighteen. I wonder how much longer I'll live. Well, we'll go on with the fortune and see."

"I don' tol' you fo'tune."

"You're only half through and you know it. Now it's your turn to open the Bible and find the verse, first the right-hand page, and then the left nearest the heart."

"I can't do it now, Possum."

29

"You've got to."

The sweat came out on Sarah's smooth dark cheeks as she opened the book and her lean black finger ran down the page. As it stopped, she uttered a low moaning sound, as of pain.

"Second Samuel, Chapter Twelve, verse eighteen," Sophia read. " 'And it came to pass on the seventh day, that the child died.' "

" 'At the wrong place, Possum. You started to open it way back from there, and de pages stuck. 'At ain't yo' true fortune. You go back where 'em pages stuck."

"Very well." Sophia flipped over with her hand about half the pages in the book. "Now run your finger down and we'll see. It's Saint Matthew, Chapter Two, and the verse is number eighteen. Sarah, you didn't do much better."

"What is it, Miss Sophy?"

" 'In Rama was there a voice heard, lamentation and weeping, and great mourning, Rachel weeping for her children, and would not be comforted, because they are not.' "

"You didn't find the right place you foun' befo'. 'At spoil de fortunetellin' for tonight. You run along now, while I mend 'em socks, and you git a book to read."

"No, I'm opening it again—the last time. You've got to find the verse on the left-hand side. Maybe it will tell us something that will change everything."

"Miss Sophy, dey sompin hee I don't like. Dis is de wrong night to tell fortune. Listen to 'at wind. I never heard it cry like 'at befo', like a little los' child. Ol' Debbil, he round hee close. It him what make us stop on 'em verses, instead of de right verses 'at tell yo' fortune true. De rain on de window, it sing instead of rattle, and it's a song I done hee an old witch sing when I was a li'l girl. De dead are up and out of de graves tonight. Dey come nights like 'is, de ol' people see 'em and sit close by the fire and not say nothin'. I ain't gwine open 'at book."

"The fortune will be told me just the same. Maybe it will be worse because you broke your promise."

"Yo' mighty ha'd on me, Miss Sophy. You ain't 'fraid of nothin', even de Lawd, and you bent and dete'min as ol' Mass Sam, who wouldn't tu'n aside for a ragin' lion. I'll run my finga down until I feel 'at little jump inside my head but I won't look at what it say, and if you look at it, it yo' business not mine, and I won't take no blame."

"That's all right. Go ahead."

Sarah's finger began its tremulous journey, almost paused, moved again. When it stopped, Sophia glanced at the heading, the chapter number on the same page, and started to glance at the verse when her eyes raised to meet Sarah's wide and popping eyes.

"Sarah, you moved your finger——"

"No, I didn't, Miss Sophy. 'At de very one whay it stopped——"

"Well, I'm not going to read it. I'd never know whether you cheated or not. Anyway, what's the use of knowing— it won't change for better or for worse what's going to happen." As she continued to gaze at Sarah, a look that made the colored woman think of conjure women came into the beautiful face. "A long time ago, Sarah, there lived the adopted son of a king, and his name was Oedipus. It was in the country that Mr. Paulos, who runs the Daisy Restaurant, came from. He went to a fortuneteller, who told him that unwittingly he would kill his own father and marry his own mother. He tried to run away, but it wasn't any use. The evil fortune caught up with him. Well, I'm not going to try to run away. I'm just going to close the book."

She did so, and she could swear that she had already forgotten what she had read at the top of the page, and the chapter number.

"Now, 'es go and make some nice ham sandwiches," Sarah proposed. "We got mo'n half of 'at fine country ham us had for Sunday dinner."

"A little later, Sarah. I think I heard Dear Papa come in and I want to see him."

Sophia ran out to find her father in the hall, newly shed of his rain-wet hat and coat, standing there apparently aimlessly, his eyes very bright, a dazed expression on his wonderfully chiseled face, and an opened telegram in his hand.

"Darling, something very important has happened," he told her, in a voice that did not hold quite firm.

She took his free hand and waited.

"Before I tell you what it is, I must tell you something that I hadn't got around to yet, because the reports I've been getting were not quite full. The gist of it is that quite a number of this year's graduates of Fairbanks College have been taking examinations to enter professional schools and especially teaching. They made quite a remarkable showing, and it has come to the attention of some of the biggest people in the country. In fact I can say we've done something toward spiking the brutal, blasphemous lie that only white men, not colored, are made in God's image. Well, this telegram is from President McKinley. You can read it now."

His hand trembled as he passed her the page. She held it and read:

I WISH TO OFFER YOU THE DIRECTORSHIP OF GOVERNMENT EDUCATION IN THE DISTRICT OF ALASKA. YOUR TASK WOULD BE TO ESTABLISH OTHER SCHOOLS AS RAPIDLY AS POSSIBLE. YOUR IMMEDIATE HEADQUARTERS WOULD BE SAINT MICHAEL NEAR THE MOUTH OF THE YUKON RIVER, AND A DEPUTY OF YOUR SELECTION WOULD BE STATIONED AT SITKA. YOUR SALARY WOULD BE $5000 A YEAR WITH ALLOWANCES. ALASKA WOULD BE SERVED AND I WOULD BE PERSONALLY GRATIFIED. IF YOU TELEGRAPH IMMEDIATE ACCEPTANCE.

Sophia handed back the telegram and asked quietly, "May I go with you or do you want to go aone?"

"My darling! Of course you can go, although you must be back in Boston in time to enter in January." Then, in a glowing voice, "Alaska schools may be all right in their way, but I doubt if any of them can quite come up to Radcliffe."

She remembered there was a gold rush in Alaska just now. Almost anything could happen to one who had caught the notice of the Three Sisters.

2. The Young Northman

In the afternoon of July 6, 1898, the iron steamer *Victoria*, manned by a crew cold sober after its revels on July Fourth, was about to sail from Seattle to the old Russian town of St. Michael, far and away toward the Arctic Circle on the Alaskan coast. Wonderfully enough, despite the rush of gold seekers buying deck space to sleep on every other Alaska-bound vessel, not all of the *Victoria*'s cabins had been engaged. The reason was a great joke to those passengers and crewmen who loved the old *Vic* and her comfortable, leisurely voyages, but not to her owners. For years now she had had the government contract to carry the mails addressed to Dutch Harbor and the Yukon River towns and interior trading posts, by which she must run on schedule on the Outside Route, and not go gallivanting through the Inside Passage to roaring Skagway.

On the passenger list was a name not uncommon in the Northwest—Eric Andersen. Somewhat red of eye and heavy of head when he first came aboard, he was almost immediately cured by the sight of one of his cupmates of two nights before, and of two of his Northland neighbors. The former was heading toward the Nome peninsula on a fool's quest for gold. The other two, sourdoughs like himself, had trapped last winter fifty and a hundred miles from his diggings, although as soon as they could assemble their belongings, including their pretty squaws, they would be heading upriver to Dawson.

Tall, loose-jointed, blond girls with whom he had danced at the Norwegian social club on the night of the Fourth had considered him somewhat young to be called a sourdough. In the first place the word was almost always used with the prefix "old." Actually a storekeeper who had spent a rainy winter snug in Ketchikan, in a climate fully as harsh as San Francisco's, could call himself that. The real sourdoughs let this pass. They knew, too, that a high-smelling method of making bread—using sour dough from the last baking in lieu of yeast—was not the essential hallmark. The new definition, almost always ribald, that drifted through the vast territory every few months was good for laughter but did not pin the matter down. Eric could recognize a fellow sourdough as soon as he opened his mouth. More than that, he had a complex of feelings, which he could not quite put in words, of what made a sourdough, a real one, no better but different than any other species of man in the wide world.

At twenty-three he himself was a real one. He had wandered up from Tacoma to work in a fish crew at the age of eighteen. Previous to that he had made a journey rather common for embryo sourdoughs—from Minnesota west—and his parents had begun the trek in Hammerfest, on the Norwegian coast. Since then he had roamed the District wide and far.

The Norwegians are a tall race. Eric stood an even six 'feet, but his body was so compact and proportionate that he looked shorter. He did not have the pale or red coloring common among Norwegians: his hair exactly matched the fur of the Far North, back-country martens he sometimes caught in his trap, and was as fine as that, blowing in the wind unless he plastered it down with grease. Not sea-blue like so many Norwegian eyes, Eric's eyes were a pale, magnetic green between thick dark eyelashes and under heavy dark brows, and his teeth were even, perfect, and a lustrous white. Otherwise—so a girl at the dance had told him—he looked like any other fellow.

This was far from true. The girl had been too young to see much more than young and healthy maleness. Of course no fellow looks like any other in close scrutiny; and the marks of an intense individuality, which is the one thing common to all sourdoughs, had come on him early. He had seen the ice go out of the Yukon three times. He had begun to be large like the river, and small like someone all alone on its banks. His face had begun to give signs of a chisel working, which is at once sad and splendid in a man of twenty-three. Other young people, who by the nature of things cannot pick and choose and must take human kind as it comes, do not like to see it in a contemporary and manage to skip it.

He and Lars Gustavassen and Otto Swanson got together by the rail. It gave them a good feeling, which all enjoyed, hardly knowing it was there. In the back of every sourdough's mind is the endless awareness of having spent vast periods of time alone and, if he lives on, of the certainty of doing the same hereafter.

Lars and Otto were slightly older than Eric and looked more phlegmatic, although Otto was known to have one of the most terrible tempers north of the Kuskokwim. All were dressed similarly and not very well, the outfits expensive but tacky, since none had the slightest notion of what was becoming to him. All three wore gold nugget stickpins in factory-tied neckties; Eric had a large nugget ring. In each coat lapel was the badge of the Yukon Order of Pioneers, a lodge-like type of fraternity. Their present interest centered on the gangplank by which fellow passengers were boarding.

A good many of these were instantly recognized by all three, in which case they were greeted loudly and jovially. "Hi there, old wolverine," or, "Howdy, Andy!" or, "There's old Bill Holbert; I didn't know he was outside; hey, Bill, where did you get that dude hat?"—these were typical salutations. When a boarder was recognized by only one or two of the three, there followed a brief, muttered biography, stripped to its essentials, to enlighten the ignorant. "That's Mr. Goldstien. He's a big fur buyer—one of the best drivers in the Nort'—and I t'ink he's planning a big trip next winter, to be coming up so early. He already bane west to Kamchatka and east to Demarcation Point." This last was a span of sixty degrees—about thirty-five hundred miles.

Red Ole Iseksen was "King of Sand Point." He was said to own a harem of a round-dozen pretty Aleut girls whom now and then he passed around to favored visitors. Sand Point was away to the westward, beyond Kodiak, although not as far west as Unga, which was the headquarters of the robed bishop of the Orthodox Greek Church, with childlike blue eyes, a face which to the knowing would have suggested Count Tolstoy's, and a venerable beard. He was not the only churchman to come aboard. To the watchers' astonishment, there were two more, each neatly dressed in black with inverted collars. One, the elder, had no baggage, and obviously had come aboard to say good-bye to his fellow, whom he appeared to treat with the greatest deference. Actually this last was a type of minister none of the three had ever seen. Except for his garb they would have guessed him an English lord, such as now and then passed this way to shoot Kodiak bears or the giant Kenai moose—the democratic kind instead of the haughty. He was tall, slender, lithe, notably handsome, walking as though he owned the ship and yet with such a pleasant manner and easy smile that Eric felt none of the upsurge of resentment that he felt toward dudes.

"I know who he is," said Lars, in a low, excited tone. "I read about him in an editorial in the Seattle *Post*. He was the minister of a swell church in New York. It was where the Vanderbilts and the Rockefellers went—the Church of —a long name I can't remember. But *his* name is the Reverend Arthur Dudley. He's only thirty-five, yet he was about to be made Bishop of Long Island. Instead he decided to become a missionary at Allapah Bay!"

"Allapah Bay!" Eric echoed in amazement. "That's fifty miles on the Godforsaken side of Point Hope and it's not a bay, only a dent in the coast. We stopped there when I worked on the Alaska Fur Company boat. *Allapah* means cold, and when an Eskimo says something is cold, by Yesus, it *is* cold! The *Bear* comes in once a year for survey. Maybe a trader or two and maybe not. The rest of the time there's only the Eskimo village and the tundra and the sea."

Otto uttered his deep laugh. "Well, he won't stay long. The first time a squaw's mukluk passes near his nose he'll long for them incense pots."

The three sourdoughs were quiet awhile, because each was thinking of his own break with the peopled places, the easy lands. Then Eric thought that Otto should not have mentioned the rank-smelling mukluk because it hit too close to home. That pertained to all three of them in some degree—perhaps to almost every young sourdough who lived away from the towns. But Eric himself lived close to the great river, all year beside it except for occasional journeys, and that caused him to have ideas of relations between man and man, man and woman, even man and God, that he could not discuss with Otto and Lars, or hardly mention to any sourdough lest they think he was putting on airs.

Then his jaw dropped as he gaped. Coming up the gangplank was a tall man, as distinguished-looking as Eric had ever seen, and lightly before him went a tall, slender girl with pale gold hair. She was alien to the West, let alone to Alaska, yet all he could think of in the way of comparison was the northern lights.

2

Out of a home population of never more than three or four millions the Norwegians had made their mark throughout the Western world, perhaps second only to the mark made by about an equal number of English, Scotch, Irish, and German settlers on the American shore in the spine-tingling last decades of the eighteenth century. It came about partly through the Norwegian's genius for quick and direct action. Their brains work fast, they are swift to realize what they want, and their bodies are, by and large, marvelously agile. That is one reason they are among the greatest seamen that ever spread a sail.

There was no porter carrying bags to show the newcomers their way. The stewards were setting the tables for dinner and dock laborers were so scarce these days of the gold rush that most hand baggage was lugged aboard by its owners or checked on the dock for later delivery to the staterooms. When the frock-coated gentleman and the summery girl gained the deck Eric was there to meet them, having moved so suddenly that Otto and Lars gaped at him with open mouths.

"Sir, they're shorthanded today," he explained, "but I

know this ship from taffrail to bowsprit, and if you'll tell me the numbers of your rooms, I'll take you there in a yiffy." Too late he remembered that these nautical terms did not apply to modern steamers but to old windjammers, and he feared, too, that he had not minded his accent as carefully as he liked to do on social occasions.

The fact remained that the two newcomers did not appear in the least astonished and their grave gaze upon him was in no way derogatory.

"We were told we could expect very fine hospitality from the Alaskan people, but we hardly looked for it this soon," the tall man said. "Our numbers are one and two."

He led the way down the stairs and along the dim corridors. Cabins one and two were the best on the ship, and the thought struck him that he had thrust his company upon his "betters," a term used sometimes by English emigrants in Dawson; or at least he had made a fool of himself. True, he had never admitted publicly to having any betters. That was the teaching of his father, Olaf, who had spoken to him solemnly when he was old enough to understand.

"T'is is not Old Country," Olaf had said. "T'is is U.S.A., where men are created free and equal, by Yiminy! Honor t'em t'at deserve it and shake hand wit' every man, but if any man turn up his nose at you, you smash it for him goot."

The fact remained that when Eric had turned the keys in the two doors the gentleman and the young lady seemed in no haste to be rid of him.

"Do you live in Alaska?" the former asked.

"Yes, sir, about five years. I've got a little place far up on the Yukon."

"Are there any Indian schools near where you live?"

"No, but there's a big Indian village two hours away by dog team. Would you like to have your portholes opened? We'll be in Inside Passage waters most of the afternoon and you'll catch a good breeze."

"Thank you."

"It's a nice t'ing you're on the starboard side instead of the port," Eric went on as he opened the ports. "That means you'll have a good view of the Aleutian Range all the way to Dutch Harbor, one of the finest views in the world. The wind's on the port side usually but there's plenty for everybody." Eric smiled a slow smile, thinking of those plentiful winds.

When he turned to go the gentleman made a friendly gesture.

"What is your name, if you'll please tell us, and where are you bound?" And when Eric had answered, "Well, Eric, we're to have the whole journey together. I am Dr. Hill, a schoolteacher, and this is my daughter, Sophia."

They gave him their hands, the professor's smooth, unacquainted with hard work, yet strong. The girl's hand differed greatly from any he had ever touched, and he was shocked into a new and deeper degree of perception of her whole person. He felt at once powerfully attracted and estranged. His excitement was increasing in leaps and bounds and he could hardly conceal it. At first he had tried to see her in generalities, a mighty pretty girl whom he might spark a little as the journey progressed, especially in the long stretch from Dutch Harbor to Point Dall, when there was not much to see but gooneys and gray seas. Suddenly he knew that she was not the sparking kind, and that she was not mighty pretty but truly and touchingly beautiful. Strangest of all, he was no longer afraid of her—in the sense that she might disdain him and wound his pride—although he knew better than before that her father was a big gun and she herself a great lady. She might wound him deeper than that, through no fault of her own. This last was as dim an inkling as he sometimes felt before the wild breaking of an Arctic blizzard.

A man may look lightly upon a woman, or with a marksman's gaze. Although the latter is likely to be embarrassing to both parties, Eric risked it, and the risk paid off. He had a picture that he doubted could ever fade, no matter where he journeyed or how long he lived. If the dressing of her pale hair and her style of clothes said she was eighteen, she still looked sixteen. Her shaping was completely unique, or at least it seemed so because of her posture—her weight, which was little, on the soles of her feet, her heels appearing barely to touch the floor, her legs wonderfully straight, and her body looking as if a powerful man had pressed his hands under her ribs on each side and lifted gently.

But her face was the truest index of the mystery he sensed so strongly. At the moment it expressed surprise and wonder, perhaps a deep-seated and subtle exultation. Her eyes were wide open, the whites framing narrow blue-gray irises that rimmed the immense pupils. He was still puzzling over the structure around the eyes—their clean setting, as of a glacier pool that ever suggests a jewel set in flawless marble, the smooth forehead and the slight bony protuberance of the eyebrows in relation to the cheekbones, the shadows within the sockets and the sheen of taut flesh without, all this of new discovery to him and of thrilling amazement—when another feeling crept into his mind and jarred him out of his spell.

It began with his noticing, vaguely at first, that the impressive man beside her was looking at her too. He seemed to have forgotten Eric's presence and he was smiling down at her, his gray eyes aglow with pride. And then Eric knew, before he had any cause to know, that these were deep waters, beyond his sounding; and he knew also, more than as a foreboding, and indeed as a stunning fact, that he and Dr. Hill had met in implacable conflict.

3

"I want to see a great deal of you, Eric, on this voyage," Sophia's father told him, with what seemed great cordiality, at the door. "I believe you are just the man to tell me what I will be in for, in the way of doing my job in Alaska."

Eric bowed his head with a suggestion of Old World courtesy picked up from his emigrant father and went his way. It was his own way because he knew no other. He felt the need of subtlety and finesse; he lacked tact and his direct moves often ended in a bearlike, blundering charge. Nevertheless, he would take Dr. Hill at his word. He had not imagined that dark feeling, but apparently it applied to only one thing, and Dr. Hill would not let it interfere with other things of moment. And good skippers took advantage of every break in the weather and the passing carelessnesses of hostile seas.

His first move would seem especially awkward, Eric thought, except to another squarehead. This did not mean that squareheads lacked imagination—the gift was bounteously given to the whole Norse race—it only meant that they understood one another quite well. They were clannish in the extreme and had been so since the days of the Vikings, and in their wintry homeland, of meager natural wealth, all had been steeped in the doctrine of live and let live. The purser's name was Stefen Jorgassen. Although three years older than Eric, he had roamed the Tacoma waterfront with him, sharing many a boyhood adventure. Just now he was scurrying all over the ship on various errands, and Eric soon cornered and caught him.

"The last time we were shipmates you admired this ring," Eric said, slipping off the band of interlinked gold nuggets.

"I sure did. I asked you if you'd sell it. I wanted to give it to my old man, who collects souvenirs of Alaska."

"If you still want it, I won't sell it, but I'll give it to you if you'll do me a favor."

"It must be a pretty big favor. I think it would weigh out twenty dollars."

"That's only one day's wash from the Gertrude Placer Mines on Moosejaw Creek," Eric told him, waving his hands and grinning.

"Well, what do you want me to do?"

"Seat me at table with Dr. Hill and his daughter Sophia."

"Eric, that's swell company for a Scandinavian cradle rocker."

"Man, I've got a sluice."

"Don't you mean snoose?" the purser asked, with typically heavy squarehead humor. Snoose was their word for snuff, cosily tucked under the upper lip. "Anyway, it's still pretty swell company. I haven't seen 'em, but the whole ship's agog over that girl, and they've got cabins one and two. They'll probably sit at the skipper's table."

"Cap'n Borne and my fat'er are old friends. I don't t'ink he'd mind."

"I don't think I can do it but I'll try. The seating won't be made till supper; at dinner it's catch as catch can."

Eric made off, his spirits wilting. Although he had succeeded in bluffing it out, the term "captain's table" had revealed his adventure in a new and dismal light, such as spread over the snow at Barrow between noon and one at the time of the winter solstice. He could combat cold, hunger, and hard luck well to his credit; he could mush out another mile when more dog tired than the dogs themselves, and he set a face like flint against the most insidious foe, which was loneliness. Because he had gone ahead in spite of all these, kept digging, held to his goal, he had begun to think he could fight anything. Now he realized he was wrong. There had been no captains' tables in all the vast and lonely country he had made his own. Maybe that was why he had gone there and stayed there still.

A few minutes after the ship got under way the dinner

bell rang. Among the sourdoughs it was as bad manners to rush to the dining saloon as it was to eat fast, and they began trekking down as solemnly as though entering church. Since the two Hills must have impeccable manners, Eric thought to make a good impression by being the last to arrive. When finally he entered he took a hopeful glance at a half-filled table. They were not among these late-comers and instead were sitting at a table nearest the passage door. Apparently they had come straight from their staterooms at the first clang of the bell. Now they were stuffing in their food with a marked efficiency while their tablemates fiddled awkwardly and in awe.

After dinner they retired to their cabins and Eric did not see them again until the *Victoria* was nearing Port Townsend, when they took deck chairs. Both of them were reading books, now and then calling attention to some interesting passage, holding short talks or long talks, sharing brief, low laughter. They seemed unaware of the slow pitch of the old snub-nosed *Vic* when she entered the wide strait of Juan de Fuca under Vancouver Island. They were being closely although covertly watched by quite a number of sourdoughs. If these had been disappointed by the steady stomachs of the two cheechakos, they were more chagrined at not being watched in return. Dr. Stanley Hill and his daughter Sophia—the word had spread like wildfire that he was the President's choice for Director of Education for all Alaska—did not seem to know they were not alone. It was an old ship's custom on Alaska waters for everyone to watch everybody the first day out, and the Hills were not playing the game. It was proper for all passengers to mingle freely and to know one another's name, destination, and a few family and business affairs before lights-out. As far as they knew, the Hills had not introduced themselves to anyone.

The truth was, Eric brooded darkly, they lived in a world of their own. This he could never enter, and it was cold comfort that the biggest guns in Alaska could not enter it either —the rich cannery men from Seattle and South Bellingham, the owners of the big placers and the fur and trading companies, and Swedish Captain Borne, at whose table they would sit tonight at supper. The traveling English big-game hunters were not nearly so self-sufficient. Haughty at first, if left to stew in their own juice they soon started chattering like Mother Carey's chickens. The Hills were not in the

41

least haughty, could never be rude to the lowliest deck hand, but they could never be lonely as long as they had each other, and that meant they were not quite human.

Yet it must be a beautiful world they had made together, Eric thought, or it could not have fashioned the wonderful countenance of Dr. Hill, which lighted like a child's, or the strange beauty of his daughter, its like unknown on any ship he had ever traveled, street he had walked, road he had wandered, vision he had conjured up. He was only twenty-three. If he lived to be eighty-three—and no few sour-doughs had made it, tough as walrus hide, mean as old minks—he could not believe he would ever behold its like again.

So he scarcely glanced at the card that a steward handed him. All the passengers were getting similar cards, designating their seating in the dining hall; and Eric felt a sharp start of surprise when he saw that the table number was one. Ordinarily—until now—he would have expected that to be the captain's table. Disillusionment set in quickly when he thought of the unpredictable ways of ancient, bald, and stringy Pike, the *Victoria*'s chief steward.

Pike liked to assert his independence of any rules. If it occurred to the old codger to start numbering tables from the back instead of front, no one could stop him: and sometimes he enjoyed scrambling the tables so that passengers milled about in a maze. The name scrawled on the card read E. Anderson, the Swedish instead of the Dansk-Norsk form of his surname. There could easily be such a person, a big gun instead of a derringer, among the passengers. Eric had not got about the ship as usual this time.

Even so he felt half dazed as he went to the stateroom that he shared with a down-river trader. He was wearing his best blue serge suit and he had bathed only four days before—a summertime luxury which in the deep of winter did not exist—but he removed his celluloid collar, wiped it clean, and washed with great care. Then he put on his newest necktie, orange-and-red as brilliant as a Stateside sunset, since the sunsets on the upper river had pale, unworldly colors. Trying in vain to remember the color of Dr. Hill's necktie, he felt discouraged and changed it for a solid dark green. Suddenly he found himself doubting the large nugget stickpin, only to thrust it into the knot with a firm hand.

Waiting by the port rail for the supper bell, he fixed his attention on Port Angeles and the harbor about which every drunken squarehead sailor waxed lyrical, "the best in t'e vide vorld." Behind it towered Mount Angeles and the distant dreamy summits of the Olympic Range, but these last did him no good, they made him more anxious, they quickened his longings instead of easing them, for the peaks suggested a never-never world he could not enter, and they were too beautiful.

When the bell rang he neither hurried nor dawdled and took a place about halfway down the line. "Where's my table, Chief?" he inquired sturdily of old Pike, who was at the main entrance of the dining hall, taking in the cards.

"The cap'n's," Pike answered blandly.

"Vot?" Every once in a while Eric relapsed in this fashion.

"Do you want me to spell it? You dumb Swedes make me sick. And see you don't eat with your knife."

No Norwegian liked to be called a dumb Swede, even by Pike. It steadied Eric as he made his way to the head table, at which seven people were already sitting, one with pale gold hair. Sophia sat at the right of Captain Borne, Dr. Hill on his left. The empty chair stood at Sophia's right, and the thought that broke first in Eric's brain was that the purser had craved the nugget ring with a good deal of force.

However lacking in superficial polish, squarehead sourdoughs practice the essence of good manners. Captain Borne rose as promptly as did Dr. Hill, and three of the four other men quickly followed suit, although the fourth, a rich mining man whose name Eric knew, got up like a bogged cow moose. Plainly he did not think that the young oaf belonged at this table.

All the men shook hands with him. Sophia bowed her head gravely; the other woman gave him a curt nod. Since Pike was shorthanded, the platters were placed on the table and passed. It was business now, Eric thought, still he was not very troubled about how to proceed. Although he had never learned to switch the knife and fork from hand to hand in the American style, his Norwegian way of eating was at least neat—cutting with his right hand, spearing with his left—and he decided to stick to it. Actually he knew no sloppy eaters among men who had followed the sea; getting food down in a heavy gale had taught them skill.

He had consumed half his steak before he perceived that Sophia and Dr. Hill had alone kept up with him, for the simple reason that they employed the same methods. It gave him a little glow of joy, out of keeping with such a trifle.

"What kind of meat is this?" Sophia asked him, pausing to savor it.

"What do you t'ink?"

Her eyes brightened. Like a child, she loved guessing games.

"Well, it tastes a little like the venison my father's friends sometimes bring him, but it's more delicious. Maybe it's bear meat."

"You wouldn't like bear meat so good, but we t'ink this the best meat in the North. It's caribou, brought frozen down the river and kept in cold storage. I wish you could see the caribou in their great herds. Sometimes they stretch clear across the horizon. Wolves hang off to catch fawns and yearlings, but they don't bot'er the old stags that can strike like a studhorse."

"Do they come close to St. Michael?"

"No."

"Still I might see them."

"I hope so. Speaking of wolves, I don't hate them like so many fellows do. I don't even shoot them when the rare chance comes—except in winter when their fur is good and brings t'ree dollars a skin. They're mean as the devil. They kill every male dog they can get their teeth into, and dogs are our very life. They won't go into a trap or hardly ever into rifle range. Yet they make a go of it where few animals and fewer men can live. Everywhere you go in the North— and in Lapland in the Old Country—you find wolves. When they sit in a circle and wail at the moon when the weather's fifty below the short hairs stand up on my neck. They are feeling somet'ing—trying to say it—and I wish I knew what it was."

She gave him a wide-eyed glance, then dropped her head and spoke quietly.

"I'd like to know too."

"The only animal I hate is a wolverine, and he can't help what he does, and I can't help cussing him. You'd think that might be a bitch—a female wolf, but it's not. He's a—"

"Let me tell *you*. He's no relation to a wolf. He's of the *Mustelidae*—the weasel family—the biggest member. He steals bait from the traps without getting caught, and eats the animals he finds there, and breaks into the trapper's

44

hut and ruins all his food and belongings. The Eskimos use the hides for their mukluks——"

"Excuse me, my dear." It was Dr. Hill's vibrant voice, as he turned from his conversation with the captain. "I was listening—out of one ear. Not mukluks—parka hoods. It is the only fur that won't gather ice from the wearer's freezing breath. Isn't that so, Eric?"

"Yes, sir, it sure is."

"Captain, you were saying——"

"That's just like my father," Sophia said. "He has ears all over him. And he's always right—damn him."

Eric was surprised, but not in the least shocked, because her eyes were shining. Instead he felt again that strange inkling of conflict.

That virtually closed the conversation between him and his lovely tablemate. Captain Borne engaged her in talk about the grand *Victoria*, in contrast with old hookers he had sailed around the Horn.

There was to be no entertainment after supper, not even dancing in the social hall, for the west wind was rising, the ship was not far from open sea, and the cheechakos had better get to bed before they got sick. As soon as the group broke up, Eric made haste to find the purser and give him his prize.

"I can't accept it," the officer told him ruefully, with an odd expression.

"Well, you earned it ten times over——"

"Eric, I didn't say a word to Cap'n about you sitting at his table. I didn't have the nerve, since you never struck it rich. Old Pike told me what happened. Cap'n was so overwhelmed by having a presidential appointee on his ship that he personally invited Dr. Hill and his daughter, then asked him if there was anyone aboard he'd especially like to have join the company. Who should he say but you? Cap'n's eyes bunged out, I tell you. My boy, you have a way with you. You let no grass grow under your feet."

Eric walked away, too dazed to reply.

4

The journey progressed. So did a relationship, more and less than a friendship, between Eric and Sophia. It was active on his part, passive on hers; she neither encouraged him nor rebuffed him. The ship seemed an island by which

45

great ocean currents and wild scenery swept into view and slowly dropped behind.

These sights were their first common interest and possession. In consciousness of these, Sophia became more sharply conscious of Eric, to whom they had first belonged. He was native to this northwest country and had projected himself in a way whereby the whole vastness of land and water that they were entering had become part of him. He could not get enough of showing it to her through his own keen, understanding eyes. He feared that she would get tired of his telling her about it, usually through the means of anecdote. Yet her eyes never stopped shining at brief, pointed tales of fish boats, grizzly bears, old Indians, potlatches, Swedes, Norskers, Danes, and Finns, mostly with elaborate nicknames, and especially cheechakos (newcomers). Many were humorous, some hilarious, and no few dramatic or tragic in the extreme. At these last, the look in her face changed and her eyes became wide open and her beauty so moving that he could hardly believe it could have ever come near to him, ever pass his way.

On shipboard to Alaska in July there is a great amount of daylight to be used. Sophia read with her father in their deck chairs about three hours every afternoon, in which time Eric did not come near her, but most of the rest of the day she seemed to take pleasure in his company. At such times, Eric noticed, her father usually busied himself elsewhere, either in talking to other Alaskans or in studying and taking notes from a phonetic dictionary of the main native languages. It seemed that he was exposing her not to Eric but to Alaska.

For reasons of weather Captain Borne laid his course close to the land till he passed Dixon Entrance, then turned sharply west-northwest toward Kodiak, his first port of call. The blue-green of the islands dimmed and disappeared, the big flock of yelling gulls turned back, and the sea had a different aspect. Eric was seated by the rail with Sophia when the first gooney made its dramatic appearance, flying in lovely ever-changing circles about the ship, dipping and soaring in utter grace and silence.

"I never heard of a gooney before," Sophia said.

"Sailors call them that. I t'ink it's a kind of albatross."

"I suppose you've never read *The Ancient Mariner*."

"You'll get tired of asking me such questions before long."

"Well, would you shoot an albatross?"

"No, it's bad luck. All the old sailors say so."

"The Ancient Mariners." She smiled to herself.

"We old sourdoughs don't shoot anything we can't eat or use."

"I'll never be an old sourdough, Eric."

He sat very still, then forced himself to speak.

"That isn't settled—is it?"

"I suppose nothing is ever settled—except one thing. But my father spoke to me again last night about going back to the States. There—I'm already talking like an Alaskan."

"How long does he want you to stay in St. Michael? Surely for one round trip of the *Vic*—maybe for two."

"I hate to say this—I don't even like to think about it — he wants me to go right back. Then I'll miss only a few days of the September term at college."

"I have to say this." She could not possibly know the compulsion, he thought. "Can't you persuade him to let you stay for one round trip, then you can leave in the middle of October, when the weat'er is still good on the coast, and be home in time for T'anksgiving? Alaska is a kind of college too, like you've never seen. Seeing my big river is a special course."

"Your own big river?"

"I should have said our big river. Still, I've got a special claim on it—or it has on me. I stuck to it instead of going to the Klondike wit' all the ot'ers."

"I don't doubt what you say. You're the sticking kind."

"I was going to stick to you as long as possible. I mean, to stay in St. Michael as long as you were there. My little placer will get along all right, so will my cabin, and my dogs that I left at the Indian village, and old Slewfoot."

"Who is old Slewfoot? You've not mentioned him before."

"An old grizzly who thinks he owns the place. He's been shot in the hind foot and throws it when he walks. He goes away and comes back. In November he moans and groans for a few days, then mushes off through the snow to some hideout in the mountains and I don't see any more of him till April. Then he comes straight to an old log where I sometimes leave taffy for him."

"Taffy?"

"I make it out of molasses and he loves it. You know we

47

sourdoughs get lonely sometimes—it's such a big and empty country—and even a bear is company."

"Isn't he dangerous?"

"Once I almost walked on him when he was asleep in the sun. He jumped up and roared and I got out of there, by Yiminy."

Sophia laughed happily, a loud, childish laugh, then grew grave.

"I would like to see Slewfoot—your great river too."

"Did you know the Yukon is a greater river than the Columbia or the Colorado or the Rio Grande?"

"Yes, I knew that. One of Dear Papa's games—long ago —was for me to name the five biggest rivers on the continent, the five highest mountains, and the ten largest lakes and the ten biggest cities."

"You speak of him as 'Dear Papa' quite often."

"Do I? It's my pet name for him."

"He loves you so much that I t'ink he'll let you stay if you want to real bad." But Eric did not think that.

"I'd like to stay awhile, Eric."

"When you go, I'll have nothing to remind me of you but the northern lights."

"I've never seen them—I'd love to—but I don't think they're a bit like me. They're all spirit—and quite a lot of me is flesh." She colored slightly, then went on. "I'll give you a pin that my great-great-grandfather used to fasten his stock."

"Then I'll give you my nugget ring. It's too big for your finger, but maybe you could wear it on a chain."

Actually, though, Eric's mind was not on his words. Something Sophia had said just now had made his blood leap and a pleasant tingle run over his body. He wondered if he dared say what he was thinking. It would be a great risk; this was an undiscovered country. Still, he was used to taking risks—a kind of coldness came into his brain, as when he was sighting at a difficult target—and he went ahead and ran them. That was the part of a man.

"Sophia?"

"Eric."

"Will you meet me tonight—alone?"

She looked at him with a question in her eyes. He could not answer because he did not know what it was. Then she said, very quietly, "Where?"

"On the foredeck. People have stopped walking by eleven o'clock, and the crew rarely goes there."

"When?"

"Tonight."

"It doesn't seem possible—but I don't—quite—know why. Eric, I'd like to meet you there and I will if I can. If I'm not there by half-past eleven, don't wait for me. It will mean—that I've decided against it."

That was right, it would be her own decision, not her father's, not his restraint. It was only a dim chance. But that was almost like the giving to some poor devil a good chance for life when he was alone and lost in the great cold. There existed a great cold that he only dimly perceived until now. A man must laugh a lot, live an awful lot, drink a good deal if that helped and didn't hurt him too bad. Take snoose or bed down with squaws if he wanted either bad enough, or got too lonely. Once in a while he must pee in the Yukon River, for luck and to swell the stream. After a while the luck, like the ice, went out.

5

Twilight still held, clear and fine, until ten-thirty; then the night closed in with almost a tropic rush, the moon barely visible and the stars extinguished by haze. The old *Vic* was famed as a good sailer, and her iron hull held heavy lading, so she rolled only a little in the light southeast wind and did not pitch at all, a favorable circumstance for people wishing to keep rendezvous in her bow. Scouting carefully, Eric saw that the nearest lamp was above a side entrance to the cabin illuminating dimly the passengers' promenade close to the rail, while a chest filled with life preservers against the forward bulkhead lay in complete shadow.

That much had been provided. It remained of utter unimportance if Sophia, waiting on her cot, reading, musing, listening to faint sounds from her father's cabin, took thought upon the rash act Eric had asked her to commit, and decided against doing so. As far as his brain could move, it seemed the sensible, almost the inevitable decision. Their pasts were without communion, their futures insulated from each other. He retained, beyond any reason he could find, denying all reason, the inkling that she might, in spite of all, keep the assignation. If so, it would be from impulses he did not understand, not one of which was the ordinary healthy wish of most young women to kittle in the dark.

What troubled him most was a question hanging in some dim realm of his mind, the same realm that had to do with superstitions, omens and auguries, signs which no lonely dweller in the Arctic solitudes could keep from noticing and hardly keep from believing, the world of the unseen. He searched for the question and pinned it down: Did he truly want her to come? If she did, his life would never be the same hereafter. He had been changed already by meeting and talking with her; if he did more than that, he himself would be greatly changed. No comet of this splendor could come near a star without causing vast upheavals in its depths and if they touched, the comet would quite possibly blow up. A small, skinny woman, a physics teacher, speaking of Encke's comet coming near Jupiter in 1891 in a Tacoma classroom, had said as much.

Eric stilled the clamor in his heart and answered his own question.

I want her to come, he thought. I want it more than finding rich gravel. I've plenty of time to strike it rich, but my only chance to get Sophia is now, this very month. I can find another mine but never another Sophia. It's a slim chance, but I'll play it with all I own. She's what the old Norse called fey. She's the mermaid that my dad saw, when he was a little boy, on Froya Rock. She's the one who comes to me in dreams and climbs into my bed and goes with me to heaven. Once she came and told me when the ice was going out, and I bet in the Fort Yukon pool and won. I saw her in a funnel-shaped mist that led me to open water and I speared a seal and was saved. She is the glimmer I saw through the frozen trees when I was lost in the Skeenjak. She's the honk of the first goose in the spring sky, lonely as hell but so beautiful. She's the first caribou, little and sharp, on the sky line, and the first hummingbird sucking the first wild rose. She's all of these and, besides, the northern lights.

As though he had spoken a potent incantation, he heard a soft sound that made him turn, and there she stood.

6

Where she stood there was almost no light at all. But he had been waiting so long that the camera-like mechanisms of his eyes had shifted to night sight and took a dim and ghostly picture of her to keep always. Her head with its pale mist of hair was lifted and a little turned, as though in startled anticipation. He stood in the black shadow of the bulkhead where he could hardly believe she could distinguish his shape. Then he remembered the strange largeness of her pupils even in sea light and noted that her eyes had fixed on his. She had told him a little about the Samses' house and its dim rooms half shuttered by the moss-hung trees without, and how her old nurse had called her Possum because she could see in the dark. She was already in some silent, wondering communion with him.

He had thought to break the ice by telling one of his sourdough anecdotes, which always delighted her. A little north of here a friend of his named Chris Yohnson, full of booze, had fallen off his fish boat on a calm summer night, swam to a small iceberg adrift from Malaspina Glacier, found to his great joy that he had not lost his bottle, drank from it until he was pleasantly warm, fell sound asleep, and knew nothing more until some tourists spied him, thought his frost-rimmed clothes were the fur of a polar bear, and almost shot him! However, Eric quickly changed his mind and let the story go untold. He felt compelled to say something quite serious—say it aloud to turn aside bad luck.

"Sophia, a minute or two ago I was t'inking to myself that you are fey."

She nodded and waited.

"What does fey mean to Americans?"

"To some people it means able to tell fortunes. To others it means half in another world. Neither seems to fit me."

"I was t'inking that, then I yust happened to remember how my fat'er used it. It comes down from the old Norse legend. I take it back. You're not fey. Hear me, Jonah, I take it back."

"Sometime you can tell me its old meaning but not now."

"Can you sit on this chest wit' me? It will be hard sitting ——"

"Yes."

She climbed up beside him and in the cool night he was at once aware of her body warmth; then he did not know what to say next.

"I started to say it's a fine night, but maybe you t'ink it isn't very fine wit' little moon and no stars."

"No, I think it's lovely. There is a little light in the water. I turned off the light in the cabin and put my head out the

51

porthole and watched, and all along the hull there are sparks and streamers of light."

"It's what we call phosphorescence. I noticed a little—not much compared to what you'll see in Bering Sea. It's caused by tiny living things disturbed by the ship. They're like water fireflies."

"It's dark and fine and almost still. And, Eric, if there was much more light, I couldn't be here."

"You bet you!" It was a squarehead saying that he had tried to avoid in Sophia's hearing.

"Eric, I met you in the dark as you asked, and I can't stay very long. We'd better not talk about scenery. Aren't we supposed to do what almost all young couples do when they first begin to go together? But you understand I never have—— I'll be awkward at it—and maybe you'll be embarrassed. I hope not, but if you are, remember I won't know it in the dark."

"Yes, you'd know it, but queer enough I'm not. I yust feel very happy and half choked up."

"Then that's all right. I think that's the way I wanted you to feel—and expected you to feel. Otherwise I wouldn't have come."

"Can this make any trouble for you?"

"No. My father doesn't know about it. If he did, it would still be all right. He wants me to be like other young people—within limits."

"I want to kiss you, Sophia."

"You can, in a moment—I believe. But I'm going to kiss you first. Then if I jump up and run away, don't think it wasn't pleasant—or that it's anything that reflects on you. It would be because I'm not like other girls—not better, heaven knows, but different. Please keep your lips still, Eric, this first time."

He nodded and turned his head. She laid her lips softly against his and did not move them for a long while. Then she turned away and smiled, a slow, forlorn, sweet smile.

He had felt no passion in her or in himself, not even its suggestion, yet he had recognized a great moment in his history, an experience touching and beautiful. He came of no stoic race, but indeed of one of the most sensitive and emotional of the human family, and he was profoundly moved. For a long while he did not attempt to speak. The smell of the salt air he knew so well became sharp in his nostrils, different than before and yet, it seemed, strangely familiar, as though he had breathed it in another existence. The immediate spell passed off, he returned to his own place, yet the wonder of the visitation remained.

"You didn't run away," he said at last.

"No."

"I don't know what to say. I wish I could say something."

"You don't need to say anything. You don't understand what happened. I do—a little—but it's nothing I can tell you. You can do something though. We came here to do the same as other young people. Can we?"

"No. It's all different."

"Why is it different? That worries me."

"I don't know. I hardly know what I'm saying. Sophia, will you lie in my lap?"

"Yes, but only kiss me. As much as you like."

This last was impossible. She did not know the dimensions of his longing, or even his fear of committing trespass. Although her breast pressed lightly against his powerful chest, he could hardly breathe. In a little while her arms moved slowly about his neck, her hands clasping behind it, her need mainly a greater comfort of position. Still she was accepting his kisses with increasing pleasure, then began to respond to them. Her lips grew more round and full and sometimes they clung to his as if in a new wonder of sensation. Then she drew back her head and made a strange remark in a low and jubilant voice.

"We're really *spooning* now, aren't we, Eric?"

He was not estranged from her, even a little. He sensed only a strangeness in her which frightened him a little. His impulse was to press her close, and then to take her out of herself, more into him, by a kiss of unrestrained, full-flowing passion. But a sound disturbed him momentarily.

"It's only a seal or a porpoise swimming around the ship."

"Let's look at it, Eric. Let's run *like hell* down the deck, to see if we can catch up with it. Maybe we can meet again tomorrow night."

They caught up with the swimmer only because now he idled along, and they could not distinguish his shape because he was almost totally submerged. The moon was somewhat bolder than before, and in the faint glimmer that lies close to the water on such nights, Eric could see an erect dorsal fin, about which hung faint, phosphorescent sparklings.

"It's neither one," Sophia said quietly. "It's a big shark. I saw one when Dear Papa took me fishing."

"They're common in these waters," Eric answered.

The intimation of ill omen pertained only to him, he thought, thank God. Sophia did not feel it and was following the weaving fin with eager eyes.

7

The chief engineer of the *Victoria* had the same attitude toward her outmoded power plant as an old man of pith and wit has toward his heart, arteries, and stomach. If well tended, they might serve him well for another twenty-five years. He knew better than to overtax them except in emergencies. When her safety valve was hissing and popping she could cut the seas at fifteen knots. At ordinary times she snored along just over ten. Still, that came to twenty-four times ten, day in, day out.

At this rate about four days would pass from the moment her train of sea gulls had turned back to the southeastern islands until another flock would come clamoring to meet her close to the Kodiak shore. Eric hoped to meet Sophia all three of the remaining nights, only to be disappointed on the second night because of a ship's party in the social hall, with singing, waltzing, and square dancing by piano, accordion, and mouth-organ music furnished by three gifted members of the crew. Since the affair lasted until twelve, and Sophia was its bright, particular star, she could not have slipped away even if she had felt so inclined. It was not he, or any squarehead, who distinguished himself waltzing with her; this honor went to Dr. Hill and the Reverend Arthur Dudley, both of which cheechakos made the young, high-stepping sourdoughs look and perhaps feel like oafs. In fact the minister won the prize as the best dancer, a cribbage board made of walrus ivory. If some hard-shell Baptists looked askance at such goings-on, the gay, distinguished, prematurely gray man of the cloth seemed not to notice.

On her third day's westward sail, the *Victoria* began to be buffeted by a heavy, crossbeam sea. For his own and his crew's comfort as well as his passengers', and with due thought to the danger of heavy mining equipment breaking

54

loose in her hold and knocking a hole in her iron hull, Captain Borne ordered half speed. The storm was of that sort which, once setting in, hangs on with an even, relentless, unbreakable grip for an unpredictable period. The sky was a dismal, dark gray mass. The wind did not raise or lower or veer a compass point. Eric could have expected it in the North Pacific, he thought, but that did not keep him from cursing it bitter and black, and the curses of a dog-driving, hummock-fighting, upper Yukon Norwegian sourdough are a thing to hear and remember.

The effect on the passengers of the monotonous heavy rolling of the vessel was interesting and varied. Seasickness hit or missed with the impartiality of bullets in battle. The few to be seen reeling about the social hall or hanging on to their plates on the wetted-down cloths of the dining saloon were a motley lot, by no means the hardiest of the company. On the whole the squareheads fared fairly well, some born in a rolling steerage in mid-Atlantic, most having shipped on fish boats and little windjammers. Sophia came down for meals, which were hearty enough, then rushed straight back to her father's cabin to administer such medicines as were believed helpful—sarsaparilla, bromides, and brandy. The Reverend Arthur Dudley made no more of the lurching roll than would far-journeying Saint Paul. He walked about with singular grace, watched with wonder and awe the big gray surges of the sea, and consoled those sitting about in postures of revulsion and dejection. A spindly little girl, whose parents lay in agony below, locked her legs about a stanchion and stitched neatly all the day. The hollow-chested bookkeeper of a rich and burly trader roamed about with a dreamy expression, unaware of the storm. The worst was a flashy drummer of mining machinery on his first trip to Alaska, who made his table steward ill by his ferocious appetite, and drove the deck sufferers to distraction by constantly reiterating that the trouble was all in their minds and not in their stomachs and the best medicine would be a good lively game of shuffleboard or quoits.

Eric felt uneasy but did not succumb. About eleven o'clock of both nights he made wistful pilgrimages to the foredeck, knowing he would find it deserted, which, of course, he did. At meals Sophia addressed most of her brief remarks to Captain Borne, once asking if there were any sharks about—she thought she had seen one the night before the storm—and were water fireflies real or a sourdough

55

yarn, like glacier worms? Then in a rash display of spirit raised by this flirtation he whacked his knee quite hard against her. She paid him back with a painful kick on the shin, so, on the whole, he felt more hopeful of the future.

On the fifth day out the wind suddenly died, as though the elements were out of breath, and the quick recuperation of the sick was a wonderful thing to see. The decks, the promenades, and the social and dining halls became again scenes of human animation. The grayness of the sea turned to turquoise blue, with a spray of diamonds on the crest of every wave. Only a pair of gooneys seemed hardly to realize the change of weather. Throughout the storm they had flown about the ship, sometimes hanging almost motionless aloft, then slipping sideways and darting in great swerves. Now their flight was in lovely curves and soarings, but their attendance was as faithful and their purpose as unknown.

Perhaps, Eric thought, they were enjoying each other's company on some sort of adventure which only another albatross could understand.

Shortly after dinner Sophia came on deck in such a dress as he had never seen—of white wool with close-fitting bodice, soft lace collar, pearl buttons, long sleeves, its skirt tight at the hips, flaring at the bottom. Taking the chair beside him, she asked what seemed random questions about his family childhood, and birthplace.

"I came from Nort' Da-kota on the Minny-sota side," he said with elaborate accent. Evidently this was an old joke among squareheads.

"And now you live on the Yukon!"

"Back east we didn't live far from the Missouri, and that's no creek. When I mentioned the Yukon to a girl from Chicago visiting in Seattle, she asked me whether it was spelled Y-u-k-o-n or J-u-k-o-n—and she wasn't so t'ickheaded after all. 'How's any one to know, when a dumb Swede pronounces it by Yiminy?' she said. She was a real lively girl, pretty as a ptarmigan."

"Did you court her, Eric?" Sophia's face remained quite still.

Eric flushed slightly. He was as puzzled by Sophia's asking as by his own inability to lie.

"We got pretty cosy in a cloakroom."

"As cosy as we were the other night?"

"It wasn't anything like that, Sophia. Nothing ever could be."

56

"Why did you name your mine the Gertrude? Was it after a girl?"

"No, it's my mother's name. I named the creek it's on Gertrude Creek. It's quite a stream—about fifty miles long —in the States it would be called a river. You see, up there anybody can name creeks and mountains and lakes after people he knows. You say it a few times and the old-timers call it that and unless there's a special reason, the name's never changed. There's a very beautiful lake not thirty miles from my diggings where Gertrude Creek was dammed up by a landslide. Whether or not I ever see you again after this trip, I'm going to call it Lake Sophia. There are a lot of quaking asp on its shores and they turn pure yellow gold in the first frost. The water is deep blue."

"How big is it?" Sophia asked, looking at him strangely. "A whole mile long?"

"A whole twenty miles long, and not a soul comes to see it, except an Indian hunter once in a while, and me."

"How much gold do you get from your mine, Eric?"

"It averages an ounce a day from April to October when I can run down water. That's just a living, but someday I'm going to find that sluice yust paved wit' gold. That's why I didn't go on to the Klondike when I heard of the big strike. One of the reasons."

"The others?"

"It's not in my bones to follow the strikes. I don't like gold camps. When two Swedes found pay dirt ten miles from me I felt uncomfortable, but it played out and they moved on."

"The winters must seem awfully long."

"Not so very. I trap, and if fur's scarce, I can make ten dollars a day cutting wood for the river steamers."

"I've got to go now."

"How about tonight? It will be chilly in the bow, but if you can come I'll bring a blanket."

"I will if I can. At eleven o'clock."

Eric arrived at the meeting place well ahead of time, with his own Chilcat blanket, blue, fringed, and with the bear design, under his arm. These were becoming scarce since the gold seekers began to swarm the passes. Tonight the moon hung big and coldly bright, eclipsing all but a few far-scattered stars, but its beams did not fall on the chest against the bulkhead; there the dark stayed thick, and, that far, luck was with him still. And then the luck became fabu-

57

lous, incomparable to any he could imagine except its own continuation, when a shadow cast by the lamp over the cabin entrance leaped and grew long beside the rail. The form took shape in the moonlight and moved toward him and then was close beside him in the dark.

"My father hasn't gone to bed, but he thinks I have, so I suppose it's all right," she murmured.

"I don't like to have you be afraid of him."

"I'm not. You don't understand. How could I be afraid of anyone who loves me as much as he does? I just don't want him to know about this until—I know something."

He waited a moment, then said, "That part is your business, not mine." And this he could not explain, although it was perfectly patent, perfectly clear to him.

"Are you afraid of him, Eric? I have reasons to want to know."

"Only that he'll come between you and me."

"That's the answer I wanted. Now what?"

"Will you lie as you did before? I'll put the blanket over your legs. I can stand as much cold as a poochkie."

"What is a poochkie?" she asked, when her breast was against his.

"I can hardly tell you now. It's a bird—a little auk, I guess—he lives on the cliffs of Diomede—and now——?"

"Yes, Eric."

Their kiss was the same as their original kiss. He recaptured the same overwhelming feeling of triumph and surprise. Sophia was so innocent. No, that was not true, instead she was so inexperienced. She had an inward, perhaps a deep knowledge of man and woman. It might be deeper than his own.

After many kisses, when she was warmed and drawing long deep breaths and her slightly parted lips became unearthly beautiful against his own, their tongues touched lightly, almost by accident it seemed, although it was a bold move on his part, prompted not only by desire but by the inkling that great boldness was essential to victory. If it failed he might lose all, because thereby he revealed himself, his innate appeal to one particular person as a man and a lover. The response was a soft sound and then immediate pressure. The clasp of her hands back of his neck tightened.

In the haphazard affairs of his roaming and roving he had felt passion more demanding and intense, but never so sweet. His lovemaking had been usually of a boyish and

58

headlong sort, somewhat crude, which many of his young sourdough ilk thought was the only natural sort. Although he had more imagination than most, he had never dreamed that mouth making love to mouth could be within itself such a complete and perfect human experience. And soon he must hold her high against his breast to prevent what would have shamed him. But it need not shame him, he thought with a new daring, a greater grasp of life. It would not have done so had he understood the slow tremor that passed through Sophia's body, increasing, then ending in complete stillness.

There followed a pause in their wooing of each other, and it was in that interval that both were, not knocked back into reality because they were amid that now, an intense realization of their own beings, but rather shocked into remembrance of the outer world, which for a few minutes had seemed to cease to exist. Another shadow leaped and grew long beside the rail. Sophia had barely time to unclasp her hands and swing her quick, long body into a full sitting position when a tall man emerged from behind the cabin into the moonlight.

He appeared to be making a last round of the deck. The moonlight showed him tall and striking-looking, and his identity did not remain one instant in doubt. Eric felt a cold wave through his body, as runs through a room in a heated cabin when, on a winter night, someone opens the door. Yet his brain remained calm, all his faculties gathered and ready for the crisis.

Dr. Hill's long strides continued and for a few seconds it seemed he would encircle the bow and pass on. He was only a step or two from concealment behind the cabin when he stopped, turned his head, then walked slowly to a position a few feet in front of the two motionless watchers. Then he spoke in his easy, flowing voice.

"You know, that's what you call delayed perception," he said. "I saw you, yet I didn't see you—it didn't register until I had almost passed by. You were rather unsociable not to speak to me."

"We were not sure you'd like it," Sophia said quickly.

"Your being out so late? I didn't know it—I thought you were sound asleep—but I certainly don't blame you, on such a pretty night. How are you, Eric?"

"I am all right, t'ank you," Eric answered in a steady voice.

"Well, I'll be on my way. But, my sweet, you'd better run to bed in a minute or two. The captain tells me we're getting into Kodiak fairly early tomorrow. We'll want to walk about and look at the old town and maybe see a b'ar. I've told you good night once, so I'll see you in the morning. Good night, Eric."

He resumed his long easy stride and quickly disappeared. Sophia was the first to speak.

"He was splendid, wasn't he?"

"Yes, but I honestly don't know why he shouldn't have acted just as he did. Do you?"

"No, he having arrived at a lucky moment—for us. A moment before we wouldn't have even seen him. There's more to it, though, than you know. And, Eric, you were splendid too."

"Then will you kiss me good night? It will mean an awful lot when I get to bed and lie there t'inking."

"I want to."

And the kiss she gave him was soft, tender, and lovely.

8

On Kodiak Island the party of passengers did not walk far enough to see a bear, although a few of them, including Eric and Sophia, saw Windy Willie, a famous character even in a land where characters are never uniform and rarely commonplace.

Windy was hardly forty. His perfectly good name was Terence O'Hara. Most of the time he was a solid fur buyer in the old Russian town, drove hard bargains, and eschewed whisky. But when there came visiting strangers, he turned into a latter-day Baron Munchausen.

"Ask him if he's seen a bear lately," Eric prompted Sophia, when Windy was pointing out the old Russian church across the road from his store.

"Ma'am," he answered instantly, "I guess you'd call the day before yesterday quite lately. You must understand that the Kodiak bear is not only the biggest bear alive but the biggest meat-eating animal on dry land. If a royal Bengal tiger and a Numidian lion attacked him simultaneously, neither would have the chance of a babe in arms. Their skins have been known to stretch sixteen feet. When he r'ars up on his hind legs he looks as high as this here church, except for its steeple. On each side of the little creeks where salmon run, you'll see what looks like deep wagon ruts, the span as wide as a wagon. They're made by the feet of the Kodiak bears, going up and down the creek to fish."

This was an odd mixture of exaggeration and solid truth, as Eric knew well. The Kodiak bear was indeed the largest land carnivore known to man, considerably heavier than the giant polar bear on the wild Arctic coasts. Unstretched skins twelve feet long were not uncommon; the hind foot frequently measured eighteen inches from claw-tip to heel. Eric had seen one when he went ashore from a fish boat at Karluk on Shelikof Strait, and when it stood up to look at him its stature had seemed monstrous. The double ruts worn on each side of the watercourses in the western Alaskan muskeg were one of the wonders of the District.

"I was hunting caribou," Windy went on. "I'd brought only three shells, for two young bucks was all I wanted, with one shell to spare in case I saw a wolverine. I'd shot 'em both and was gutting the carcasses when a bear smelled that fresh meat. He came loping out of the alder bush, and then he saw me, and, ma'am, he gave a growl that would make your blood run cold, and came straight at me."

"Goodness!" Sophia exclaimed.

"He was only fifty feet away when I first saw him. I had to get my hands out of the deer, and they were slippery with blood, so when I grabbed my gun I almost dropped it. By then the bear was almost on top of me and I had to shoot from the hip, and I didn't shoot too good, either. I aimed between his little red eyes but hit him just below the lower jaw and broke his neck. As he fell his paw broke the leg of one of my deer. The skin's in the store if you want to see it."

He beckoned the way, and there, hung from the high rafter, was a green bearskin fully ten feet long. Sophia stared in disbelief.

"I've taken a lot bigger skins, but he was big enough, for a fellow with only one shell in his gun, and cramped besides," Windy remarked modestly.

"You win, Mr. O'Hara," Eric said politely.

"You'll notice the bullet hole in the neck. And over here is one of the deer. I hadn't time to quarter him yet. And you see his front leg is broken."

The party of hearers went forth rather humbly. When Eric had a chance to speak to Sophia, he had a rueful expression.

"You believed that story, didn't you?"

"Well, it seems to be pretty well documented. That's one of my father's sayings."

"I can assure you it was made up out of whole cloth. Some Aleut hunter shot that bear and traded the skin for a sack of sugar. He or some other shot that lame deer. But I wish you'd asked him if he's seen a whale lately. He would have shown us the rope that he'd fastened to the brute with a spear—he cut it yust in time from being yanked down to Davy Jones's locker. On the beach would be his boat, with its bow staved in. I think he makes up stories to fit the objects that he comes across. I doubt if he's ever shot a bear."

"Is he afraid of them?"

"I can't say Windy is a coward in any way. I've never seen any sign of it, and we used to stop here often when I was halibut fishing. I t'ink he feels that the facts can never come up to the yarns he dreams up and loves."

"Eric, you're providing me with a very interesting introduction to Alaska." But she said it with a dim smile, as if the introduction was all there ever would be.

9

A day behind schedule, Captain Borne quickly landed the small freight consigned to Kodiak and weighed anchor in early afternoon. His course was generally west by north, as he made for Shelikof Strait on the shortest route to Unga. And since, strangely, Sophia had invited Eric to sit with her on the deck in a somewhat secluded place, they gazed together at beautiful wooded Afognak Island, northward of Kodiak, and one pillar of the sea gate between the two.

It was now late afternoon, a time of day that human spirits fall, for most of the day is gone, along with most of its hope. It is a lonely time, because night is near and the greater part of that night will be passed in a solitude more profound than that of the Arctic wastes, the soul laid bare and wandering dim paths, in dreams aware of the impenetrable void between it and every other soul. No one knew better than Eric this open secret that all men know, which their brave concept of manhood, or some loyalty to God who made them, will not let them tell or hardly contemplate; but Eric also knew how to set it aside. That was to make friends, make merry when the chance came, and to seek some kind of oneness with nature. Just now he was in the greatest quest he had ever made, to put loneliness away as long and as far as possible. But Sophia had smiled in that odd way, and he was frightened.

"Take a good look at Afognak," he told her, as he waited for something. "It's the last big woods you'll see except a little on this end of Kodiak. From then on, the trees cease. I mean there isn't one all the way to Dutch Harbor, over a t'ousand miles. There's only alder bushes, muskeg, and tundra."

"Why? Is it too far north?"

"No, the peninsula dips southward, and so do the Aleutian Islands. God knows there's plenty of rain, and the temperature hardly ever touches zero, while way up where I live it goes to fifty below and there are countless trees. Some t'ink it's the wind that never stops blowing from here to Attu, but no one really knows."

"The wind. I don't like to think about it. It was blowing hard on the night Sarah told my fortune. Part of it was good, I believed that part and rejected the rest. But none of it was true." She paused and fixed her eyes on his. "Eric, I can't meet you alone any more."

The blow struck within and he did not let its effect show in his face. He waited a little while and then asked, "Do you want to tell me why?"

"I don't know why—at least I can't put it in words."

"Did your fat'er say something to you?"

"Not a word. In fact he said hardly anything to me and kept looking the other way."

"Then you sensed his disapproval?"

"I don't think disapproval is the right word. You asked me, and you've got the right to know, and I'll tell you. He was deeply downcast and severely shocked. I suppose he still thinks of me—tries to anyway—as a little girl. His movements were awkward and fumbling, he was very white, he couldn't get his words out, and some of his sentences were incoherent. That was when we came down to breakfast. He's brooded all day but puts on a good show when he talks to anyone else."

"Won't he get over it soon? I've heard of other fathers who took it hard when their daughters started going out——"

"No, and I won't either. It's not only what he feels and can't say; it's also what I feel and can't say. *They removed from the Red Sea and camped in the wilderness of Sin.* That was part of the fortune that was told me. I know it wasn't sin, what we did last night—it was natural as breathing. Yet I have a feeling of dreadful guilt—as though I'd betrayed the one that I love most. It's a wrong feeling and yet it's there, stronger than I can tell you. Please understand it doesn't bear against you personally. If it were any other man it would have been the same."

"Of course you know I was going to ask you to marry me. I was yust waiting for the most favorable time. I wanted to ask you the moment I saw you."

"Of course I knew, but I'm glad you told me in plain words. And I'd love to marry you, Eric, if there was a chance. I'd love to go with you to your mine, live in your cabin, live by the great river, and see the snow and the river ice go out, and see the northern lights. The trouble is, as near as I can put it, I couldn't make you happy. I could never belong to you."

"I wouldn't want you to belong to me. I'd want you to be free."

"I never can be. I'm bound in a way I can't explain or hardly understand. A doctor would say my personality has been damaged by something that was no one's fault, and it might be true. I say, no matter how it sounds, that I'm a prisoner of love. It's too strong and I can't break free. I suppose that means that in my heart I don't want to break free. It's as though I couldn't live without it."

Eric sat still with his hands open in his lap and although she looked there with a kind of dread, she could read nothing in his weathered face. Then he took from his pocket a little can, and put a little of its contents under his upper lip.

"Excuse me," he said. "It's a little snoose—it's kind of soothing to us squareheads—it's saved a lot of us from yumping in the river. Now I'm going to my cabin and t'ink over what you say. I won't get anywhere with it—I'll yust beat my head against the wall—but I'll tell you now I'm not beaten yet. I don't know what I'll do. I'll try everyt'ing."

"It won't do any good. That's why I wish it was somebody else than you. You're so hard to defeat and you'd take defeat so hard."

Her eyes became very bright and she looked long at the trees on Afognak Island.

10

The coasts of the Alaska Peninsula that the ship skirted became wildly green. Having never visited Ireland, Sophia had never seen such vivid, living green, and its nearest likeness was the Carolina salt marsh in certain seasons, and new-sprouted rice, occasionally planted on some of the old manors going to rack and ruin on the Combahee River. The most brilliant green was the alder thickets, growing in emerald bands on the rising ground and part way up the hills, and the muskeg, a narrow strip of lowland just back of the sand, visible only at close range. Sometimes areas of tundra lay between, this a darker green and, in certain lights, olive color.

Behind the hills rose the Aleutian Range, with snow-covered spectacular peaks. The whole effect was that of beauty, although of an enchanted, unworldly sort. Quite true, not one tree stood up to balk the wind. Sophia kept looking for one—or so she told Eric—it would be a sign of something, if only an exception to prove the rule; and he thought it would mean more than that to her, for he perceived now that she had been suckled in superstition. The best he could do was show her a fox on the beach, a herd of the small barren-land caribou at the foot of a hill, and finally a bear with two cubs fishing in the muskeg. They passed a few Indian villages and once a white trapper's hut.

Elsewhere the land was incredibly void of human beings. It suggested to the imagination an uninhabited planet. They came to Coal Bay, an immense jagged gash in the coast, and behind it towered Pavlof Volcano, one of a handful of peaks that bore a name. Eric thought its height was only about nine thousand feet, but it shot up almost from sea level and its effect on the mind was stunning.

The ship put in at the old Russian town of Unga, where the bearded bishop disembarked, a little freight was left, and five bales of furs, four of seal taken in pelagic hunting and one very small of sea otter, were lightered aboard, for the *Victoria* would not stop here on her return trip. An old Aleut came on deck with a sea-otter skin, hoping to sell it to a passenger. It was dark, lustrous, with silver hairs, the most precious and perhaps the most beautiful fur ever worn by woman. And Eric did not miss his chance to tell Sophia about the strange sea creature, if only to hold her eyes awhile and see them light.

Once they had thronged all the Alaskan coasts south of the Kuskokwim, and their shimmering pelts had brought the Russian traders who first conquered the territory; and in their greed they had half exterminated the sea otters and decimated the Aleut hunters. They were playful creatures that now lived their whole lives in beds of kelp, and the mothers cuddled their cubs in a way too human for a chick-enhearted man to watch. "They'll soon be extinct," Eric said. "They can't make a go of it against the traders, even way out here. I sometimes t'ink that the sea otter and the big bears and us old sourdoughs are kinfolk. We have ways we can't change and we need a lot of room and maybe we'll all pass out toget'er."

This was only one of the many hours Eric spent with Sophia on the deck. She seemed always pleased to have him join her, and sometimes overjoyed, and if he had no reason to believe that his suit prospered in the least, certainly their affair, however changed in meaning, had not ended. His days were bittersweet and brief, his nights dragged from his lying awake and from dreaming interminable flickering dreams. One night he dreamed of wolves howling at the moon, then somehow he had found himself among them; sitting in their weird ring in the snow, mingling his voice with theirs in an eerie chorus.

A few minutes every day, sometimes for longer periods, Eric passed with a man whom he could properly call a new friend. He had been inclined to dislike him at first because of his rather dour manner and stern countenance, although when he smiled there came forth a big smile, pleasant to see. He came of Scotch ancestry, and, first officer of the *Victoria*, he was known as Mate Locke. Eric admitted from the first that he was a good officer, alert, intelligent, tolerating no slackness in the men, and possessing what Eric thought was a good mixture of caution and daring; all of which he knew as well as anyone, causing the hands to regard him as conceited. Certainly he was a proud soul, and probably found it difficult to make friends.

In their first good talk he had explained to Eric that he was making only one round trip on the *Victoria*, to spend the time profitably before he took the bridge of a big new freighter with modern engines, at present making her way from an English shipyard around the Horn. Now he replaced temporarily a mate who had been lured away from the sea to the gold fields.

"I'm Canadian Pacific," he said. "I started with them when I came west and I'll end with them, because it's a big company with big ideas. My new berth won't be as comfortable as this but I'll learn more. When those big liners that the company is planning to build are off the ways—it will be some years yet—I want to be in line for master."

Mate Locke had had no time to talk with Eric during the storm but afterward they held good sessions. And when the ship was off Belkofski he had said something of immediate moment in Eric's life.

"I've told you enough for you to know that I'm an ambitious man. Eric, you are the same."

"I t'ink that's so."

"I'm not speaking now of your mine. You'll either strike it rich or hit for greener pastures. Hoping you'll excuse me, I'm speaking of your courtship of a beautiful girl, as beautiful as I can remember seeing, a girl of unusual education, and a highborn lady besides."

"How did you know of it?"

"The whole ship knows you're badly smitten. Everybody, I mean, except Dr. Hill, who can't see the woods for the trees. But I think I'm the only one except you two who knows you've run into rough weather. You haven't been meeting her lately on the foredeck."

"Where did you hear that, Mate Locke?" Eric asked quietly and politely.

"I didn't hear it. I don't listen to gossip— I keep my eyes open. Well, I hope you'll soon come out into the calm. I respect ambitious fellows and their bold ventures. Just don't lose your nerve."

"It takes a lot of nerve, I tell you."

"You've got it. And remember this. I'm a Canadian but you are an American. The old caste system still lingers on in such English possessions as Canada; even there it's breaking up fast. In America only its shadow remains—except, perhaps, in the Deep South. Your Declaration of Independence gave it a swift kick, and Washington finished the job when he kicked out King George. You are an Alaskan, a pioneer in a great country. Don't think little, think big. Fight like hell to win."

"T'ank you, I sure will."

"As for me," Mate Locke went on after a slight pause, his expression and his voice revealing tension, "I'll never forget her as long as I live. I'll never command a bridge so high and fine that she won't visit my thoughts. Just to be shipmates with her is a great experience."

The ship sailed by False Pass, a narrow waterway navigable only to boats of shallow draft between the last cape of the Alaska Peninsula and Unimak Island. This last was a mighty island with the most wild and rugged scenery they had yet seen, and crowned with three snowy peaks. One, a perfect cone, considered among Alaska's most beautiful, had been named Shishaldin, but the sailors called it Smoky Moses because of the volcanic vapors that ever streamed from its summit and scattered in the wind. Before the Russian traders came, it was the habitation of fifteen hundred Aleuts. Now it lay desolate except for giant bears of the Kodiak species, smaller fur bearers, deer, hawks and eagles and migratory birds, and the ptarmigan of piteous cry, and even little birds that whistled sweetly, and the salmon that rushed into the creeks to spawn and die. When the *Victoria* had passed its long, wave-worn beaches, there remained only a night's run to Dutch Harbor, the metropolis of the West, where she would turn into Bering Sea.

She steamed into the port soon in the morning. The town boasted a Russian church, a large trading post, a warehouse, the offices of a postmaster, a marshal, and an Indian agent, several small houses occupied by Russian half-breeds, and about a hundred *barabaras*, which were whalebone earth-covered homes of Aleut Indians. And here the passengers, expecting nothing new in the way of sights, were treated to a small measure of excitement.

It began soon after the trader and two officials who had been alerted by mail extended a welcome to the new school director. As the passengers watched, they noted, too, a young man and a very young woman, obviously aliens to this furthest west of all American outposts, standing by with anxious faces. Afterward the welcomers called Captain Borne and Dr. Hill aside for a hurried consultation. It had gone on hardly five minutes when the captain summoned Eric.

"Our friends here have a problem which they have asked us to help solve," Captain Borne explained. "It concerns a part of Alaska that you know better than any of us. Mr. Foley, will you tell Eric, too, what you were starting to tell us?"

Mr. Foley was better known as Foxskin Foley. A tall, thin man of about fifty, almost bald, he had been one of the detachment of American troops who had saluted the Russian flag when it had been hauled down from Baranof Castle in Sitka. A successful trader, he was known to deal more fairly with the natives than many in the business.

"Eric, you see those two young people yonder. Their names are Frank and Fannie Ford, from San Francisco, and they're crazy to get to the Klondike. They had no money to pay their passage by the short route through Skagway and the White Pass, but in Seattle the skipper of a halibut boat offered to fetch them this far on the long route if Frank would work his way. I don't think Frank would be much of a sailor, and I know that old bull seal and I reckon he thought Fannie might pay their passage, one way or another. He put 'em on shore here, where Frank thought he could make money for the rest of his trip catching sea otter. Well, you can guess how a rank cheechako who'd never been to sea would shine at that. Take a look at him."

Eric did so, a quick, trenchant glance, and the impression he received of the very tall, long-jawed blond man in his twenties was not one of ordinariness—because Eric saw the ordinary man as a brave and capable fellow—but of discontent and futility. His wife of about seventeen offered a far more interesting study. In the first place, she was pretty, small, brunette, with quite delicate facial structure and large, arresting brown eyes. She had dressed unsuitably for this scene which might betray vanity. And the tortured smile that she threw to Eric as their eyes met touched him and could very easily imply a degree of desperation.

"Frank says if they can get to St. Michael they can work their way to the Klondike on a river steamer, she as a stewardess and he at odd jobs. Eric, are the Yukon boats as shorthanded as they were, or have enough gold seekers gone broke that they're a glut on the market?"

"I t'ink the boats are still shorthanded. When I came down the last time I stood a trick in the stokehole, ten dollars a day, to help the old scow along. I t'ink they could make it all right. You should see some of the cheechakos that have come down-river, traveling first class, wit' big pokes of gold."

"Cap'n can't take deadheads and he says he doesn't want Frank in his crew." Foley turned to Dr. Hill. "Sir, they'll need two hundred dollars, eighty for steamer fare to St. Michael, and the rest to buy their outfit. I've raised thirty of it here. Would you think it proper to pass the hat among the passengers to make up the rest?"

"Perfectly proper, if the captain gives his permission."

"Sure."

"And I'm going to ask Eric to do the hat passing in my

place. He's one of Alaska's own, while I'm a cheechako. Will you, Eric? Make a little speech to tell the passengers what it's for."

Eric nodded gravely and took off his hat and turned straightway to a little crowd of passengers.

"Ladies and gentlemen and old sourdoughs," he began in a deep and quite resonant voice, "there are two people who've been stranded and need help to get to St. Michael and the gold fields. We've got forty dollars, counting my contribution——"

"It's fifty now," Dr. Hill broke in, dropping a bill in the hat.

"T'ank you." And then with a grin, palpably enjoying the situation, "One time in Minnesota we all went to a camp meeting. They had a big preacher from down Sout', and before they passed the plate for him he said he didn't want to hear the money drop in, he wanted it to fall soft and not jingle. Well, if I said that here, the cheechakos among us would have to pay the fare. All sourdough money jingles but with a good ring to it, and dust and nuggets are welcome too. The ladies needn't contribute but the men will kindly remember when they were stranded somewhere wit' no grub."

Dropping in a ten-dollar gold piece, Eric passed the hat. Many of the men did the same; the least donation was five dollars, in coin, bills, or nuggets, and one old miner ostentatiously brought out pocket scales, measured twenty dollars in gold dust from his poke, and added it to the pile. The grand total topped the goal set by about forty dollars.

The crowd cheered, highly pleased with their own human kindness, and some of the women went over to beam on Fannie. Eric, however, was fated for a moment of acute exasperation, to be followed by many troubled reflections and misgivings. It occurred after the donation had been delivered to Frank. Waiting his chance he called Eric aside.

"I thought they'd give more than that," he complained peevishly. "Some of them passengers are millionaires and could put in a hundred dollars and never miss it. Outfits are mighty costly up there. I've got to buy dogs if I'm going to prospect in virgin country, and a winter supply of grub."

Eric almost bit his tongue, held his breath, then said something in Norwegian. "That means," he explained, " 'don't look the gift horse in the mout'.' And, Frank, you be damned careful to stay out of virgin country, unless you want to turn into a pillar of solid ice. You stake your claim near a camp, where someone can hear you holler."

"I can look out for myself, and for Fannie too. But I'm much obliged to you for what you done, and since you know all the sourdoughs, tell me about one or two who've got plenty and are easy spenders." He paused, then added with a show of dingy teeth, "and if he has an eye for a pretty woman it won't do no harm."

"I don't get the idea," Eric answered, in a neutral tone.

"What's a man's wife for but to help him out when he's down on his luck? Fannie won't go too far, just play him along, and if the old fool's wallet gets flattened a little, it will be a good joke on him."

"I'm a miner, not a pimp," Eric answered brutally, turning away.

11

Eric at once caught up with a small group making for Mr. Foley's store. It included the proprietor, Dr. Hill, Sophia, Reverend Dudley, Mr. Pike, whose pantries were running short on several items, and a middle-aged, Middle Western couple bent on an adventure tour of the Alaskan coast. The glances Sophia gave him were slightly different than of late, although he could not have possibly told in what manner. Her voice seemed deeper and more rich. He thought that she might be pleased with his way of taking collections and his little speech, and of course she did not know how easily Alaskans are shaken down by a hard-luck story, or dream of the unpleasant aftermath.

But there was more to it. Her pale olive cheeks had a spot of rose, her eyes were superbly lighted, her pale hair had a golden sheen in the lovely Alaskan sunlight.

"That girl you helped out is very pretty," she remarked to Eric, out of hearing of the rest.

"I thought so too."

"You could have her if you like. She despises that man. She's got more to her than her silly clothes would show."

"I t'ink she's in for trouble—big trouble."

"I didn't say she's worthy of you, Eric. You know, you are a natural leader."

"I sure didn't know it."

"My father felt it the first day. He's highly intuitive about everyone but me."

All of them entered the store, looked at the shelves laden

71

with brick tea, canned pork and beans, and, oddly enough, canned sardines, cube sugar, block salt, bolts of cloth, thread that had long since taken the place of sinew, tinware that had supplanted native pottery, lanterns burning kerosene instead of stone seal-oil lamps with wicks of moss, rifles and shells succeeding bows, arrows, and spears—all things for which the Aleuts traded their beautiful furs, whalebone, pearl shell, and fossil ivory. These goods were kept in his warehouse, Mr. Foley explained. While a half-caste clerk waited on Mr. Pike, he would take his guests there for a quick look. During the short walk the party was reduced to the host, Eric, Sophia, Dr. Hill, and Captain Borne, as the others drifted off.

They had hardly entered the roughly built, musky-smelling building when Dr. Hill noticed two beautifully made fly rods laid on pegs in the wall. He stopped to admire them.

"Do you like to fish?" Mr. Foley asked.

"I love it, but I don't get to do so very often."

"Can you handle a fly rod?"

"Since you ask, I'm rather expert with one. I used to fish for trout in the Berkshires when I was young."

"Well, I can give you some fishing like you never dreamed. Right now—not two hundred yards from this spot. We're about the same height. You're heavier but you can get into a pair of my old pants and mukluks. It's generally believed that salmon coming upriver can't be caught by hook and line. That doesn't hold with the silvers that are swarming into our creek, and they weigh as much as eight pounds, and the way they can horse about in that fast water is something to see. You'll use salmon eggs for bait. You can catch just as many as you have time to play and land." In his enthusiasm he seemed quite a different man.

"Can I give my catch to the Indians?" Dr. Hill asked, flushing with pleasure.

"Better yet, you can give them to Pike for the passengers' supper aboard ship. One thing that the Indians are not shy of is salmon."

"I'd like to go along and watch," Captain Borne said.

"You're more than welcome. Sophia——?"

"I had wanted to look at the furs."

"Show them to her, Williams," Foley shouted to a stringy antediluvian clerk sitting in a crude half-walled office, writing in a book. "If you're busy, have Charley do it." Charley was evidently the Chinese stitching deerhide bales in the rear.

A moment later the three bustled off, and the noise in the warehouse ceased. Williams did not look up from his book. Charley continued to stitch. Eric and Sophia breathed in the rank smell of fox, mink, seal, wolverine, and otter skins, mingling with one another and with what Eric thought was the strange smell of precious ambergris. They did not speak.

For a moment they walked about aimlessly in the big dim barnlike building. They looked at some fossil walrus ivory, a lustrous, inimitable black. Then Sophia called to the old clerk, "I'd like to see some silver fox. Maybe I'll buy one."

Williams knew he had been addressed, but apparently he did not hear plainly. He wrote another line, closed the book, rose slowly from his chair, and approached the young people, in a slow cautious walk. In the way of old men he did not speak to them until he was close by, then he shouted.

"What did you say, ma'am?"

"Could I see some silver-fox skins?"

"I think they're all baled. You can ask Charley. Now I must go to my house. Charley will show you anything you want to see."

He walked away and forgot the visitors and the door closed behind him. In silence, as though working a charm, they walked to the rear of the building to deal with Charley. He was a handsome man of about thirty—Eric thought he was a mixture of Chinese, Aleut, and Russian.

"Charley?" Eric called, not knowing what he should say next.

"I heard what you said to Mr. Williams," he said in what was no doubt missionary English, perfectly correct but strangely accented. "We have no silver-fox skins; we have shipped the last; the old man has forgotten. We have nothing unusual here but a very large bearskin, perhaps the finest I, for one, have ever seen. It was taken on Unimak Island and has red fur and white claws. It is in the loft, rolled up under the bench. Would you like to see it?"

"Very much."

"There are the stairs. If you wish me to go with you——"

"It isn't necessary."

"Very well, missy." And this address was not from missionary English but from pidgin English. Charley's tongue had slipped.

Sophia led the way up the narrow unbanistered plank stairs. The loft was fairly small, with a railing, perhaps to safeguard Williams if he ever had business there. Some bales of skins were stacked here, and there was nothing else but the bench under which Eric found the bearskin. It was loosely rolled and when he had laid it flat on the floor he saw that it was indeed a remarkable skin, huge, thick-furred, with the ivory-looking foreclaws that are not rare in the Kodiak species but which add greatly to the value of a pelt. However, he noticed that it had been fleshed too closely and the fur would probably fall out.

He saw all this at first glance and immediately forgot it. His mind was on Sophia only. His whole being was fixed and concentrated upon her and he did not speak and his thoughts moved tardily if at all, being arrested by his pre-occupation with desire. Her hair still looked palely luminous, and that increased his desire, and so did her big-pu-piled eyes and the obscure one-sided smile of her long lips, and so did the slim shape of her body, and even the light way she stood and the upward toss of her head had the same effect.

And then a sound came up the stairs. An appreciable time passed before it could distract his attention from her to take hold of it and deal with it. It had been Charley's voice and the words were, "I go to lunch now. Stay as long as you like and look at anything you please." Then Eric heard the door shut and the charm that had been working had been cast, and Sophia and he were all alone in the empty, silent, wildly scented building.

It came to him to say that there was nothing unusual about them being left here, that nobody in Alaska guarded against theft, that all doors were unlocked day and night. He did not because a more urgent matter was forcing his lips and tongue to another course. Anyway, she probably knew this Alaskan way of doing, for it had romantic appeal for people and had been widely told.

He spoke at last, deep in his throat because his breath was short.

"Sophia, will you take back what you said?"

"I don't have to take it back. I haven't met you alone. We've been left alone."

"What does that mean?"

"What you can make it mean."

He took her in his arms and after their first fierce kiss he lifted her and laid her on a strange bed and lay down beside her. After an unearthly moment of deep, full communion of their mouths he unbuttoned her blouse and pushed down her shift. She wore no corset to delay and balk him; men like Dr. Hill did not approve of garments that restricted exercise and full breathing. He cupped his hand over one lovely breast, small, firm, warm, perfectly formed, and he felt the nipple come erect against his palm. Then she turned her head and whispered in his ear.

"Do more than that to it, Eric."

He took it between both hands and lowered his head and did her heart's desire. Then after a long while she whispered again, not knowing what she was saying, although Eric knew too well, and then she, too, knew what she had said in a soft and loving voice.

"Dear Papa . . ."

He drew his lips from her breast and lay still and his skies were falling and he could not speak when she spoke sharply.

"Eric, this is your only chance. Our only chance."

"Tell me, for God's sake."

"Take me now, or let me go for good. I'll try not to resist you. If I do— and that awful guilt may make me—use your full strength. Rape me, Eric. That's what I'm asking. I can't give, but you can take and perhaps . . . perhaps . . ."

Her words died away, and soon her struggle began, not to attack, only to defend, yet it was very strong. She did not cry out, her nails did not flail, but her body writhed before at last it grew still. No sign of renewed ecstasy came into her face. But when he rose at last and stood looking at her with eyes black with shame, his face livid, waiting for he knew not what, hope swelled his heart again when she burst into childish tears.

"I am yours, Eric," she sobbed, "and I am free."

3.   Northward Sail

When Dr. Hill and Mr. Foley returned from fishing, the faces of both men prideful of the catch, Eric and Sophia were roaming about the native town, looking at worked walrus ivory, skillfully fashioned kamlekas, these being waterproof outer garments made of gut, and *oomiaks* and *oomiak-sooks*, middle-sized and very large skin-covered boats. Also their nostrils were filled with the inimitable smell of smoked or sun-dried salmon hanging on racks, and their eyes delighted with many Aleut faces, some of them old, weathered, and wise, and many young, fresh, and engaging. They ceased their leisurely perambulations to hurry to meet the angler and his beaming host. The salmon weighed easily fifty pounds, and, on two strings to share the weight, still looked silvery and bright in the sunlight.

Eric knew there was a new expression on his own face as well as on Sophia's; he did not know both were strangely alike. He did not think Dr. Hill would notice either just now, he being full of his own triumph; Eric was more inclined to fear the sharp trader eyes of Mr. Foley.

"Doctor, you weren't bragging when you said you were expert with the fly rod," Eric ventured.

"I was bragging, Eric, but Mr. Foley maintains it had more substance than the story of Mr. Windy Willie's bear hunt. Sophia, I never dreamed there was such fishing this side of the Other Shore, and quite doubtful of it there. I swear to you I never had my bait ten seconds in the water without a smashing strike. Mr. Foley, how many fish that I hooked made good their escape?"

"One, when he lodged behind a rock and the hook tore out. Miss Hill, your father handles a fly rod in a different fashion from any angler I've ever seen. You know in England the first rule with a big fish is 'show him the butt.' I've had English bear hunters fish here and they make a big point of it. That means to hold the rod with the butt toward the fish, with the whole bend of the rod for him to play against. Your father does that but holds his rod high over his head as well, to keep the fish near the surface, handling his line as deftly as a musician handles strings. He's deadly, I tell you. I thought he was going to break my rod, he struck so hard when the fish ran, but he knew just what it could take. I've never seen a fisherman lose so few fish."

"You give me too much credit, my friend. But you've also given me the finest sport I can remember in a coon's age. Darling, did you have an interesting time?"

"Very. And speaking of the Other Shore, a well-educated part-Russian Indian told me something interesting. Long ago the Aleuts knew how to embalm their dead. He said some mummies had been found on Atka Island, and beside them lay their fish spears and bone hooks." Sophia spoke gravely, big-eyed, and it might be a remarkable piece of histrionics to mask her feelings, Eric thought, but most likely as natural as breathing.

"I'll have to look into that when I have time. I'm rather glad, though, that embalming is a lost art; God knows I don't want any poor clay preserved an hour longer than necessary." He was speaking only to her, forgetful of all others. Eric perceived again their profound companionship, and a little bell in his brain rang a dim and far-off alarm.

"Doctor, I wish you'd get the President to make Dutch Harbor your headquarters instead of in the cold North. It's halfway between St. Michael and Sitka."

"It would be most pleasant. And now I'd best take these fish to Pike."

"Isn't that coals to Newcastle?" Sophia asked, her eyes shining.

"A bad pun, darling, and hence a good pun."

"I'll take those fish," Eric said quickly. For he needed to get off by himself.

By the time he had completed his errand, all through passengers had returned to the ship, hungry for supper. Five had packed their bags and departed, among them the trader sharing Eric's stateroom. To his great joy, a piece of luck that surely showed his star in the ascendant, none of six newcomers had been assigned the empty berth. He had told Sophia of the possibility and now he could hardly wait to tell her of the fact.

The chance came when she was waiting on the deck for Dr. Hill, who was scrubbing off fish slime. She stood in a deserted part and seemed to be daydreaming. His heart thudding in spite of Lady Luck, he blurted out the news.

"I'm so glad," she answered.

"Yesus," he breathed.

"Do you sleep like a log? Of course not."

"No, I'm a great dreamer, and when I set myself, I can wake at the slightest sound."

"No matter anyway. Your door will not be locked. Eric, if it happens, it will be about two in the morning. Papa reads till midnight, then sleeps like a baby."

"Make it happen, Sophia."

"Trust me. I'll never fail you. If I don't come tonight it

will be because of circumstances I can't avoid, then there will be tomorrow night. I have to warn you about something, though. I told you I was free but some time will pass —and a good many things have to happen—before I can truly realize it and act upon it. Dear Papa has to realize it too and accept it, and that isn't easy when we love each other as we do."

"Yust do your best."

"I was thinking, just before you came up, what you told me about the ice going out of the Yukon. It goes out in great turmoil and struggle. There must be breach after breach until the pressure piles up and it moves as a cataclysm. But the ice never goes out of the Arctic Ocean, does it?"

"It breaks up in awful violence and sound, and draws back until the bays are clear and the Eskimos can launch their boats. There are great ice floes and ice fields further north, then solid ice again."

"I used to dream often of ice and snow. I dreamed of it again last night. I seem to be lost in it—and there's only one light—and it goes out. Love me, and be patient with me. Now leave me alone here to meet Papa."

At supper he spoke very little to Sophia, who was in grave conversation with her father across Captain Borne's empty chair. The captain stood on his bridge, taking the *Victoria* out of Dutch Harbor and around the peninsula to the southward of Unalaska Island, making for big Umnak Pass into Bering Sea. He did not venture immediately north between that island and Akutan because the channel had not been well charted and the waterlogged hull of a derelict floated just under the surface somewhere in its narrow waters.

When this menace to navigation was mentioned at the supper table—it had been found and then lost by a fish boat not many weeks before—Eric recalled a story, whether true or fictitious he did not know, told him by Mate Locke. Locke had evidently believed the tale, despite its extreme strangeness. Eric thought of telling it to his tablemates, reconsidered, then decided to essay it—squarehead dialect be damned. His main impulse sprang from the realization that he must put his best foot forward in Dr. Hill's presence and not lag. He must give play to such mind as he possessed, which actually, in his secret estimations, he held in high respect. Beside that, he wanted to please Sophia.

"I heard a good story of the sea, whet'er or not it really happened," he began, in his full resonant voice that at once locked his hearer's interest.

He began to tell them about a ship such as he had never seen. She was the acme of luxury—except down below where immigrants traveled—and plied between New York and Southampton at twenty knots, competing with the *City of New York* and the *City of Paris* for the carriage trade. Her gross weight exceeded thirteen thousand tons.

On this particular voyage she had shipped a fool. Although rich and highborn, he indulged in mimicry, song and dance, parlor tricks, and in practical jokes of an elaborate order. In mid-Atlantic on a day of thick fog, while her captain stood taut on her bridge, the fool and some friends were sitting below it. "Do you want me to give those fellows up there a start?" he asked. His friends said no, for God's sake, behave yourself; still he persisted in his rattle-brained idea. Cupping his hands over his mouth, he perfectly imitated the deep resonant whistle of a big liner, and such were his powers of ventriloquism, assisted by a light breeze on the bow, that the sound seemed to come out of the gray smother directly ahead of the ship.

The consequences were far greater than the fool had ever anticipated.

"The cap'n got busy, as well he might," Eric said, with a slow grin. "He ordered the helm hard over and full speed astern. Well, those engines were mighty big, and the piano slid across the social hall, and all the dishes fell off the tea tables, and the booze hounds in the bar spilled their drinks. The fool was scared stiff and his friends were so ashamed of him that they yust faded away. But what do you t'ink?"

All his hearers shook their heads, meanwhile waiting in suspense, and Sophia's eyes had lighted.

"A shape took form in the fôg and there lay a big derelict. The cap'n missed striking her by half a cable's length and he would have sunk his own ship except for the fool. He saw that her boilers were cold and her hull encrusted wit' salt so she looked like a ghost ship. When not long after he got drowned in a harbor-boat accident, he died believing that the sound in the fog was the voice of God."

"It may have been," Dr. Hill said quietly. "By heaven, I won't say it wasn't. Sometimes I think He moves among men only through the hands and minds of men."

The rest were made thoughtful, and five minutes passed

before the table conversation again got into full swing.

Supper over, Eric went to bed and to sleep. Time stood still and had seemed endless when he was wakened by the soft opening of his door. For an instant a shape stood there in silhouette against the dim glimmer in the corridor; then the door closed, and a thing that he had dreamed, but had never really believed, had come true. A small lamp, made like a ship's lantern, stood by his bed. He lighted it, the little flame increased. Sophia was wearing a robe of glimmering silk over her nightgown and bedroom slippers, and her flowing pale gold hair appeared faintly luminous.

She took off her slippers, placed them in easy reach on the floor, and hung her robe over the foot of the bed.

"Will that light show under the door?" she asked in hushed tones.

"I don't t'ink so. Everyt'ing fits very tight on the *Vic*."

"Then leave it on."

"Good. I want to see your face."

He stretched out his arm and she lay in its hollow, her mouth against his. There followed a courtship in which both were inexperienced, but which the native tenderness of a strong man kept in rhythm with slowly mounting passion. He made love to her whole body, remaining perceptive of its loveliness, her gift to him instead of his conquest, and perceptive of living poetry in spite of no long steeping in the beauty of written poetry, such as served Sophia and cast its magic glow over her thoughts and feelings and actions and had somehow become reflected in her face and form. He had felt it while watching the effortless cosmic sweep of the river under the silent hills. He had heard it in the cry of ptarmigan flying alone on a vast, empty plain. The lamp burned dimly; the port and starboard lights of the vessel shone over the dark sea and might be watched with unceasing wonder by a band of Aleut hunters in their wave-tossed oomiak; the waves made a singing sound along her hull; and always before when such harmony had touched him, he had been alone.

What the two sought, they found. Despite the high pitch of ecstasy that was for each his own—love-blessed, as exquisite a human experience as life can give, because it is the way that life itself is given—their greatest discovery was of each other, warm and close and sharing. Her maiden pain dropped into a lost and irrecoverable past. For good or ill, their fates were inextricably joined.

Their last port of call was St. Paul, one of the two main islands of the Pribilofs, two days' sail from Umnak Pass in Bering Sea. The word port was a misnomer. It had no bay, no shelter for ships except what they could find in its lee, this changing with every wind. The few vessels touching here often must hang off for several days in the summer season before they dared come nigh; when September gales set in, it remained virtually isolated until June. Yet throughout the winter, Aleut Indians, planted here by the Russians long ago, seal killers, skinners, and fleshers, went forth in their skin boats to fish and to hunt whales, in weather that would cause a seasoned sailing skipper to reef all his canvas and heave to.

In summer there was other traffic in and about St. Paul and her sister island St. George, and this was among the most interesting in the wide world. Since time out of mind these naked windswept beaches had been breeding grounds of the fur seals. Every year they returned from the sea like salmon to the rivers, never learning the danger here, the cruel instinct unchangeable, and every year their herd, the last of the great herds, was visibly less.

Eric told Sophia they should begin to see signs of this traffic a hundred miles this side of St. Paul—and other sights not nearly as pleasant.

The lovers had met in Eric's stateroom on the second night out of Dutch Harbor, and again on the third night. This night she gave him a pearl stickpin of considerable beauty and value. "It was one of the few nice things that my grandfather Toland Sams was able to keep when he lost his plantation on the Combahee," she told him. "He gave it to me before he died, and said I was to give it to my true love. But, Eric, don't wear it until I tell you. That will be a day or two before we get into St. Michael."

"I'd like to wear it tomorrow. We're engaged, aren't we?"

"Yes, but there's still a lot of ice to break. I want Papa to see it that long before you ask for his consent. The sight will shock him terribly—and then perhaps the final shock will not be so great."

"All right. I'll talk to him when you say, but yust now I can't think of anything more frightening. Sophia, I've never had anything like this before. I could have bought a pearl pin, maybe, when I was flush, but it would have been out of my class—we sourdoughs know about class, even if wild horses couldn't drag it out of us—and this is legacy besides. All I have to give you is my ring. I was willing to give it to the purser to sit at your table. Still, it's made from the first handful of nuggets I took from Gertrude Mine, and that I washed, hoping and praying, with a pan."

"It's a wonderful engagement ring for an Alaskan bride. It's too big for my finger but I'll wear it on a chain, as you said. I'll put it on the same day you wear your pin."

She stayed longer than before—about two hours—and the lovers embraced at her arrival and again just before she left. They knew each other as lovers do—that strange complex of sensation and emotion that can never be clearly anticipated or recaptured in memory—and in addition they seemed to draw close to a mystery and wonder that must lodge within the soul, impenetrable to thought. Then they could scarcely bear to part. Sleep was so lonely, dreams so wandering.

Rather early the following morning, when most passengers were dressing for breakfast—or wondering whether to dress at all, since a moderately heavy sea was running—the man Frank Ford came up to Eric, who was standing by the rail.

"Not much to do on this damned ship," he remarked.

"Shuffleboard is a good game," Eric answered with an expressionless face.

"It's not my style. When the people play cards they play seven-up and whist. Poker's my meat, with the sky the limit. But not a hand has been dealt on this ship since I came aboard."

"You can have plenty of that in the gold camps."

"She's twenty years behind the times. You ought to see some ships running between San Francisco and the Orient; then you'd know what a real ship looks like. The *Vic* has good beds and fair food—I'll say that for her. But, you know, Andersen, I don't sleep as well as I ought to in them beds."

"So?"

"I've made a habit of waking up around midnight and lying there making plans. And there's a board that creaks when anyone walks by just outside our stateroom."

"I wouldn't t'ink many people would be passing that time of night." Eric's voice had changed a little—not roughened, softened if anything—but apparently Frank did not

82

notice it, for his manner became more bold, and his dingy smile more disagreeable to see.

"Oh, a few do—going to bathrooms and such as that. Well, the night before last the board creaked when I hadn't heard any footsteps. Whoever it was, was walking on tiptoe. I was curious what the person was up to so I partly opened the door and caught a glimpse of her under the lamp down the corridor. I couldn't mistake that pretty shape that belongs to only one young lady on this ship. I took it she was making for the head, so I didn't think any more about it."

"That was probably a good idea."

"But she stayed about an hour. I heard her when she came back. When it happened again last night, I watched where she went—and it wasn't the head. That time she stayed two hours. Well, she was an innocent girl when I first saw her in Dutch Harbor—not all them fine young ladies are, but she was—and I've done a lot of thinking about it, Eric. Some men would feel duty bound to tell her father."

"Are you one of those men?" Eric asked.

"No, my way is to live and let live. Still, I might give some good advice. It isn't an ordinary case of 'Ole couldn't vait'—like in the story. You know, how the license clerk told Frieda that she looked as if she might have a little Swede in her. There won't be any license clerk in this case. The man she's visiting isn't in her social class or money class either. He hasn't got a dog's chance, and I don't know what her father would do if he found out what's going on. So my advice to that fellow would be my own doctrine— live and let live, with me."

"How much do you want, Frank?"

"A hundred dollars to help me out with my outfit. You own a little mine—it wouldn't hurt you—and I'd forget all about it."

There was a broad band of violence running through Eric's nature. He did not let it move but his eyes became the color of polar ice.

"I won't give you that, Frank, so you'll forget it. I may give you something else. If I'd lose my footing and fall against you, you'd go over the rail. Stand right there by it and don't move till I tell you."

"I never——"

"We're aft. Nobody could swim and get you. Before the ship could haul around, you'd be in the water half an hour, and that's too long, with this sea running, and you'd forget everything you ever knew and tell nobody nothing ever again."

Frank glanced into Eric's eyes, then his whole face looked dingy.

"I never intended to—that's the God's truth. Do you think I'd try to make trouble for a shipmate who'd passed the hat for me? Now you be careful, Andersen. Someone would see you shove me and I'd yell for help and everybody would know you done it. Keep your temper, I say. I thought you might do me a favor, that's all."

"I think I'd be doing everybody a favor, including Fannie."

"Speaking of Fannie, she's going to be on that river boat up the Yukon while your girl is heading back Outside. Her father has already arranged for her transportation. I got that straight from the purser. Fannie's right taken with you, Eric—I know the signs. I'm not jealous of her—what's the use of being jealous of any woman—and not to do any bragging, she's the best in the West Coast."

A slight change came over Eric so that Frank knew that he was safe. Perhaps he thought that his proffer had made him so, and he could not know that instead it was the news he had told. Eric had put his mind on it and his thoughts flew to what he might do, the best and surest thing. Anyway, he could do nothing about human dregs being washed northward in these days of the gold rush. Probably there were no few; and thank God he and Sophia were going to disembark on his own unpeopled shore. This last was his certain aim.

"Now get the hell out and stay out," Eric said.

Frank walked away, his lips twitching as though he were about to weep.

3

Still fifty miles from St. Paul, Eric showed Sophia and Dr. Hill an early sign of the sea traffic that made this and its sister island the subject of wonder of all men who followed the sea and of nature lovers and savants the world over. It was an animal about five feet long, sinuously shaped, its feet tucked under its body so that it suggested a small dolphin leaping out of the sea in long arcs, vanishing from sight, then leaping again, a wonderfully rhythmic action and swift progression.

"That's a mother seal from the rookeries on one of the two islands," Eric explained. "She's been out fishing, and now she's going back with milk in her breast for her *kotik,* her baby seal. The beaches swarm with pups, but she'll go tearing through them, knocking them right and left, until she finds her own, and there's no use of any other baby grabbing at her as she goes by. But an awful lot of seal mothers start out and never return. The sealing boats ring the island and kill them coming and going. It's a wasteful process, not only because half the seals that they shoot go to the bottom before they can launch a boat and pick them up. Besides, when they kill one they kill three—the mother, the baby that no other mother seal will let suck, and the unborn baby in her womb."

"I've heard about it," Dr. Hill replied. "It's a damned outrage."

"We'll lose all our seals if it isn't stopped. The sealing on the island is pitiful. The bachelor seals, that is the males not yet big enough to maintain a harem against the other bulls, are herded away from their playgrounds—there's no other word; they do nothing but play all summer except for going out to fish—and then clubbed. They amble along to their deaths never knowing that men are their enemies. But the sealers know better than to bot'er the old bull seals guarding their harems on the beaches. They'd get thrown from bull to bull like a rag doll and be torn to pieces."

"I wish we weren't going there," Sophia said.

"Sometimes a bull without a harem goes berserk and charges the beaches. The other bulls throw him just as easy and he's lucky to get away torn and bleeding. Each has his own space and that's private. But if you can forget the slaughter—that the herd of two million that the Russians found is now down to a quarter of a million—well, it's still one of the great sights of the world."

"I never want a fur coat."

"I don't think you should say that, Sophia," Dr. Hill reproved her gravely. "Eric is himself a trapper when he can't run his mine. Eskimos and coastal Indians couldn't live without killing hair seals and sea lions and walrus. White men up here have got to live, or leave. Few men can live anywhere except by the taking of other lives. But killing must be as merciful as possible, which many men forget, and it must not be wasteful or we show ourselves knaves and fools. Three fur seals' lives or more for one pelt are too many."

They fell silent, and Eric was thinking how simply Dr. Hill had spoken, yet how forcefully. The latter was as much the consequence of his voice and appearance as of his whole manner of sincerity, the marks of a man of considerable greatness. Sophia had had her eyes fixed on him, and Eric had seen them slowly widen and an intense look come into them. Love was its element, such love as she might never know for another, and no guilt lay there now, although there might be unbelieving wonder at what had happened, and a fatalistic waiting for what might yet happen.

They had seen the seal on their first visit to the deck in the gray, windy morning. The sight became a common one as the day wore on, often three or four seals in their graceful bounding voyages visible at one glance. Dr. Hill brought up the odd fact, which Eric did not know, that the fur seals, swimmers without peer except for dolphins and mysterious whales, were not born with the prowess but must learn it at the risk of drowning; and then generalized that all high art must be learned, the development of a potentiality, and the born swimmers such as fish, dogs, alligators, and turtles were competent in the first instance, and clumsy in the last. "One reason man reached the top of the heap," he said, "is that he's born knowing nothing."

The *Victoria* was making against the wind. The ship pitched, but the chances of her boats touching shore tonight were greatly increased. When still five miles away, with the low-lying island visible only as a dull green smudge in the dark gray sea, her passengers began to hear a sound strangely like the uproar of bleachers at a football game, rising with the gusts and dying away between. "It's the seal herd raising hell as usual," a sourdough said.

At two miles they found the sealing boats lined up in the lee of the island, and they dared not draw closer in this weather because they had no power but the wind itself, which might change or suddenly increase to a gale, for this was Bering Sea, the most stormy of the Seven. The crews blew their horns in salute to the big ship, but Captain Borne, a humanitarian who hated pelagic sealing, did not deign to reply.

A sea mile further, he had no choice but to drop his iron. And there she lay, pitching and swinging, while the wind shifted a point or two without ever changing its main sweep, rose and fell a little, not abating its main force, for three nights and two days.

Two people aboard rejoiced in the long wait, and Eric wished he could remember some weather magic he had seen an old shaman practice to keep the wind in the quarter he desired, to blow ice floes from his sealing waters. Both knew the simple fact that the closer they were bound, the less chance there was of their separation by fate and circumstance. Eric felt the bond strengthen at all hours, awake or asleep, for his dreams kept track of his hopes, fears, longings, and summarized all these and somehow sent dispatches to his conscious intelligence. Sharing ecstasy and beauty, answering the same needs, overcome by the same passions and finding the same relief, they had increasingly clear intimations of each other's identity, which is at once love's search and half-glimpsed finding, and each had passing visions of his own identity, the most obscure of all mysteries man must meet in life. True love can change its form or what seems its nature, although no proof was ever found of its death while the heart beats on. Eric knew that he was its captive in a way that abjures that strange dimension, time. But truly he did not know and perhaps could never know if Sophia was in the same boat with him, or if they were in different boats on a dark and stormy sea.

4

On the third morning of their anchorage the wind died away with long moanings. When Captain Borne brought his ship two cables' length from the shore a lighter came alongside to take in visiting passengers and freight. The island was rankly green this time of year, its low cliffs and shelves hung with weeds, and there was no abatement of the wild clamor of the seals. This and the cries of innumerable sea birds gave the island a kind of vitality, and Eric found hard to imagine when it would lie silent, forsaken by all but its Aleut dwellers and gray foxes, the time of long nights and never-ending gales.

The scenes of its greatest activity, animated beyond description, were of course the seal-thronged beaches and the grassy playgrounds of the *holleschicki,* the bachelor seals, immediately behind them. A United States commissioner led all sight-seers—many passengers chose to stay on board —and pointed out the more dramatic details, such as great jagged rocks worn ice-smooth by the fur of bodies constantly in motion. Each of the harem owners ran night and day in a bounding motion suggestive of a bear about his band of timid-looking cows—a strangely inapt term for his slender, sleek-looking mates—protecting them from covetous neighbors or from lust-crazed bulls who had failed to win mates of their own, and preventing their escape to some pasture greener in their inconstant eyes. The roughhouse and the biting that went on was beyond belief, and the roaring, barking, and bleating, every voice in the city raised in discord, created an unforgettable impression on the visitors. Meanwhile the babies romped or slept quietly, or half drowned themselves learning to swim.

The beach kings let their captives go back and forth to fish and to nurse their babies, or at least they winked at it. A stranger thing was that lanes had been left at intervals on the beaches for the bachelors and "idle bulls" to go back and forth to sea. It betokened an organization as remarkable as that of mound-building ants.

"The bulls haul out first," the commissioner said. "For some weeks they fight among themselves for space on the beaches, and most of them win, but some lose. When the cows begin to haul out, the bulls snatch as many as they can get, and they get knocked about, I tell you. Now this is the greatest wonder. For three months the harem owners don't eat or drink; they are just too busy. I never heard of love going that far."

But Eric had become sensitized in the last fortnight and the thing that touched him most was a sad thing—that the seals born on these beaches must irrevocably return to them every summer as long as they lived, coming back from their long and unknown journeys about the Pacific Ocean, crowding the passes into Bering Sea, hauling out to meet strange and unthinkable death waiting for them at home.

The houses in the native village were government-built of frame, not nearly so high-smelling as their now forgotten *barabaras* on the Aleutian Islands, but probably more chill in the winter gales. On the walls of every house hung what looked like foot-long lengths of rope. When a woman cheechako asked about them the commissioner seemed embarrassed, then replied that they were certain organs of the seal, dried and saved for medicine.

"Those organs are bull-seal genitals," Dr. Hill told Sophia in a voice low but audible to Eric. "One of the traders told me about them. They're ground up and sold in China as an aphrodisiac. They're not the testes—there might be some sense to it in that case—but the phalli. But I guess the venerable Chinaman will never know the difference."

It did not seem right, Eric thought, for a father to speak so frankly to his young daughter. Phalli was a new term to Eric but its meaning perfectly obvious. Then he thought harder, with the conclusion that he had confused right with the notions of proprieties of the day, two different kettles of fish. The fact remained that somewhere along Dr. Hill's high-minded and intelligent course of teaching Sophia to confront reality, something had gone wrong.

But instead of its symptom, Sophia's murmur in his ear, unladylike and ribald by most people's thinking, was prompted by her rash and headlong attempt to effect its cure. The other people were wrong. In this case it was not the least unseemly. She was deeply in earnest, as her face, the low intense sound, and even the way she stood told him plainly.

"Eric, I wish we could make love in one of the native houses. Fertility is rampant on this island, and I believe I'd catch a baby."

He gave her the quick smile that she had come to watch for; and a few minutes later the passengers began streaming back to the lighter. Captain Borne decided to spend the night at his anchorage, so he could take advantage of high tides in the shallow waters, not yet carefully plumbed, between St. Paul and big Nunivak Island; and Dr. Hill talked late with the commissioner on the subject of improving the government school for Aleut children. So it happened that the two lovers made their love within shouting distance of the shore, the clamor of the seals unremittent in their ears, and the smell of blood mingled with village smells and of green things growing rank in the short summers was wafted through the porthole. It remained open because the night was windless and quite warm, remarkable in Bering Sea, and a good night for their pursuit. He saw her beauty wholly in almost impalpable reflected moonlight off the quiet waters which his cat-green eyes could search.

Tonight the microscopic water fireflies were excited and wildly active. When, very late, they watched through the porthole, the *voyageur* seals leaped up in cold, gold flame. Every sea bird that lighted on the water caused lovely luminous rings to spread and slowly fade away. When the time came to part he stood as always at the door, and tonight he whispered a breathless question.

"Did the charm work?"

"I think it did. I believe I felt the planting of the seed. I'll know very soon."

"Yesus, I hope so." And it took a deal of strength of mind —why he could not tell—to hold that hope firmly in his heart and not let it weaken when those sinking spells came on.

"Eric, you said we're two days' run from St. Michael."

"Yust about two days, if the weat'er don't get bad."

"That's all right. Tomorrow night when you come down to supper wear your stickpin, and I'll wear my ring."

When they met at supper table the following evening Eric felt pale, while what looked like dark roses bloomed in Sophia's beautifully planed, pale olive cheeks. He wore the pearl in the knot of his factory-tied four-in-hand necktie, she had hung the nugget ring by a little gold clasp from a black velvet band around her neck. Neither appeared to attract any notice at first. Nugget rings abounded in Alaska; probably most of his tablemates thought that the pearl was an imitation. Not so, Dr. Hill. He did not start, his pleasant expression did not change, but he was markedly quiet throughout the meal, and so absent-minded that more than once he must ask Captain Borne to repeat a question. Toward its end the somewhat disagreeable woman, the bejeweled wife of a mine owner sitting across the table, made a startled remark.

"Mr. Andersen, that's a real pearl!"

"Yes, ma'am."

"I thought you dug for gold, not dived for pearls."

"I'd do a lot of diving before I found any in the Yukon River."

"It's a beauty, too. It must be about three carats. If you want to sell it, I think I can give you what you paid for it and perhaps a little more. I'd like to have it for a ring."

"I wouldn't want to sell it, t'ank you, ma'am."

As the party was getting up to leave, Dr. Hill stepped quickly to Eric's side.

"Can I see you a few minutes in the social hall?" he asked in a pleasant voice and with what seemed a return to his usual charming and cordial manner.

"Yes, sir. Right away, if you like."

"Right away, then."

When Eric had made one round of the deck, his thoughts in turmoil, he found Dr. Hill waiting for him in the almost deserted hall. Sitting well out of hearing of anyone, that distinguished man, with handsome gray head and scholar's face, gave him a friendly nod and his quick boyish smile, then offered him a cigar.

"No, sir. I've got a little snoose under my lip. Most of us squareheads have been sailors one time or anot'er, and we get out of the habit of smoking, because a smoke is so hard to light in a fresh wind."

"Very well. I may take to it for windy days at St. Michael. I wonder if you've guessed the subject of this little talk."

"Yes, sir, I t'ink I have."

"You and Sophia have had a wonderful companionship on this ship. I've approved of it highly—she's been quite lonely all her life, my fault entirely—and you're a representative Alaskan and I like you very much. I think it quite wonderful if in that relationship she gave you her grandfather's pin and accepted your nugget ring. What I wanted to speak about is the danger—a better word would be the great mistake—of a deeper relationship. You at least would be very vulnerable to such. My daughter is an authentic beauty, wistful and altogether lovely, and a new type to you, I think. Also you are an earnest and emotional young man."

He paused and Eric spoke sensibly and well.

"She's all that you say and I am a man of deep feelings."

"I have to warn you, Eric, that for you both to fall in love—and it is quite possible, I know—would be disastrous to you both. In the first place, she is going Outside on the return voyage of this ship. I want her to do so—she has been accepted for one of the best of the female colleges—and she is an obedient girl, who realizes that her eager mentality must be fed; and when the time comes she must marry a man of somewhat the same background and tastes. I would never say her equal, in disparagement of you. You have gifts and qualities and attainments that are different from hers but not inferior in the eyes of God or of any man of studious judgment. So-called social position is based usually on wealth or success, sometimes on lineage, but neither she or I have ever held by it. I hope I've taught her what I

91

learned myself, that these things are not the true measure of an individual."

"I'm not her equal, Dr. Hill. I never said that before about anybody. In her case it's plain as day."

"I respect that view without accepting it. What I must consider, though, is the life she would have with you if, in spite of all I could say to you or to her, you two should fall in love and make the tragic mistake of marriage. That is a harsh word—tragic. My knowledge of my daughter permits me to use no other. She is not delicate of body—in fact she is quite sturdy, considering she has done no hard work and does not excel in athletic games. The games she loves are mental, tests of her ability to learn—the great game that some people play against man's native ignorance. It is of ever-recurring excitement. New vistas are repeatedly opened, and then a new blank wall is seen, challenging the mind. What would happen to that, Eric, way up on the Yukon? She would have no books except the few you could ship in from outside. She would hear no music, see no pictures; her appetite for knowledge and for the great achievements of man in the arts and sciences would be frustrated. It is a voracious appetite, Eric. Once aroused it is insatiable and its feeding is the most continuous joy. She would not meet any people of her own tastes. Marriage is a beautiful relationship between two young people in love but it can't stand alone. Well, I've said all I have to say. You may reply or not, as you choose."

Deep lines came into Eric's face as he made grave reply.

"What you said is true about books and pictures and meeting educated people, and there's loneliness besides. Still, you haven't said it all. I'll have to t'ink about it, if you please."

"Can you promise me to reconcile yourself to parting with Sophia when the *Victoria* sails from St. Michael? If you will, I'll do nothing to curtail your companionship with her until then."

"No, sir."

"Thank you for hearing me out. And if she shows signs of becoming involved too deeply with you—I mean too deeply for her future hope and happiness—I don't know what I'll do, but I'll do something."

They rose and bowed their heads to each other, Dr. Hill as a gentleman born, Eric in Old World courtesy picked up from his parents. Then each went his way.

The long day passed with only a brief interchange between Eric and Sophia. This happened in the afternoon. She paused briefly at his side and spoke quickly.

"I can't come tonight, Eric."

"I was afraid not."

"Something might happen. I don't know what. We'll see it through in St. Michael."

She turned away, a look of lovely sorrow on her face.

Eric spent the day in reverie, and up out of the deeps of his mind rose wandering thoughts and images born of childhood impressions that he hardly knew he had received. He had never seen the Old Country of his parents, but they had spoken of it often in his young days. They had come from Hammerfest, further north than the great bend of the Yukon, in a climate moderated by the north-flowing ocean currents, yet still severe. Their lives had been shaped by the round, naked mountains behind them and the desolate sea before, and their imaginations quickened by wild and ancient legend. His mother could play a concertina quite well and he was raised on North Country folk music, including the eerie melodies of the Laps, for Gertrude's grandmother had come from Lapland, and perhaps from her he had inherited his dark hair. She had performed at concerts in the small, music-loving Minnesota town where he was born, and, the first time he had heard Grieg there was hardly a stanza that did not seem an echo of some half-forgotten song.

Today that music ran through his head. The darkness of spirit that is ever around the corner from the Northman's gaieties came deep upon him. Sometimes its visitation had caused him to get roaring drunk, sometimes he had sought escape by going "down the line" bull-like in his venery, to its wretched end. Today he dwelt, as did a prince of the Norsemen, upon non-being. He did not wish to die in this cold, gray sea, but to become one with the silence and solitude and eternal ice of the tundra held a bittersweet allurement. He would not live very long, he thought, if he lost Sophia.

Tonight his stateroom was instinct with desolation he had rarely felt even in the Arctic wastes. Stephen Foster's songs, loudly but not badly sung by an assembly of passengers in the social hall, rising above the singing swish of the wind and the lap of waters along the ship's sides, did not relieve it and seemed to increase it. Foster had never seen the South that had inspired his melodies—Eric remembered reading that—and he himself would never go there, down upon the Suwannee River, to an Old Kentucky Home, or to the fields where the darkies wept or Black Joe labored, or where his love lay dreaming. For if someday he should take Sophia home, to her old home, she would not return with him to his bleak, beautiful North; the borrowed and brave love she had tried to feel for it would be revealed in its true colors. An old Norwegian folk tale told of a fisherman's daughter who had wedded a merman, and when she had visited the little village where she was born she never returned to the green caves beneath the sea. No longer would he be able to hide the truth—that the short summers and then the snowy wastes and the wind raving and the deadly cold were only fit for squareheads.

If he did not win her he could never see her homeland because it would hurt too much.

Long after midnight he stood by his porthole, watching the intermittent gleamings of stars, and the wan glimmers of the young moon on the restless waters. After that he slept dreamlessly, the kind of sleep that comes when all dreams end.

The next day was the last day of this voyage. Captain Borne intended to lie at St. Michael for four or five days, time for expected river freight to arrive and be stowed, then weigh for Dutch Harbor and Kodiak, the only ports of call unless there was mail or freight to deliver at intervening points. Passengers packed their bags, and went about saying farewells and exchanging addresses with one another and members of the crew. Dinner at one o'clock was one to remember—fresh tomato soup, king-crab salad, turkey, wild duck, salmon and beef steaks, vegetables from a government experiment farm on St. Paul, baked potatoes from eastern Washington, fresh peaches from California, and fresh strawberry shortcake. Pike was seeing to it that the table stewards would be well tipped. He wanted to lose as few as possible to the gold fields.

After dinner Frank Ford stood on the foredeck, hoping to be the first to spy Point Romanzof, behind which, in a little dent in the coast of Norton Sound, huddled St. Michael. On his face was a grim expression, as though he was already steeling his will and setting his muscles to strike it rich. Fannie Ford sat as if crumpled in a deck chair aft, smiling her tortured smile at anyone who would smile at her, otherwise with an expression of desolation.

Point Romanzof on the low-lying treeless shore came into easy view in midafternoon. Three hours passed before the *Victoria* had rounded it and the people at the rail made out the spire of an old Russian church, second in antiquity and beauty only to the cathedral at Sitka. When the passengers disembarked most of them repaired to a new, ramshackle hotel, built to accommodate passengers on the river boats, and inordinately costly. On the short walk there from the wharf they saw their first Eskimos, not choice specimens of what was once a sturdy, healthy, artistic, and resourceful race and which remained so in remote regions where white men did not find it profitable to stay. And for the first time Reverend Dudley heard an outcry that he was fated to hear times beyond counting, at the Diomedes, Kotzebue, and Point Hope on his further journey northward.

"Kow-kow pechuk," the entreaters whined with anxious faces, extended palms, and small, strange eyes. *"Kow-kow pilitay."*

The grub is all gone. Give me grub.

The hotel beds were lousy, but supper was at least bountiful, with caribou venison, fish, bannocks, and canned beans. Exactly the same offering was made at breakfast, but Eric could not eat, thinking of the appointment he had at the desk at nine o'clock with Sophia, and what might follow. And his thoughts crept again and again to what must be her first impressions of his own Far North, the shabby town, the bleak coast, the tundra stretching wide, the Eskimo women in greasy calico worn over their hair-seal shirts and pants, the omnipresent smell of smoked fish and half-decayed meat, and, in dramatic contrast, the sight of the *Victoria* on her mooring lines, no great beauty of a ship, but white, clean, proud, and bound soon for the warm lands.

Eric tried to recapture even an intimation of the ecstasy Sophia and he had shared in their stolen embraces. He could not and could only know it had come to pass. At fifteen minutes after nine she had not shown up. Then at his first glimpse of her on the stairs her step seemed lagging, and only quickened when she caught sight of him, and only then did her drawn face resume its beauty.

"I asked him to stay awhile in his room," she said. "That you wanted to talk to him."

He hesitated, his tongue balked, then he blurted out, "Sophia, do you still want to go wit' me?"

Her color rose and she answered, "Man of little faith."

"I can't help it. I forget what all this is like when I'm away, and maybe I never saw it clearly until I tried to look through your eyes. What your fat'er told me was true—as far as it went."

"You love it, don't you?"

"It's my own, although sometimes I hate it."

"Then it's my own too. I'll love and hate it with you. I'll go with you as long as I live."

"T'ank God! Now I can talk to your fat'er all right."

They went to his room, knocked, heard the cordial call to come in, entered. He tried to hide his surprise at Sophia's presence too.

"How are you, Eric? Take a chair. I'll sit on the bed. Sophia, I'm under the impression that Eric wishes to speak to me alone."

"No, I want to stay. This is a little different than it would be back home."

His color slowly faded. "I don't know what you mean."

"I'll tell you, Dr. Hill." Eric's voice was quite steady, lowered because of the thin plank walls of the room, and the voice of a man. "I came to ask for Sophia's hand in marriage."

Dr. Hill glanced once into his daughter's face, then with a quick spring rose and went to the window. "I never dreamed it had gone that far! What have I done, in permitting this association——?"

Neither of the two lovers spoke. They waited, sitting still, until he could compose himself. When he resumed his seat he had recaptured not only his self-control but his poise and distinction. He was perfectly grave, and only the brilliance of his eyes betrayed his repressed excitement.

"Of course, Sophia, you are party to this request. Only the measure of your partisanship must I doubt. Eric, my first question is this. Have you told Sophia of our conversation in the social hall?"

"I'd told her the trut' about that in different words long before then."

"I can't believe that not only you would brush it aside but that she would also."

"We didn't brush it aside. We faced it and decided to go ahead."

96

"Then you are both victims of infatuation. It's my fault. I shouldn't have sheltered her as I did—been so selfish with her. Don't speak, Sophia. Well, it must end. You two must be parted at once. I forbid——"

"I must speak, Dear Papa. Don't forbid anything—because that won't do any good. I'm of legal age to marry without my father's consent. I want your consent if you can find it in your heart to give it. I love you."

"Yet you'd leave me to marry a stranger in a strange land. Even counting in miles, his cabin by the river is as far from St. Michael as western Texas from Beaufort—by summer travel on the river boats the journey is as long as across the Atlantic. From October to April a vast snow field lies between. Eric, how many days journey by dog sled?"

"More than sixty, loaded down and wit' good luck," Eric replied.

"My God, either of us could fall sick and die without ever seeing each other again."

A look of lonely dreams came into Sophia's face.

"It's awfully far, I know. But you said I'd marry a stranger in a strange land. You could say the same of Ruth."

"Why do you mention her?"

"It was part of an old fortunetelling."

"You think it's fate. Sophia, there's no such thing. There is only circumstance, and efforts that fail or succeed, and human will. Boaz, whom Ruth married, was a mighty man who made a good home for her, and their descendant was David. Eric, have you any reason to believe, practical reason, I mean, such as position, prospects, natural gifts, that you are a good match for my daughter Sophia?"

"No, sir, I do not."

"Then I refuse your petition. You cannot marry Sophia with my consent."

A silence set in that was like one of those natural silences that seem unnatural, as when wind ceases or clouds lower or a hard rain stops or when a whole city hushes its murmur at the round, reverberating toll of a bell. Eric sat with bowed head. Dr. Hill's face was like stone, except that his eyes, fixed on the wall, were intensely dark. Only Sophia seemed waiting for something, an inward thing, perhaps for her heart to still so she could speak. Then she gave one puzzled glance about the rude, meanly furnished room, and she did speak.

"There's only one thing more to tell you, Dear Papa, and I'm the one to do it. I'm the only one that knows it. I'm going to have a baby and Eric is its father."

Both men turned their heads to look at her. Her lips had curled a little. Eric's face had turned pale, whereby its weathering and its good plainness became more apparent. Dr. Hill looked incredulous, as though he had no other refuge than disbelief. Then he spoke brokenly.

"Sophia—if that is true—it doesn't mean I would give my consent. A love affair can pass away. A baby can be cared for. A tragic marriage——" Then his voice failed and he turned away, his hand over his eyes.

"There doesn't seem to be anything to say. I wish there was——"

"Even if you're mistaken, still the act——" He paused again, and then said quietly, "Will you leave me, both of you? Right away, please. Go downstairs—anywhere. I can't contend with it in anyone's presence."

"May I kiss you?" Sophia asked as might a child.

"Not now. Please go."

She and Eric went out, closing the door behind them. He followed her aimless course down the steps, his thought in turmoil. At the bottom step she stopped, turned with her eyes round and staring.

"Go back. Fast as we can. *Run*——"

Their swift feet resounded on the planks of the rough hall, then Eric yanked on the doorknob. The door did not open and the thought burst meteor-fast, almost unrealized, through Eric's brain that the old romantic Alaskan custom of unlocked doors held no more on the paths of the cheechako. Sophia caught up with Eric and rapped loudly and insistently.

"Who is it?" came Dr. Hill's voice, hoarse and changed from the familiar, as though he had been wakened from heavy sleep.

"It's Sophia. Let us in, please."

"Not now, my lovely. Leave me awhile——"

"Unless you let us in, Eric will break down the door."

Eric did not wait for the reply but kicked with all his might, and the lock tore through the cheap wood of the frame. Dr. Hill still sat on the bed. Eric had seen his hand draw swiftly back from a pillow and knew Sophia had seen it too. They drew close to the bed, ready to spring.

"What's under there, Papa?" Sophia asked quietly.

"Nothing that matters now. Once I came to you and was going to open a closet door, and you asked me not to, and I did not. The wheel has half turned round and the positions reversed. I ask you not to look under the pillow. I swear to you before God that the temptation has passed. It was only an impulse without relentless force. I have my work to do, what I'm trained for, what I have succeeded in doing until now, and in which I must continue to succeed."

His voice was choked at first but it cleared as he went on and gathered power.

"I love you more than anyone that ever was, or is, or ever can be," Sophia told him, with great sorrow, into his eyes.

"That's the way that I love you." He turned to Eric, his tear-wet eyes searching deeply. "You heard what we said to each other. Under those conditions are you going to break the engagement?"

"No, sir."

"You, too, Sophia, wish to go ahead?"

"Yes."

"I will not oppose you further. You shall have as fine a marriage as can be held here, and I will give you away according to the old, wise ritual. After that, I want to forget you, Sophia, except as a dream in the night, a wraith before my eyes. Don't let me see that beautiful face that has been my light, the eyes that are my jewels and the pale gold hair, the form of a dryad. If we meet by accident, kiss me lightly, tell me of some little triumph, and go your way. When the time comes, do not look at my face in death. Take the rough road and travel it as joyously as you can, and leave me to my labors and my solitude that can never again be breached. This is farewell."

"Good-bye, Dear Papa."

Shaken by sobs, Eric's arm about her waist, she turned away and left the room, in which phantoms gathered, its air strange and chill with desolation.

4. The Great River

In the hours following Dr. Hill's renunciation Eric moved in what seemed a waking dream. As such, it was deeply troubled, haunted by intimations he could not seize and by vague fears he could not identify. His thoughts flowed at an uneven pace, now rushing, then lagging like the waters of Gertrude Creek in its rocky bed, and sometimes they seemed to swirl. Back of them remained the reality to which every little while he turned in surprise. Then he was shaken out of his half daze until his thoughts began to weave again.

It was Dr. Hill who planned and directed the appointments of the coming marriage. He took great pains, which Eric perceived was his duty as a gentleman and the father of the bride, once he had given his consent. Quite palpably he tried to avoid coming near them when they were together and did so with visible strain, and it was nearly noon of the second day when he caught up with them on the board sidewalk fronting the wharf and disclosed, in an even voice, the arrangements he wished to make.

"I want to report what I've done and ask what you think of it," he said. "There's no suitable place in the town for the wedding—except a few homes of people I don't know and the cathedral, where only the Greek service is performed. Well, there's a small Protestant church too, whose minister is a missionary of forbidding aspect. I think he'd regard the Episcopalian service which Sophia knows best as the invention of the devil. So I asked Captain Borne if it could be held in the social hall on the ship, and he seemed greatly pleased with the prospect. What do you think?"

"That would be very nice," Sophia answered.

"You, Eric?"

"Yes, sir. T'ank you very much."

"Your license can be obtained at the courthouse. I've asked Reverend Dudley if he would perform the ceremony. He said he'd love to, but he wanted to talk to Eric before he made his decision. I don't know why. It's rather puzzling. He said he'd see you, if you are free, in his room at two this afternoon. Don't be too disappointed if he declines. I think he's trying to find the answer to some spiritual problem. He's a fine man and of course an unusual man to have resigned his pulpit in New York and be waiting for a trading schooner to take him to an Eskimo village in the Arctic wastes. If he declines, you'll have no choice but the half-Russian justice of the peace."

Walking slowly as they talked, they came to where the sidewalk ended in a muddy path over tundra, so they turned back.

"I'd like to invite all our shipmates, passengers and crew, and a few officials here. Somewhat to my surprise, the materials for a festive affair after the ceremony are available. There is a considerable stock of champagne, bought for miners coming down the river who wish to toast their luck. It was made in the Sacramento Valley by a French colony and not expensive according to St. Michael ideas. I've ordered three dozen magnums, enough for one round and extras. Pike has abundant punch cups at our disposal and is delighted to use them for about the third time since the ship was christened."

"I think that's wonderful," Sophia said. "Pike and his good men will do it up brown."

"I wasn't so lucky about edibles." He turned and looked strangely at Sophia. "There will be no cates and dainties, and dates from Fez, such as were stored in the castle when Prospero rode across the moors."

" 'Its little smoke in pallid moonlight died,' " Sophia answered, her eyes filling with tears.

Eric did not know to what they referred, but he felt no jealousy or resentment, only wonder at the occurrence of all this and his part in it, and a resolve to live up to it as far as plain powers permitted.

"If you agree, the marriage will take place at eight o'clock tomorrow night. The reception will be over by ten, and that will give you plenty of time to catch the steamer leaving at midnight for the mouth of the Yukon. I have reserved a—a stateroom. It's the nicest on the ship and at a specially low rate. Eric, you can pay for it at the office."

"That will be fine," Eric said.

"Now I'll hurry back to report to Captain Borne. Eric, you can tell Sophia the result of your talk with Reverend Dudley."

He turned away and Eric and Sophia walked on slowly in silence, hand in hand.

2

Eric knocked on the door of Arthur Dudley's hotel room exactly at two. He felt more excited than he could have explained to himself, and, to his astonishment, the distinguished man who admitted him looked shaken. No less surprising, he wore a gray suit without a clerical collar.

"Thank you, Eric, for coming," he said in his rich voice. "May I serve you a drink of whisky?"

"T'ank you very much."

"I'll have one with you. I need a bracer—what I'm about

101

to tell you will not be easy to say. I've said it before to no one but an old boyhood friend in New York. There are two reasons that I'm telling you. One is, this is the first time since I've left there that I have been forced to take action, one way or the other, on a problem of awesome depth. The other reason is that you are a young man, a serious man, and a very human man. This is a problem to which ordinary human feeling is more pertinent than any amount of education or so-called spiritual insight. The matter lies in the heart."

Reverend Dudley—so Eric thought of him—had spoken in low tones, not to be overheard, and with a great deal of light in his fine eyes. Eric nodded his head and waited.

"I suppose there is what is called a story behind almost everyone's coming to Alaska to live in this faraway and great, sparsely peopled territory. Many of those stories are strange, some of them tragic. Even the gold seekers who hope to get rich and go back are by no means of ordinary ilk or they would not undertake such a rash adventure; many are driven by forces beyond their control. My story is short and it would have less meaning, perhaps, if I had not been a clergyman. I use the past tense. For the moment I am—nothing."

"You seem a clergyman to me," Eric said.

"Thank you. My pulpit was in one of the strongest and richest small churches in New York. I loved being a clergyman; the mysteries of God, of what we call salvation—all the terms of theology are subject to countless interpretations—captured me in my adolescence. I became a dedicated minister—at least I thought so. I had mundane gifts such as a good voice and presence, imagination and education to preach an interesting, sometimes I believe an inspiring sermon. I was not unctuous. Meditation, prayers, dwelling on the lives of the patriarchs, the saints, and especially the story of Jesus that has electrified such countless million people made me not only a successful minister but, I had reasons to believe, a good minister. I never married. I remained celibate, which the fathers of the Roman Catholic Church saw fit for priests. I thought all my sexual energies were sublimated—another term without a precise meaning. I was wrong."

A great deal of strain came into the high-bred face; the hands were clenched and their cords stood out. He relaxed

102

with a long sigh, then his tone changed. It was not bitter as much as self-denunciatory.

"One night a young woman came to my parish house to ask my advice on a difficult marital problem. She was the wife—almost the bride—of a young and brilliant lawyer in my congregation. Although I was not in love with her in the least, I was overcome by lust. One moment there was none; the next it charged every cell of my body. That much, at least, is human. She was not in love with me, she was in love with her husband, but she looked up to me as her true priest and guide. You see the case is getting blacker every minute, the sin of adultery in an unmitigated degree. But you don't know the worst."

"I'm a poor man to judge the worst, Reverend Dudley," Eric said.

"No, I believe otherwise. Listen. In order to seduce her, I employed hypocrisy of the most shocking sort. I talked of spiritual affinity being heightened in this case by physical affinity. Bah!"

The Reverend Dudley rose and spat on the floor.

"She was a trusting girl," he went on quietly when he had resumed his seat, "and I obtained my goal. When she had gone, weeping, I did not kneel in prayer because I was ashamed to address God. After awhile I dressed as you see me now with the vague intention of going to my bishop, confessing, and asking to be publicly condemned and excommunicated. Then I realized I could not do so without some risk to the girl's reputation and destroying a great deal of the faith that people have in ministers. Instead, after a sleepless night, I came to the decision to resign my pulpit on what would seem at least a creditable reason, that I wanted to become a missionary in some remote part of the world. I did want to. Only by that exile, I thought, could I ever atone, make peace with God, face myself in the mirror. Most missionaries are ordained ministers, but not all. I intended to keep the empty title of Reverend until I reached my destination, then be a teacher only, help the people all I could, and never perform another sacrament. I made my plans, carried them out, and here I am, on my way to the Arctic."

"Reverend, nine men out of ten have been overcome with lust and used every trick they could t'ink of."

"That is some comfort. I have been saved from ever

thinking I was a saint. That's the story. Now Dr. Hill has come to me and asked me to perform the sacrament of marriage, one of the great sacraments. If I can, I can perform others. I long to perform them, to go on being a clergyman in great humility before God; this is the test. So I'll ask you one question. Please answer yes or no."

"I will."

"Are you, after hearing that story, willing for me to perform the wedding ceremony of Sophia and Eric? I decided that you, as the husband, were the one to ask—the only one I could ask."

"Yes, sir, I am."

"That's all I need to know. I will."

3

Eric would not attempt to shine at his own wedding, did not wish to, could not if he tried. He engaged an old Eskimo woman, once the squaw of a Russian official famed for his neat dress, to clean and press his blue serge suit; he polished his shoes and bought a good linen shirt, starched collars, and a new necktie. This last the storekeeper taught him how to tie in a perfectly good four-in-hand at the first try. Eric had been a sailor and a fisherman and was deft at handling lines.

The squaw's daughter went forth to a creek bank and returned with an armful of bluebells, geraniums, fireweed of beautiful deep rose, immense violets, iris, larkspur, monkshood, and delicate fern. The hotelkeeper's half-Russian wife, who painted creditable pictures and who yearned for the refinements of life, made them into a bouquet which few florists, using hothouse flowers, could have surpassed.

After thinking it over, Eric asked Mate Locke to be his best man. He needed no reason other than that the officer had encouraged him when he had been downcast, and the two liked each other. He was somewhat surprised by Sophia's choice of matron of honor and maid of honor. The first was Fannie Ford, who appeared incredulous and almost overcome, the second a full-blooded, mission-schooled Malemiut Eskimo girl who worked in a curio shop next to the hotel. In this choosing, Sophia appeared to ignore or defy the contempt that many northern Alaskans, especially newcomers, show all Eskimos—regardless of the fact that they could not possibly survive with primitive tools on the hostile coasts where the undegenerate tribes made their brave fight against appalling odds—and which southern Alaskans are prone to feel toward Indians. These white men called all Eskimos "huskies," all Indians "siwash." Actually Chikarik was an extremely pretty girl, vivacious and intelligent, and in a dress Sophia gave her, her black hair fixed in a glossy loop with ivory pins, and carrying a bouquet, she made an excellent impression. Fannie's dress lacked taste, but her big black eyes glistened with tears and her full heart lent her countenance something more than common prettiness.

Eric decided that he could never know Sophia's high heart, would never dispute what it told her, and such part of it as she gave him was his forever.

Sophia was as astonished as she was touched by the number and variety of their wedding presents, although Eric could have told her to expect just this, knowing the Alaskans. Her shipmates had ransacked the shelves of the stores, and the gifts covered two big tables brought from the dining room. They included a samovar of copper hammered out in Muscovy when Great Catherine reigned; pieces of Japanese and Cantonese porcelain bought with the pelts of seals and sea otters in long-ago voyages; a Chinese god of good luck cunningly worked in pale jade, six inches tall; a slightly disfigured but still lovely icon from some forgotten church; a silver cross set with amethysts and opals; Eskimo carvings in fossil ivory; a gold locket once worn by Baranof's native mistress, said to contain a lock of his hair; cured skins of white fox, orange-throated marten, glossy and almost black, ermine, and a rare fisher; an immense polar-bear skin rug, not well mounted but ice white; more than two dozen pieces of silver; a musket that had fired a salute when Old Glory was first raised at Baranof Castle; bottles of champagne and a whole case of *pâté de foie gras* shipped by mistake to a local grocer; the inevitable cribbage board; and, conveniencing old sourdoughs who did not know a suitable wedding present from a sack of salt, a small silver bowl heaped to the brim with gold nuggets and dust to a total weight of three pounds.

All this exotic opulence went into eclipse when the pianist began to play what Eric knew only as "Here Comes the Bride," and Sophia entered the hall on her father's arm and made toward a kind of bower, erected by the crew of planks covered with white cloth and roofed with ferns and flowers. From his place Eric watched her with a filled throat, awe-

105

struck not so much by his own luck—for many common men like him had been visited by beauty—but by beauty itself as it adorns the rugged world, beauty in manifold forms, scattered here and there as by a spendthrift God, after the gates of Eden had been closed and locked. He came and stood beside her, the music stopped, and Reverend Dudley's voice, low and deep and full, flowed into the hush.

"Dearly beloved, we are gathered together . . ."

The solemn service came to its close. None of the women wept, but the old men's weathered faces twisted into beauty. Dr. Hill, who had remained standing, braced a tense arm against his chair, and as soon as he could, Reverend Dudley turned his back to hide what his faraway and fashionable congregation had never dreamed of seeing —tears rolling down his cheeks.

The pianist began to play the piece that Eric knew as "Two Souls Went Up the Aisle and Only One Came Back." Jollity broke forth, all the noisier because of the deep and silent currents that had just flowed, and soon Pike and his little corps of stewards were in their glory. Not only was there wine, pale gold and sparkling in the cups—he had searched his pantries and in his youth he had served as a waiter in the Bohemian Club in San Francisco—but in the dining hall where the party had repaired stood a huge wedding cake, heavy with frosting in elaborate design, and across the top in bold lettering was the word SKOOKEM, which to old Alaskans is a shibboleth to all good fortune. Toasts were drunk, all of them heart-warming and one, composed in raggedy verse by a sailor, was written down by a score or more of hearers, tucked away in wallets, and bid fare to become a sourdough classic.

When the revelry ended and Eric and Sophia rushed to their rooms to finish packing, she thought she had seen the last of many well-wishers for only God knew how long, but she was wrong. They had hired every lighter available and made out to the river steamer to see the benedict and his bride off and away.

Two who had participated in the service remained in their hotel rooms. One was Arthur Dudley, to whom it had served as a catalyst, and who needed to be alone awhile with his surging emotions and solemn thoughts. The other was Dr. Hill.

106

"I can't go," he said with a white face. "You'll have to excuse me. Will you take me at my word?"

Sophia answered with two lines of poetry, and Eric did not know it was in continuation of an interchange between them that he had heard yesterday; he knew only it was one of their ways of communication when other words failed.

"And they are gone: aye, ages long ago
These lovers fled away into the storm."

Dr. Hill looked deeply into her eyes and answered.

"The Beadsman, after thousand aves told,
For aye unsought-for slept among his ashes cold."

4

Amid noisy singing of "Auld Lang Syne," not discordant because when one singer got off key another missed it in the opposite direction, the river boat sailed.

As Eric and Sophia stood at the rail, watching the far-scattered lights grow dim, she asked one troubled question.

"Eric, I know so little about Alaska. Did we do right to let all those people, whose names I didn't know a month ago, give us presents? Many are expensive although few of the people are rich—some very rare and fine. Shouldn't we have told them not to bring any?"

"Not by any means. I do know Alaska pretty well. It was wort' it to them many times over. You see, any kind of social affairs are pretty rare up here. When we do have parties the men get off and play poker and drink, and the women talk of little things. There isn't really very much for anyone to talk about and everyone knows what the others are going to say before they say it. Even when we get together it sometimes seems to me that each of us is still alone. That wedding had something they've rarely seen or felt. All the sourdoughs and the sailors were so happy to be invited; I don't know about the cheechakos. They'll talk about it a lot and remember it when the ice has gone out a lot of times."

"Why do you speak so often of the ice going out? It has special meaning for you."

"For every sourdough. It's the real beginning of spring."

"Well, let's go to bed. I want you to hold me close. I need that awfully badly, for I am sad, as no bride should be. In the morning we'll be on the river, and I'll be happy again."

It was six hours run to Aphoon Pass in the Yukon delta, so the morning broke with the vessel still at sea. She passed the village of Kotlik at the mouth of the pass about six, and the great tide of the young moon bore her safely over the shallows. "This is not the river yet," Eric told her at breakfast. "Wait till you see the real river." He spoke proudly, confidently.

They saw it about noon at the point of the delta, one of the greatest and most noble rivers in the world. On a visit with her father to Natchez she had seen the Mississippi, but it was a river of bridges, of dikes, and of many ports and people, and so the majesty beheld by Indians and by Joliet and Marquette was partially concealed. Here there was nothing but the river, alone in a vast plane, reflecting the sky. Its only peers in solemn grandeur, she thought, must be the Lena, the Ob, and the Yenisei, flowing through the Siberian wastes, names she had learned in her study room, her father's library. When she spoke of this to Eric he reminded her of the Mackenzie in Canada, which he had never seen and whose name she barely knew.

"She's the sister of the Yukon," he said, "as long, as great, and one long arm of each almost touches the other in the region of Frances Lake, way off by Mount Hunt. I knew a man who went out there looking for gold."

"I don't suppose he thought it much of an adventure, but just this is a great adventure for me. Eric, I'm going to be happy. I'm never going to look back."

He could not see that she did so as the boat nosed up and up the great waterway, her paddle wheels chugging. She spent almost all of every day beside him on the deck, and her glance was forward. He was quick to point out to her little breaches of the vast emptiness of river, plain, and sky, such as Eskimos or Indians fishing or hunting, their far-spaced forlorn-looking villages, the mouths of nameless rivers, rare roadhouses for winter travelers on the ice, trading posts, and the ancient Russian hamlets of Andreafski and Holy Cross and Russian Mission. A great bend occurred just below the latter town. The ship's course had been south and east, now it was north-northeast, as the river began to skirt low mountains to the northwest. From then to the mouth of the great Koyukuk River, rising in faraway, wintry Brooks Range, it flowed in an almost straight line, hundreds of miles without a considerable bend, and its slow sweep suggested eternity.

The two saw little of their fellow passengers, even those shipmates who had come up on the *Victoria*. These were not trying to leave the newlyweds to themselves; rather they felt a vague embarrassment, as though the visible entering into the Alaskan interior of a girl of this unknown order, and what she would be in for there, presented an anomaly with which they could not contend. Frequently Eric bethought himself with a cold chill of doubt, fear, and guilt, stunned at what the devil he had done. But Sophia's obvious happiness, touching deeply the old-timers, soon restored his good spirits.

Fannie Ford, earning her passage in the galley, looked at Sophia with troubled awe. Frank Ford, working at odd jobs, gave both her and Eric a wide berth.

Again there were trees and lean forest. At the mouth of the Tanana, an enormous tributary where a steam launch took off a few of their shipmates, and the loss of whose waters did not seem to contract the upper river in the least, the steamer entered the region of the ramparts, a narrow valley with abrupt walls and rugged scenery about a hundred miles long. Where it ended abruptly the ship entered the so-called flats, extending for two hundred miles; here the river spread ten, fifteen, or twenty miles in a maze of channels, and there was little to see but sand bars and low, thickly wooded islands as far as the eye could reach. In shallow water between two of these islands a moose was spied swimming powerfully, his antlers spreading wide. A small boat was quickly launched, the animal shot, hauled to the ship's side, and heaved aboard, the whole half ton of him, as a supply of fresh meat.

"I can't eat any," Sophia told Eric when the spilled blood had been washed off the deck.

"Don't say that, my darling. I've got to shoot lots of moose for our winter fare. Please try."

"I'll try and succeed. I forgot where I was. Excuse me."

Two thirds of the way through the flats, at the mouth of the unexplored Porcupine, the river made a dramatic bend so the ship's course changed from northeast to southwest. Here the river touched the Arctic Circle, the most northerly point of its great flow, and when its waters were again united and had swept in one solid stream fifty miles against the laboring ship, there came in sight Eric's little landing and the cabin he called home.

He did not call her attention to it at first, because it

looked so small, all but smothered by the arms of nearby forest. He had to come to it at last, and then her searching gaze following his pointed finger could hardly find the green dot on the green shore. Why had he painted it green? Perhaps that it might escape the attention of broke cheechakos making down river in any craft that offered; perhaps from some impulse toward oneness with the forest. Even he could not see his sluice, it was so well screened by thickets.

They had already packed and said farewells; now the captain came and told them something in his big, bluff way.

"I'm not goin' to have that young lady hopping off this ship while I nose her in. We've never carried anyone like her before and I'm as democratic as the next'n, but I'm going to heave her iron, and run out the gangplank, and see her off in style. My stevedores will tote your gear clean to your shed. As for them gold seekers pantin' to get to the Klondike, it won't hurt 'em any to stay poor for an extra ten minutes."

All this was done. Sophia, waiting on what served Eric as a dock, hardly glanced at the house a hundred yards up the trail, because she was in strangely quiet communion with the passengers lining the rail. When in a little while the vessel weighed, with chugging engines, they broke into a song that was a sentimental favorite among the oldsters, a lovely song in all truth, and why they had chosen it to express their farewells none of them knew.

> *"Oh! don't you remember sweet Alice, Ben Bolt,*
> *Sweet Alice, whose hair was so brown . . ."*

Its haunting strains came down the waters, carried by them it seemed, until it died away in the distance, Eric and Sophia waiting hand in hand. Then without a glance at the diminishing ship they walked up the trail together.

"It's a beautiful setting," she said. "It's a little house instead of a big house, and it's not on a point jutting out into a bay but back in the land, yet it makes me think of our house in Beaufort."

"The trees shelter it from the worst of the nort'east wind although she blows hard enough sometimes, I tell you."

"There were great live oaks around our house. They were old and gnarled, not young and green like these spruce. I remember one night when the wind off the bay was almost too strong for them, and they groaned like people."

They said no more until he had removed a chain from the

log wall to the doorknob. "It's not to keep people out," he explained. "If thieves wanted to come in they could break through a window, and honest prospectors could take off the chain if they came along shy of shelter. It was to keep out wolverines, who can worry a door until it opens, or maybe a bear who smelled some jerky and leaned against it."

They went in and the open door admitted enough light to reveal the interior, although the windows were boarded up. It was what Sophia could have expected, no more or less. It was perfectly clean, for no dust gathers along the Yukon. There were two rooms, the largest containing a combined heating and cooking stove, a wood box, a homemade bedstead on which lay a thick moosehide mattress and neatly folded blankets and a fur-covered pillow, two chairs fashioned by the same hands, pans on nails driven in the wall, a cupboard containing dishes and a chest for clothes, and a rug of neatly stitched caribou skins, more to hold heat than for looks. The smaller room was for goods that would suffer from freezing if stored in the shed and for immediate use on those days when the hardiest sourdough was loath to stir out of doors. Utility was the test of every article. Even the fur-covered pillow turned out to be no touch of luxury, but a sensible need.

"That's wolverine fur," Eric explained. "Sometimes, toward morning, I was too sleepy to get up and mend the fire, and if it was forty below outside, that cold got in, sneaked in, and a caribou-hide pillow would get covered with frost from my breath. That's my own invention."

"I'm glad it's big enough for two heads," Sophia answered, smiling.

"I'll take off those clapboards in a minute. I've got to work our mine until the freeze-up, to fatten my poke a little, but in the winter I'll make a bathtub for the back room, so you won't have to use the washtub, and maybe I can add another room to put our presents."

"You needn't hurry, Eric. The house is lovely as it is."

"I don't see how you could say that, Sophia."

"It's comfortable and snug. It's our shelter against the winter cold. Its loveliness lies in—well, in its spirit. You built it yourself and took great pains with it; it's not thrown together, it isn't a shack. You were making a home for yourself and your wife, whoever she might be. Well, I'm your wife. I want our first baby to be born here."

"That will be in May, when the river is full of ducks and

geese, and it never gets real dark, and there's only a heavy twilight in the midnight hours. The moose and caribou cows are nursing their calves, and flowers and birds, even hummingbirds, are everywhere. We won't be bothered by heat or mosquitoes either—there's always a good breeze this part of the river and the little pests are blown away, and black flies too. It's a fine time to have a baby."

She looked him in the face and answered soberly.

"It won't be then, Eric."

"I don't understand."

"What I told my father wasn't true. It was a lie. Why I had to tell it I won't try to explain; it belongs to the past, not the present. But it won't be long before it's true. I feel that in my bones. I'll nurse him at my breast and as soon as he can talk he'll say, 'By Yesus, I'm hungry,' and we'll feed him moose and caribou meat so he'll grow tall and sinewy, like you; and I'll know I'm victorious, and the fortune that was told me will be proven false, and I'll sleep with you with never a bad dream."

5

In their first two weeks at the cabin Eric shoveled gravel eight hours a day and still had abundant daylight to show Sophia the immediate neighborhood. Dressed in the roughest clothes she possessed, she followed him into the dim woods, seeing many of their inmates, fished for trout in Gertrude Creek, and helped him clean blue grouse as big as barnyard hens, which he shot neatly through the head with a light rifle. On a Sunday, since he had been taught by his Lutheran parents to rest from lucrative labor, he took her on a ten-mile jaunt upriver in his big sailing skiff to a large Indian village known as Tekuh, which meant gun, and which might have been named for an old brass-mounted Hudson Bay musket found at its site, perhaps beside the broken skeleton of a too venturesome explorer.

These Indians were Kutchins, hence belonged to the northern division of the Athabaska tribe, one of the great tribes, to which the Umpqua Indians of Oregon and the Navaho and Apache of the Southwest also belonged. Their village was a considerable establishment, with fish wheels, drying racks, many seines, and a fleet of *bidarkas*, which were light, fleet boats. They had had mission influence during the Russian occupancy—a dedicated and high-minded priest of the Greek Church had come all this way to teach

112

them—and he had been a good missionary, making no great to-do over their secret loyalties to their pagan gods and their idea of morals, but had instilled in them ideas of cleanliness, simple hygiene, and even thrift, which seems to be alien to the nature of Alaskan Indians. He had long gone to his reward and the mission was in ruins, but his half-Kutchin son, who had gone to Russia for a two-year course in medicine, had returned to his birthplace to marry, to live, and to employ such medical skill as he possessed. He was called Father Pavlof, he saved nine out of ten of the babies born in the village with no medicine but a strong vile-tasting liquor that the whites called sourdough booze—this as a disinfectant—and abundant soap and water. Although he cooked and slept in a cabin apart from the other villagers, including his full-blooded Kutchin wife, he dressed like an Indian, shared in the village fishing and hunting, dances, and in its religious rites, after which he probably made atonement before a holy picture of Our Lady of Kazad. Because he had worked two years in a Hudson Bay post before he went to Russia, he had picked up a little English.

Eric had no business with him today. Such, he hoped, would occur before a year had passed. Today he would deal with his wife, H'kah, whose name meant goose, and who was the best seamstress in the village. To that end he had brought several tanned caribou skins, a wolverine skin, and the skin of the leopard seal.

A staring crowd had gathered about Sophia when she had disembarked, remaining perfectly silent until an old hunter uttered a word that caused sharp pricklings at the back of Eric's neck. The word was Yukhoi, and Eric knew it because he had heard it sometimes on winter nights when a Kutchin companion had pointed at the sky. It was a naming which the other watchers accepted with nodding heads, and they would know her or speak of her by no other as long as she lived on the Yukon, and as much longer as the old men told and passed down tales.

Yukhoi was the Kutchin word for the northern lights.

None of the watchers followed Eric and Sophia into H'kah's house. No one was present but her daughter Sant, which meant summer and had apparently been given her for no reason other than that she had been born on midsummer night, when there is no night as far north as Tekuh village.

Sant was about sixteen, her hairdress and decoration showed her to be unmarried, and as the child of a half-breed and a full-blooded Kutchin woman, she could claim to be one fourth white. She made no such claim, it never crossed her mind, and no ordinary observer would believe it. Her clean face might be a shade lighter than her mother's but it was cast the same and had the same qualities that had once attracted Pavlof to H'kah—good although primitive molding, brilliant black eyes that appeared slightly slanted, signs of an alert intelligence, and a wide, beaming smile showing glistening teeth.

She was not smiling now. She gave Sophia one wild glance before her face took on utter impassivity.

The thought had occurred to Eric to employ her as an interpreter between him and H'kah. Partly through some remnant of her father's pride in his own pale skin, partly because he thought it might serve her well in an American-owned territory, especially if she went to mission school, Pavlof had taught her a good part of what English he knew. He did so by always speaking to her in this language, and thus he saved from forgetfulness his own scant knowledge. Immediately Eric decided against the attempt, telling himself he would do better, with less danger of bitching the business, by using signs and a few Kutchin words, of which he knew about fifty.

He showed the caribou skins to H'kah, pointed to Sophia, and said, "Parka." H'kah measured her with keen black eyes. When Eric pointed first to his shirt, then his trousers, again pointing to Sophia, the woman nodded. Eric held up the wolverine skin and made a gesture indicating a hood. Displaying the leopard-seal skin, he said, "Mukluks."

"Dollar?" H'kah asked.

Eric held up five fingers.

"And that," he told Sophia, "is all there is to it."

As they were leaving, Sant made an abrupt motion, then looking into Eric's face, she spoke a word in a tone of inquiry.

"Ohtziyeh?"

Eric shook his head slowly and followed Sophia out the door.

6

A few days later Eric dug into a bed of somewhat looser gravel. No richer than the old, it was easier to work, and in a glowing half hour he hit upon a splendid idea. By diverting more water from the big spring above, and redirecting and widening his flume, he could hurl a considerable jet against the bed and wash into a bigger sluice three or four times as much gravel as he could shovel by hand. Moreover, the mine could operate all night and a great part of the day throughout the summer season. The bed appeared large, and he saw no reason why, while it lasted and luck held, he should not retrieve daily about ten ounces of gold nuggets and dust instead of one.

Greatly excited, he dropped his shovel and hurried home to tell Sophia, who was cooking their usual hearty midday meal.

"I haven't struck it rich," he told her modestly. "That comes when gold lays like cold lard in a pan. It's only an idea that I can't do much about until October, for I'll need a full poke to hire Indians to build new flumes and sluices. Maybe it won't work. Getting the water down is a hard problem, and I wish I was a better engineer and figurer. But if it does work, I think we might get out as much as fifteen thousand dollars between the spring thaw and next fall's freeze-up."

"What would we do with all that money?" Sophia asked, taking his hand in her usual way, and with the pensive look he knew so well.

"Build a better house, for one thing, a house to be proud of. Take trips Outside, maybe clear to Hammerfest, where my folks were born. Put the rest in the bank."

"We don't need a better house. It would be out of keeping with Alaska and the river. I couldn't keep it up except with a native girl to work here or by missing trips with you into the woods. If you ran a big mine, wouldn't you have to hire help? Then we wouldn't have this reach of river all to ourselves. As long as the gold is in the gravel of your claim, it's the same as in the bank. I'd like to visit your kinfolk in Norway, but not until I've seen the caribou herds, and gone with you up the Pelly and Porcupine. This winter I want you to teach me to use snowshoes and drive dogs, and to go hunting with you, and trapping. One reason I'll love this country is that there isn't much to spend money for. Let's enlarge your mine a little at a time. It will be a lot more fun to do it ourselves instead of hiring Indians."

He was not in the least crestfallen. But he held her in

his arms, her lips laid softly against his, until the moose steaks scorched.

A few days after this a river steamer nosed into shore and unloaded crates and boxes full of presents. Until now, when he had lived alone, the mere passing of the boats had made him stop work and watch them out of sight, or get up at night to see their lights, for he knew all the pilots, and they usually blew their whistles as they approached his little landing. When they had stopped he had boarded and fraternized jovially with passengers and crew, in haste to go, reluctant to return. Today he felt vaguely uncomfortable all the while she lay at his little dock. He told himself that the passengers were almost all cheechakos whom he did not know and many of the crew had been newly recruited in Seattle, so it was not like old times. Actually it seemed that he was anxious about Sophia—as though he had to defend her against something that he did not understand.

Since they had no place to put the gifts at present, Eric stored them, gold dust and all, in his shed.

September drew to its close, with lengthening nights, and hard frost before dawn, the quaking asp the color of Sophia's hair, and the waterfowl crying and circling in great flocks, then taking off southward. At night wild geese and swans, who had gorged and gabbed all summer in the ponds of the Arctic muskeg, honked overhead where the stars twinkled, and most of them were young on their first journey Outside, and some were very old. When one night their clamor wakened Eric and Sophia, and they lay in the dark and listened, she murmured a question.

"Eric, how long does a swan live?"

"The old Norwegians say they sometimes live to be a hundred. I shot one once, to eat, with scars all over his bill from fighting, and his black feet were wrinkled like an old man's hand."

"The poet Tennyson who wrote *Enoch Arden* that you liked so well in school has a line about the swan, how it dies after many a summer. It occurs in his telling of an old story that I want to tell you. In classic myth the goddess of the dawn was named Aurora, the same word as in aurora borealis, the northern lights. She fell in love with a mortal, whose name was Tithonus, and he asked her to give him immortality. She gave it to him without thinking, then the Hours, her attendants, were jealous and somehow kept her from giving him immortal youth as well. So while she re-

116

mained forever young and beautiful, he grew older and older. The poem tells how, when he was unimaginably old, he begged her to take back her gift of immortality so he could die and become earth in earth. But it was said that even the gods could not take back their gifts and it leaves you wondering whether or not he could ever die."

"I t'ink that in a way you are Aurora and I am her lover," Eric answered after a long pause, his skin pricking. "When I am old you will still be young and beautiful."

"It's only a story, Eric."

On the morrow a river steamer making the last upriver journey before the freeze-up hove into view and whistled hoarsely. To Eric's surprise, she put into his dock and discharged three big boxes, so heavy that deck hands had to help him carry them into his house. On one of them was tacked a sealed envelope, addressed to Mrs. Eric Andersen, Gertrude Mine, Upper Yukon, and in Dr. Hill's handwriting.

Sophia opened it and read:

My beloved:

Here is yours and Eric's wedding present. I ordered it by telegraph from Seattle and it arrived in time for me to send by the last boat.

I got to thinking that if I were going to spend the rest of my life in a land largely cut off from what we call civilization and could take with me only one luxury, one thing of no immediate practical use, let us say one pleasure-giving object, I would choose the new encyclopedia. That is what I am sending you.

Actually it may prove useful to Eric in his mining as well as in learning more about the animals and birds he sees, the relationships of the natives to other peoples, botany, geology, forestry, and so on, and surely it will help feed your avid mind in your leisure hours.

I feel that I am making a good start in my new life in Alaska. I hope that you are doing the same and will be happy always.

Faithfully,
Papa

Eric seemed more shaken by the gift than was Sophia. When she saw his face, pale and deeply strained, and perceived he was close to tears from the upsurge of repressed emotions, she came and drew down his high

117

head and kissed him with deep love.

"I'll make shelves for those books as soon as I can," he told her stanchly.

"I may never open them, Eric. Dear Papa was mistaken. It's a wonderful gift for the girl he raised and knew, but I'm not that girl any more. I've had enough book learning. Now I want to learn with my eyes and ears and nose, and especially with my hands, doing things. I want a baby, your baby, to love and care for, and you will give me one soon. Be true to me and love me. That—and to be your wife—is all I ask of life."

"Well, I'm going to read them," Eric said after a long pause. "I'm a fast reader. I'll read an hour or two every night, more than that on stormy days when we can't go out. Two people who love each other don't have to talk. It will take years to go through all twenty-four big volumes, and much of it I won't be able to understand, but when I'm forty—and you are thirty-five—I'll be better fit——"

"Don't say it, Eric. I can't stand it. Read as much as you like, educate yourself for leadership in Alaska if that's in your fate, but don't break my heart by implying that I married beneath me. I married a true man and a strong man. If either of us isn't worthy of the other, which God forbid, I am the one—I tell you so in all truth. I'm not a liar. I don't tell or live any lies—forget about those I told Papa. Now let's look at the river—better yet, go into the woods where it's dim and still."

So she put on her hair-seal shirt and pants and her mukluks—for the deep shade, although chill, was not cold enough for a parka—and soon they were following a moose path into the forest. Its purity and quiet sorrow that can be felt but not explained healed their wrenched hearts and soon they were walking with stealing steps, in a mysterious closeness. Eric had brought his heavy rifle, more from habit than from any need, and he did not fire it when a woodland caribou, that great deer with the shimmering mane and tall proud antlers, twice as large as the far-wandering barren-land caribou, leaped from his covert and stood staring. The harvesting of their winter supply of meat must begin after the freeze-up, when it could be hung, kept, and used.

Light snow fell and melted away. On a night in early October heavy snow began to fall just before dark, gathering on the windows, and in wakefulness and in dreams Eric

118

knew that it fell heavily all night, although in silence, with no wind to pelt it, and it might be that little creakings and stirrings on the roof told him of its gathering weight. In the morning the whole land was changed. Every tree stood mantled in snow; the limbs of the young spruce bowed down; all green was gone, whiteness lay everywhere except on the river that mirrored the dark gray sky. Eric looked at it from the doorway and told Sophia it would remain until spring.

"It's beautiful," she answered.

In mid-October the wind blew steadily and hard all afternoon, a biting wind out of the north, and the temperature fell from thirty-two to eight degrees above zero in four hours. At twilight the rushing sound suddenly ceased, and he filled the wood box and laid by extra fuel, for he knew this weather. All night the still cold deepened, ghostly in its lack of substance, but little rivulets everywhere ceased their soft murmur, and creatures living in shallow ponds dug into the mud of the bottom and lay still. Three times he went out to look at his thermometer, its silver column ever shorter, and once there came a faint flicker of the northern lights in the cloudless sky. He waited, hoping for a display to show Sophia; for it might somehow mitigate the bleakness of the bitter cold, but it died away.

Clad in his parka, with his hood raised, in the morning he tramped ten miles on snowshoes to the Indian village to get his dogs and sled, which he had left in Pavlof's care for he had not wanted to catch fish and care for them in these busy first months of his marriage. The beasts were malemutes, named for the Eskimo tribe that had originally developed the breed, gray, narrow-eyed wolfish beasts, not as large as huskies, but strong, intelligent, and willing. The villagers stood in the doorways as he started home, his sled full-laden with smoked fish. All but one remained motionless; the girl Sant raised her hand level with her head and kept it so until he vanished in the thickets.

7

On his return he introduced the dogs to Sophia, who had come a little way over the firm snow to meet him. They growled at first sight of her, but quieted when they caught her scent, different in their brute brains from Eric's, but permeated with it. Although the ensuing night was milder than the last, the thermometer dipped below zero, and the thin ice on the river bays thickened. In the next few days it began to fringe all the shores, slowly widening, and by the end of October it had spread across the channel. When snow fell again, wildly blown in small dry flakes of extreme coldness, the river was no longer a gray-green rift in the white covering of the land. It lay everywhere, softening the shape of things, enveloping all, at once pure, beautiful, and unworldly. Eric used the word "forbidding" to describe it. Sophia did not protest this, although she did not think so, perhaps because it gave new meaning to their small warm island within the wooden walls.

The first clear, moonless night gave them a great show of northern lights. Warm in their parkas with the hoods raised, they watched it nearly an hour, its multicolored flickerings in the north spreading sometimes in shimmering waves throughout the dome of the sky. Sometimes it formed bands of pale green and rose, sometimes what looked like search-light beams except for their slow climb. "Some old-timers swear they've heard it crackle and hiss," Eric told her. "For me it always plays in silence."

Every day that weather permitted, the two went hunting in the forest for woodland caribou. On one of these trips she caught her first clear view of Slewfoot, the grizzly bear who dwelt hereabouts, too set in his ways to seek other lairs in the hunting, grubbing, fishing season. He was in new fur, with a fine square head that Eric said resembled his own; and he was larger and more impressive than Sophia had imagined. Soon, though, the deepening snow and cold would drive him to a den in the distant mountains. There he would sleep in a sleep like death, and since he looked so grizzled, not enfeebled in the least, Sophia wondered if he would waken when spring came.

Such game as he chose—young bulls mostly, never cows—Eric's heavy rifle killed cleanly at close range. She came to take pride in his quick, good aim and to share the intensity that came upon him at the instant of firing, and even to feel a sense of triumph that might be related to that of security, as the splendid untrammeled life came to a sudden end. Always he butchered the carcass while it was still warm, the dogs wildly excited by the smell of blood. Then he loaded on the sled all four quarters, the fatty hump and tender backstrap, tongue, liver, heart, and sometimes some of the gut to use for storing pemmican. She learned to help at these tasks, feeling no more revulsion than had some of

120

her ancestresses who had gone with their husbands to the western frontier.

The days shortened and the nights grew longer, as if by a disorder of nature. In the long darknesses of late November and early December the cold set in in a deep and silent tide; the most prolonged and bitter onslaught that Eric could remember at this time of year. Then for three days and nights it was cold beyond description, any warmth left on earth beyond imagining. The thermometer might lie but not other phenomena that Eric had beheld before. When the door opened the moisture in the room condensed instantly to wraithlike clouds whisking about the room, and the chill that enveloped it must resemble, Eric thought, the chill that comes upon a man bedridden with age or sickness; before the doctor and the watchers can notice any change he knows full well that his life is running out through his clammy skin and his breaths are numbered. When, dressed in furs and parka, Eric must make sallies into the great cold, his breath made a crackling sound as its moisture instantly turned to sleet. The dogs slept the clock around, their noses tucked under their tails, except for a moment or two when they roused up to eat the smoked fish that he tossed to them.

After its terrible onslaught the cold abated and on December twenty-first and twenty-second the temperature was barely zero. In this period the sun did not rise above the low mountains and a haze restricted its wan light, so instead of a midnight sun there was a midday darkness. The winter had far to go, long to linger, with its great gales yet to come; the fact remained that this was ebbing, not flowing, and the days would lengthen swiftly.

The milder weather let Eric and Sophia go ptarmigan hunting with his light rifle in preparation for Christmas dinner. She could wear snowshoes quite well, although her ankles soon tired; anyway Eric would not venture with her very far into the woods, because sometimes a December blizzard strikes without warning. Actually they saw no ptarmigan, although snow-white rabbits and ermine crossed their path; so Eric brought from his shed a frozen goose that he had shot in the last days of the migration. With dressing made of highly seasoned breadcrumbs, hot biscuits, jelly, rice and gravy, and canned peas, a bottle of champagne to bubble in the cups, a sprig of greenery for the table, they fared well.

In late January broke one of the great storms, which Sophia saw only as snowflakes driving wildly by the window. She heard its raving and felt its chill in the corners of the heated room, for the wind found tiny apertures in the walls and under the roof that Eric himself could never find in good weather. In the eighty hours of its duration he ventured no further than the shed and the pickets of his dogs, and, even so, Sophia burned her brightest lamp at the window in case in that blind turmoil Eric should make a wrong turn and wander away.

January was a long, dim, and awesome month, with fearful cold. But the sun was coming back, and February brought back sharp division between night and day, real days beginning when the sun rose boldly, ending with its setting with ever-longer stay; and its beams gave forth an appreciable warmth. By March first, spring was coming up the trail. The little thaws of surface ice and snow under the midday sun stopped in late afternoon, the sound of their faint tricklings died away, and by twilight all the land was again fast frozen and wrapped in silence. But a few rough-voiced hardy birds were returning to the woods, wolves no longer wailed at the icy moon, the fall of snow from the tree branches gave glimpses of dark green, and a silver gull winged over the cabin before it cried forlornly and fled southward.

"It's like those first days after the flood, before the waters receded," Sophia said, "and the dove returned to the Ark."

March 23, 1899, was a memorable day for Sophia although she did not tell Eric so, or what had happened. But after breakfast of the morning of April 3rd, following a long night in which Eric had twice roused up and gone to the door and told her of whispering waters, she sat at table and made a mysterious remark.

"Eric, you'd better take a little snoose."

He looked at her, did so, and his hand shook, spilling a little of the brown powder on the cloth.

"I may be mistaken, but I don't think so. From age twelve to March twenty-third this year, my body has kept time like a clock, a twenty-eight-day clock. On that day it stopped. I've waited ten days before I let myself believe it, although I was perfectly sure. Since then—even before—there have been some other signs of which Sarah told me, not only a faint sickness in the morning but itching nipples

122

and heavy sleep. Two hundred and eighty days from February twenty-fourth—that's the way the doctors count—is December first. It's a cold dark time to have a baby, but that will put the hallmark on his sourdough-hood. Have you anything to say?"

"Not a word yust now."

"Eric, I can't tell you how I feel or imagine how you feel. The words you sing to Mendelssohn's wedding march aren't true—two souls going up the aisle come back two souls. I thank God that marriage doesn't turn two souls into one; his own soul is everyone's private possession and refuge. But the souls of two people brush close at times like this. Isn't that so?"

"I t'ink so."

"Don't fear for me, Eric. I have compared my body to that of young colored women who've had babies, and they are just alike. There will be plenty of room between the bones. I've good muscular structure and the muscles have strengthened a whole lot since I came here. Don't even think of sending me out on the last boat. Pavlof is not much of a doctor but he hasn't lost a single baby since I've been here, at least you haven't told me of any. I want my baby born in our own house, our own bed. I want him to be a native Alaskan. I said 'him'—if it's a girl I want her to be an Alaskan girl, seeing the snow as soon as her eyes are open, smelling the spring in her first spring, that wonderful smell of the spruce. We'll show her the northern lights. We'll wrap her up two weeks after she's born, and you'll put both of us on the sled and give us a wild ride over the ice. We'll name her Gertrude—Gertrude Andersen. She'll be tall, and maybe have green eyes, and I think she'll be beautiful."

"She couldn't very well help that," Eric said, looking at the face he loved.

"I think it will be a boy. If so, I want to name him after you, and another Eric. Have you ever heard of Eric the Red?"

"I read the saga. Mamma got it for me. She was proud that he came to America so long before Columbus. I read it t'rough."

"He was a sourdough, in a way of speaking. He came to Vineland, *Furder Strandi,* which Papa thinks was Labrador. If you had been he, he would have been named Eric the Black. I want him to be a dead shot, to know how to handle dogs before he's ten, to make fish weirs, to pole boats, to

123

keep alive in the great cold. You tend to that part, and I'll
be his teacher until we have to send him to the best schools
in Alaska. I want him to become the governor of Alaska,
if you yourself never do."

"Me, Sophia? I'm only a trapper, a squarehead, a piker
miner."

"You failed to mention one thing—you're my husband.
When we first married I never doubted that, with my help,
you'd become governor. But when I dream about it now,
you're just about to take the chair and something—I don't
know what—it's black with a white top and it disappears—
gets in the way. But if you don't make it, he will. Your son
Eric."

"Yesus!"

"Now open a bottle of champagne. It will be cool enough
in the back room. That's good sourdough procedure, and
Dear Papa said it was utter poppycock that a leaven of
alcohol in a pregnant woman's blood can hurt her unborn
baby. So why not, since we've struck it rich?"

She rose, went to the door, and opened it. There was
faint sound everywhere, the murmur of waters, snow falling off tree limbs, and, barely discernible and perhaps imagined only, might be a knocking sound far and away up
the river. A white dot, almost out of sight, northward bound
for the shallow pools of the Arctic muskeg, was a lone
swan. She gave her clear, far-carrying call.

5. Tithonus

With progressive speed and gathering power, the sun wore
away and tore apart the river ice. More and more water
flowed over it as it melted on the surface and close to the
banks, and short and shallow creeks dumped floodwater
from melting snow with countless tons of rotted ice into the
main channel. As the main structure weakened, pressure
beyond conception built up behind it, rifts appeared, sections moved, only to jam with other sections; the grum-
bling, groaning, knocking sounds became continuous and
re-echoed miles away. In mid-April occurred the cataclysm;
with a tremendous roar the last supports broke free, the
cracks instantly became crevices, the whole ice moved, fragments and floes grinding and heaving, ice sheets four feet

thick tilted endwise, all in such turmoil that it stunned the mind, the Götterdämmerung of the Arctic.

Thereafter spring held fast; and its growth everywhere —grass, flowers, buds swelling, leaves coming out in full and vital greenery, saplings shooting up, the sprouts on the spruce boughs richly green in contrast with the old silver-dusted blue-black of the parent tree—ever reminded Sophia of the growth in her own body, and she felt a oneness with every live thing, and it brought her tranquillity and what Eric felt was a different and richer beauty.

Again the river and the ponds teemed with waterfowl, wings flashed everywhere, and silver gulls scrabbled and screamed. Eric did not attempt his project of a big jet to wash the looser gravel into his sluices and was content this year to build a small flume with planks hand-hewn by Indians at the village. Even so, its little torrent moved twice as many tons each day as he had previously shoveled, and his take in gold was twice as great. He had money to order lumber from St. Michael and time to enlarge the house by an additional room, and a small, crude bathroom.

More prospectors came and went, and toward summer's end an upriver steamer brought word of a rich strike on Nome peninsula. Thereafter the down-river boats were packed with gold seekers quitting the Klondike for what might prove a new Golconda, mainly men who had either delved in vain or spent their winnings, yet whose eyes were beady, faces strained, and voices ragged with excitement. On one boat came two gamblers and half a dozen women. Because the ship put into Eric's landing to replace a broken paddle, he had dealings with one of these.

She was coming out of her stateroom and at sight of Eric she started to turn back. It was too late: knowing he had seen and recognized her, she came boldly on. At least she gave the impression of boldness and that was the one she wished to give, although Eric remembered the defiance that sometimes caused a bull moose, very old, or perhaps a yearling, mortally wounded, knowing that his magnificent life was draining fast, to stand with his head up facing his deadly foe, or even sometimes to advance. When Eric looked closely at Fannie Ford he knew she was no bolder than she ever had been, only more defiant.

She wore more finery than before, and with less taste. In spite of her paint, she still looked terribly young, and the mascara under her eyes did not change their desolate expression. Eric came gravely forward, unsmiling, there was nothing to smile about; nor did she smile.

"How are you, Fannie?" he asked.

"I'm all right. If I weren't do you think I'd be traveling first class, fare paid in dust, on this grand ship? Isn't it elegant? People say the grub's better than on the *Vic,* now that the *Vic* sails chockablock with gold seekers."

"Where's Frank?"

"How in hell should I know? We've quit, nearly a year ago. The last I heard he was at Cripple Creek, working in a restaurant. How's your lady wife?"

"She's in good healt', t'ank you." Eric hesitated, then spoke on. "She's going to have a baby in December."

"Oh, my God!"

"I can't hardly believe it either."

"That's not what I meant, and you know it. When I married Frank I expected to have one by this time. It's a good thing I didn't. Wouldn't he be a father to be proud of? And, of course, you've heard how I'm making a living?"

"No."

"No one told you about Frankie? That's my name now. I haven't any last name. When I have to sign, I write Frankie Filmore; it sounds grand."

"The old Alaskans don't mention women's names. I don't see many cheechakos."

"Well, I'm not one of the most successful of the camp followers. The men who dance with me complain that I'm sulky. I'm not; I'm nearsighted and the lights hurt my eyes. Isn't that interesting? Still, I make two or three hundred a week, more than Dr. Hill makes, I bet. Sometimes I get presents, never under fifty in nuggets and dust, sometimes as much as a hundred. Have you, too, struck it rich?"

Eric shook his head.

"I suppose you guessed all I've told you."

"I won't answer that."

"Will you do me a favor, Eric? It's a small one for you, pretty big for me. Not tell Sophia? She said I could call her by her first name."

"I won't say a word about it."

"Now it's Nome. The Chink who washes out the sweepings of the dance hall gets more dust than you get from your mine. Have you heard the song, 'After the Ball Is Over?' It's a big hit in the Klondike."

126

"After it's over, you can let me know, if you wish."

"I don't think I ever will. Good-bye, good luck, and—you know the rest of the expression. I never use it; I've been told I use very ladylike language. Anyway it doesn't apply to you."

She went into her cabin; Eric went to see about buying some medical stores from the steward's cabinet, then to shore.

The ship sped away down-river with the current behind her; the late summer sped with sometimes a chill south wind scattering its small, white clouds. Signs of fall appeared, and in late August a hard frost goldened the leaves of the quaking asp before its time. When Eric began to harvest winter meat Sophia went as far into the woods with him as he would let her, but that was not very far, for he feared the rocks that sometimes slipped underfoot on the hillsides, and he could not quite believe in modern doctors' advice to pregnant women, despite Gertrude's having told him that in the Old Country the peasant women did a full day's work in the fields until the pains began. In September he sailed upriver to talk to Pavlof.

"Father, on December first of this year my wife expects a baby," Eric said. "It may be a day or two before, or after, but I don't want you to leave the village during that time."

Pavlof waited a few seconds before he answered; his half-Indian countenance betrayed no feeling; then he spoke quickly, leaning forward with a sudden spread of his hands.

"I no deliver white woman's baby since long time ago I study in Moscow."

"Indian and white women have babies just the same."

"No, Indian baby come easy, white baby come hard. Squaw work like hell till pains begin, joints loose, muscles strong. Squaw wide across ass, plenty room between bone. White woman no work hard, joints tight, muscles weak. Your wife she narrow across ass, maybe room for baby come through, maybe not. Think maybe you better take her Outside to have baby."

"No, she insists on staying here."

"Then maybe you better send for white doctor. Good doctor in Dawson, he come down-river before freeze-up—*whish* —one day, one night. He stay with you till baby come."

"No, she wants you. She says she has plenty of room

127

between the bones. And her muscles are not weak; she's stronger than most women Outside. If you should have any trouble, you have forceps, haven't you?"

"Got forceps."

"Have you forgotten how to use them?"

"I no forget. Sometimes when Indian baby got big head I use 'em."

"Do you boil them beforehand?"

"Boil forceps, pretty near boil hands, boil cotton blanket. Old priest at school, he raise hell if we no boil everything, I no forget."

"You'll do all right, Father. Just be sure and be here when I come for you. Remember, twenty-one days before the darkest day. Stay within call from five days before then until five days afterward, and I'll give you five dollars for every one of those ten days. If you leave the village even fifty days before the dark day to go hunting, don't go more than two miles, and tell H'kah where you are going. I'll shoot once every minute and you answer my shots until we find each other. Do you understand?"

"I do what you say. But your wife born baby easy if come one month too soon."

As Eric walked down the village row, Sant came running from her mother's house. Her dusky face looked clean from a late washing; her hair had been dressed with fish oil; her deerskin shirt and mukluks were richly decorated with many-colored beads and she wore a necklace of small, iridescent shells.

"Mist' Rick!" she called. "Sant send present to pretty wife."

"That's mighty nice of you, Sant."

"Shut hand till you get on trail, no let people see. It— what you call?—good-luck charm. Old shaman, he give H'kah before Sant born. It make me born easy, no trouble, no hurt H'kah too bad."

"Sant, you speak better English than the last time I talked to you."

"I talk plenty to Father Pavlof."

She slipped something made of bone into Eric's hand, then stood looking down.

"Indian say white men no sleep with wife, three, four months before baby come."

"I still sleep with my wife."

"I mean, no play buck rabbit. White man mighty smart.

128

No get baby, baby already made, doctor say can hurt baby."

"Many doctors don't believe that these days."

"You come many times to talk-talk with Father Pavlof?"

"I don't think so. He understands what I want of him. I'll come for him when it's time for the baby to come."

"Maybe you get hard up, remember old time. Sant no forget."

She walked swiftly away. Eric did not look at what was in his hand until he was clear of the village, then with some astonishment, because the bone carving did not appear seventeen or more years old, or else it had been newly polished. Although he had seen many totems, this was of a new sort.

About three inches long, it had been crudely carved of the long bone of a moose, and appeared to represent a manikin, with the head tightly fitted into a bone ring. Eric did not like the look of it very well, although without knowing or even questioning why. He started to pocket it, only to hold it in his hand while he launched his boat. Adrift on the current, steering with his oar, he made from the creek mouth into mid-river. Then he dropped the carving overside, watched it glimmer in the clear water, then disappear.

2

For Eric and Sophia, September and October was a time of waiting. Actually that was all it was, even though the routine of his tasks and hers went uninterrupted. They rarely mentioned the coming crisis and tried to conceal the fixation of their minds upon it. In June, after consulting Sophia, Eric had ordered a box of new books from Seattle, not heavy reading but mostly pleasant and good—a book of Riley's poems, the lurid novel *Thelma*, brand-new *The Gentleman from Indiana*, *Trilby*, which her father had not wanted her to read, *Peter Pan*, the immortal *Tess*, a Gilbert Parker novel of Canada, a Burnett novel and several others. They arrived in September, and Sophia appeared to lose herself in them, although again and again her eyes would wander away from the page to gaze through the window, and mostly in Eric's absence she worked on the layette. The cloth too had been ordered from Seattle, although there were several items for which Eric furnished the materials. All these things she showed to Eric before putting away—including an eiderdown quilt faced with silk, a similar quilted silk nightcap, and, her final triumph, a parka and hood made of young caribou skins as soft as chamois.

In November they stopped trying to conceal anxiety, perhaps sharpened by what seemed the malice of the weather. The autumn season had lasted briefly, the river had locked October tenth, now winter gripped the land, with deep-zero cold spells alternating with gales. In this month Eric made two trips to make sure of Pavlof's preparations, riding his dog sled and racing his team, in a rush to go and frantic haste to return. Yes, everything was ready. Pavlof would not stray from the village until Eric brought his summons. Eric himself became deeply worn, gaunt in the face, unaware of his long repression of his body's needs, sleeping fitfully with ever-troubled dreams.

The upper Yukon country, whose winter temperatures sometimes fell to forty or even fifty below zero, was likewise subject to unseasonable spells of extremely mild weather. In the early morning of November thirtieth, a wind from the southeast began to blow, moist and so warm that Eric must shed his parka to do his tasks in comfort. He looked at his thermometer and found it rising fast. At four in the afternoon it had risen from eight degrees below zero to thirty-three above, the highest reading he could remember between November first and March thirty-first at this time of day, and the crust of the snow had definitely softened. Shortly after this, snow began to fall in large, soft flakes, and continued to do so all night. Snowshoeing would be a hard chore until the snow packed again. On the early morning of December first Sophia noticed a symptom of which she had read in the article on obstetrics in the encyclopedia.

Just at noonday of December first she felt a rather sharp twinge of pain midway in her abdomen, followed by a dull pain as of a cramp. It passed off; she did not speak of it but she glanced at the clock. In twenty minutes the same thing occurred, the twinge slightly sharper, the cramp more severe. Again she waited and in eighteen minutes came the third of these little attacks of pain. Eric was at the table, waiting for dinner; she served him and sat down opposite him. Both made their usual swift hearty meal, then she spoke.

"You'll have to go now, Eric."

His eyes met hers in intense interrogation.

"The pains have begun," she went on. "They are very

mild and far apart, but rhythmic. I was almost sure it would happen today and it has. There's no reason to think it's a false alarm—the pains are indescribable but unique in my experience. You mentioned the soft snow—you've spoken of it before and I know it means slow, hard travel, but you needn't hurry; don't exhaust yourself. The first stage of labor, the dilation of the cervix to let the baby through, lasts at least eight hours, often twelve hours or even longer. Nothing bad can happen before then."

Sophia knew that she should have put the word "usually" before the verb. Rather rarely, but not considered phenomenal by doctors, the dilation stage of labor is short and the expulsion stage terribly long, instead of vice versa. She had spoken from impulse—instinct was what it was—not to alarm her husband, not to put him to an exhausting ordeal, and perhaps to hide her terrors. The three precepts of Dear Papa, pounded into her head ever since she could walk, had been harsh but were the makings of a *grande dame*—never show you are embarrassed, never show your feelings are hurt, never show you are afraid. They applied even to a wife's conduct before her husband in a marriage such as this between a sourdough and his cheechako girl who had known poetry but not how to wash dishes.

Eric glanced through the window. "I'll have him here in six hours."

There could be no running of dogs today; the sled would only delay the journey. In five minutes he was ready for the hard trek and had kissed and joked with Sophia. Within ten minutes he was gravely doubting if the round trip could be made in the time he had set. The shoe sank nearly a foot with every step; its lifting without picking up snow required a distinct effort. His pace was steady, as rapid as possible without his hurling himself into exhaustion, but when he glanced at his watch after going only two miles, the hands stood at forty minutes after his departure. At that rate he would take three hours and twenty minutes to reach the village. Happily the light wind was working eastward, colder weather would come soon, or else he missed his usually right guess.

The grueling labor caused the minutes to seem to lag; actually they were passing at their ruthless rate and adding up to hours. At the midway point that he knew so well he had spent one hour and forty minutes of his allotted time. He wished that Sophia had told him of her first twinge of

131

pain, for he would have been out the door like a bullet and a whole hour would have been saved. Always she was too considerate of him, afraid of sending him on fools' errands, and too secretive. None of these three could he resent; the last was a small price to pay for his great winning.

Yet his spirits fell, that darkness of heart he knew sometimes came swiftly upon him, and his sense of unbreachable solitude had never been more heavy and more dull. He trudged alone in the heavy snow of the river ice two miles wide, no living thing showed itself alive, for the distant forest was one great rough-topped low hill of snow. After death, there might be all whiteness instead of blackness. Whiteness occurred from the dissolving of all colors, each canceling the others, and he could not think of a hell more desolate than one soul trudging alone through forever whiteness. There wasn't any hell. There was only nothingness, all that the soul could ask. Once Sophia had recited to him a verse of a poem about young Englishmen trapped by the cholera epidemic in India, and it had spoken of the nearing hour when "the haughty yearnings of the soul could sting no more." That must be nothingness, for as long as the soul lived it must yearn. That was the nature, the being, of souls.

He pulled himself together to realize that he was walking too fast for this kind of snow. His legs ached steadily and a sharp pain seized his ankle at the start of every stride. Once he thought a snowshoe rabbit crossed in front of him, but when he came to the place, there were no tracks. Well, rabbits were hard to see—white in a world of whiteness. Instead of lagging a little, he tried to hurry, only to find this impossible without danger to his object. Even he, Eric, in whose strength he put such trust, could collapse under enough strain. He resumed his former pace.

At three quarters of the way he noticed with dull surprise that his legs no longer ached, the sharp pain had gone from his ankles, and his stride appeared effortless. That could not be right, he thought, because actually the walking was harder than before, because the snow was packing from its own weight and the rising east wind and the deepening cold were forming a crust which he broke through at every step. "Every man is two men," he mumbled. "When one gives out, the other spells him. When that second man is done, both fall together, and unless they are given food and rest, they die together." And it was a great thing in the

hearts of men—that secret assurance of dual self in his hour
of need. Maybe some men did not have it. He wondered if
Frank Ford had it. There was no one to say, "You yellow
bastard, show yourself a man."

Eric had started out at five minutes after one. Fifteen
minutes after four he saw the village lights glimmer through
the heavy dusk; somehow he had gained ten minutes on
what he had thought was his pace of three miles an hour.
He went first to the outlying cabin where Pavlof ate and
slept. It had no light, no one answered his call, no one slept
in the bed, and so he made for H'kah's house. She looked
up from her bannock making; sitting in a corner, Sant did
not seem to see him.

"Where's Pavlof?" Eric demanded.

"He's gone hunting, but white doctor here."

"What?"

"Father Pavlof say he come back at what you say?"—
H'kah counted swiftly on her fingers—"six o'clock. But he
say you better take white doctor, big doctor from White
Horse, for he know how to take baby better'n Indian doctor."

"Where is this white doctor? What is his name? I want
him this minute."

"H'kah don't know name. He come on new moon, stay
with Tootsun. Tootsun live alone, her man drown last summer in river. House six, seven houses up hill. You see light."

Eric hurried away, climbed the hill, saw the light through
the cracks in the door brighter than other village lights. He
knocked and went in. A white man Eric had never seen lay
stretched on the bed. The full-burning fish-oil light showed
him plainly—a man of about forty-five, somewhat fat, of
medium length, with a stubble of dark beard. He wore store
clothes, dirty and shabby. He had a rounded face, not as
weak as would seem to go with the rest of him and with his
occupancy of this rank-smelling hut. He sat up at sight of
Eric and put his unshod feet on the floor.

"You're Andersen," he said. "I was more than half expecting you. Yesterday too——"

"Did Pavlof tell you——?"

"Yes, and he went off under my protest—he'll be back
at six. He refused to believe that I couldn't handle the case
better than he. Is your wife in labor?"

"The pains started at twelve o'clock."

"How far were they apart?"

"About twenty minutes."

"My name is Scott Harris. I've a degree in medicine from the University of Pennsylvania. But don't let that deceive you. Let me say first that your wife's all right. It's her first baby, Pavlof told me—the first stage of labor can be expected to last at least until eight, more likely till midnight, and it's only a little after four."

"Well, how soon can you clean yourself up and start?"

"I asked you not to let my medical honors deceive you. I don't live up to them. Besides giving physic and pulling out splinters and putting on bandages, I have practiced no medicine for ten years. I've been following the camps, the Cassiar—Forty Mile Creek—stinking little camps on the Lewes and Pelly, and finally the big camp on Cripple Creek. Always with a squaw to rustle grub. I add that juicy detail because it lends veracity to my argument. I made whisky-money dealing cards—I drink good whisky—but not much more. Speaking of whisky——"

"We're not speaking of whisky," Eric broke in.

"Forgive my garrulousness. You, of course, are anxious, although I assure you there's plenty of time. To get to my point—if Pavlof isn't here by six I'll go with you and do what I can. I've got to have a sled and dogs. I can't walk ten miles. On my word as a gentleman—I was born one, you understand, regardless of what has happened since— the chance of a good delivery are ten times better with Pavlof than with me. I watched him deliver a baby only the day before yesterday. As far as the essentials go, not the frills, he's a good obstetrician. My hands are too unsteady to use forceps; if no forceps are needed, she doesn't need anyone except to cut and tie the cord."

Eric looked at him dazedly, suddenly almost too tired to speak.

"Then there's nothing to do but wait till six."

"Now I'll prescribe for you. That much is within my province and skill. You must rest and had better sleep an hour. The snow's crusting and you can make it back in a little over two hours, if you are in any shape. I never saw a man as dog tired who can still keep his feet."

"I'll lie down if you'll call me——"

"The instant Pavlof appears. He's got a watch and he'll keep his word——"

"He broke his word to me."

Dr. Harris got up and poured from his bottle into a tin cup.

"Drink this," he ordered. "You're too tired to sleep well without a soporific."

Hardly knowing what he was doing, Eric drained the cup.

"You must forgive him," the other was saying as Eric's drink began to take hold. "His teacher was a white doctor and he has too much respect for white doctors, even the relics of same."

"You say the first period of labor is eight hours?" Eric asked, greatly stronger now, able to stand without swaying.

"Sometimes twelve with the first baby, or even twenty-four. Your wife will be all right."

"I'll go now. I'll lie down in Pavlof's cabin——"

"Sleep, man, not just lie down. Have another drink to make sure. Two drinks never hurt anyone, let alone a sour-dough."

He poured another, as deep in the cup as before. Eric craved it, to restore his courage and his hope, to drive the mists off his brain, to make everything seem brighter, not so dark, so he swallowed it quickly. He did not remember thanking the giver or leaving the hut; the next he knew he was lying on Pavlof's bed, his mukluks and some of his more cumbersome clothes dropped on the floor. He began to dream before he fell fast asleep.

It seemed he had been dreaming a long time when he smelled fish. It was a sharp, new smell of fish, not merely the fish-infiltrated rankness of the room, to which he had become accustomed and no longer noticed. Then he came vaguely aware that someone was in the room. The new-comer was doing something beside his bed, there were soft sounds, and then the caribou robe he had drawn over him was lifted and someone warm and smooth-skinned lay beside him. A hand found its way under his clothes, down his body. . . .

3

For an hour after Eric left for the Indian village Sophia maintained a philosophical attitude toward the coming ordeal. The stabbing pains, followed by severe cramp that died away, came at considerable intervals; between them she fed the fire and filled the big tub steaming on the stove from filled tubs in the back room. At the worst the pains were no harder to bear than hard toothache, and anyway they were in the contract. They were the lot of woman, she thought tritely, if she wanted to be whole and fulfill her principal function. She would not let herself dwell on fear, because it was such an insidious thing; once it found entrance into her mind it seized it and made it sick, whereby every other thought became twisted. Even so, it stole upon her when she was off guard.

In the second hour she noticed a disturbing fact: not that the pains increased in severity—she had expected that—but that they struck at narrowing intervals. It caused her to remember an article in one of the women's magazines to which she subscribed, copies of which arrived one by one, or in batches, according to the frequency or the infrequency of river boats. She had read it before her pregnancy and had forgotten it until now. It had dealt with childbearing among primitive peoples and the author had ventured the bold guess that a diet heavy with lean meat, instead of endangering a pregnant woman, hastened both the first and second stage of labor. He did not think that muscle tone was the total answer: he thought that the ductless glands, the use of which Vesalius had tried to explain but whose presence in the body baffled modern doctors, would, when stimulated by protein, excite the womb into supernormal activity. The magazine editors had added that the views presented above did not reflect the ideas of most reputable physicians but had been published because they were so open-minded.

Dr. Hill had taught Sophia to be open-minded. Suddenly she regretted that fact, because just now it opened the door to terror.

She shut it again, and, and, she thought, bolted it. The pains were lasting longer and the interval between them was hardly five minutes, when, at the end of the second hour of Eric's absence she drank a glass of warmed canned milk and lay down. The house was utterly silent except for occasional cracklings of the fire. By now, she thought, Eric was almost to the Indian village and would be starting back, accompanied by a dark-skinned doctor with deft hands. If Dear Papa was sixty days distant by dog sled, Eric was less than four hours. At sound of his step the pains would not ease, she would have to bear them, but this sense of deep and sinking loneliness would be banished, and fear would no longer knock on the closed door.

Four hours. Four hours! *Four hours!*

And now she remembered another writing which she had found in a drawer at age sixteen. It had been in her grandfather's scrawl, and when she had asked Sarah what had been its occasion, Sarah had answered in a voice betraying some embarrassment, even shock—and Sarah was hard to shock—"Why, Possum, Ol' Mas' Sams wrote that when you was being bornded, and sent it in to Miss Julia to make her laugh. She was at what dey call a lying-in hospital in Ch's'ton, and him and her auntie Mary Sams and your papa and me was waitin' in a kind of sittin' room, for de big docta' didn't want no one in the 'livery room when he was takin' a baby, for fea' dey get in his way. Old Mas' Sams read it aloud befo' he sent it in. He would say anything that come into his haid."

Sophia also had been somewhat shocked, not at the blunt language of the verses but at her grandfather's thinking that his daughter Julia would enjoy them. It had not fitted into the concept that Sophia had of her mother.

In spite of her retentive memory, Sophia had no idea that she could recall the verses. However, she made an effort to do so, and a few words at a time, then with lines that she revised over and over, she pieced the whole thing together. Between pains she muttered it aloud:

> *Bid your cervix quickly dilate,*
> *Lusty pains come at a high rate.*
>
> *Haste the second stage, expulsion,*
> *To born the brat your swift compulsion.*
>
> *Bid the flesh and bone be pliable,*
> *For to fits we all are liable.*
>
> *Curse like pirate, whoop and yell,*
> *Bear down hard, and grunt like hell.*

But as soon as she had said it, that door barring out terror opened a crack, and she felt its chill. It was as though she had spoken an incantation, perhaps of evil augury. Julia had had a good doctor in reach of her hand; Sophia was alone. Lord, let this kind of pains last till Eric comes! I don't care how hard You make them, if only the baby doesn't start down too soon. Maybe I can do it alone, so many women have, but if—if . . .

For she remembered that while she had let Eric feel the

137

baby's kicks against her belly, sometimes in the last month she felt a hard knock of which he knew nothing, and which she quickly expelled from her mind. What could it have been but the baby's head? It must be a big head to hit so hard.

At half-past four, when the windows had darkened and the snow beyond glimmered wanly, when surely Eric had reached the village and was starting back, a pain that began like the others had a different end. It became a great paroxysm of pain, higher in her body than before, which made her cry out. She sat up, staring at the walls as though they were unfamiliar, almost unable to believe it had happened. She waited, panting and terrified. At the end of a long minute, and she could almost hope it had meant something different than she had thought, the thing came again, and this time the baby moved; she felt its motion in such agony as she had never dreamed God's children need ever bear.

Time stopped for her soon after that; the world she had known ceased to exist; there was only pain. In the brief and lessening intervals between the seizures she forgot Eric, she forgot Dear Papa, she herself became dim as in a dream, she could only wait in horror for the next one, knowing its inevitability. Again and again the shattering blow fell, and in her desperate attempt to think, to remember such things as would keep her from unintermittent screaming, she thought of an elevator falling and crashing in ruins, she thought of a pile driver she had once watched, falling, striking, rising to fall again. In one interval she was glad of a strange thing —that Eric had not left his revolver within her reach. For with that she could take two lives.

It went on unchanged except for shortening intervals for a period she could not measure, because it seemed endless. Then the blows suddenly stopped, the baby did not move, and a new kind of pain began, and somehow she knew that it was a futile pain, which she must undergo without gain. It came only with her great, irresistible, and useless straining.

This too lasted beyond her final, dim conception of time's passing. But there is a last frontier of pain which the human mind will not enter. The intervals began to lengthen as her muscles weakened, and she drifted away into dreams just before the crest of each wave of this ineffable sea of pain in which she was drowning. Her lips moved. If he doesn't come soon we will both die. Then as though she were cast up on the shore of that sea, a finally merciful nature let her escape into profound trance.

4

Eric had been asleep less than an hour when a clock in his brain told him it was half-past five. He was wakening when Pavlof, gray of face, came into the room.

"You didn't go with the white doctor?"

"No." Eric began jerking on his outer garments. "Get ready as fast as you can."

"Pavlof's heart get weak. I run away but I come back. Now I get sled and dogs. The crust freeze and we both ride sled and go like hell."

They were under way in ten minutes, Pavlof bringing the instruments and medicines that he used, the dogs running. Eric's thoughts ran ahead of them and did not turn backward now; there was something behind him to which sooner or later he must give attention, not atone, because that was impossible, only face as a man. That was for the future. The present was the backsweep of the snow beside the sled.

When the dogs slacked their pace or when they came on stretches of soft snow, either Eric or Pavlof or both sprang off, ran ahead, and mercilessly drove them on. Landmarks that Eric called Seven Mile, Half Way, Three Mile came into view in the icy moonlight, drew close, and dropped behind. Eric had no time to take out and look at his watch; he guessed it was still short of seven when he saw glimmers of lighted windows and the pale smoke from his chimney.

No one answered Eric's shout. He tied the lead dog to a post before he entered the house, so it came about that Pavlof went in ahead of him. Eric came in time to see him bending over the bed, on which lay Sophia in what might be death, but which Pavlof's alert face told him might be unfathomable deep sleep. Her white hand lay in Pavlof's dark hand, his sensitive index finger on her wrist.

"I find pulse," he muttered. "It very weak and fast, we got to work quick."

As he spoke he threw off his parka and seal-fur shirt. Eric began pouring boiling water into the washbasin. Pavlof dropped his forceps into the tub, then rapidly and with great thoroughness washed his hands and forearms. Dip-

139

ping and then soaping the hairbrush, he rubbed his close-cut fingernails through the bristles. Then he turned once more to the bed.

"Baby down, but no get head through bones. I feel now."

His hand went up into the womb, then paused, his fingers probing. "Head big, it stuck," he told Eric, without looking up. "I try to turn a little. If no can get through then, I mash head. If him alive, no know it; if dead, no matter."

"Do what you have to, Pavlof, to save Sophia."

Pavlof's wrist moved slowly, strongly. Then he said, "I get him out now, I think. You no touch forceps."

Pavlof fished them from the boiling water, held them firmly. He worked briefly, the head was born, immediately after, the whole body. Eric glanced only once at the baby that made no sound, that lay still, and whose scalp was diffused with blood and small face smeared.

"You got ammonia?" Pavlof asked.

"Yes." Eric ran for the bottle.

"Pass it under her nose. If she coughs, chances good. She'll get rid of afterbirth in about ten minutes."

Sophia did cough, and her eyes half opened.

"Make her drink coffee," Pavlof commanded.

As always, the pot was steaming on the stove. All but a little had boiled out; of what was left Eric half filled a cup and began to pour a little at a time into her mouth. Some of it ran out but she swallowed some, and Pavlof took time to grin at Eric when he felt her pulse almost miraculously slow its flutter and then strengthen.

"That plenty now. She sleep good now, she all right. But baby no good. Baby dead."

"What killed him? Our being so late?"

Pavlof dropped his bloody arms. "Yes, we too late. Baby's head stuck in the bone, muscles kept pushing and by'n'by it cause vessels to break in brain. Pavlof kill baby by running away."

"You thought the white doctor could do better——"

"That big lie. I knew him no good; I tell big lie to Pavlof, cause he scared to take white baby, maybe mother and baby both die, then he go jump in river, for no one call him Father Pavlof no more, and Indian laugh at me, no longer let me sit in front in the Kashga when old men talk." He turned away to examine the placenta that the contraction

140

of Sophia's womb had expelled; then he listened to her breathing.

"She all right now," he said. "Everything come out. But baby come out dead."

While Sophia slept Eric made a box out of spare planks, and, dipping a little cloth in ink, he wrote "Eric" on its side. Meanwhile Pavlof shoveled snow from a place they had chosen on the tundra near a tongue of the forest, and then built a big fire to melt the frozen ground. This last was slow work; at dawn it was hardly half finished, and Eric decided to use dynamite, which he kept in store for blasting out boulders that occasionally blocked the working of his gravel bed. When the blast went off he ran at top speed to the house.

Sophia was sitting up in bed, staring, haggard and very white.

"Eric! Have I had my baby? Where is it?"

Eric put his arms around her and answered, tears rolling down his face, "In a box."

Some seconds passed before her mind could take hold of this. Then she asked quietly, "You came too late?"

"Yes, Pavlof and I came too late. We were delayed at the village."

"Was it a good baby—except that it died?"

"A boy, perfectly formed, but it had a big head."

"Could I have done anything that I didn't do? Did I give up too soon?"

"God in heaven, no. You passed out."

"Was the light burning when you came? I dreamed it went out."

"Yes, it was burning good. All of us did the best we could."

"It wasn't good enough. But don't cry, Eric; I'll try again as soon as I can. Forgive me if I cry."

In Rama there was lamentation . . . Rachel weeping . . .

5

There was not much visible change within and about the house on the upper river. As soon as she was able, Sophia began doing her household tasks; and as her strength returned, she went with Eric into the forest. She almost never spoke of the lost baby and never went to look at a little

141

place in the tundra bare of lichens; and these would grow again when spring returned. Eric raised no marker because Sophia asked him not to. "The baby never breathed," she said. "It has no name, it had only the promise of a name. The sooner we can forget its failure to live except as part of me, to become a person, the better for both of us. You buried it deep, didn't you? I want it to become a part of the always frozen ground."

Eric nodded, remembering how he had written that hoped-for name on the box, unable to speak.

"And Eric, if I should die—and it's everyone's right to say what he wants done in that case, his last will and testament—I want the same kind of burial. I don't want any marker where I lie. I don't want anyone but you to know the place. I expect to live long and have several babies, the others will have a better chance; this is just in case of the unexpected. Now let's snowshoe into the woods. Take the shotgun; maybe you can shoot something good for supper."

Forgetfulness did not come easily to Eric; the story of the stillbirth had complications, or at least side issues, that Sophia did not know. The memory of these did not readily become dimmed. They were not easy to live with but they would not recede into the past because they fetched him up face to face with an ever-present fact: a human weakness which, despite the low-life escapades of his bachelor days, he had not confessed to himself that he possessed. He did not believe he was treacherous or had a yellow streak; but he had risked all his gains, all he loved, to gratify one sudden body hunger, and this at a time that his dedication to that love should have been most high. Would not such a man, a little short on grub, steal from a cache?

In the first days of March, when there was nothing but the pale sun and lengthening days to promise spring, he made an excuse to mush to the Indian village. He could not sleep well until the errand was accomplished; what he learned there might murder sleep, an expression Sophia had once used, the origin of which he did not know. He intended to ask Sant a question, face to face, and she could not deceive him because he knew Indian ways too well; probably she would not try. However, he was glad enough to change his plans when he learned that she had gone up the creek to fish through the ice and would not return until nightfall. So he addressed himself to Pavlof, coming straight to the point.

"You knew what was between Sant and me before I married."

"Sure. Everybody in the village know."

"How many know that she came to your house when I was waiting there for you?"

"No one know it but Sant, H'kah, and me. H'kah told me or I not know."

"Is that true, Pavlof?"

"Sure. Sant like a fox when she itch hard enough, sneak out, sneak back, nobody see. She got that much white blood in her."

Eric drew a deep breath. "Well, is she all right?" Then, strengthening his voice, "Is she going to have a baby?"

"No have baby. She come sick last month, same month before. I saw bloody rag. You no worry, Mist' Rick. No one ever know. North Light—Indians call her that—never find out."

Eric felt like shouting. Not only fear but gnawing guilt seemed to float away. These two were often closely connected, Eric thought grimly a moment later; frequently they slept in the same bed; now and again they were mistaken for each other.

He made haste to inquire of Pavlof's welfare.

"Did the people laugh at you about our baby?"

"No laugh, no care. Baby come, baby go, all same to Indian. Father Pavlof still sit in front of old men. But if North Light die, old Indians feel sad, old squaws cry like hell, maybe burn down village and move upriver, Pavlof luck all gone, Indian luck all gone. They never see anyone like North Light."

Eric tried to speak fully, but he could only say, "I never have either."

On the way home his spirits were high, as the dogs knew well as they ran at his shout across the deep-packed snow. He was thinking that Sophia was not essentially changed by the loss of her baby; she had felt it within her body, kicking, moving, heaving itself about, it seemed; but she had never looked into its living eyes. He found himself wishing that she had shown more grief, because he had sense enough to know it had struck deeper than she had ever revealed. It might be there had been two blows, one the loss itself, the other to a thing for which he could find no name but pride. The having of her first baby was a prideful thing to a woman. It was not only a fulfillment of natural function,

143

the payment of debt to her being, but itself a personal triumph. Those blows did not show in her face as far as he could tell, unless sometimes he saw a reflection of their pain deep in her eyes. Often her eyes wandered to the window and she daydreamed.

He had cause to think of what childbearing did to a woman soon after his return. It came about from the government's first, halting effort to deliver mail to the far-scattered river settlements during the freeze-up. The delivery was every two weeks as far upriver as Holy Cross; from there to the mouth of the Tanana it could be looked for about once a month; travelers occasionally brought mail to Fort Yukon; from thence to the Canadian border it was catch as catch can. However, there was more winter travel than before, because of the washing of creek gravels below the Klondike, and when a well-outfitted party of five mushed upriver on some heart-glowing errand they did not disclose, Eric felt no great surprise to receive a letter.

It was from Dr. Hill, and it read:

Dear Eric:

I hope this reaches you before the ice breaks. Of course you remember Fannie Ford. She left Nome and came to St. Michael to see me. She brought two things—a baby and a strange request.

It is not Frank's baby. She has seen nothing of him since their parting in Dawson, of which you know. I demanded complete honesty of her and she gave it—she doesn't know which of several men is the baby's father. Of course, that did not recommend the granting of her request, but she had gone a long way down and is trying to get back, and I found that on deep thought it did not really affect the main issue.

Her request was that she become a teacher at an Indian school. She has had a high-school education, speaks good enough English, and seems apt in learning native words— she learned at least a hundred Eskimo words during her stay in Nome. She was debased by Frank, still I seem to sense in her a fair strength of character. She adores the baby girl and will do anything to give the child a decent chance in life.

Teachers for the lonely outposts and Indian villages are hard to find. The pay is meager, a bare living in fact, the hardships great. Usually they need dedication to some great

*religious order or missionary society to volunteer their serv-
ices. So I have decided to give her a trial.*

*She has resumed the name Fannie Ford. This alone will
help to obscure her life as Frankie Filmore in the gold
camps; and Alaskans are not prone to weigh men and
women down by their past mistakes: the view up here is
always to the future.*

*The Secretary of the Interior is eager that I re-establish
a school at Tekuh village, near where you live, to replace a
very fine school conducted by a priest of the Greek Church
some twenty years ago, and now defunct. When the river is
open the government will send lumber, stoves, and other
equipment, and will employ you to supervise the building
of a schoolhouse and living quarters for the teacher. For the
present I have appointed Fannie to a temporary post at the
Russian Mission; she can teach there until the spring of
1901. Then I would like to have her start at Tekuh village.*

*It might be she will be some company for Sophia. The
great hour of her life was as matron of honor at the wedding. Please let me hear from you as to whether Indians can
be hired to erect the buildings, what pay they would expect, your charge for supervising, and whether any free
labor could be expected. We operate, as you know, on a low
budget.*

*You will be pleased to hear that the Reverend Arthur
Dudley paid me a visit on a trip to Nome to get smallpox
vaccine. He has become fluent in the language of the coast
Eskimos and told me that he has not regretted his decision to
go to the Arctic, and that he never will.*

My love to my lovely daughter,
Stanley Hill

"Well, what do you think of it?" Eric asked, when Sophia
had read the letter.

"I'm glad he gave her the chance. It's just like Dear
Papa."

"Would she be any company for you?"

"Not much, because I don't need any except—you and
what I'll have before then, I think. Eric, did you know she
was a camp follower?"

"Yes. She came by here on the ship with the broken
paddle blade. She asked me not to tell you, but she's not a
camp follower now."

"That's just like you, too."

"I don't want any credit for that, or for what I'm going to say. I'm mighty common clay, Sophia. The village is no trip in my sailboat, the wind or a pole to help me upriver, the current to help me back, and the gravel will go on washing into the sluice. So I'm going to work free."

"Good for you! It's your next big step on the way to the governorship of Alaska."

6

The spring broke fast; the ice went out on April tenth; that same day brought a flock of busy sparrows to the riverbank. And the lovely northern summer quickly sped.

Eric had sent his answer to Dr. Hill's letter on the first down-river boat, answering its questions from solid knowledge of Indian ways; but although he met midstream every up-bound boat and spoke to her captain, no lumber or stoves had been consigned to Tekuh village. Evidently there was a hitch in the plan, not surprising to anyone who knew the slow and ponderous turning of the wheels of government. Out of that same knowledge, Eric did not go to the village and explain the project to the elders. Indians wait to be shown. They could see, smell, and feel lumber, but not the promises of distant officials. He wanted to start no talking and grunting until the goods were in hand.

Once the captain had answered Eric's call with no, there was no lumber for Tekuh, but, come to think of it, there was a small shipment of dressed lumber for Eric himself, and dinged if he hadn't almost gone by without putting it on shore. Come to think of it, Eric had ordered it from Eureka Mill six months before, beautiful, durable California redwood, with the idea of building a small porch for summer afternoons. It was discharged on his little dock, he paid for it in gold, and the ship went on her way.

But Eric could not make the improvement now. Despite the long days, with working his mine, enough hunting to keep the table laden with succulent deer meat, wild duck and geese, grouse, even plover for new taste, and taking many a jaunt into the woods and along the river in his boat with his ever-eager companion, he could only store the stuff in his shed. Then he remembered with a slight shock that he had not even fulfilled his promise to Sophia to provide a real bathtub. By Yiminy, he would order a skookem bathtub from Seattle, lined with porcelain.

The summer turned curiously dry—the clouds gathering, then dispersing without dumping their much needed rain. Grass became scant; the spring shoots of the trees stunted and parched; even the river, fed by the melting snows of the Chugach, St. Elias, and Selwyn mountains and by the watershed of the Porcupine River, did not come to its full flood. Eric began to notice a scarcity of game such as woodland caribou and moose; and when freezing weather set in he had to hunt far and late to harvest winter meat. Usually at this time scattered bands of barren-land caribou roamed southward on their migration from the Arctic plains, veered off when they smelled man, swam the river half a mile down. This year he saw not one.

Too late for green things trying to grow, the October snows pelted, lay deep, and packed. The season of darkness set in, always the hardest to bear in the Far North country, a time of low spirits and heavy hearts and sorrowful reflections. There spread pale and icy sunlight for an hour or two before and after noon, and these hours cramped as December advanced, till they were not worth counting. There had been several severe cold spells; then, on the afternoon of December twentieth, after an icy wind, cold smote the land in ferocious onslaught. At midnight Eric need not look at his thermometer to know that its bottom had dropped out. There was enough sign elsewhere—the wraiths of frozen moisture careening about the room when the door was opened, his own crackling breath when he went out to feed his dogs, the deadly stillness everywhere.

On the twenty-first the sun did not top the hills, and only a wan glimmer spread over the snow at noon, and the cruel cold held fast. Just after two an astonishing thing occurred in the little house. Eric and Sophia heard a shout, then a hard rap on the door. Eric pocketed his pistol, for murder was no longer almost unknown in the region of the gold camps, then opened the door. Pavlof slipped through, his mustache frost-rimed despite his parka hood, and stood leaning forward a little from the waist, his mittened hands open.

"What is it?"

"Tootsuh"—this was the name of a young Indian in the village—"see six caribou by big bluff on Pike Creek yesterday. He shoot, miss, but caribou no run far this weather, so Pavlof go look for 'em today. Meat almost gone, fish scarce in village, squaws fish through ice of creek. Too cold today.

I go look for caribou, if I find track, follow 'em, maybe shoot 'em, but no find track."

"You want me to give you some meat? Is that it?"

"No, Pavlof no beg yet. Leave hut plenty early so find light to shoot. Pavlof start back, walk two, three, four mile, then see white man. He come out of woods, stagger, stagger, mighty sick. I come up, take hold of him, he fall. 'Help me,' he say. 'Help me get to Andersen house. I give you all my gold.' "

"Who was he? Did he give his name?"

"No give name. I never see him."

"What did you do?"

"Not do anything but cut wood, build big fire, come here. I no carry him, Mist' Rick, and he no can walk. He smell bad, think his legs froze and start to rot. I not strong enough to carry him ten mile, both of us die."

Eric turned quickly to Sophia. "Four miles this side of the big bluff on Pike Creek is two hours by dog team on such snow as this. I think it's a fool's errand, yet I've got to go. I'll be back within five hours from now—at the most six."

"Of course. There's plenty of wood; I'll be all right. Don't take needless risks."

Eric sat on the bed, pulling on extra woolen socks to wear with his mukluks. Over his deerskin shirt and pants, he put on hair-seal garments, then got into his parka. The dogs were hard to rouse; his and Pavlof's mittened hands made hard work of putting on their harness. Yet in twenty minutes they were mushing through the heavy dusk, the dogs in a slow lope, both men riding the sled.

In a little under two hours since Eric had cried, "Mush!" they saw the gleam of Pavlof's fire, almost burned out. Beside it lay a long dark object that did not move. They came up into the glimmer, where the traveler lay on his side, his arms crossed in front of his face. Eric moved them, his brain registering their pliability, almost certain proof that life was in them yet, before he looked well into the ghastly face and cried out, "Good God, it's Frank Ford."

It was what remained of Frank Ford, not much; because Eric knew from the smell that a large part of him was rotted and dead.

"Who is it?" Frank mumbled.

"Eric Andersen."

"You've come too late."

148

"We'll put you on the sled——"

"What's the use of that? Can you give me some whisky? I'll open my mouth and you pour a little down my throat. A big drink, if you can spare it. I want to talk a minute to my old friend."

When the alcohol had stimulated the failing heart Frank spoke again, in a tone that, despite its weakness, was faintly boastful.

"I would have made it to your house if that cold spell hadn't caught me. I took my last drink and got sleepy and lay down to rest a little while and the drink died on me. Now I'm a goner sure. Still, isn't this the way for a real sourdough to go?"

Eric could not answer.

"I *am* a real sourdough, Eric. This is my third winter in the North, and I'd of struck it rich next spring as sure as God. You're a good fellow, Eric. You passed the hat for me in Dutch Harbor. Reach in my pocket and get my poke and keep what's in it."

"I'll give it to Pavlof. He's the one who found you."

"Will you do me one more favor?" Frank asked, when the ounce or two of gold lay in Pavlof's hand.

"Sure."

"Don't dig a hole and bury me. I was always afraid of holes, but not much else, I tell you. Leave me here till the fire goes out, and let my skeleton lie in the big woods till it falls apart. I've always loved nature. That's why I left the city and came up to the man's country, the great outdoors."

"The fire's going out now."

"So is the fire you lit in my stomach with the whisky. It's going out, I tell you, and I am too. Frank Ford. That's who I am. Frank Ford, from San Francisco, a he-man if you ever saw one. Frank Ford . . ."

The voice sank to a mumble and died away. When Eric turned to mend the fire, Pavlof spoke for the first time.

"No good. He dead. White man dead."

7

When Eric's shouts as he drove off on his mercy errand had died away, loneliness assailed Sophia, deep-striking and dark. The season was so dark, the high tide of the Northern winter, the snow that she saw from the window glimmered faintly under what remained of the wasted moon, infinite snow, forsaken, silent, austere. The reflected light of the sun, bleak enough at midday, was all gone; and at three o'clock the night was in full flood, not to ebb in the least for eighteen hours. The house was warm, but just beyond its walls the cold was implacable.

She tried to read a little, then found she could not follow the sense of the little marks on the white page and dropped the book. To her dismay she found herself walking about the rooms, looking out every window, and there could be only one cause for that, which was unfaced fear. What was she afraid of? In vain she searched her mind for the answer, for Eric had gone forth well equipped to confront the bleak weather; he was a sourdough who knew how to take care of himself; Pavlof was a stout companion; and the journey, which every sign told her was futile, would be short. She wondered if she could be afraid of herself. The darkness had got hold of her, somehow; and her loss, more than a year ago, brought no re-awakened grief but an empty, futile feeling of failure, and what seemed a diminishing of her vitality.

About four o'clock she was trying to darn a pair of Eric's woolen socks when she thought she heard a light tap on the door. For a few seconds she thought it was a hallucination, then it came again. Between then and her getting up she had time to wonder if Eric and Pavlof had failed to find the sick and exhausted traveler and he had somehow found his way here. It was not Eric's knock, or else some terrible thing had happened.

When she opened the door, her first feeling was of profound relief. A young Indian woman was standing there, and as soon as she could slip into the room, with a blast, like a solid wedge, of cold air, Sophia believed that she recognized her as Sant, whose name she now knew meant "summer," and who had asked Eric a question in her tongue on Sophia's first visit to the village. On her back was a well-wrapped pack.

Without a word she came close to the stove and removed her fur mittens. There was no expression on her face that Sophia could read.

"Are you in trouble, Sant, to come across the snow on a night like this?" Sophia asked from an instinct of sympathy. She had heard that the young squaw knew a little English.

"No me, but all Indian in trouble. Not much meat left,

not much fish. Men go hunting, no shoot anything. So I give you present."

"You mean, in exchange for grub?"

"No. For you to keep."

She slipped her arms out of the leather straps of her bundle, laid it on the bed, and Sophia thought that it moved a little. Sant took off its caribou-skin covering, disclosing a sack of the same material. Out of it she brought a light-skinned baby only a few months old. It was awake and blinked its black eyes in the light.

"I give you baby to keep," Sant said.

"Whose is it? Why should you give it to me?"

"I no can take care of him. My milk dry up, got no canned milk to feed baby. You got plenty canned milk. He good baby, almost white, you like him fine; he work good for you when he get big. He belong Mist' Rick. Mist' Rick made him."

Sophia said something she need not say because already she knew the answer.

"You mean my husband?"

"Um."

Sophia had been taught never to show inward hurt. It was a hard lesson, deep-taught; it had almost become automatic, it hardly required effort. Her face did not change greatly in Sant's sight; only her eyes changed, became indrawn and turned intensely dark.

"Maybe he take place of little baby born dead," Sant said hopefully.

Sophia shook her head. "No, he can't do that."

"Mist' Rick make him on the day your little baby die."

"On the first day of December? How old is the baby?"

"Three months, pretty near four months. He good, strong baby."

"There was a white doctor there when my husband went for Pavlof. The white doctor made him, didn't he?"

"No, Mist' Rick made him. But I no tell Mist' Rick, no tell anybody, people think white doctor make him, but that big lie. For two, three months I tell nobody but H'kah, Sant going to have baby, thought maybe had caught cold, fool Pavlof about baby, let him see bloody rag. Then belly began to swell, so I told big lie about white doctor, 'cause he gone then. You look good at him. You see Mist' Rick make him. North Light, I tell truth. If I lie, hope old shaman put Jonah on me, so I dry up and die."

151

Sophia leaned over the bed and looked deeply into the small face. The cheekbones were Indian, the eyes had an Indian look, but its skin was far lighter than Sant's, lighter than Pavlof's.

"I can't tell," she said.

"You no believe Sant? Ask H'kah, ask Pavlof. When Mist' Rick come back, ask him. He no lie, he tell you how he make him when he come for Pavlof though soft snow."

"I'll give you one more chance. Is this my husband's baby? If you lie——" Sophia could make no threat, only fall silent.

"I tell truth, swear by Lady of Kazan. She look down from wall in Pavlof's house when Mist' Rick and me in Pavlof's bed."

"I believe you. I know you are telling the truth. Yes, my husband will keep the baby, at least he'll help you keep it. Now will you go? I have something to do. Do you want a cup of hot coffee first?"

"No, I no have coffee. I go quick."

Sant leaned over the bed, gently sniffed the baby's cheek, then put on her mittens and parka.

"You keep bag," she said. "Good for carrying baby. I name him Joe Harris. I go now."

In a few seconds she had put on the snowshoes she had left at the threshold and faded into the wan darkness. Sophia stood in the doorway a few seconds in the savage cold. A sense of doom had come upon her, and it was building, blackening with every breath. A dream she had often dreamed was going to come true. It had not been a bad dream, after all. It had been a sweet dream, really, and provision had been made for its coming true.

Yet she took a Bible from the bookshelf and opened it in the middle. The heading read "Job," but that wasn't right —this was not the book to which she had turned that windy day in Beaufort, the printed word at the top of the page at which she had barely glanced. She began thumbing through the pages until her eyes lighted on "First Kings"; then she stopped with a great start. That was the right book . . . and the chapter was . . . the chapter was . . . *twenty-one!*

Sophia found the verse on which Sarah's finger had stopped, after its quick upward movement. It dealt with a conversation between Ahab and Elijah. Sophia read on until she came to the twenty-third verse, and then she knew the prophecy that she had refused to read, but which had been holding all the time.

And of Jezebel also spake the Lord, saying, The dogs shall eat Jezebel by the wall of Jezreel.

No, it was not literally true. No dogs would eat her, no wolves came close to the cabin wall. It was true only in spirit.

She got wood from the box and fed the fire. Some of its heat would hold for several hours in the close-built house; there was no danger of the full cold breaking in before Eric returned. Even if it did, her own caribou parka, in which she wrapped the baby, would preserve its life. She closed the hood over the baby's face and fastened the edges with safety pins, leaving plenty of vents for it to breathe.

Then rather quickly, for her preparations were made, she undressed and put on her nightgown and bedroom slippers. She stood only a moment at the door, glanced at the books in their rows, the solemn volumes of the encyclopedia, the good novels Eric had sent for; then her gaze made a quick sweep of the walls, the chairs, finally resting on the bed where she had lost her own baby. Then she opened the door narrowly and slipped out.

The cold seized her instantly in its deadly grasp. When she had caught her breath she knew one great onslaught of pain, but it was not nearly as terrible as that she had once suffered in vain. She reeled a little, but kept walking about a hundred feet, and the pain was already turning to an awful numbing ache as she lay down in the snow, on her side, one arm pillowing her head.

A little time passed, not much, only a few minutes by the clock. It did not even seem very long, because her eyes were getting heavy and her thoughts were no longer clear. She perceived the flicker of the northern lights that increased to banners and streamers up the sky, and these spread and spread, and suddenly they rushed to form a solid arch of purest iridescent pearl, supporting the dome of the sky. It grew dim and slowly died away, and this was what she had dreamed.

Now the hard numbing ache began to pass off, because the nerve ends had frozen. She could not have moved now, even if she tried, she was so deeply captive of the cold that she no longer felt it. She made a last effort to know herself, to remember Sophia, and it might be that her frozen lips moved a little, but more likely only her thoughts moved.

153

"Dear Papa! You died that morning in the hotel room, and now I'm dying, and we'll be together always."

Then it was as though his arms were around her, and she felt his warmth and strength, his lips laid quietly against hers.

8

Eric had been hard pressed to obey Frank Ford's last injunction, even though his resistance was instinctive rather than reasonable. This deep forest was a good enough place to lie. To melt with fire enough frozen ground to hide the dead would be a task of hours, and wolves had forsaken the region to follow the moose and deer to a better range. He would ask Sophia if he should go back with dynamite and do the office.

So he called, "Good-bye, Frank," roused the dogs that had lain down in their harness, and yelled, "Mush."

He was five miles from home when Pavlof, walking beside the sled, announced he would take a cutoff down a big moose trail that he knew to the village. Eric said all right; and in sudden haste to leave the lonely woods for the cabin warmth, he mounted the sled. The dogs, rested a little, or hungry for their meal that they had usually at two o'clock, were easily driven to an easy lope that sped the long stretches of scattered woods and plain. The snow was firmly crusted, almost as smooth as ice, perfect conditions for travel.

He was more than halfway across the river ice when his lead dog gave a strange outcry. Eric had been expecting him to bark as he smelled wood smoke; instead he raised his head as he ran, and howled. It was somewhat like the wail of an old wolf as he sat in a ring with his pack on a moonlit night, yet eerily different. The bitch behind him did the same, and in a moment one after another of the team howled at intervals, so the sound was continuous, one beginning the wail just before another left off, a song without melody that he had never heard in his five years of dog driving. It was as though their hearts were aching and they had no other utterance of the pain.

Soon Eric saw the window light glimmering through the trees. He shouted to the dogs and they broke into a headlong run. They came to where the lamplight within was reflected on the snow, and made for their pickets; Eric sprang down and fastened the lead dog. Ordinarily he would have

154

stopped to unharness them, but they stood with bristling ruffs, so he left them and sped to the door. "Sophia!" he called, as he removed his snowshoes. He called once more as he knocked and threw the door open.

She was not there to meet him. The thought struck him instantly that she must be in the rear room, the new room, or the small bathroom. He glanced about in a dazed way, noting that the fire in the stove burned low, for the room had begun to chill and the front draft showed red from glowing coals, not yellow from flame. He was looking the second time at the bed when he noticed what seemed to be a bundle, not even two feet long, wrapped in what seemed to be Sophia's parka. It was in his throat to call to her when instead, on some dreadful impulse, he took three strides and removed the pins with which the edges of the hood had been brought together. His heart already knew what would be inside; only his eyes must make sure. He took one glance into the small, pale-colored face, then ran wildly to the other rooms. All were empty and hollow, and that meant that Sophia was not here, and so there remained only one place that she could be, and that was in the snow.

He ran three times around the house, a madman now— ran in ever-widening circles until he saw her, because her raiment was white as the snow, and her hair was too fair to show clearly. Then he knew, with that awful knowledge men must confront not once or twice in the course of their lives, that she was not there truly, that she had ceased to be.

Instantly his sanity was restored. He walked to her and laid his bare hand on her icy face. Without a sound he picked her up, her position unchanging, not soft now, but stony hard, and moved toward his door. Just before he reached it he stopped. The room was still above freezing temperature and the cold was now her element, and it must not be changed.

Quickly he laid her at his feet, in the same position he found her, and put on his mittens to keep his hands from freezing. Again he picked her up and carried her to his shed, where the temperature was far below zero. A work table stood there, and there he laid her down.

He shut the door behind him and stood motionless beside her in the utter dark for nearly an hour. His thoughts moved, knowing the whole truth now, or as much of the truth as one soul could ever know of another. He did not weep, because he could not. The only sound was his breath's faint crackle in the intense cold.

This he hardly felt, since he stood so still in his hooded parka that no air stirred. His own element became darkness; and because time seemed to have stopped its flight, the thought could not occur to him that it could ever change.

Yet at the end of the hour he uttered one racking groan, went out of the shed, carefully closed and latched its heavy door. Then he tramped into the house, and his first act after removing his mittens was to feel the baby's face. The parka hood had dropped over it and it was perfectly warm; the baby breathed quietly in peaceful sleep. His next act was to replenish the fire. Always look to the fires, he thought, when there was any life worth saving in the Northern winter. Then he found himself at the cupboard, getting a can of milk. He poured it in a pan with cold water and set it on the back of the stove to warm. The baby would wake soon and want its warm teat, so he made ready an empty bottle with a cloth stopper through which it could suck.

Again he went to his shed and stood by the table about twenty minutes. He was not now so bulwarked against the cold; his garments were the same but his strength had diminished. When he left the shed he set outside the dressed lumber he had bought for flooring, his store of dynamite, shovel, rock drills, and other tools, and again latched the door behind him. Ice crystals in the upper air no longer dimmed the wisp of moon, now full overhead, and he had enough light to transport the lumber, saw, ax, hammer, and nails to the back room of the house.

He thought to wait until later in the night before he began his task, then decided there was no good of that, no one would be helped, nothing would be saved, and the carrying out of Sophia's last will and testament would be only delayed. A wooden table served as a workbench. If the dogs heard the sounds of sawing and hammering they did not rouse up; once when he opened the door he saw them lying in their harness, every nose tucked under tail, in deathlike sleep. Long after midnight he heard a low wail from the front room. He went in, tested the milk with his finger, poured it in the bottle and affixed the stopper. He shook a little of it into the cloth and put it between the baby's lips. As soon as he received its taste and smell, he sucked greedily. Apparently he had been already weaned of the breast

156

and had sucked seal oil and meat broth, perhaps lightly sweetened, in Sant's arms.

When the bottle was almost empty the baby went back to sleep, Eric to his labor. At moonset it was done, a stout box a little over six feet long, two feet wide, two feet deep, with a cover to be nailed on. Taking his lantern, he entered the shed once more, and shone its light on the beautiful marble face. Latching the door, he walked forth to a little shelf on the low hill, and there he began to shovel away snow, then to drill into the frozen ground.

It was a hard chore to insert the dynamite and fix fuses with mittened hands; sometimes he had to bare them briefly. Then he lighted the main fuse and ran. A moment later came a reverberating roar, louder than thunder, frozen ground welled up and fragments shot high to rain down with heavy thuds. An irregularly shaped pit, big enough to hold the box with room to spare, and six feet deep, had been blown out of the forever frozen ground.

He shaped it with his ax, then returned to the back room and carefully lined the box with an eider-down quilt that had been Sophia's birthday present a preceding summer. On it he laid her pillow, and then slid the box through the wide doorway onto the snow. It was made of light wood, and hence of no great weight; he had no trouble getting it across his shoulder and carrying it to the edge of the pit. When he had brought out the cover, hammer, and nails, he went back to the house and made fresh coffee. After he had drunk he unharnessed his dogs, fed each of them in turn, and picketed each. Glancing at his watch in the lantern light, he saw that the hands pointed to eight. His tasks had taken about twelve hours, and now they were nearly done.

Once more he went to the pit, and with his pick and shovel lengthened it to give him room to stand. Until ten o'clock of the twenty-second, the day that the sun began its northward journey, he stood quietly in the shed, or else rested briefly in a chair beside his son.

At ten a glimmer of light revealed the hills in bold silhouette and began to steal over the snow. Then he went to the shed and again laid the beautiful form across his arms and carried it to the snowy brink of the pit, where he placed it in the box just as he had first found it. Then he stood looking down at it, and his rigid throat cords relaxed at last and he began to speak.

"Sophia, I am now going to carry out your last will and testament. You will become one with the frozen ground, and I'll replace the torn earth, and I'll raise no mark, and no one but me will ever know where you lie.

"Sophia, I would come with you if I thought you wished me to. It would be such an easy thing; and to live on, and do what you would want me to, will be a hard thing. But it will become easier with the middle years, and only in the last years will the world turn so gray again.

"Sophia, you remember what you told me about Tithonus and Aurora. What I said that day was true. I will grow old, and you will be forever young and beautiful.

"Sophia, wherever your spirit has fled, or what ghost of you remains, if only in my own heart and brain, hear my solemn pledge. I will do what you wanted of me, what would have given you the most happiness if you had lived. Within my soul I will keep faith with my memories of you. I will live, and seek happiness, and try to justify your taking my hand and coming up the river with me and staying with me almost three years. I will develop what powers I have. I will make them greater by never flinching from what you would want me to do. I will try to become a leader among the Alaskans.

"Good-bye, Sophia, Northern Light, light of my eyes. I love you forever and ever, world without end."

He got down into the pit and strength came upon him to lift down the box and its beautiful content to the leveled floor. He looked once more at the dim face, the lovely form, then quickly nailed on the cover. Then he climbed out and began to refill the pit with naked, ice-veined, rock-hard earth he had blown out. When spring came he would plant moss and grass, and in the lengthening days and warm sun of spring the top of the grave would become one with its surroundings.

When the task was done he picked up four small white stones and carefully placed them. They were common stones that no one would notice, that would in no way separate the rectangle they enclosed from the rest of the landscape. Then he shouldered his tools and walked to the shed and left them. He looked at the shadow of a spruce tree cast by the glowing sky and it seemed to him a few inches shorter than yesterday. The hour was exactly noon, the river flowed under its ice, time continued its implacable advance.

BOOK TWO

6. The Growth of Eric

The night passed at last, with Eric rising twice to mend the fire, to heat milk and give it to his son, and to see to his welfare. About eight o'clock, when a gray glimmer of false dawn began to steal over the snow, he rose and went out, looked at his thermometer, again fed the baby, and fed the fire with homemade charcoal that would heat the house above freezing temperature for about eight hours on a windless day of not extreme cold. Then he harnessed the dogs and loaded the sled with a case of canned milk and of canned peas blanket-wrapped against freezing, frozen meat for making broth, and finally put aboard the warmly bundled baby. Then he started up snowbound river ice to the Indian village.

The hard-packed snow gave him passage in two hours. He went first to H'kah's house, where he found H'kah, Sant, Pavlof, and two visitors squatting by the fire. Sant rose, her face stiff with unknown emotion, and unwrapped the baby and held it against her breast. At Eric's request, Pavlof turned out the two guests, giving one of them a prideful errand—to set fires in the Kashga, which was the medicine lodge, dance hall, and assembly place of the whole village. Then he spoke to Sant in English, asking Pavlof to explain in the Indian language any words or phrases she might not understand.

"Sant, you tell everyone that white doctor, Harris, make this baby?"

"Um."

"You've told no one I make him?"

"No one but North Light."

"Keep to that word. Always. His name is Joe Harris. If you do, can keep baby long time, I give food for him, for you, too. If you tell one person, I take baby, you no see him no more. You understand?"

"Um."

"Why no I tell people I make him? White man reason you no understand. Tell people white doctor gave you dollar, let him make baby."

Sant spoke quickly. "I tell people he pay me five dollar. I

show 'em five dollar in dust. I take from his poke while he asleep, drunk. His squaw no there, no know it, he gave her hell, but no hit her, she say if he hit her she no give him grub, break whisky bottle."

"I will tell reason all of us keep secret. It is for sake of North Light's spirit. It same Yukhoi, plenty high, plenty bright." And Sant looked a little puzzled until Pavlof spoke in the village tongue.

"Um," she said, nodding.

"Now go to Kashga. I tell all people something."

In a few minutes almost all the grown people of the village, including women with babies on their backs, had assembled in the big, chill room. The elders squatted in front, the young men and women stood packed close behind them and by the wall; Eric stood facing the assembly, Pavlof beside him. He told his lies in a deeply earnest voice, Pavlof translating them in an excited rush of words.

"I speak to elders, but all of you listen. I have seen baby white doctor make. His name Joe Harris. He fine baby, make fine man, his blood three parts Indian, five parts white. I adopt him."

When Pavlof had translated, the people's grunting showed that they understood perfectly well. Adoption was a common practice in their village.

"I give Sant grub and she keep him long while. After while he go school. But he no stop being Indian; he be Indian and white man both. I want him be big Indian know Indian talk, Indian ways to fish, hunt, trap, shoot gun straight, throw spear, make weirs, paddle boat fast as hell, everything Indian do, he do. Same time be big white man, make Indian and white man good friends, help Indian."

The elders were greatly stirred by this. One of them arose as though to begin dancing, but Pavlof shook his head and Eric went on speaking.

"Does anyone know where white doctor, Scott Harris, went when he left here?"

When Pavlof had repeated the question the squaw with whom the doctor had lived in the village spoke in her own tongue. Pavlof interpreted her reply.

"He go to Circle City. Tomchili go there, sell furs, saw him there."

Circle City was one of the youngest of the gold camps, the highest big camp on the river below the Canadian border, and was only a day's mush over well-packed snow.

"I go see white doctor," Eric went on. "I give him five dollar he give Sant, five dollar more, so he give baby to me."

All the people, even the squaws, grunted their approval.

"Now I tell you sad thing," Eric went on, his face changing, his voice still firm. "While I go with Pavlof, try to help half-dead white man on Pike Creek, North Light go outside into cold, she freeze, die, I bury her."

When Pavlof had translated in a shaking voice, a long silence held. Every listener stared incredulously. Then an old woman gasped the single word, "Yukhoi?" Pavlof nodded.

"But her spirit is still here," Eric said. "You will not set fire to the village or leave it and make another. As long as you see the lights in the sky you will know she is still beautiful, and your luck is not gone, your luck will still hold."

The same old woman gave forth a wail as charged with sorrow as the long rising and falling song of the wolves ringed under the moon on a winter night. At once she sprang up, ran out of the Kashga, weeping and howling. Instantly all the other squaws except Sant surged toward the door, young and old crying out, and in a moment they began trotting in file up the hard-packed village road in pitiful lamentation. When they got to the end of the village road they turned back in a long loop, still wailing the grief they could not tell, not trying to ease it, only time could do that; they were only expressing it as instinct enforced. Their hearts' longing for beauty had been answered for a while, then struck a mortal blow. They trotted in step, and their footfalls on the ice-hard snow made strange accompaniment to the chorus of their cries.

Sant stood with bent head, weeping, terribly afraid until Eric spoke to her.

"It's not your fault, it's my fault. North Light wouldn't want anyone to know that. Do you know the reason for my lying, the only reason?"

"I know."

"If the time comes that I believe she would want me to tell the truth, I will. You see—I never knew her feelings. I could only guess at them—and so often miss."

He stood in the doorway, his hand over his eyes. In his heart he was grateful for the eerie mourning of the squaws, because it told what he could not, what his white man's tongue could not utter. More than an hour later, when he

161

had finished making preparations for the baby's care, he started back across the snow. At only a short distance he caught a glimpse of a small pack of wolves, not more than seven, this many rarely seen even in midwinter, that had been hunger-driven into coming near the village, lurking there to steal frozen meat or fish. Now they were making off at a swift run, perhaps their wild hearts aching at these cries so like their own, uttered by awesome man.

At two miles Eric could still hear the dirge, eloquent in the silence of man and all he was, and the thud of feet like a distant drum.

2

A few days later, over wind-packed snow, Eric made the easy trek to Circle City, a city of tents with a few log or clapboard huts and trading posts, and there he inquired of the inevitable saloonkeeper where he might find Dr. Scott Harris.

"You need a doctor," said the barkeeper, whose occupation demanded a swift study of faces and appraisal of the whole man. "You look mighty haggard and your eyes don't look right to me. But Doc Harris practices medicine only in his spare time. He hasn't got much of that, between drinks and card playing. He may look at your tongue and order a tonic for you, and that's about all. If it's anything serious you better go to see Dr. Dawes at Dawson. Remember that name—Dawes—Dawson."

"Well, I want to see Doc Harris anyway."

"He'll be around here later as he moves from joint to joint. You may find him at home, which is a tent, three rows up, six tents down the line. If he's not there, his squaw will tell you where he's likely to be at."

Eric found Scott Harris at home, snug by an oilstove, warm within from strong drink, his squaw away rustling grub by one means or another. Harris greeted him politely.

"Mr. Andersen! I haven't seen you since you came to me about your wife a December night at that village, the name of which I've forgotten. I think Pavlof said she lost the baby but she pulled through. I'm glad it wasn't I who officiated. I do wisely merely to tinker at my art, and leave the earning of my food and drink to a quick estimation of percentages at stud, draw poker, and suchlike games—and of course to the industry of the women of the country. What brings you here?"

"Doctor, I came to lay in some supplies. Do you recall spending a period in bed with a young squaw named Sant while at Tekuh village?"

"Not at the moment. I seemed to recall being unusually loyal to that squaw—I've forgotten her name—at whose house I boarded. That doesn't mean I didn't do it. The state of being even mildly intoxicated can cause curious lapse of memory, as you, of course, know. Why in God's name do you ask?"

"She's had a very light-skinned baby and says you are its father."

"That might well be. But I trust she doesn't expect anything but my congratulations. That's all I ever give to the mothers of my offspring."

"It's a fine baby, and I'm taking an interest in him. I want to provide for his care and education. You see, he is five eighths white, and I have named him Joe Harris. If you protest that name, of course I will change it. I ask that you give me your word not to hunt him up or have anything to do with him, now or in the future. If you will I'll give you the five dollars that you gave Sant, and ten dollars as a token of appreciation."

"So that's what became of that five dollars in dust! I was out of my mind! Make it twenty extra, and it's a deal."

"All right."

"Of course keep his name Joe Harris. I have not the slightest objection. I never hunt up my bastards or have anything to do with them except for the original sin. You see, Mr. Andersen, I have a very convenient philosophy of life, based on Darwin's book. Its essence is the survival of the fittest to improve the species. I possess a somewhat superior mind, regardless of what I've done with it. Also, I am a remarkably virile man, considering my age and astronomical count of bottles. It is very rarely that a heavy drinker is also a begetter worthy of the patriarchs; one power seems to sap the other. I happen to be both."

"It sure is remarkable," Eric agreed.

"Thus I consider it my biological duty to drink as much whisky as possible, so that weaker men may get less, and to scatter my seed as widely as possible, as does the buck rabbit, the stag, all males of the gregarious species, and even the lowly tumbleweed. It was the tumbleweed that I saw rolling on desert sands, the most nearly round tumbleweed, the best tumbleweed, tumbling faster and going further

163

than inferior tumbleweeds, that inspired me to take Darwin to heart. Now I feel that I have more than justified Nature's aim when the seed that made me, one of countless millions, jumped the gun as it were, and won the race with its competitors and staked its claim."

"Here, Doctor, is twenty dollars in gold, as by our agreement."

"Joe Harris! Not a bad name for a half-breed Indian. I am sure I will hear of him later. I will no doubt meet you later, considering the sound constitutions of both of us, and if you wish to pay me for the begetting of any other bastard who might take your fancy, be sure and hunt me up."

"T'ank you, and good day."

"Thank you, Mr. Andersen. I assure you this has been quite a novel, even memorable, experience."

It was the same for him, too, Eric thought.

Eric bought his supplies and returned to his echoing, empty house. Then he began making preparations for a long and arduous journey, such a great journey as few men have made alone at this time of year. He reduced part of his winter meat to pemmican, storing it in gut. He assembled a primus stove that burned kerosene, fuel, a small strong tent, a waterproof tarpaulin, a caribou sleeping bag with caribou robes, two large cooking pots and one small, ax, tent stakes, one heavy and one light rifle with ammunition, such edibles as flour, salt, sugar, and rice, coffee, extra strings for snowshoe webs, matches as well as flint and steel, a hunting knife, a carborundum stone, pick and shovel, his best clothes and pearl stickpin, soap, two lanterns, snow glasses, and all his gold. On a journey of such length it was impossible to carry enough food for the dogs along with all the rest, so his equipment included tackle to fish through ice, drills, dynamite, and fuses. When he made a farewell scrutiny of the house, its storm windows were boarded up and nothing was here that the cold could hurt. The cold could not hurt anything he was leaving.

His last act before departure was to lay kindling in the big stove, with matches handy, for any wanderer in sore distress, and leave the door chain so that a half-frozen human hand could unfasten it. This was an act of faith by a sourdough to old Alaskan ways.

He had told Dr. Hill that the winter journey by dog team from the little house to St. Michael was of sixty days, the sled loaded, the driver walking. This one took seventy-two days, the weather being fairly good, the luck above average. Once his supply of dog food almost ran out, and he went hunting in the forest, and killed an old, lean, half-decrepit bull moose. Twice he met with blizzards, one of which immobilized him for five days, the other for three days. Snow-covered ice-hummocks delayed him from time to time, there were minor accidents to his equipment, and he did not travel farther in one day than aching muscles and weary bones warned him. He stopped at Indian villages only to buy dog food. As far as possible he swung wide of small new gold camps and prospectors' huts, and not once did he sleep in a bed except of his own making, on spruce boughs cunningly laid, or on the frozen ground. He wanted no company but the snowy wastes and their far-scattered inmates. The journey was not only of his body. His soul seemed to range out and far, forward and back in time and space. It was not a pilgrimage of penance; he asked no blessing, he sought no forgiveness other than had been given him, without asking, by a memory that never dimmed and indeed became clearer, more meaningful, with every desolate, long-drawn day.

On the twenty-second day of March, a time of feasting and ritual performance throughout the Northern pagan world for immeasurable ages, Easter time in the Christian era, he caught sight of the snowy roofs and the tall spire of St. Michael. Just as he was, driving his dogs, he inquired for the house of Dr. Stanley Hill and followed the directions given him. It was now late afternoon; lamps were being lighted. The light in a window through which Eric gazed revealed Dr. Hill sitting near a lamp, a book in his hands. Eric removed his snowshoes, parka, and hood, and knocked on the door.

"Eric!" Dr. Hill burst out at first sight of his face, his own face turning white. Then, trying to collect himself, rallying his courage, he asked, "Where have you come from?"

"From the house where Sophia and I lived on the upper Yukon."

"You say 'lived.' Can't you say 'live'?" God, you've brought terrible news. I can see it in your face."

"Yes, I've brought terrible news."

"Come in. I'd better not hear it until I drink whisky, I tell you so in all truth. You need it too. We are two men, but sometimes manhood needs help through some awful moment, and that moment has come."

165

He shut the door behind him, took two glasses from a cupboard, poured in the raw drink. As Dr. Hill lifted it to his lips, his hand shook and he had to wipe his face. Eric downed his portion in one gulp, but it was without warmth.

"I must sit," Dr. Hill said. "Will you sit, too?"

"Yes, sir, because it's a long story."

"The end is what I guessed, when you said 'lived' and I saw your face?"

"Yust about the end—the terrible news you guessed. There is a little more that comes afterward."

"Please turn up the lamp. It's burning down. I can hardly see you."

"No, sir, the lamp is burning all right."

"Please give me a moment, until I can control myself."

"I will."

Neither man glanced at the other or made any sound for about five minutes. Each sat with his face in his hands, and neither saw the other's rigidity of body, the awful inward storm that sweeps through it when a man weeps in silence. Finally Dr. Hill spoke in low, steady tones.

"I am ready to listen if you are ready to speak."

"I am ready." Eric drew a long breath. "Before I met Sophia I went sometimes to an Indian girl in Tekuh village."

"Go on, Eric."

Eric told the whole story of his life with Sophia, beginning with her joy in the little house, their trips together, her confession of the lies she had told his listener. At this point Dr. Hill asked a question.

"But what she told me—that she was going to have a baby—could have been possible?"

"Yes, sir."

"Then the untruth was of no significance. You and she were already engaged, you were already bound to each other. I would have had no choice but to give my consent. Perhaps—I do not know—she made it easier for me to do so. Please go on."

Eric told of that March day of her announcement, the champagne they had drunk, the lone swan's call. He told of his care of her, such as he could give, and of his instructions to Pavlof, then of his trek across soft snow on the afternoon of December 1, 1899. As he began to recount the events in the village, the learning of Pavlof's absence, his talk with the half-drunken doctor, and the two drinks he had taken, his voice showed signs of faltering. But he set

It lower somehow and drove it with his will and his words came clear.

"I lay down in Pavlof's house to sleep until Pavlof returned. I was half asleep when Sant got in bed with me. It's no excuse that I'd been under great strain for about three months——"

"Sophia shouldn't have let that happen," Dr. Hill broke in. "I should have warned her about that. In my haste—under the blow—I failed to do so."

"She thought I'd be true. She had asked me to be true—I never dreamed I would yield to such a temptation. Sant was gone when Pavlof came, half an hour earlier than he said. We raced the dogs, but Sophia was unconscious when we got home. The labor hadn't taken near as long as she had thought it would. Pavlof saved Sophia and took the baby with forceps, but it was dead."

Eric told of Sophia's grief, of Sant's deceit when his guard was down, and of his own failure to confess the broken troth. Then he spoke of the dry summer and of the winter's first, fierce onslaught of cold. He went forth with Pavlof to find Frank Ford dying in the snow. . . .

"Frank Ford," Dr. Hill echoed. "Poor devil."

"If you please, I would like to stop a minute. The worst happened on that day. I can go on, though, if the waiting is too hard for you to bear."

"No, stop a minute. Do you want a little snoose?"

"No, sir."

Eric did not wait a minute, hardly half a minute. His green eyes turned intensely dark, his hands lay open, his throat cords stood out, almost rigid. Then, continuing to gaze into Dr. Hill's face, he spoke in a rush of words.

"While I was gone, Sant came with her baby. My baby. She didn't know any better—she had no milk and the village was almost out of grub. Sophia wrapped it up, built up the fire, and in her nightgown went out into the snow. I found her lying on her side, one arm under her head. She was dead. Sophia was dead."

Dr. Hill got up and walked about the room. Eric did not watch him, he sat inert, hearing the footsteps back and forth. The darkness pressed against the window, the fire crackled, occasionally a firecracker sounded in Eskimo Town, perhaps in celebration of nearby Easter, for almost all of these natives were members of the Greek Church. The warm, well-furnished room swam before Eric's eyes. This was his long-awaited moment of greatest strain.

Dr. Hill returned to his chair. "You said there was a little more."

"Not much more. I buried Sophia in ever-frozen ground, as she had asked when she expected the baby. She had asked me not to raise a marker and I didn't; I laid down four small white stones. I took the baby back to his mother, who named it Joe Harris. I provided for it, and for Sophia's sake concealed that I was its father. If I live I intend to care for it well. If I die I've written for Joe to inherit the Gertrude Mine in care of a friend."

"Why should you say 'if I live'? Why shouldn't you live?"

"I said that, because I thought you might want to kill me. I wouldn't blame you. I'd point the gun at my own breast with my shirt open, the muzzle against the skin, and all you'd have to do is come up and pull the trigger. The powder burns would show and no one would doubt it was suicide."

"Were you tempted to suicide, Eric?"

"No. I wanted to live to try to do all Sophia had asked me. But I caused Sophia's death and it would be your right to kill me, and if you want to, go ahead. I won't flinch."

"No, you didn't cause Sophia's death. If anything outside of fate, if anyone caused it, I was that one. I broke faith with her in a far greater degree than you did, when I asked that I never look at her beautiful face again. She would have lived except for that. She had no one to whom to turn—nothing to turn to but the snow. We have both been fearfully punished, Eric. If there is any hell, we needn't fear it, because we've had it. Now will you excuse me? Tomorrow we'll talk about the future—and about Joe Harris."

Both men rose, and when Dr. Hill held out his hand Eric shook it. The next moment he was driving his team down the empty, hollow-sounding road.

3

The morrow brought icy wind from the northeast blowing across the tundra, so that Dr. Hill, weakened by grief, did not venture out. It was the following day that he met briefly with Eric in the lobby of the rickety hotel of haunting memories. The baby named Joe Harris was hardly mentioned. The older man spoke mostly of the progress, along with many setbacks, of Alaska schools, then with great earnestness of the projected school at Tekuh village.

"The lumber, stoves, window glass, desks, even blackboards and chalk, also the materials for the teacher's quarters, lie in the warehouse waiting shipment on the first river boat," he said. "I've had printed at the government printing office a dictionary of Athabaska-English, in which I arranged about a thousand of the most useful words, and the village has been allotted a hundred copies. If that school can get going and keep going, replacing the old Russian school, the authorities will be encouraged to start schools at other villages remote from the coast. If you are still of a mind to supervise its building, getting all the free labor and the cheapest labor you can, I will consider it a great favor."

"I will. I told Sophia I would offer my services free, and she was greatly pleased."

"I was concerned about my plan to send Fannie Ford there," Dr. Hill went on, "since the village is about a day's mush from Circle City. But she has done well at Russian Mission, exceedingly well, in fact, she is engrossed in the work, and I decided that having gone through what she has, she would be better able to resist the temptations of a new, rich camp than a girl from the States without much experience. So she and her little girl—her name is Victoria Ford, after the ship where Fannie had the loveliest experience of her life, and she is about seven months older than Joe Harris—will be able to come up to start her job in August."

"The school and her quarters will be ready then, if somet'ing don't go wrong."

Presently the two men parted, to meet only rarely and briefly in the time before the ice went out and the first boat of the year could weigh. Eric put off his sled and most of his own supplies at his own landing, then accompanied the freight clear to Tekuh village; here he disembarked and helped the Indians get into shelter any materials that the weather might damage. Amid a great deal of talking and grunting, Eric had Pavlof assemble all the people in the Kashga. There he told them that North Light's father had chosen their village to have one of the first schools for Indian children on the upper river, to obtain great good as well as great honor among all villages, and the lumber and the stoves and all the other things of which they did not yet see the use had been sent them by the President, whom some Indians called the Great White Father of the people.

Each day Pavlof would number off one man in every four to work on the building, and every other man who loafed from the spring fishing and hunting must also work. Later there would be work for the squaws, too.

Eric returned overland to his house, and the following day began the replanting of moss and grass over a small, raw place in the ground, and made minor repairs in his flumes. The next day he sailed upriver to the village to choose the site for the schoolhouse and the teacher's quarters; and the leveling of the ground and the setting of stone pillars deep in the permafrost was well begun. Eric appointed as foreman the young brave Tootsuh, whose name meant crow, a kind of Ulysses among the Tekuh villagers, who in his travels had worked as a housebuilder in Dawson. Thereafter, the laying of the sills and the erection of corner posts went swiftly forward.

Early in the spring Sant had married Sih, tall and young and famed in the village for his marksmanship with rifle, bow, and spear, a cunning trapper, and an excellent fisherman. The past was dead except for the recurring glimmer of dreams, so when Eric called at their new house she received him with friendly and prideful smiles, showing her white, strong, even teeth, told him of the lusty growth and increasing prowess of Joe Harris, and only fell silent and solemn when Mist' Rick and her lord, Sih, talked of grave matters. Eric had wondered, and had been somewhat fearful, about his attitude toward the baby, who at summer's end would be one year old. These misgivings disappeared almost at first sight; and to see if they would likely recur, he set little Joe on his knee and studied his face with great care.

He was five eighths white and his skin somewhat lighter than Pavlof's, but the cast of his features and the growth of his hair seemed almost altogether Indian. Actually he was a handsome baby; the movements of his hands and his eyes showed good endowments, and his robust yell indicated a great deal of vitality. Very plainly, no sin of the father had been visited on the child.

You've got a stiff job before you, young fellow, Eric was thinking, to beat all the Indians and a good part of the white men at their own games.

By August first, both schoolhouse and teacher's quarters had been erected and painted, and Eric personally bossed the job of installing their furnishings, for at this task Tootsuh was at a loss. He added some comforts and supplies that the Great White Father had not got around to sending, and was waiting at the landing when, on September first, a river steamer making upriver came into view.

Followed by a fleet of badarrahs, laden to the gunwales with shouting Indians, he paddled his own boat into midstream. Then he was too busy taking off Fannie, her baby, and her baggage, to get a good look at her; this occurred only when she was seated in the stern of his boat, and he was rowing, facing her, into shore.

Of course the most obvious change in Fannie since he had seen her last was that of dress. No trace of finery remained; she was dressed sensibly and well, and for the first time since he had met her, she took pride in her appearance, for pride and vanity were not even closely related, one being an inward strength and the other an outward show to cover up a keenly sensed weakness. Not a trace of her defiance remained; she was at once exultant and touched by the welcome being given her by Eric and the yelling Indians. She was less pretty than when he had first seen her at Dutch Harbor; and by the same token drew closer to beauty. Her eyes were still big and soft, her smile had ceased to be a grimace and had become almost serene. When people pass through smoke and flame, Eric thought, usually they come forth charred. Once in a while a person emerges stronger than before.

"You've a very pretty baby," Eric remarked, when his eyes had searched too long. "How old is she?"

"A year and seven months. She's a good little sourdough, too. She takes everything as it comes and makes the best of it."

"Fannie, do you want to go to the Kashga first—or to your quarters?"

"I'd better go to the Kashga. It's a very nice welcome they're giving me and I want to show my gratitude."

"You bet you," Eric said, greatly pleased—in fact he never said "you bet you" except with great pleasure.

"And, Eric, it's awfully nice of you to meet me." Flushing, she went on, "And that sounds like a new song I heard in St. Michael. 'It's awfully nice of all you boys to see me to the train; so long, Mary!' And it's so much nicer to be coming than going."

He was not sure of her full meaning and could only guess at it.

As soon as they landed he took her at once to the Kashga, the baby tucked under his arm. At once the whole village gathered, the elders squatting in front with Pavlof in their fore, the others crowding behind them and against the walls. All smiles and all sound disappeared as Fannie faced the assembly. Eric had told her that if she needed an interpreter, Pavlof would do the office. She had replied that she could make out all right, and she did so. Eric could catch only a few words of her brief address. By these he knew that she had started well as a teacher.

When she finished there was a good deal of nodding and grunting. Then an old squaw, privileged by her countless wrinkles, by her motherhood and grandmotherhood of good hunters and strong youths, cried out the single word, "Mitshee!" It was one of the few Indian words that Eric knew, and it meant "Daughter." The grunting and nodding that followed told plainly that this would be her name in the tribe.

Soon after he took her for her first inspection of the school, all the villagers trailing along to watch. Eric showed her the desks, those in the rear big enough for striplings, decreasing in size in the rows until the front desks were of a size for six-year-olds; the blackboards with the chalk in troughs, the stove and wood box, and storm windows for protection against winter cold, lamps for the winter dark, a washstand for dirty hands and faces. "It's the best school building west of Russian Mission," Fannie told him. "I'm going to make it the best school."

When Eric and Fannie went to her small two-room house the Indians returned to their own houses. She had something to say to him, and came out with it when he had lighted a little fire to remove the evening chill. They were seated in two Stateside chairs, which had been the subject of much grunting and feeling by the Indians.

"Eric, you were with Frank when he died. Dr. Hill told me so."

"Yes."

"He was always afraid of small, cramped places. He used to say—especially when he had had some drinks—that if he died in the wilderness, he wanted to be left there, and not buried. Did he tell you that or was he too far gone?"

"He told me, and I did what he asked."

"Did you ever go back to look for his bones?"

"No."

"I've got one other question. You needn't answer unless you want to, but if you do answer, please speak the truth. Did he die game?"

"Yes, he died mighty game."

"I'm glad. He had a certain gameness—it cropped out now and then, along with other qualities. Perhaps it was braggadocio, but it had the same effect."

"Did you take it hard, Fannie?"

"No, I was glad he didn't have to get into more holes—except that last one, and you saved him from that one. Thanks, Eric."

5

The school prospered well. Fannie took pride in this, but gave the most credit where it was due—to the eagerness of the Indian children to learn and their parents to have them learn. She had long ago perceived that dark-skinned people in a land dominated by white people suffered from a psychological handicap, which, under the right conditions, could be a spur to achievement. Few of the Indians of Tekuh village had not met white people of a different stamp from Eric, North Light, and Daughter. Those had addressed them in a different tone, had looked at them with a different gaze; often they treated with more courtesy a drunken low-white than a wrinkled elder of the tribe, his head packed with lore of forest, the tundra, and the river, his hand not as cunning as of yore, when it could launch the arrow, hurl the spear, build the deadly weir, snag the pike and the white fish under the ice, trap fur in the snowy wastes, do all the things, mainly with homemade tools, by which he, his family, and his tribe survived in a hostile land.

The children knew of this down-upon looking by the whites without being told. By the time they were five years old it had become a fact of their existence. Under Dr. Hill's coaching Fannie did all she could to counteract it, encouraging the villagers to celebrate their old festivals and feasts and to keep as many of their customs as made for survival and progress in the changing times. She never meddled with their religious practices except when a shaman used his power to harm. She declined to believe that God had dealt any differently with the souls of Christians than with the souls of numberless Indians and Eskimos who had lived and died before the first missionary hove into view;

although she told the children the story of Jesus, who healed the sick and made the blind see and had taught charity and mercy until he himself was killed by human intolerance and hate, the story of the Christ she did not attempt to tell. Always she taught them to take pride in their native gifts and their heritage, for pride had been such a hard lesson for Fannie herself to learn.

She concerned herself with Indian morals only when they involved the matter of health. In regard to this the government had worked out a simple, rough-and-ready technique of treatment. Most of the young people in the village made love when the opportunity offered, regarding it in the same way as the gratification of any other appetite, and began sexual play in early childhood, as had countless numbers of her own countrymen. However, when the couples married, under ordinary conditions they maintained a rather high level of fidelity. Unlike the Eskimos they did not lend their wives to visitors; as a rule a brave would share his wife with a friend or kinsman only in times of great need. When a man or woman brought back disease from the gold camps Pavlof and she did their best to impose quarantine; and by taking the elders into their confidence and by seeing that its violation caused a loss of face, their efforts met with considerable success. Only rarely must they dispatch one of the tribe to the government doctor at Fort Yukon.

Often Fannie must search herself to see if she was rid of racial prejudice she had picked up at Dawson and Nome. That research was not very thorough; complete tolerance is a hard thing for anyone to come by in dealing with more primitive people of another color; and she lacked the intellectual power to be truly introspective. She no longer objected to the fishy smell that hung over every one of the villagers; even in the closed schoolroom in winter days her nose got used to it. She realized that their bathing the whole body in winter was impossible and a matter of considerable difficulty in summer, and anyway the fur worn next to the skin somehow seemed to prevent the accumulation of much dirt. As for vermin, she could only take care of herself, her growing child, and that child's usual playmate, who was five eighths white.

That the concern she felt for two-year-old Joe Harris was considerably greater than for other toddlers in the village she did not attempt to explain. Perhaps there was reason enough in his being the grandson of the village chief, without whose co-operation she could get nowhere. She did not like to think that Joe's white blood was a factor, yet in her heart it was; for little Vicky must have a playmate and he was the most "suitable" of any in the village. Eric, too, was concerned with him, asking about him, seeing to his diet, and contributing to his support, apparently because of some arrangement he had made with Dr. Harris and because he had no one else for whom to care. Sometimes she caught herself wishing that he was all white. She could not help but see that, of the two children, he learned more quickly and was by far the stronger. With Eric backing him—she had great respect for Eric—and hence with Dr. Hill in the distance, only his Indian blood would keep him from going far. If he were all white, there might be a future glimmering beyond this present. Actually Joe looked more Indian every day.

When Joe played with Vicky—he already knew the footpath between H'kah's house and Fannie's and took it alone every day except on days of storm or intense cold—she always spoke to him in English and made him answer in that tongue. He was growing up bilingual—so Dr. Hill would put it. When he was three—Vicky a few months older, that time like sunrise in a child's life after the uncertain light of dawn when it begins to learn the structure of the language—she perceived that Vicky was likewise bilingual, a fact that should have pleased her, she thought, for certainly it would please Dr. Hill, yet which she could not keep from dismaying her a little. Vicky had the run of the schoolhouse and nearby Indian houses where she heard native speech; and it might be that when the children strayed beyond her hearing, they employed that tongue.

In the spring of 1905, with Joe going on five and Vicky's fifth birthday behind her, Eric sailed upriver, bringing two packages for Joe—both of them thin, one about three feet long and the other about four—and a quite wonderful doll for Vicky. The giving of these gifts did not prove to be the main reason for his visit. Instead it evolved from a letter Eric had received on the first upriver steamer.

In Fannie's snug sitting room, Eric read it aloud:

Dear Eric:
   The United States Marshal in the judicial district embracing Nome, the Seward Peninsula, and great parts of the Arctic coast has been forced to resign because of ill-

health. For the time being his tasks are being performed by deputies.

Some days ago I received a telegram from the Secretary of the Interior asking if I could suggest a suitable successor, preferably an Alaskan, who has a good working knowledge of our native inhabitants. I immediately thought of you.

Your headquarters would be Nome; however, most of your activities would be far afield. Nome's population is dwindling every year and now stands at about four thousand winter residents, eight thousand in the summer. Lawlessness has almost ceased there; most crimes of violence in that district occur among Eskimos and Indians debauched with whisky, and the stopping of that sale would be one of your most important tasks.

You would have a great deal of authority in your own person, which is a satisfactory condition for an ambitious man. Your salary would be $4,000 a year with traveling expenses. I realize that this sum does not go far in this part of the world; however, perhaps you could supplement your income by leasing the Gertrude Mine. You would be subject to reappointment or non-reappointment at the conclusion of the President's term of office.

I hope to hear from you, by the first boat, that you will accept.

> *Sincerely,*
> *Stanley Hill*

"Well?" Fannie asked.

"What do you t'ink?"

"Why ask, when you've already made up your mind? However, if you want me to second the motion I'll do so gladly."

"I wouldn't like living in Nome. T'ank heaven, most of the time I'd be on the move. There would be no trouble about leasing my mine on shares. I know a Swede who'd take it tomorrow. I know a big company too, who'd spend t'ousands of dollars on diverting the stream above and have a skookem placer. But the gold-bearing gravels would be washed out in a couple of years, and I'd have a lot of money in the bank but no mine. I t'ink I'll take the Swede."

"Would you have him live in your house?"

Eric's face changed expression. "He'd want a snug little cabin close by the sluice."

"Would you enjoy the work—and the authority?"

176

"I'd enjoy the work. My hands have got to be busy, and, what head I've got, the same. Alaska's changing and only a few old-timers can live to themselves any more, wit' the weat'er and the game and maybe a squaw for company. The day of those old lone wolves is almost gone. I've got to learn how to work wit' other men."

"Every man likes a job where he can use his full powers. Sophia would have wanted you to accept—you know that better than I."

"She sure would. If it turned out I had the ability to be a leader in Alaska, she'd want me to be one. She wouldn't want me to flinch from it—for any reason."

"What reason could there be? You've already proved you've got it, just in getting this school started at the lowest cost to the government—Dr. Hill told me that—of any school outside of mission schools. Also, you've been very lonely these four years. You can't go on that way."

"Everybody has to go on that way, I t'ink—not only in Alaska but everywhere. I don't know anyone who isn't awful lonely a good part of the time. In Alaska we get a double dose, such a big country with so few people. Some real old sourdoughs like it—they're what Dr. Hill called misanthropes, I guess—but they'll move furt'er and furt'er back into the woods until they die off. Well, yust saying all this has cleared it up in my head. I've already written the letter of acceptance and I'll send it off on the first boat. I don't like to move away from the river and the rest, but I won't pull up my roots. I'll be back when a new President is elected. Now will you send Vicky to get little Joe and his stepfather Sih? I want to give Joe his presents and Sih some instructions, which you'll have to translate."

The little girl beamed with pride, perfectly understanding her instructions, and immediately trotted off. In a few minutes the stalwart young native and the little boy stood at the door. Although Fannie had a feeling that she did not try to explain against inviting any of the grown Indians into her sitting room, and did so only with ill ease, she forced cordiality into her voice and had both visitors enter. A frequenter here, Joe had eyes only for the packages. Sih, knowing himself for a good hunter and Eric's friend, came in with great dignity.

Joe's eyes were deep-set, close together, and a brilliant black. Their gaze was markedly intent. Eric thought he had bought the right presents.

Joe unwrapped the shorter of the two, breaking the twine with a good jerk, to disclose a small-sized but well-made air gun.

"What is it, Joe?" Eric asked.

"*Tekuh*," the child answered, trying to work the lever.

"Say it in English."

"Goon."

Joe made a hasty but sharp examination of the air rifle, tucked it under his arm, and began to open the longer package. From the torn paper came forth a single-shot, business-like-looking .22 rifle, obviously finely fashioned and expensive. While Joe's black eyes were going over it, inch by inch, and his chubby hands were feeling it, Eric turned to Fannie.

"Tell Sih I will speak to him about the guns."

Fannie translated in fluent Athabaskan.

"Tell Sih that Joe is to have the air gun at once, and Sih is to teach him how to shoot it. The first thing that Joe must learn is never to shoot it except when he has a clear view of the target and knows that no person or dog or anything to take harm is in the way. He may shoot it at ptarmigan, squirrels, rabbits, anything good to eat, at nothing that is not good to eat except a mark. He must learn to get a fast sight, as the best white hunters do, not take a rest and a long aim as do Indians. Look hard as he can through the sights and pull the trigger while he's looking hard. Do you understand?"

When Fannie had translated this, not without difficulty and repetition, Sih said something in a somewhat excited tone, although his face remained impassive. Since Sih brought in the name Kentucky Jack—he pronounced it Kontook Jock—Fannie need not translate the remark. Sih understood perfectly; Joe must be learned to shoot as did Kentucky Jack Hardman, who had won the rifle tournament at Dawson the year before. That meant to swing his piece with a full-arm movement and fire before anyone could believe he had found his aim.

"I want him to have the .22 when he's eight," Eric told Fannie. "That may seem young to you, but he'll have the feel of a gun by then, and the lesson not to fire until he's sure of his aim and target will be burned in. It may be too long for him, but the Kentucky rifles used by the frontiersmen in our Revolutionary War were mighty long, and what they did with 'em was a caution. Tell Sih the main part of that. Tell him, too, that no other person in the tribe, boy or man, is ever to shoot it. Tell him I could have got a repeater, but Joe is to learn to kill with the first shot. Joe is to be taught how to care for it, to clean it with ramrod and an oiled rag as soon as he finishes shooting. Say that when I come back here to stay, I want him a dead shot. He must make a careful stalk, get close, shoot quick, and make sure. He's not to waste ammunition—get that through his head. He's never to carry the gun cocked; he must cock it on the way to his shoulder. By the time he's nine or ten he's to shoot game birds through the head so as not to hurt the meat. And there's one thing more, very important. He can't hunt with the rifle all the time. Part of the time he has to use bow and arrow, for someday when he's a man and needs grub bad, a little spring might break and he'd be helpless. I want him to learn all that the Indians know about hunting and fishing, and shoot a rifle like Kentucky Jack."

Fannie went over this carefully with Sih, until his nods and grunts told that he understood perfectly. Then his face was as eloquent of pride as a wooden mask sometimes worn long ago in Indian ritual.

He went forth stolidly, carrying the .22 rifle; in a rather different voice than usual Fannie told the two children to go out into the spring sunlight to play. As she shut the door behind them, Eric saw that her eyes were big and intensely bright.

"Sit down, Eric," she said.

"All right."

"I've got something to say. Maybe I shouldn't say it—it's a pretty hard decision for a woman with no more schooling in the social graces than I have had—still, I'm thinking it, and I believe you'd want me to come out with it. I never realized fully what a truly great interest—that isn't even the word—you take in Joe Harris. He's in your life to stay and in a mighty important way. He might be—I believe he is—the most important living human being in your life."

She paused. He answered quietly.

"I would say that's true."

"Well, it's hard to account for if he's the son of a no-good doctor whom as far as I know you met only once. Well, I'll go ahead. I won't leave it up in the air. Before you married, you used to go with Sant. Pavlof made a little slip once—I guessed that much. I think at the very time Dr. Harris was here—probably the very night you came to get Pavlof—

179

you were suddenly overcome with passion, and Joe is your son."

Eric's face hardly changed, but his voice dropped very low.

"If that's so, and since you loved Sophia—I say loved, at least she was your ideal—you must hate me."

"Not me, Eric. You forget what I've been through in Dawson, and in Nome. I know those sudden passions in men, almost unbearable. When I had to seek some kind of excuse for my life as a camp follower that knowledge was all I had." Fannie's expression changed, her face flushed, and a woman different and far more true than he had yet seen in her was looking steadfastly into his eyes. "It was a poor excuse; still, I think some of the best camp followers, and among them are some awfully bad ones and some not so bad, may have shared it with me. I'll tell you this, too, for whatever it may mean. When a man came to me after three months on the creeks, a decent man as far as I could tell, shaming himself to go to a common prostitute because he had no one else to whom to go, I—I served him gladly. I tried to make him understand our fellow humanity. I went with him that night instead of with some man of the camp who could get all the women he wanted, and once or twice —once or twice when he was broke, I let him do it free. Forgive me, Eric, for breaking down like this," she went on, her eyes filling with tears. "Don't confess anything more. I've confessed enough for us both."

After both had kept silent a long time, Fannie spoke again.

"I'll love your little Joe and do all I can for him. Joe Harris. I know why you've hidden the truth, and I'll never tell it to anyone."

"I know you won't. And now I'd better be going. I hope Vicky likes her doll."

"She'll love it too much; I wish you'd brought her an Indian doll."

"I didn't t'ink of it. I wouldn't have known where to get one, a nice doll, not just a carved piece of wood—but I guess they're all right too. I don't suppose I'll see you for a good while."

"You might. One of the girls I went to school with is living in St. Michael, the wife of a rich trader." The woman who had looked into his eyes a moment ago had vanished, and Fannie, a woman of many frailties, was speaking now.

"I've been given six months' vacation—I didn't take it the last time it was offered. She's invited Vicky and me to stay with her as long as we can, and I accepted for next summer."

"I hope to see you there, but I won't be there often. Good-bye, Fannie."

6

Nome, dwindling every day, was still the largest community in Alaska. It had one quite good hotel, several with ornate façades, numerous flophouses, flashy saloons and gambling halls, restaurants, stores advertising the latest styles in clothes, mail every week, rows of houses that became shacks as they straggled onto the tundra, its native town and whore town, and mudholes beyond counting. A government building housed Eric's office as well as the district court. The former marshal told him the routine of duties. Since the deputy had been a political appointee and had never driven a dog sled, Eric assigned to him the keeping of the peace within Nome itself and took the administration of law throughout the vast hinterland. Toward this end, he had brought along his own dog team.

He looked over the dockets, to find that lately there had been almost no crimes of violence in Nome or the nearby gulches. Most of the cases had involved claim jumping. Whisky-running on the ships touching Nome had almost dried up, although no small amount of rotgut still flowed from unknown springs, usually brought in on native boats, backs, or sleds. The stopping of this traffic became Eric's first major task.

Arriving in October, well before Christmas he was almost certain that the main local distributor of the concoction was the owner of the Alaska Rose Trading Post, a veteran of the upper Yukon gold camps called English Eddie. Eric's deputy, sent on the somewhat distasteful errand, discovered that Eddie's stock of trade goods, visible on the shelves, was surprisingly scanty and poor; yet Eskimos and Indians hung around all day, and came in unusual number after nightfall. On obtaining official permission to examine ship ladings, he found that English Eddie had shipped more fur so far this year than any other trader in Nome. After a little study of Eddie's comings and goings Eric asked the United States Judge for a search warrant for the post and the owner's living quarters in the rear.

181

"Search warrants aren't looked upon with favor when they involve our white citizens," the judge remarked, grinning, as he wrote out the document. "Still, it's high time these slow murders of our native citizens were stopped, and I hope you can do it without too much pistol fire going and coming."

"There won't be any," Eric promised.

He chose the third night before Christmas for the raid, and in the afternoon of that day called in his deputy to discuss plans. Almost at once the latter gave utterance to surprise.

"You expect to raid that dive with only two men?"

"I'd rather it would be only one—you. It's your province to handle such matters in Nome. But the stuff will be well hidden—and with two of us looking, the chances of finding it will be better. So, if you don't mind, I'll go along."

"If I don't mind, good God! English Eddie has a terrible temper. He's bluffed out everybody but the Canadian Northwest Police. He won't take kindly to this one damn bit. And if we should happen to find his stock——"

"We're going to find it if it's there, and it must be there, because he's got nobody running back and forth to supply the customers. Meet me here at ten, and we'll go right over."

When the deputy had gone Eric wondered if he had spoken too lightly of the business. It would be the first raid on a white man's property in about two years. Actually he had not tried to impress the deputy or even himself; he was simply not afraid. This he could not quite explain, since English Eddie was something of an unknown quantity and rather widely feared in the underworld of Nome. "I've weat'ered out too many blizzards to be much scared of one man," he decided finally.

At ten the deputy came into his office, with a big revolver slung on his hip and a bulge on his left breast. He was a good officer, Eric thought; his face showed determination and his eyes were steady, not wobbling in the least; the fact remained he had not much experience in the North.

"If I were you, I'd leave that gun here."

"If you tell me to, I will, but it seems to me foolhardy."

"There's nothing foolhardy about it. The chance of a fatal accident is a great deal less. I'm carrying no guns. Our protection is our stars—English Eddie knows exactly what they mean."

"All right." The deputy took off the holster and started to the door.

"Why don't you leave your shoulder holster, too? Eddie would see it as plain as I do, and that changes the whole affair."

"Well, if you want to go the whole hog—I will too."

So they went and found English Eddie behind his counter, a few other Eskimos standing about, and one Eskimo with a bottle at his lips in a dim corner.

"Where did you get that whisky?" the deputy demanded.

"He brought it in here," Eddie shouted, "and it's none of my business or yours."

"I bring in bottle," the native muttered, with a drunken leer that Eric had seen too often for his comfort, a drunken Eskimo being one of the most revolting spectacles in the North. He had often wondered why it was a worse sight than a drunken white man, and could never find the answer. Perhaps it suggested a child's drunkenness, which he had once seen on a street in Circle City. The child's father had given him the drink, too drunk himself to know what he was doing, and Eric had been able to do nothing but make the child vomit, and go his way.

"That's all right," Eric told his deputy. "Maybe he did bring it in. Eddie, we have a search warrant to look through your establishment for rotgut whisky."

"So the new marshal has taken to searching legitimate places of business," Eddie replied, smiling what someone had once called a "dangerous" smile, a description that had flattered Eddie greatly. Evidently he did not expect a very thorough search.

"You take the left side of the building," Eric directed his deputy, "and I'll take the right." Eddie was standing on the right-hand side.

"Wait just a minute. Where are your guns? Under your coats, I guess."

"We haven't any guns."

"You mean you've come here to serve a search warrant on English Eddie without packing guns?"

"You bet you. But we're wearing our stars."

Eddie was severely jarred. The situation had suddenly become immensely complicated. A businessman behind his counter could be expected to submit to the orders of armed officers and would not lose prestige among his equals and inferiors, but law without guns to back it was an abstraction with which he could hardly deal. A little sweat came out on his florid face.

After a futile search of the store Eric pointed to a doorway in the rear.

"Does that lead to your living quarters?" he asked.

Eddie rushed from behind his counter and posted himself there, all two hundred pounds of him, a picture of belligerence.

"It sure is, and you're not wanted inside."

"If you read the warrant you'll find it includes your whole establishment," Eric answered, pausing politely.

"A man's home is his castle. That's an older law than any on the books of the U. S. Government. Every man has the right to protect it. I learned that in England."

"When did you visit England, Eddie? You were born in Chicago. You moved to Washington State ten years ago. Since then you've been following the gold camps. Your real name is Franz Holberg. We don't give a damn about that, but we're going to search your place."

"Well, you're two to one. If you come one at a time, by God I'll——"

Eric was not much kin to Windy Willie. He never liked to say or do anything that smacked of heroics; the fact remained that he was the United States Marshal, keenly feeling the dignity of that office as almost any squarehead would, and he had a little snoose under his upper lip to quiet his nerves. He walked straight toward English Eddie, his arms free. The latter saw the badge that did not cost a dollar gleam in the lamplight and perhaps he saw something in Eric's face that caused a disagreeable fact, which throughout his life he had usually managed to ignore, to stand stubbornly before his eyes. He closed his fist and drew back his arm, then suddenly let it fall.

"Oh hell, go ahead and search for you won't find nothing, you stinking bastards," he bawled as he threw open the door.

Then Eric was faced, too, with something that looked like a disagreeable fact—that of anticlimax. Eddie's living quarters consisted of one large room containing a neatly made bed, four chairs, a clothes closet, a dining and reading table, oddly enough a bookshelf, a small flat-topped cooking stove whose front draft showed red coals, and a large heating stove whose drafts showed flame. On a wan hope, but sensing defeat, Eric started for the clothes closet.

"I hope this room isn't too cold for your majesties," Eddie said, with what seemed heavy sarcasm. "I lighted the heater just before you made your royal entrance."

Something, Eric did not know what, made him stop, then in an absent-minded manner walk to the big stove. The room was perfectly still as he opened its big door. The stove had a false metal bottom, a hole in which showed a candle placed so that its flame flickered in the front draft. In between were stacked at least sixty bottles of transparent liquid, enough for Eddie's Christmas trade.

Eric uncorked one of the bottles, sniffed and tasted it, and with great dignity put Franz Holberg, alias English Eddie, under arrest. The next act of Eric and his deputy was deliberately conspicuous—the lugging out to the street of all but two of the bottles, and breaking them in a neat pile. Long before they had finished the task a small crowd of Eskimos with a scattering of white men ringed the scene, the former sniffing deeply and grunting sadly.

English Eddie was duly arraigned, tried, and sentenced to a thousand-dollar fine and sixty days in jail. Thereafter the flow of rotgut in the city of Nome conspicuously dwindled.

7

The word got out, through an Eskimo's telling, that Eric and his deputy had made the raid and the arrest unarmed. Although nothing was new about it Outside, in Alaska it made a considerable impression on the populace. Nome had been born the same year as Joe Harris, who could not yet talk quite plainly. A hundred revolvers had cracked to celebrate last Fourth of July; and gun toting was still widely practiced as a matter of gold-camp tradition, although real gun fights could be counted on the fingers. Actually the city's leaders and almost all of its permanent population moved immediately behind him. In their eyes he reflected an Alaska yet to be.

In the early summer of Eric's third year as marshal a trading vessel plying the Arctic coast brought a letter from a trapper who signed himself Nick Novikof, and forwarded by a trader at Point Hope. Almost at its first words Eric's attention became riveted. Those words were Allapah Bay, the parish of the Reverend Arthur Dudley, whom Eric knew.

While hunting and following his line of fox traps with

185

dog sled in the hard cold of the preceding winter, Novikof had found the frozen body of an old Eskimo woman, with a piece of thong tied fast around her scrawny neck. She had been killed since a snowfall of a few hours before, and by following their tracks, he soon came on a party of five Eskimo men and four women making for Allapah Bay. They readily confessed killing the woman—the mother of one of the men—but because of the poorly breached barrier of language they were able to give no sort of an excuse. Since they were very low on grub—their sled had fallen into an ice crevice and most of their supplies been lost—the trapper had given them the haunch of a caribou he had just killed, to see them through to Allapah Bay. On his return to Point Hope he had written a brief, factual letter, almost without comment, to the U. S. authorities in Nome.

Below his signature was this line, added by the trader at Point Hope:

I am sorry to ask that a U. S. Marshal be sent clear up here to see that justice is done, but the way we white traders would have handled it in the old days would bother the missionaries.

Eric obtained a warrant for the arrest of Ooliet *et al.*, the dead woman's supposed son and companions, and set sail in a trading vessel. On the second day the vessel made a brief stop at Little Diomede, and Eric saw the poochkies. He had always wanted to see the poochkies, perhaps only because he liked the word, and because almost every Arctic traveler he had ever met mentioned them sooner or later. Actually they were only auklike birds that perched like parrots all over the cliffs and ledges of the two islands jutting up from Bering Strait, and were continually flying and crying in thick flocks.

Into these flocks Eskimo boys threw a primitive kind of chain shot, many thongs tied together midway, each end fixed to a stone. These spread in flight and almost every cast would bring down a poochkie. In the pan they fried in their own fat, and, if the eater did not mind a strong fishy flavor, were pleasant to eat. And Bering Strait itself, Eric thought, was a momentous bit of geography. It was only about a hundred miles wide, with the easternmost cape of Siberia on the west and Cape Prince of Wales, the westernmost jut of the Alaskan mainland, on the east; and the narrow passage linked the Pacific and Arctic oceans. Dr.

Hill believed that all the native peoples in the New World, from the sophisticated Inca to the subtle Eskimo, sprang from Asiatic wanderers who had crossed this strait in their skin boats.

As the long sea miles sped, thrust backward by the propeller of the small steam launch, the hours of twilight that an upper-river man counted as summer night failed to show up. The sun slid along the horizon, without much upward or downward motion, and ever it painted the clouds pale lovely colors, and the sea itself had a peculiar hue. It was also wondrously calm, with low, inconspicuous tides. From the north came a scintillating glimmer that the crew called the ice blink. It was the reflection of the sun on the eternal ice.

Beyond bleak Kotzebue the ship stopped at Point Hope; and here, too, the white man had brought rack and ruin, and the people stood about the landing crying, "*Kow-kow pechuck, kow-kow pilitay.*" They were no great improvement over the Eskimos at Nome. They had good dogs picketed in front of their moss-roofed huts, which were reached through a low passage through which the enterer must crawl, this to fight cold and wind.

Eric sat awhile in a back room of the trading post, having a drink with the proprietor, a powerfully built Norwegian with the good Viking name of Thorsen, but Eric soon found that he did not like him very well.

"You're Norse, aren't you?" Thorsen had asked, almost without accent.

"Yes."

"Then I can speak to you man to man. I know what your business is up here—to look into the murder of the squaw Meeluk. Mind you, she was murdered by her own son, a heathen Eskimo called Ooliet. Maybe the others helped kill her, but he was the main one. If the United States Government stands for that, I'll move to Herschel Island on the Canadian side of the line."

"What reason did Ooliet give?"

"You can listen to that, and see what you think of it, when you get to the Reverend Dudley's village on Allapah Bay."

Eric thought awhile and then asked another question.

"Where did that band of natives live?"

"Where would you expect? On Allapah Bay—they were part of the Reverend's little flock. They'd been off around

187

Icy Cape and were heading home. They almost never got there, too; a blizzard came up soon after Big Nick Novikof caught up with them. They had to make a snowhouse, and except for that haunch of caribou the old fool had given them, they would have all starved, a good riddance for Alaska and saving you a trip and the government a hanging. And now that preacher—so he calls himself—is going to stand up for them, mark my words."

"Does the Reverend Dudley preach?" Eric asked, on an odd impulse.

"I guess he don't. He calls himself a minister and as such, he's supposed to preach, not interfere with what we're trying to do up here, law and order and the advancement of civilization."

"You seem to feel pretty strongly about him, Mr. Thorsen."

"Understand, I've nothing against missionaries—in their place. Some of them do quite a lot of good. But Dudley isn't a regular missionary. As for his private affairs—I haven't anything to say about them because they're not my business. But I object to what he teaches the natives—not to be humble before white people, and to carry on with their heathen ways. I object to him selling them supplies at cost; how are white people going to stay up here unless they can make a decent profit? I've known some of my natives to trek forty miles to save a dollar on a sack of flour. I think he should be run out of the territory."

Eric ended his visit with Thorsen rather quickly. He did not feel that the trader's opinions should have very much bearing on the outcome of his enterprise.

He felt even less so at his first good view of Allapah Village. The houses looked bigger and warmer than any he had seen on this coast; there was no litter but more equipment for Arctic life—kayaks, oomiaks, fish nets and racks, dogs, and sleds. When he landed and saw the people he was pleasantly jarred. Their hair-seal blouses and pants looked clean; they stood in a different posture from the Eskimos of Nome, no palms were outstretched, no one whined, and there was a big smile on every face. Old-timers had told how the Eskimos, when first met with, had been a markedly happy people, seeing the funny side of everything. These Allapah villagers still looked happy.

In a moment a tall man burst out of the trading post and came running down to the landing.

"Is that you, Eric?" he shouted, when still at a distance.

"You bet you."

"Well, I've been looking for you, and how glad I am to see you!" Then, as he came close and shook Eric's hand, "I literally thank God that it's you who've come on this business instead of a cheechako. You see, I'd heard you were marshal of this district, but I was afraid you'd be off somewhere and a deputy would come in your place. Now come on up to my quarters. There's no hurry about talking to the people involved—they're going to stay put—and I've a bottle of good Hudson Bay rum that needs broaching."

Listening to what he said, Eric was also seeing how he looked. Arthur Dudley appeared younger, more lithe, more vital, happier than when they had last met. Eric guessed that his spiritual problems had been resolved. His native-made clothes had a certain dash. His shirt was of young caribou skins, the skins cut in squares, russet alternating with pale tan, suggesting a plaid, and the collar was lined with ermine. His pants were of leopard seal, deeply fleshed to make them soft and pliable; on his feet were fur-lined moccasins decorated with beads. He had never fulfilled most people's mental image of a minister; Eric wondered if he still counted himself one and administered Christian sacraments.

"Am I to call you 'Reverend'?" Eric asked in his straightforward way as they were entering his snug quarters, which might be called a rectory although it did not look like one. "You see, I don't know your present status."

"I wish you'd call me Arthur. There's twelve years' difference between our ages, but I think we are both young pioneers. That friendly address would please me very much."

"Then I will."

"Actually I dislike the word reverend. Its Latin root is fear, and nobody fears me unless it is the Devil. Sometimes I think he does. I've caught him bending more than once and administered a swift kick. I feel sure I am revered at Allapah Bay, using the word in its usual meaning. Occasionally I've been called aboard a vessel to perform a sacrament; once when an old trapper was dying of consumption, once to marry the mate to his half-Russian girl—they had no time to get to a priest of the Greek Church before the baby was due. I told them the priests—they are very understanding fellows—would make no to-do about the baby except to christen it, but they were a very proper pair, and I was glad to oblige. I perform no sacraments among the villagers, partly because the Father, Son, and Holy Ghost comprise a good part of the ritual and are untranslatable into the Malemiut dialect. Anyway they have done very well with their animist religion, and I see no reason for them to change."

They were sitting now in a kind of study, its walls lined with books, the chairs of bone or ivory structure, extremely comfortable, with eider-down pillows. Dudley bowed his head slightly, then called through the open door of a rear room.

"Ermine?"

"Yes, Arthur," a young woman's voice replied.

"Will you fix rum and water for my guest and me, and a limeade—if that is what you want—for yourself. Not too cold for me, please. How about you, Eric?"

"I'll have mine as you have yours."

"After that come in and join us," Arthur went on, speaking to his invisible hearer.

"All right."

"How do you keep yourself occupied, if you don't mind telling me?" Eric asked out of simple curiosity.

"Eric, I'm busy as—what is it?—a one-armed paper hanger suffering from lice. By the way, that joke—tapestry instead of paper—antedates Chaucer. I have become a better than passable seal harpooner. When the seals appear in the leads you must harvest them at once, tomorrow they may be gone, and I take an active part in the hunts. I can handle a kayak in not too rough weather. I am an enthusiastic fisherman and fowler. I conduct a school teaching a wide variety of subjects. I run a trading post, buying furs at what I can get for them, selling goods at cost, and this practice doesn't enhance my popularity with traders up and down the coast. They are particularly upset because some of their own villagers come all the way here to deal with me. I wouldn't be worth while by any thinking but the Eskimos'. They say Ugruk, or whatever his name is, is going to spend time somehow, sleep, eat, loaf, so he might as well spend it on the trail, not die any sooner because he make trip. They are profound realists. Also they always learn something here, and the other traders have learned they mustn't be too greedy if they want to stay in business."

Just then a young Eskimo woman entered the room with

a tray of drinks. She was dressed becomingly in fur-trimmed, bead-adorned skins, and Eric thought her the prettiest he had ever seen. That might be because she was clean and trim, her hair dressed becomingly, and she wore her native costume with a flair.

But as he rose with Arthur to greet her he received another even more startling impression. Somewhere, somtime, he had seen her before.

"Ermine, you remember Eric Andersen."

"Of course, but I don't think he remembers me," she answered, with a girlish giggle. "Let him guess."

Eric did not guess; suddenly he knew.

"By Yesus, you're Chikarik, who was in our wedding!"

"The word means ermine," Arthur said, beaming with pride.

Ermine put down her tray, came close to Eric, and gently sniffed his cheek. Then all three sat down as old friends, enjoyed their drinks, and talked the usual talk of the North.

Eric spoke above innumerable inner voices, for his mind was dealing with a bygone scene aboard the *Victoria*. He silenced them at last, his thinking became objective, and he marveled greatly at the cordiality and freedom from strain of the present scene. Perhaps its simplicity was the real cause of his wonder. It seemed to have no complications; for long years now he had not felt as much at home.

When the glasses were empty—they were not glass, but the bored-out stubs of male-walrus ivory—Ermine excused herself, first asking Eric to be hers and Arthur's guest for supper. He accepted gladly, and when she had gone Arthur rose and closed the door to the inner room.

"I spoke to you very frankly once," he said, resuming his seat. "Now I would like to speak to you frankly again. I have nothing to confess of any mark, as I had before; I have no crucial question to ask. But you are of course curious about Ermine and me; you see the relationship is a world apart from that of the usual white-man-native-woman affair, and if the matter ever comes up in your hearing, I hope you will set the speakers straight."

"I sure will."

"The first part of the story is confidential. I told you of the sudden lust that overcame me that dreadful night in my rectory. Fool that I was, I thought it would never come again. The occasion was in my first summer in the Arctic, a day on which all the visitors were celebrating one of their

191

festivals. A young squaw—her name doesn't matter—came into my warehouse, where I was alone. She was unmarried, I was under great strain, yet I resisted the temptation. Then I knew I was not that rare sort of man who doesn't need a mate. Quite clearly I perceived that I could never be happy, my life's purposes could never be fulfilled, until I had one."

He stopped, smiled in retrospect, and went on.

"It had come about that I had talked a good deal with Ermine—her name was Chikarik and it still is; Ermine is my pet name for her. I was interested first in what seemed to be her success in what we call civilized life. I was soon to learn that the success was not as great as I had thought. She told me she had no future worth looking toward. She could not bring herself to marry one of the debased Eskimos of Nome. As a rule, only a rather low sort of white man would take her for keeps, and she knew too well how he would treat her. He would always be ashamed of her. You've heard the saying that when an Eskimo girl begins to look pretty to you, you have missed too many boats. Actually a good many Eskimo girls are truly beautiful, except that various things interfere, often a conditioning of mind, to blind our eyes. Of course tattoo is disfiguring, labrets are ugly; I'm glad to say our young women wear neither. Usually there is a fish smell and often dirt. But I knew that Chikarik came from one of the undebauched villages and had been chosen for mission school because of the quickness of her mind. Also I knew that she was beautiful to my sight.

"So, Eric, I wrote her a letter, sending money for her passage up here, and, if she wished, for her return trip. I told her I wanted to talk to her on a very serious matter. She came, I perceived again what a remarkable young woman she was, a member of a truly remarkable race, and we spoke frankly. Knowing I would never leave the Arctic except for trips, at the end of our talks I kissed her and proposed marriage. She was eager to rejoin her people, she made nothing of the fact that I was nearly twice her age. I was lucky enough to appeal to her in various ways, and she accepted. The results are what you have seen."

"That's yust fine," Eric said, his face flushing.

"When I say marriage, you understand that I mean Eskimo marriage. A few Eskimo women have been married to white men in the Christian service; I decided that

192

for once it could be reversed. Ermine's mind is silver-clear and quick, but I didn't think she would understand what this means: 'O God, who has so consecrated the state of Matrimony that in it is represented the spiritual marriage and unity between Christ and his Church; Look mercifully upon these thy servants . . .' I have pondered it a good deal and still have no idea what it means."

Thinking of Joe Harris, Eric wondered whether Arthur and Ermine had children, but did not feel free to ask. After his host had shown him some very ancient Eskimo ivory carvings, Eric rose to leave.

"I'll see you at supper—rather early, if you please, say six o'clock. We're going to have a snow goose, shot on a pond on the tundra. After supper I want you to talk with Ooliet, I doing the best I can to interpret. Our Eskimos have never learned to lie and you'll find out the truth about the death of that old woman on the ice. Then you can do what you believe to be your duty."

8

The supper and the company both proved excellent in Eric's opinion. The goose had not been parboiled or soaked in salt water to remove its wild taste, nor had its delicious flavor been destroyed by overcooking. It was stuffed with bread crumbs mixed with an aromatic water root Eric did not know; the only other dish was a water-cress salad, dressed with melted goose fat. There were no canned beans or peas; the only exotic on the table was a bottle of good Chianti, of which Ermine did not partake.

"We Eskimos can't drink anything containing alcohol without going crazy," she explained calmly.

When the bottle was empty all three walked to the house where Ooliet lived. Arthur called him out, and there came with him his young wife and a very old man whom Ermine believed to be the wife's grandfather or great-uncle. Arthur led them to the beach, where they squatted, casting long shadows from the low sun. The clouds along the horizon were of pale rose and gold, and Eric had not seen their like except in the Arctic. The still sea reflected their hues.

Sophia moved into Eric's mind, and he could imagine the expression on her face if she had stood with him alone, looking out on this lonely sea. Perhaps into her mind would steal a stanza of poetry which she had particularly loved, which had ended "Of perilous seas, in faery lands forlorn."

The Arctic Ocean was not a perilous sea except for its ice, but she had told him that the young man who wrote the poem had originally written "keel-less seas," which well described these waters, for except on the steam launch that had brought him here, there was no keel between him and the Pole.

Arthur spoke to the fine-looking Eskimo, who looked about thirty years old, and he made reply.

"Ooliet said that Meeluk—meaning breasts, it is a pet word for mother, as mamma, of the same meaning, is in English—was not his mother but his grandmother. She was *okukshak*—very old."

The Eskimo spoke again.

"This is almost incredible," Arthur said, his eyes shining. "He said that his grandmother was 'able to walk' when someone he calls 'Beechy' came in his great ship and touched her village. It couldn't have been anyone but Captain Beechey of the *Blossom*, who first sailed this coast in 1826. Supposing she was six years old. Good God, that means she was about eighty-eight when she was killed, an almost unheard-of age for an Eskimo. Ooliet says that she had no living sons, so he acted as her son, provided her with food and skins for her clothing, and she lived in his house."

Now the Eskimo spoke at considerable length, making short, strong movements with his arms.

"This is very interesting," Arthur said. "Meeluk suffered with what must have been rheumatism in an acute form and was nearly blind. Even the winter before last she had asked to be killed, begged him to do so, while the tears ran down her old, drawn face, but Ooliet could not bring himself to do it. He loved her very deeply, and she could still tell stories of the old times before the traders came, and counsel the people. But she still wanted to go to—well, we'll call it the Happy Hunting Ground, although that's not literal. 'The Place of Ever Feasting,' hits it better. She was lonely for the people she used to know and could not laugh any more—and Eric, when an Eskimo can't laugh, it's a terrible thing. To try to cheer her up, Ooliet took her early in the summer to a little village up the coast, to stay with her nephew—he also *okukshak* by Eskimo counting. But the nephew died, and she begged so hard to be killed that early in the winter one of the villagers came across the ice to summon Ooliet. This man was her great-nephew, I gather, but he couldn't kill the old woman, they were not close enough kin. Ooliet went for her, taking along his wife, some cousins, and others. They were on their way back to Allapah, carrying Meeluk on the sled, when a bridge of snow over a crevice gave way; almost all of their supplies were lost and two of their dogs, which had to be cut loose to save the others."

The tale went on in a rush of words until Arthur raised his hand to silence him.

"They went on," he told, "but they weren't getting anywhere over the bad ice. There was nothing with which they could mend the broken runner—no driftwood or anything —and the remaining dogs couldn't draw it except a foot or two at a time. So they had to abandon it, putting what grub they had on various backs, and Ooliet took the old woman on his back. And they had gone only a mile or so when Ooliet's cousin, who could smell weather, told them that a blizzard would soon strike."

"And it did," Eric said to himself.

"You can imagine the scene—the cold, lowering clouds, the dark, the first puffs of icy wind. Meeluk began wailing as only an old squaw can wail. So a dreadful moment was coming closer, an awful decision had to be made. And now I'm going to ask Ooliet to repeat his grandmother's plea."

Ooliet spoke in a low mutter, his face impassive.

"Kill me," Meeluk pled. "If you won't kill me, leave me here. I am very old. I was the woman of Seesook, the chief. I can no longer chew the skins to soften them, and sew them with sinew; I cannot refill the lamps with my shaking hands. For years I have done nothing to earn the seal meat that you cut up for me to swallow, I have been a burden on my people. Now, unless you leave me here, I will cause you all to die in the blowing snow. I, no longer any good, will be the cause of good ones dying, good ones that I love. To leave me is all I ask. But if before you go, you will darken my eyes so I cannot see the storm break, if you will make me so I do not lie trembling and alone, you will pay me for the milk I gave my babes and all else I gave."

Arthur fell silent, then quickly rose and turned his back on the others, his hand over his eyes. Ermine went to him, kissed his cheek, then resumed her place.

"There is not much more," Arthur said, when he had regained his self-control. "I'll ask Ooliet to tell just what happened. I want you to hear him say it, even though you don't

195

understand the words." Then Arthur spoke again to the gray-faced Eskimo.

The latter spoke briefly, the words jerking out of him, his chest heaving.

"Ooliet looked into his cousin's eyes, and nodded. The cousin came up from behind and struck Meeluk a sharp blow on the back of the head with his pole, not hard enough to kill her, only to knock her out. Then Ooliet cut a thong and fixed it about the old scrawny neck, drew it tight and knotted it. Then the party left her on the snow and continued their journey."

A few minutes later Eric was standing with Arthur at his doorway; Ermine had gone inside. Arthur glanced with not quite concealed surprise at the younger man's expression.

"I'm going to report that Meeluk committed suicide," Eric said. "It's not literally true, but I don't give a damn."

"You won't get in trouble if the truth comes out?" Arthur asked, after a long pause.

"I don't t'ink so. There are enough real sourdoughs in Alaska who'll know I did the right t'ing."

"You know, Eric, when I saw Dr. Hill in Nome he told me of a certain ambition, something he wanted to see happen in good time. I know of nothing except fate itself that need prevent it coming true."

7. The Growth of Joe

In the summer of 1908 Eric wrote a letter to James R. Garfield, Secretary of the Interior under President Roosevelt, resigning his post as U. S. Marshal. In this letter he stated that he did not desire reappointment, regardless of the outcome of the coming election, since he wished to return and resume the management of a small mining property on the upper Yukon. In reply he received a polite letter of regret.

Actually he had made more of a mark in his term of office than he realized. The great mills of government grind slowly, but many who help turn them are good men, dedicated to public service, and watching out for good men. Shortly after the inauguration of William Howard Taft, he received a letter from the Postmaster General, offering him the postmastership of Circle City, less than a day's trek, and only three hours' sail, from the Gertrude Mine.

"Both Mr. Garfield and Mr. Gifford Pinchot, chief of Forestry, have written to the President, expressing satisfaction with your services in Alaska, and recommending that you be retained in government service," the official informed him. Bung-eyed, Eric read this last, for he had never laid eyes on the great forester, and he had supposed that his reports, sent through channels, had never been read by anyone but a receiving clerk and filed away in a deep recess in the labyrinth of records.

Of course the postmastership of Circle City was a very minor plum, commanding a puny salary. Eric accepted it more to keep his hand in, in case he should ever run for office, than for any other reason. Except when the mail was in, via river boat or dog sled, he spent every Sunday, even in midwinter, either at home or at Tekuh village. At the latter place he spent most of his time with an Indian half-breed going on ten.

He had only to look at him to know that his instructions about Joe's raising had been faithfully carried out. Particularly he noticed the narrow-set, brilliant black eyes, the folds of the lids hiding the whites, leaving a three-cornered opening—eyes that had a direct and intense gaze—and felt sure he was a born rifleman. When Eric had tossed into the air ten tin cans in succession, to have one after another pierced by a .22 bullet fired six feet above his head, he knew also that Joe Harris was an expert rifleman, in a measure rarely seen except among professionals. He might be somewhere in the class with Annie Rooney, who at this age had shot running quail through the head on an Indiana farm.

Pavlof, Sih and Sant had watched this first demonstration in great anxiety, but at its end they had beamed as proudly as did his playmate Vicky; and only one watcher, Fannie, retained a troubled expression. Actually she had not watched the shooting as carefully as she had watched Vicky's face.

On one of his visits, Fannie had put to Eric a difficult question.

"An ugly thing happened on my second visit to my friend at St. Michael," she told him. "She had a little girl, Kate Harkins, about a year older than Vicky, and most of the time they were good playmates. One day Kate heard Vicky talking to an Indian in the Athabaska tongue—he was from somewhere up the Tanana. Kate remarked that she wouldn't dirty her mouth speaking Indian.

" 'When my papa speaks to a native he uses English, and if the native doesn't understand him, my papa pounds it into his head with his fists,' Kate said. 'Where did you learn it?' "

"Vicky told her that I was a teacher in an Indian village, and, goaded into it in a way, she said that her best friend was an Indian. 'Do you play with an Indian girl?' Kate asked. 'No, it's a boy, a few months younger than me.' 'You hug and kiss him and all that?' 'No, but we go hunting and fishing.' Then Kate made a face, and Vicky took the wrong way to defend herself. 'Joe isn't a full-blooded Indian,' she said, 'he's more than half white.'

"Kate jumped about, mocking her. 'Half-white, half-white,' she shouted so loudly that some other children heard her. 'I'll bet he stinks just as bad.' Then Kate stopped and began one of those terrible lectures that older children sometimes deliver to younger children. 'You poor child, don't you know that breeds are even worse than full-blooded Indians? They inherit the bad side of both races. My papa says so. A low-white man for a father, a dirty squaw for a mother. I'll go on playing with you, Vicky, because you didn't know any better than to play with a half-breed boy. But when you come to visit here again, you tell me cross your heart and hope to die you've sent him about his business. If you don't, I won't play with you nor will any white boys and girls in all St. Michael. Do you think that when we play post office any white boy would ever kiss a girl who had kissed a half-breed? It would make him vomit.' I know that Vicky ran in the house and cried, but I didn't get the straight of it for some time."

"My God, children can be little fiends!" Eric said, tucking a little snoose under his lip.

"To look at Kate, you wouldn't think butter would melt in her mouth. And she's prettier than Vicky, had much nicer clothes, and that made it all the worse."

"What did you say to Vicky when she told you about it?"

"I did my best to counteract its effect. I think I succeeded pretty well—when we came back here she and Joe seemed the same good friends. But I made her promise not to tell Joe, even when she gets mad at him—that happens pretty frequently—and I don't think she has. Now I get to my question. I did right, didn't I?"

"Fannie, I don't know. I'll have to t'ink it over. The father of the girl—is he a cheechako?"

"He's always calling himself a sourdough, but he came from Seattle and bought a trading post only a year before I

198

visited there, and he's never been to the interior." Her tone turned faintly apologetic. "And of course the Indians and Eskimos he sees are not very good specimens."

"No, they're not—because of men like him. Fannie, I believe Vicky should tell him what the girl said—not when she's mad at him, but when they've had a fine time together. He's ten and old enough to take it. He's known about the prejudice ever since he could walk—you can bet on that. I want him to realize he can't hide from it, and all his life—if he stays in Alaska—he's got to face it like a man. It may make a better man out of him, in the long run. Do you think she remembers the incident very clearly?"

"I'm afraid she does. And she doesn't want to visit in St. Michael again."

"I t'ink that dirty talk she heard might have a worse effect on her than its repetition would have on him. Counteract it all you can—if she wants to tell Joe, tell her she may do so. He'll take it all right, or I don't know my man."

When Eric had gone, he soon perceived why he was willing to subject Joe to such a painful experience. He thought that Vicky's mere telling it to him would serve her as a confession and break some ice that might be forming, not white and pure like the river ice, but dirty frozen snow, tramped underfoot. He thought, too, that one severe shock would be better for Joe than a thousand twinges of unknown pain.

Actually these did not come as often as Eric feared. Soon after Vicky's return from the visit, Joe had perceived that their relationship had changed in a slight degree but this change manifested itself only rarely, and in certain activities. She no longer put her arm around his neck as they walked into the woods or to fishing holes; when they wrestled she would suddenly break off and tell him that she did not want to play. It might be that they did not clasp hands as often as when they were little children.

To compensate for that, their expeditions into the woods and tundra became constantly more adventurous and triumphant. When he had had only the air gun they had brought back fool hens, once a big grouse, once two ducks in the same day. Even if he had not been ordered to draw close and shoot for the head, he would have soon learned the necessity, simply because the pellet did not hit hard enough to incapacitate any fowl hit in the body; in fact, more than one prize, hit in the head, took off in unsteady flight before they could get their hands on it. They made it a practice as soon as he had shot to run with all their might and retrieve the trophy.

When, at age eight, he had discarded the air gun for the .22 rifle, he made the change without the slightest difficulty and for the first time discovered what it was to know, provided his aim was certain, that the bullet would find its mark. After that, he killed cleanly. A willing and cheerful hiker from the first, before long Vicky learned how to stalk, which he seemed to know by instinct. Just to look for game was exciting; when it was sighted, and he led forth in its approach, their excitement kindled until they were almost breathless. He learned to take advantage of every feature of the scene. Sometimes they kept behind trees; sometimes they crawled through thickets; and the greatest and most thrilling stalks of all were made on open ground, approaching a pool on the tundra, where mallards gabbled, or a great Canadian goose stretched her neck to feed. It was mainly a matter of moving when the fowl's head was underwater, or, if they were approaching a flock of ducks, when their attention was drawn elsewhere. Wearing their oldest skin clothing, from which mud is easily washed, they lay full length, moved forward, and stopped the same instant. They were perfectly visible on the level plain, but Joe soon learned that wild things did not see, or at least were not afraid, of completely motionless objects. When freezing they truly froze, half with inward chills, half by a feat of will whereby they did not move a finger or their heads one inch, and kept track of the quarry only by movements of their eyeballs.

When they came within a certain distance something told Joe, "I can hit it now," and "it" meant the head, not the body. Rather early in his experience with the .22 the certain range was about sixty feet. This steadily lengthened with the passing years.

An effective way to get ducks and geese in the open was for him to send Vicky on a wide encirclement of the pool, to be followed by every sharp eye in the flock. Then if she would stand about a hundred yards from the opposite side he could make the stalk quickly. However, she always protested this procedure in an angry whisper, and would follow it only when he insisted, which was not often. Although he was finding out female tricks and oddities, the trouble was that he wanted her behind him in wildly thrilling minutes as much as she wanted to be there.

The most thrilling instant of all was when he sprang up to shoot. That bound was so fast, meanwhile swinging his gun, that he found aim and fired before even a bounding duck, such as a mallard or pintail, could take wing. Actually he could never remember aiming. All he did was *see*, as hard as he could. It was as though the rifle were becoming part of his body, to be pointed and stopped like a finger.

Once, in lovely May, they spied a magnificent swan preening and fluffing her feathers in the glass of a still pool, snow white except where the light through the spread plumage gleamed like silver. Vicky was surprised when Joe turned away.

"She'd be easy to get, and swans are awful good," Vicky said, speaking English, as she almost always did when Joe acted at all strange. "Father Pavlof brought us one last fall."

"Mist' Rick asked me not to kill any swans except when we're short of grub. The swan is Mist' Rick's totem."

"What does that mean?"

"I can't tell you in English. I didn't know what he meant till I thought about it in Indian." Then he began to speak the village language.

"We don't have the word totem. But it means a bird or an animal that is related to a person. It hasn't the same blood, it doesn't look a bit like him, but they speak to each other without words, they look out for each other, they know about each other even when a thousand miles apart, they make each other feel good when they meet. It has something to do with spirits."

Winter weather put no halt on their trips into the woods, except on days of terrific cold or storm. Now their game was snowshoe rabbits and ptarmigan, and once a young bull caribou, the stalking of which through the snow, both of them wearing snow-white parkas of rabbit skins, would recur with throbbing excitement in many a dream. They crept upwind within forty feet; then Joe shot with all his might, partly because the prize was so great, partly because he seemed to remember Mist' Rick saying he was not to use a rifle of such small caliber on big game. Hit in the forehead, the beast dropped dead. Often Vicky went with him to follow his short line of Indian-made traps—Eric had argued that if he could take fur with native rig he could certainly compete with the best in the business when his time came to use steel traps—and out of the skins of the first two dozen ermine that he caught, H'kah fashioned a muff and a cap, replete with black tails, for Vicky's birthday present, and she wore it proudly to school, and sometimes when she played alone, calling herself Queen Victoria of the North.

At fishing she was his full partner, not his follower, and this by her own right. Whether through creek ice—a cold chore of waiting, then a quick jerk of the line to snag and bring up the flopping silver fish—or in the deep eddies of open water, he had to fish hard to match her, and sometimes he failed. She was a natural fisherwoman. The fish seemed to like her bait better than his, perhaps because of some little twist she gave it with her fingers. She had a superb sense of timing, not a second too soon or late; when her sensitive hands told her that the fish had taken the bait, then her strike was bullet-swift.

Both loved their shared aloneness on these trips, although once that sharing was shaken by an unexpected happening.

In the long, lovely August of the year 1912, as Joe's twelfth birthday drew near, they were coming home with a good bag when they stopped to watch a falcon hunting fool hens. Then they learned that this grouse with a red motley was not such a fool after all, because when he sat perfectly still, as was his custom in times of peril, the falcon could not see him. She was swooping and darting within thirty feet of him and making a fool of herself, extra large falcons such as this invariably being females. She knew the flock was somewhere about, probably having seen one of them in flight, and not until another lost his nerve and flew did she stoop and kill.

"But of course their trick won't work on a man's eyes," Joe said. "I think that men must have the best all-around eyes in the whole world, even counting wild geese."

They were lying full length on the thick grass, facing each other. An urge, perhaps as strong as that which had caused the falcon to pounce with nameless fury on the fool hen and then to scream in ecstasy as she bound with it and brought it to the ground, came upon Joe. He knew perfectly well what it was; he could not remember when he did not know.

He leaned his head a little and sniffed Vicky's cheek. She did not move. Then he pressed her still lips with his own, the white man's caress that he had seen and sometimes gave Sant. Still she did not move. Then he found the opening between her caribou-hide shirt and pants, and thrust in his hand. At once she jerked it out and lay rigid.

"Don't ever do that again."

"Why not?" He was careful to speak English. "Why can't I feel you like I feel Indian girls? They like it fine."

"They're Indians but I'm a white girl."

"But you and I love each other, better than sister and brother. Doesn't that make it all right for us to play that way? You said you loved me. You say it often when I've made a real good shot. Once or twice you rushed and kissed me."

"I'm ashamed that I did. My friend Kate told me if I ever kissed an Indian—or a half-breed—she wouldn't play with me any more. She said no white boys would ever kiss me. No, I'm not ashamed of kissing you before, I was so excited, but I mustn't do it any more. That's the truth, Joe."

"Does my mouth taste any different from white boys' mouths?"

"No. It tastes good. Maybe your lips are a little harder than theirs. I do love you, Joe. I love you more than anyone except Mamma, and I dream about you almost every night. Still we mustn't play like we're both white."

"Will you marry me, when we're old enough? Once you said you would."

"I'm afraid I never can. I don't know why—I guess it's against the law. I don't think my mamma would want me to, either. I feel just awful."

Vicky broke into tears.

2

Meanwhile Eric had come to two decisions, one of them of some moment, the other important, too, when he stopped to reflect. The lesser was to order Joe a surplus Springfield rifle, Model 1903, that would carry its 155-grain bullet true for half a mile. He did not have it made over, as many sportsmen did; the army model which he had handled at Fort Yukon was well balanced and handy enough. It would be the best rifle in the village, by far the best for picking off caribou at very long range, and with it Joe could do a man's share in laying in winter meat.

His other decision stemmed from a controversy raging in Alaska and echoing in the halls of Congress and taking quite a little space in Outside as well as local newspapers.

It concerned the so-called Cunningham claims on coal lands granted by Secretary Ballinger of the Interior, and protested by an agent in the land office of the Department. According to this agent, Ballinger was dissipating Alaskan resources to enrich Wall Street.

Eric was quite sure that Ballinger had done no wrong and in fact was trying to develop the territory in the only way it could be developed, through private capital. He believed that all the to-do in Congress was a sop to the present trust-busting and anti-corporation feeling in America, stirred up by the ever-doughty, forever-combative Theodore Roosevelt, now out of office and eager to get back in. Thinking it over, knowing well he would be defeated by a heavy vote in southeastern Alaska, the most thickly populated part where he was almost unknown, still he decided to resign his post office at Circle City and to run for the office of Alaskan delegate to Congress in the election of 1910.

Eric conducted his campaign as he drove a dog sled over hummock ice, by steadily plodding along. His program was for as much home rule as he believed the Alaskans could manage, but he did not paint the future in the rainbow colors pictured by his main opponent, with Alaska immediately a state, all six hundred thousand square miles of her, good roads everywhere, thriving cities, the whole Tanana Valley in smiling cultivation, and with a governor appointed by the people instead of by the President. His addresses were brief. He was fond of saying that he "wanted to tell the whole country the trut' about Alaska," and a Panhandle paper pictured him in a better than average cartoon entitled "Trut'ful Andy visits his bosses." There he was shown signing away Alaska to plutocrats of Wall Street, receiving in exchange a big can of snoose.

Actually the picture won him a good many votes among the halibut and cod fishermen of the Southeast, most of whom were Norse, Swedes, Danes, and Finns who liked a little snoose themselves.

He spoke at Nome, St. Michael, the Kenai Peninsula towns, Valdez, Cordova, Juneau, Wrangell, Petersburg, Ketchikan, and old Sitka. When the returns came in it was immediately apparent that he had lost the race; even so the number of votes cast for him, not only in the North but in the Panhandle, made him a man to reckon with in future Alaskan affairs.

In the next two years he dealt mainly with the Gertrude

Mine, the Tekuh school close to his heart, and the advancement of a tall, lithe, brown-skinned boy who attended there. Early in 1912, affairs of great moment to Alaska began to shape. One was an Act of Congress terminating the District of Alaska and setting up the Territory of Alaska, with a legislature of eight senators and sixteen representatives. Another was the strengthening of a labor union of workers in the larger mines, who pressed for shorter hours and who were adamantly opposed by the owners, mainly Stateside corporations. Eric decided to run in his own judicial district for one of its four representatives to the new legislature convening in 1913.

That district was as big as four average states in the U.S.A., so again Eric got on the move. Now he visited not only the towns and big gold camps but the little camps to hell and gone up the creeks, the trading posts, and the roadhouses which were beside trails and on riverbanks, and were usually designated by their number of miles from someplace. He shook hands with everyone, and had very little to say. When pressed about the labor troubles he made what his opponents called a mealymouthed reply. "I believe in a fair deal for labor and a fair deal for capital, because Alaska can't get along wit'out either. If you elect me, I'll do what I t'ink best for the Territory."

A hand-printed newspaper in Circle City opposed him with fiery editorials and a series of cartoons, one of which depicted him astride a fence, with Wall Street on one side, and bent-backed miners with pick and shovel on the other. The caption was, "I yust t'ink I'll sit here till the wind blows steady."

Yet the people who met him or heard his brief speeches seemed to think that his utterances made sense, and they seemed to believe that he would, indeed, do what was best for the Territory. Of the four leading candidates in his district he polled the highest vote, and missed a clean majority over all the rest by a narrow margin.

It assured him a position of power in the coming session, to occur in Juneau. His mere election brought an invitation to a banquet there, at which all electees were to be guests of honor, and given in celebration of the new Territorial status, but he was somewhat surprised by being asked to make a short speech. The writer of the invitation and general chairman of the banquet turned out to be the wealthy miner, named Roberts, who had sat at the captain's table on that voyage of the *Victoria*, every sea mile of which seemed etched on his memory.

Mr. Roberts' opening paragraph was rather jocular. He recalled Eric's coming to table, and first mistaking him for an ignorant pan washer of the creeks. He confessed that his opinion had rapidly changed as the journey had progressed, and the magnitude of his mistake had been proven by Eric's public services at Nome, later at Circle City, and now in the "crucible of the polls."

It was no great trip upriver to Whitehorse, from where Eric took the White Pass Railroad down to Skagway, thence making his way to Juneau through Lynn Canal. He was met at the boat by Mr. Roberts and a small delegation of important Juneau citizens. Escorted to the new hotel in a Packard automobile, the first ever seen on these streets, he found that a suite had been engaged for him, by far the grandest in which he had ever set foot, let alone lain down on a bed. Mr. Roberts mentioned that the bill for a week's stay at the hotel had been "taken care of by the committee."

"I can't accept that, because I was coming down here anyway in a few days," Eric replied, "and I t'ink I'd better move to a smaller room."

"I am sorry," Mr. Roberts said, "and of course you understand it was only in the spirit of hospitality."

"He does," said another jovially, "and we all have our constituents to look to, don't we, Eric?"

It turned out that the new governor could not be present at the banquet, but other dignitaries were there, and quite a large representation of miners, some of them powerful in the union, others popular members of the rank and file, including such as were called bohunks—men with Slavic names. The menu was extensive and expensive, the cigars passed were immense Havanas with gorgeous bands, and French champagne flowed freely. To everybody's pleasure, the speakers preceding Eric spoke briefly, stressing the future development of the Territory and the necessity of good relations between labor and capital. To all of this Eric agreed.

Then the toastmaster gave him a brief nod and rose and said an astonishing thing.

"Now we are going to hear from the chief speaker of the evening."

He went on to say that Eric had been elected by the largest number of votes, in proportion to the number of voters, of any representative to the legislature. He had come to

Alaska at age eighteen and had made a little gold strike, and by "untold" labor had developed it into a valuable placer mine.

"Gentlemen, he still owns that mine, yet when you look at him you wouldn't think he was an ogre, slave-driving his employees, depriving them and their families of their just due." This was received with noisy laughter. "You could call him a capitalist," Mr. Roberts went on, "yet politically he is known as a moderate in everything, not against capital or labor either. I think he may give us some good advice about the so-called labor troubles that are at present retarding the development of the Territory. No one is in a better position to do so.

"Gentlemen, I give you Eric Andersen, a great Alaskan."

There was considerable applause, during which Eric turned brick red.

"T'ank you," he began. "Still, I t'ink there is some mistake. One of the speakers preceding me might have been the speaker of the evening but I am sure I am not. I was asked to give a brief talk. It will be brief. First I must correct one or two wrong impressions which his honor, the toastmaster, is working under."

The big room in the Oddfellows' Hall had fallen silent. The eyes fixed on him were curiously intent.

"My mine is a small mine and I have never employed any labor there. At present it is being worked on shares. I have bought boards from the Indians and supervised the building of their school, on which they worked free. I am not a great Alaskan. I'd have to do a great deal more for the nation and the Territory than I have yet done before I can call myself anything more than a good sourdough. And, it's true, I hope for good relations between capital and labor. I know our need of both, and I would fight any deprival of my rights as a mineowner. As a worker of my own mine, I don't want the hours to be too long or the gain too small."

The strange silence held and Eric wished he had a little snoose under his lip, because this was a trying moment.

"In the present dispute I can only say what I would do if I were the owners, or a paid worker," he went on, after a deep breath. "If I were the owner I'd pay good wages for reasonable hours, and if I couldn't afford that, or get new machinery and more efficiency to make up the difference, I'd say my mine wasn't any good, and I'd shut it down; and if I was a worker on that mine, I'd hold out for an eight-hour day, six days a week. That's plenty long enough for any man to work wit' pick and shovel and dynamite, and if I couldn't get that, I'd quit and look for another yob. T'ank you very much."

He sat down, but quite a number of people stood up, clapping and yelling. Of course all the bohunks did so, the union officials, the minister who had asked a blessing, and a good many businessmen. One after another of the miners joined them, until the mineowners and their representatives began to feel conspicuous, thumping their hands spasmodically and looking at one another with considerable disgust, so they, too, rose.

"That squarehead son of a bitch," one of them muttered to Mr. Roberts. "He's kicked over the applecart, and the ten-hour day is dead as a duck. Speaking of dead ducks, canvasback à la Maryland, wasn't it a swell dinner! Man, you can give a dinner!"

3

Early in the year 1911 a valuable employee of the Canadian Pacific Company, listed on the books as Captain L. H. Locke, was conferring with company executives in their offices in Vancouver.

He had had a fine record. Now, still in middle age, he was about to see the fulfillment of a dream.

"Cap'n, we're about to lay a new keel in the shipyards of Paisley, England," the president of the company told him. "In general, she's to be another Princess liner, but we've got a little tougher job for her than carrying summer tourists, and she's going to be weather-decked and have great stability, and we're going to run her all winter instead of mooring her or using her catch as catch can. She'll be about two hundred and fifty feet long, forty-four-foot beam, and draw twenty-four feet. We reckon her gross tonnage will pass twenty-three hundred tons."

Captain Locke was still known as a dour Scotchman. He merely inclined his head when the president paused.

"Well, Cap'n, she's going to be yours. You deserve her, and you'll get her. How many years have you been with us now?"

"Twenty-one, except for that little jaunt I made as first officer on the *Victoria*."

"That's a wonderful record. And speaking of the old *Vic*, I'm going to get Pike for the new liner, if I have to shanghai him from his own pantry. You see, we'll carry tourists like the others, but we're thinking about her in terms of the Alaskans, of whom there are going to be more every year, and of course our fellow Canadians in the Yukon Territory. Now, look. If we furnish them with luxurious transportation in winter, don't you think they'll stick with us in summer too, when we're competing with the American boats?"

"Yes, sir, I do think so. And if I'm to have her, I'll be glad to carry a lot of sourdoughs. I'm not a very sociable man, and I get on with them better than with tourists."

"The main thing is, you sail your ship, whoever she is. Well, that's about all—and to tell you you'll be taking her around the Horn mid-summer of next year. Oh yes. We've been thinking about her name. Why don't you give us a hand on that?"

"I'd like to." For Captain Locke believed in the importance of good names for vessels and had his own ideas about them.

"You haven't much of a selection, I'm afraid; but I'm inclined to let you have the say of such as are available. Of course you know we are naming our Princess ships after English princesses, with accent on the Stuarts, whom the ancestors of our founder supported."

"Yes, I knew they were cursed Jacobites," said Captain Locke, of good Scotch Protestant descent. Everyone smiled.

"Mary and Alice, directly descended from James I, are already taken. That leaves, let's see, Elizabeth who married Frederick V; Henrietta Maria, too much of a muchness; Catherine; and Sophia who married the Elector of Hanover, the mother of George I. Which of those appeals to you the most?"

"I like the name Elizabeth." He stopped and reflected; a moment ago he had mentioned his journey on the *Victoria*. "On second thought, if it's all right with you, I'll choose Sophia."

"Sophia. The *Princess Sophia*. You know, Captain, that's a very beautiful name. I didn't know you had this aesthetic side. Maybe we can get a real princess to christen her."

Something more than a real princess had already christened her, thought Captain Locke.

4

In the spring of 1914 Joe would complete the eighth grade at the Tekuh school. Since the year had started to come back, on December 22, the real New Year of all peoples, when thoughtful men began to reckon on what should be done in the coming year, he had wrestled with the problem of where to send Joe to high school. At first he leaned toward public school in Tacoma, where he himself had gone, but now the town had become a city, with asphalt instead of mudholed roads, hard on the feet of a youth raised in moccasins and mukluks, and where hunting and fishing would be hard to get without hired conveyance. Then the main decision was forced on him by event.

On June 28, the Archduke Francis Ferdinand was assassinated at Sarajevo. It would certainly start another Balkan war, and many had written that such a war could very easily spread with Germany craving empire and in deadly economic and naval competition with England, France panting to avenge her humiliation of forty-some years before, and Czar Nicholas rushing from one extreme action to another at the whims of his Hessian Czarina. On hearing the news, Eric decided to send Joe to a military academy.

There was a good one in a pleasant countryside in Washington State, which was popularly known as the Culver of the West. In the capacity of Joe's guardian, Eric applied by telegraph and received an application blank and a carefully worded letter. It was to the effect that since Joe's previous schooling had occurred in an upper Yukon village whose name did not appear on the map, he would have to undergo entrance examinations; however, if Mr. Andersen wished to fill in the forms and run the risk of the boy's rejection, he could present himself on such and such a date, and with our appreciation, etc., etc., yours sincerely.

When Eric, filling in the application, came to the line "Father of Applicant" he wrote stoutly, "Scott Harris (presumed)." For "Mother of Applicant," he gave Sant Pavlof. Then, grinning to himself, he wrote a postscript on the blank. He had happened to hear of this western Culver through talk of its rifle team, which competed against teams of other military colleges including that of the real Culver. Last year it had come out third in a nation-wide shooting match, much to the pride of Evergreen State boosters. Eric wondered how far the Culver of the West would go to win first place. So he wrote:

Before you reject my ward, Joe Harris, I suggest you let him test his ability as a marksman, since surely good shoot-

210

ing must be a matter of prime importance in a school stressing the military.

Eric did not grin when the time came to say good-bye to Joe at the landing at Tekuh village. The stripling was well dressed in Stateside clothes, so that he would get used to them before he sailed on the old *Victoria* from Nome. Even so, the strange attire did not make him look less Indian, and perhaps more so, for the white shirt and collar accented his pale brown skin darkened by wind and sun, the tight suit revealed a different muscular and bone structure than is usually seen on white boys of this age, and the hat curiously called attention to his humped nose and high cheekbones. He was Indianlike in another way, important to him now. His face showed no trace of emotion.

"Mist' Rick, if I should die Outside, would it be too much trouble to have my body brought up to Alaska, up the river, to be buried in the permafrost?"

The request was at odds with the last word, Eric thought, for one was pure Indian and the other was a white man's word, more used in books than in speech.

"Not by a damn sight. But what is there down there to kill you?"

"It's not what's there. It's what isn't there. There isn't the river, and the big woods, and the hunting and fishing, and the bright summer and the dark winter. I'm not sure I can live without them."

"Yes, you can, Joe, for you're going hunting now for a big trophy. Count it as that. If they let you in the school, I want you to graduate close to the top of your class. In everything I want you to show that an Indian half-breed can win big trophies from anybody going, as Yim Thorpe has shown what a full-blooded Indian can do. This first hunt may be eleven months long, counting the trip both ways. But you'll be home in July, when the geese are on the river."

"Good-bye, Mist' Rick."

"Good-bye, old sourdough."

Eric turned away, and a girl taller than her mother and with bright hues of hair and skin, yet with a suggestion of forest shadow in big gray eyes, came up to speak to Joe. He moved a little further away from passengers lining the rail.

"*Ohtziveh?*" she asked. If Eric had heard her he would have remembered Sant's using the same word as he and Sophia were leaving H'kah's house on their first visit to the village. It meant, "Will you come here?" or "Will you come back?" Eric had come back, one December night nearly fifteen years ago, and thereby a dark cloud had spread across his skies, never to give full passage to the sunlight, yet what came through shone strangely upon Joe.

"*Shohnoh*" (I do not know), Joe answered Vicky's question.

"I will always love you."

"I love you, Kah." This was his pet name for her, the village word for rabbit, and he had named her that a long time ago because she chewed like a rabbit when they had something extra good to eat.

"Remember that I'll be away too—at the nuns' school at St. Michael—and I won't get to go fishing very often, and never to go hunting. You write to me and I'll write to you. Let's both of us dream we're hunting in the woods, sneaking up on something. Good-bye, Joe. *Skookem!*"

"Good-bye, Vicky. *Hee, hee, hoh, hoh!*" And this was the outcry of the dancers in the Kashga, whom they had often watched, and its meaning had been lost long before the first white man sailed westward from Kamchatka, but somehow it seemed to invoke good luck.

She looked at his thin lips as though she wanted to kiss them, but people were watching, so she only squeezed his hand.

5

Joe had very little to do with his fellow passengers on the river steamer and then on the big white ship because a few of them, apparently of no common denominator except in this respect, appeared to resent a half-breed Indian youth traveling first class and wearing such good clothes and having such good manners. Perhaps there were more who felt the same, yet who hid their feelings as Joe hid his own. But the head steward succeeding Pike seated him at one of the best tables, as Pike himself would have done; and since Joe never spoke unless he was spoken to, and perhaps because that high-up table seated high-up people, he met with civil and even cordial treatment. For the rest he had his eyes, ears, and nose, all avidly busy. Long before the *Victoria* docked in Seattle he had come to a new comprehension of Alaska's size. It would even dwarf Texas, of which a man in a wide hat talked largely.

When Joe had his first good look at the exterior of the

school his spirits took a tumble. The campus had been described in the folder as "large and inviting and beautifully landscaped." Actually from one end of it to the other was long rifle range, a shorter distance than from Tekuh village to the Yukon River bank, and there was no Tekuh villager who would not swear in court that he lived smack-bang on the river. It was inviting in exactly the same way as a city park, with well-mowed grass and carefully tended trees. Unfortunately Joe had confused the verb "landscaped" with the noun "landscape." He had supposed that God had fixed it, not gardeners.

The walls of the college buildings appeared to be gray plaster over brick or wood, and the walks between had been laid out in straight lines and graveled. Still, there were great trophies to be won here, worthy of those being taken by the great Jim Thorpe, so he walked straight-backed to the building bearing the sign "Administration Offices," and went in. As he stood gazing about, a young man in uniform with a silver bar on each shoulder saw him through an open door and came hurrying out.

"Who are you, please?" he asked, with an odd expression on his face.

"Joe Harris, sir. I have applied for entrance to the school."

"Wait here a minute, Harris."

He went into an adjoining office, the door of which read "Adjutant." He closed that door, but the two rooms had an open connecting door; also his own door had been left open; and he had no idea of the sharpness of hearing that the quiet woods developed in good Alaskan hunters. Joe heard the conversation perfectly plainly.

"Well, Harris has showed up!" the lieutenant said in an excited tone.

"He has, has he? How does he look?" asked a deeper voice.

"Just as we suspected except for his clothes. His clothes are good enough. He's an Indian if I ever saw one."

"Clean?"

"Yes."

"Full-blooded?"

"I'd judge so, or at least three fourths."

"There's nothing in our bylaws, set up by our good and true board of governors, to permit us to exclude an Indian *per se*."

"When our lads write home that they are messing with an Indian, some of the parents in the Seattle Four Hundred may take it amiss. Look, Henry, he's two days late."

Apparently the lieutenant did not know that the *Victoria* had lain four days behind Nunivak Island during the raging of a northwest gale, Joe thought, but he would not dream of giving the excuse.

"I don't think the Old Man would employ subterfuge," the adjutant said. "He *did* go to West Point. The entrance fee has been paid, we said we'd give him his chance. Take him into the anteroom and give him those examination papers. If, at age fourteen, he passes 'em——"

"He's older than fourteen. He looks sixteen to me. I 'spect there aren't very good calendars in—what's its name—Tekuh village."

But in a moment Joe was seated at a table, with pen, ink, and foolscap at hand. The examinations were in arithmetic, American history, current events, geography, general science, and economics. Each had twenty questions. Handwriting, spelling, and neatness would be a factor in the grading. Joe wrote rapidly, although he had been told he could take three hours. Economics was the only one of the six subjects that had worried him until he examined the questions, a typical one being: Name three natural resources of the state of Washington. He answered it, "Fish, forests, and farmlands," because Joe had a quiet sense of humor, by no means rare in redskins.

He took his writings to the officer, who, after one startled glance at the first page, rushed them to the adjutant. This time Joe could not hear their conversation and waited calmly, as he might wait for a caribou at a salt lick, for something more than half an hour. Then he was told to go into the adjutant's office.

He found a soldierly-looking man of about forty, with a countenance and manner that Joe instantly respected.

"Stand at attention, Joe," the adjutant told him. "That means to stand straight, with your arms at your side. I am Major Barnes. First, I want you to tell me how old you are."

"Sir, I was born early in September 1900. My mother doesn't remember the exact date. My guardian chose September first. But by Indian counting I'm almost fifteen. They count age from December twenty-second of the preceeding year, the turn of the year, and according to that I'll be fifteen on December twenty-second of this year."

"You speak very good English, Harris."

"Sir, I am bilingual." And Mist' Rick had told him to begin every remark with "Sir" when he spoke to elders. But Eric had overdone it a little.

"Are you a full-blooded Indian?"

"Sir, I am five eighths white."

"I take pleasure in telling you you've passed the written examination. You will be proud to know that you've turned in perfect papers except for one odd mistake. In your paper on current events, in writing of the Olympic games, you spelled Jim Thorpe, Yim Thorpe. Such precision in examinations has not happened too many times at our school. There remains, however, an oral examination, conducted by our commandant, Colonel Travis. Just now he's drilling the battalion, so now would be a good time to grant your guardian's request, to see if you have the makings of a good rifleman, an important thing in our counting, since a good many of our graduates go directly into the military."

"Sir, I'd like to try it."

"The first- and second-year classmen carry wooden rifles, and on our short range shoot .22s. Would that suit you?"

"Sir, yes, if I can't stand the test with a Springfield."

The adjutant's eyes changed a little, narrowing rather than opening and Joe thought he might be a pretty good rifleman himself.

"It's quite possible, if you wish. We have the 1903 Springfield for our two upper classes."

"Sir, thank you."

The range was deserted except for their own party, Major Barnes, the lieutenant who had admitted Joe, another officer who wanted to come along, and an old fellow of all work who set up and took down targets. Breastworks provided a dead rest.

Joe looked at the paper target set at one hundred yards; it had a three-inch bull's eye.

"Take as long as you like to find your aim," Barnes advised.

"Sir, yes, but if you please I'd rather shoot freehand."

"You understand your score will be counted just the same as if you shot with a rest?"

"Sir, yes."

"Very well." His eyes looked shiny in the September sunlight. "Here is a clip of five cartridges, 155-grain bullets, for your magazine, and an additional cartridge to put in the

215

barrel. Please load, and you may fire when you're ready, Gridley."

This last address Joe did not understand, but it must be in the way of a joke, because the face of one of the officers looked frozen.

Joe had already looked to the sight. Now he stood up and fired, the six bullets gone in what must have been about twelve seconds. Apparently he did not aim at all, merely worked his bolt, swung his piece, and stopped the gun the same instant that he touched the trigger. Barnes noticed that his eyes were indrawn and hard and black as jet.

The old man walked rather slowly to the butt, keeping his eye on Joe to see that he did not start such wild shooting again. When he came to it he bent over to examine it, then very carefully removed the paper target and came on the run. His hand was shaking as he passed it to Barnes.

Major Barnes made no comment, even his face said nothing, as he passed it to the two other officers. As it went by, Joe saw all six holes were in the bull's eye and could be covered by a silver dollar. He was not at all surprised, for that was the way he had held.

Nor did the two officers speak, although their eyes were quite round. Barnes spoke at last.

"Harris, do you think you could do that again?"

"Sir, as many times as you want me to up to fifty rounds. After that I couldn't group my hits."

"In that case, I'm going to ask Colonel Travis to come over. Lieutenant Morris, will you go over to the drill field and say we've got something interesting for him to see?"

A new target was erected and the other two officers stood about saying nothing until Colonel Travis and the lieutenant appeared. Travis was about fifty and West Point was in his carriage and looked out of his eyes.

"Sir," said Major Barnes, "I thought you might like to see Candidate Harris shoot a rifle."

"Yes, Major, I would."

Joe repeated the performance except in one minor detail, this being that he had grouped the hits a little closer; natural enough, he thought, now that he was more used to the gun, and perhaps not so nervous.

Then Colonel Travis asked Joe a few questions.

"Harris, can other Indian boys, or men, shoot that well?"

"Sir, none that I know of."

"What about Alaskan white men?"

216

"Sir, I don't know any, but there is a white man in Dawson, in the Yukon Territory, who I *think* can beat me."

"I dare say. At what ranges do you shoot freehand or take a dead rest?"

"Sir, I shoot freehand at running game at all ranges. But if the range is very far, I do it only when we're hard up for meat. When the game is standing still and I can't get up to it, I take a rest at four hundred yards and up."

"How well do you score at those longer ranges?"

"Sir, with my own rifle—I know just how it carries—I can usually make a clean kill up to a thousand yards."

He looked at the other officers and they conferred together. Joe heard only a portion of their conversation.

"I wish we could put him on the team this year," Barnes was saying in his rather heavy voice. "He looks sixteen."

"Every day of it," the lieutenant broke in.

"There'd be nothing to stop us this side of the Mississippi," the adjutant went on, "and if we didn't beat Culver, I'd eat my service hat, cord and all."

"Barnes, you have all the wile and would employ the same opportunism as an old mess sergeant in the Regular Army. You know perfectly well if we ring in a marksman under sixteen and lie about his age, we'll be kicked out of the conference. The rule may be a foolish one—born shots of fourteen are no more careless with guns than skilled shots at sixteen—but we teach obedience here and must now and then practice it." Travis flashed a delightful smile.

"I suppose so, but we'll have to watch him to keep some of those tinhorn schools from swiping him. In fact I wouldn't put it past V.M.I. to shoot him against West Point."

"Well, we can bring him forth very quietly when he's sixteen—that is, if he likes it here."

"And that means——"

"Henry, do you think I'm a blinking fool?" Colonel Travis turned gravely to Joe.

"Stand at attention, Harris!"

"Sir, yes!" Joe did so.

"You are now a fully qualified student of this academy. You will go now and be assigned a room by the officer in charge. About face, march!"

6

On April 6, 1917, Joe was a year and two months from graduation. The great events of that day, re-echoing all over the world, soon to be known in the farthest gold camps up the creeks of the Yukon, caused him to make an application to the adjutant of the battalion, Major Barnes. Barnes heard him out and went in to speak to Colonel Travis, who presently summoned Joe to his office.

"Harris, I hear you wish to stop school and enlist," Travis said, without preliminary talk.

"Yes, sir. If I can, I'll come back after the war and make up the work."

"Major Barnes and I talked it over. We want you to complete your third year, which will end on June fifteenth, because our whole program is going to undergo a drastic change. If you do that, your scholastic and military record here, including your promotion last fall to a lieutenancy in the battalion, will justify us in recommending you and a few others in your class to Reserve Officers' Training Camps in the Armed Forces. The second series of those camps will begin late in August. Between now and June fifteenth the junior and senior classes will undergo rigorous training, equivalent to rookie training at Camp Lewis. As for the time between then and your call to duty in August, I'll make a suggestion which I hope you will accept. You haven't had time to go back and forth to Alaska during Thanksgiving, Christmas, and Easter holidays. You'll be way ahead of most of the men accepted at those camps, you can't get into action any sooner as an officer, and I hope you will spend those two months at home."

"I'd like to, sir."

"You won't need rookie training, which most applicants to those schools must have. Isn't your foster father in Juneau?"

"Yes, sir."

"It's only three days from Seattle. You may have time to take the White Pass Railroad to the upper river; I hope so. I'm not a sentimental man, but I served in one war, and this war is going to be truly hell. For you to go to France without a visit home would be bad for your morale. You can leave word at Juneau where to forward a telegram from military headquarters of this district."

So on June sixteenth Joe took himself off to Seattle, and by luck caught the *Princess Sophia*, of whom Mist' Rick had written and about whom all Alaska was agog. The sourdoughs had liked the idea of having a crack ship in the winter runs, stepping from the wet, chill docks to her warm

218

cabin and storm-weathered deck, and into all luxury that they could possibly desire, and they conspired together to catch her whenever possible. Captain Locke might be a bit dour, no backslapper certainly, a little standoffish until you knew him well; he remained their idea of a good skipper in treacherous waters. Who should preside in the dining saloon but old Pike, ornerier than ever, and still seeing to it that the meals were hot, tasty, and filling?

Joe wondered for what princess she had been named. He had never read about a Princess Sophia. One day, in a group of passengers, he heard one of them put the question to Captain Locke.

"She was from the southern part of the country, and she made all the other princesses look sick," Captain Locke answered, then turned away.

Mist' Rick was waiting on the Juneau dock in a rainstorm. He whisked Joe into a taxi and rushed him to the inexpensive hotel where he lived. In Mist' Rick's pleasant rooms the forty-year-old man and the seventeen-year-old sat down, and Joe heard the latest news of the upper river; the duck and goose flight this year, the prevalence of big game, the fish run, and who had died and who had been born at Tekuh village. His grandmother H'kah remained the best skin sewer in the village, despite somewhat unsteady hands. Pavlof still sat in front of the elders in the Kashga, still could deliver babies with hardly ever a loss. Sant and Sih had the best house in the village and the best boat, and Joe had a baby sister, born in the first days of spring, who had been named Mamu; almost a sacred word among the northern Athabaskas, Joe was thinking, because it meant "fire." The Gertrude Mine produced well.

"I'm very proud of the marks you made at school," Mist' Rick said.

"Thank you, sir."

"And I didn't t'ink you'd be long about deciding to join up. Maybe you've heard the old joke about one lady boasting to another lady, a beautiful brunette, that one of her ancestors came over on the *Mayflower*, and asking if the other lady could say as much. 'No,' the brunette lady answered, 'but one of my ancestors met the boat.' "

Joe uttered his short, harsh, Indian laugh.

Eric rose to get his whisky bottle, and to Joe's great surprise he mixed two drinks.

"You know, Joe, that Indians haven't a good reputation

219

for holding their liquor," Eric said. "You may be in the same boat with 'em, maybe not. But you'll have a lot of it passed at you overseas, and you might as well find out when there's nobody here but you and me, and nothing to do till tomorrow. Do you want to try it?"

"Yes, sir."

Eric handed him the glass, and both men sipped comfortably. Eric told him of the latest doings of the Alaska legislature, and of President Wilson's plans for the Territory. Then they talked of what was on every tongue, the failure so far of an Allied break-through on the Somme, the English fiasco about Reims, and the revolution in Russia. "But America isn't going to send her men for replacements under English and French commanders," Eric said. "When we come, it will be as an army."

Eric asked Joe how the drink had hit him; for he could see no telltale sign.

"It hasn't hit me at all," Joe answered. "I feel comfortable and easy of mind."

"That's all right. That's the way a drink is supposed to make you feel. I'll fix you one more and if that satisfies you, you've graduated from the course. You can take two drinks anywhere at one session, and walk off with them."

But perhaps it was that second drink that emboldened Joe to ask a question. He put it in an easy voice.

"I haven't heard from Vicky for a good while. Have you heard from Mrs. Ford how she's getting along?"

"No, but I heard from Vicky herself—in reply to my letter that you were coming to visit me before joining up. Her school let out in late May, and it happens one of her school friends lives here, and Vicky expects to visit her about the middle of July. That will give us time to take the White Pass Railroad to Whitehorse and go down-river to our old stamping ground."

Joe's eyes brightened, but he said, with some hesitation, "I don't want to miss any telegrams from the Army."

"You won't. You don't know how civilized we're getting on the upper Yukon. Telegrams relayed to Dawson would reach you by our new mail boat in at least four days. And, now, this is a little bit hard to put. As you probably know perfectly well, Vicky's going to stay with her friend but she's coming to visit you."

"I don't know whether that's true. Her letters have been getting shorter and further apart. Remember I haven't seen

220

her for close to a year and the last time was at her school, with nuns going in and out of the parlor. We talked in English. I didn't dare say an Indian word. I couldn't even call her Rabbit."

"It may not be much better here, you know—but I t'ink it will," Eric said thoughtfully.

"I doubt it. She won't want to be seen going with an Indian."

"She's thought of all that, and coming down here yust the same. Besides you'll have the academy uniform with the insignia of a lieutenant of cadets, and no other young man in Juneau is wearing those as yet. You can take her to the movies, fishing in Tee Harbor, and walking around. If there are any dances, I'd let other fellers take her there. And you and she can make little jaunts that no one knows about but you two. I t'ink you'll have a nice visit."

They put by all that when they went to Skagway and took the hair-raising White Pass Railroad to Whitehorse. Once more they put forth on the great river, and it had not changed a particle, and the land very little. Wild geese rose in clamoring crowds. Once they saw a family of black bears meandering on the shore.

"By the way, how's old Slewfoot?" Joe asked.

Eric looked sad. "Joe, he was getting mighty old. If he was only five when I first saw him, about 1896, he was twenty-five last year, which must count at least eighty in a man. I think he was fully ten at that time, he was so big and rangy. Well, last October he got so weak and scrawny I was tempted to shoot him but couldn't quite make it, and decided to let him die in his winter sleep, since he didn't have enough fat to pull him through. The heavy snows came early. I thought, oh hell, I'll shoot him a moose, and I did, but I couldn't go on killing for him. I was watching him when he gnawed the last bone. He looked out across the snow, across the frozen river to the mountains where he had his den. Then he did something I've never known a bear to do—stand up and give a long cry, almost as clear as a bugle sounding taps. Then he hit it off through the snow.

"I followed him for about an hour, he was so wobbly, and found him lying dead. That was the end of old Slewfoot and I felt real bad."

7

Joe disembarked from the river steamer at Tekuh village, and the Indians at the landing stood in a posture that Eric had rarely seen, although they made almost no sound. Eric went on to the house with a lovely ghost, one that never took a pale and ghostly form, but which was as beautifully tinted as the winter sky when the northern lights played, because she was made of Eric's memories. He saw to some improvements in the flumes and sluices of the mine, paid a visit to Circle City, which was entering into decline, and, without in the least knowing why, took a long ramble one day to the scene of the death of Frank Ford. Under a fallen log he found the skull, long naked, as good as any man's skull at long last, Eric thought, and left it where it lay. Also he found a badge of the Yukon Order of Pioneers, which he picked up to give to Fannie, although this, too, was without good reason. On some impulse that he could never explain he looked into a hole in a fallen tree trunk. There he found the remains of a leather wallet, no doubt carried there by pack rats, empty except for a sheet of paper, on which was printed *S.S. Victoria,* and which came from the ship's writing room. Below this heading, carefully and neatly written in ink, were some verses, a good many words of which were still legible.

Eric's neck prickled as he recognized them. They had been written by one of the ship's crew as a toast to Sophia on her wedding night, and had been copied and pocketed by a good many sourdoughs. It was a strange and baffling commentary on Frank's nature that he had kept it to the last.

8

Joe had spent only two rather worried weeks at Tekuh village—no news of the war reached that wintry Arcadia—when he received a telegram on the mail boat, forwarded from Dawson.

It was from an adjutant at Camp Lewis, Washington, and it read:

YOU ARE HEREBY NOTIFIED THAT YOUR APLICATION TO THE INFANTRY OFFICERS' TRAINING CAMP HAS BEEN ACCEPTED, AND YOU ARE TO REPORT HERE FOR INDUCTION INTO THE ARMED FORCES, AUGUST 25, 1917.

Somebody had lied about his age, Joe thought, with a big grin, for he merely signed the blank, leaving the school authorities to fill it in. Now he entered happily into all the

222

village enterprises, hunting, fishing, gorging, and since he was a man, he danced the dance of the returning salmon in the Kashga, shouting, "Hee, hee! Hoh, hoh!" The language he had not spoken for more than a year was sweet in his mouth. He even gave an Ingersoll watch to the shaman, after which certain medicine was made that the war would not be over until he got there, and he would win certain prizes, not all of them of metal or ribbon.

Joe saw nothing of Fannie Ford—the school had been closed and she was paying a visit to Circle City. But Eric saw her there at the hotel, and there she introduced him to a tall, fair-haired man of about forty who reminded Eric of someone he had known but could not now identify—one of those irritating half-perceived reminders that hang on the fringe of the brain. His name was Bert Gibson, and Fannie asked Eric to join them in a hamburger with beer in what was called the dining room at such Alaskan hotels, actually a cramped lunch counter, with two tables, very rarely used, in an alcove. Eric was perplexed, and then a little worried, by the shine in Fannie's eyes.

"Bert and I have something to tell you," she said, in a childish voice glowing with excitement. "You're the first one we have told, because you're such an old friend. Bert and I are going to be married tomorrow and take a camping trip into the woods for our honeymoon."

"Why that's yust fine," Eric said.

"He's been coming down to visit me at Tekuh, and invited me to come to visit here—so we could see each other in fairly civilized surroundings, and be sure we weren't making a mistake. Well, we weren't disappointed in each other, we found we felt just alike about almost everything and had so many interests in common that both of us wanted to go ahead. Of course I told him about those bad years—it was hard going, but I made it. He understood it perfectly and said, 'Let the dead past bury its dead.'"

"My very words," Bert broke in eagerly. "It was seventeen years behind her, and in Alaska there's always a new tomorrow. Up here we live in the present and future, not the past. Besides, when it came to laying cards on the table, I held plenty I wouldn't want anyone to see."

"That's yust fine," Eric said, only to realize he had made the same remark only a moment ago.

"He's greatly interested in my work, as I am in his, and we're both at an age—I'm thirty-six and Bert's thirty-eight

—when we can make our marriage the kind of quiet, nice success we both want."

"I'm sure of it. And what you yust said makes me t'ink you're going on with the Tekuh school."

"I wouldn't drop that, even for Bert. Forgive me, Bert, for saying that, but you're big enough not to want me to. We're both going to live in my quarters at Tekuh. Bert's a real sourdough—he's been in Alaska eight years—and you tell Eric what you're going to do."

"I'll keep busy, Mr. Andersen, no fear of that," Bert said. "I'm a good trapper, and I'll have no trouble making a good catch, for you know the Indians don't trap very hard, they'd rather take it easy with hunting and fishing, and I don't blame them, being what they are; they haven't the incentive to make money. That will keep me busy during the freeze-up. In the summer I expect to prospect a little—there's a lot of gold here on the upper river that's never been found—and I've got a process for drying salmon, taught me by a fellow straight from Norway, that doesn't make it smell like the dried fish of the natives and takes out a lot of the wild taste. You'd say you never tasted any better grub unless it's Fannie's cooking. I feel sure there'd be a big market for it in the States, to eat on crackers like the rich people do before dinner. It could become a big seller at delicatessens and at kosher stores. So you see I'll have plenty to do in the summer, too."

"Isn't that a fine plan, Eric?" Fannie broke in, her pretty face flushed.

"It sure sounds fine to me." And then steadying himself, "The government wants every increase in food products that's possible in these war years."

"I hadn't thought of that," Bert remarked, with great satisfaction.

"I've been very lonely, Eric," Fannie said earnestly, "especially with Vicky away. And so has Bert. And now he wants to ask you to pay us both a big honor. Ask him, Bert."

"I've heard so much about you from Fannie that I'd like to invite you to stand up with me at the marriage tomorrow."

"I'll be at the wedding and kiss the bride," Eric said, "but Bert, it's an old wedding custom, and a lucky one, for the groom to ask an old friend to be his best man. If not that, a brother of the bride. I want you to do that. I

224

wouldn't feel right about taking that important office on such short acquaintance."

"I guess you're right, at that," Bert said. "Fannie, I'll ask Bill Perry. You like him, he's a nature's nobleman, and he's sure been a good friend to me."

Fannie looked a little hurt, but she was so happy underneath that the pang did not last long. The wedding would occur at the Methodist church at six o'clock in the afternoon—such a pretty time of day—and would be followed by an outdoor reception. Soon after this, Eric glanced at his watch and asked to be excused until time for the ceremony.

As he was leaving the dining room he glanced back and suddenly he knew of whom Bert Gibson reminded him. The face was stronger than the one he remembered now so well. Bert was more the man than the other, and was a good fellow who would love Fannie and probably make her happy, but the fact remained there was something about him that recalled Frank Ford.

9

Eric and Joe kept in touch, and Eric caught the upriver steamer that would pick Joe up at Tekuh village. The two returned the way they had come, via Whitehorse and the White Pass Railroad. Joe was once more in his cadet uniform and showing the natural good manners, refined at military school, that delighted those passengers who appreciated native capacities, which seemed an anomaly to some, and caused a few to murmur darkly such remarks as, "Just put a bottle of sourdough booze in his reach and all that polish would rub off quick, and you'd see the real siwash underneath."

In Juneau, Joe went at once to call on Vicky, who had arrived ten days before and to whom Joe had sent a telegram from Dawson. She was going on eighteen, the age when any pretty face has a clean-cut look, a freshness, and a joyousness in life itself, a trust in forever spring, that causes men of middle age to look at them not with yearning for their own lost youth but with eyes more appreciative than young eyes, and at the same time a sympathetic sinking of the heart. Vicky's face was somewhat more than pretty, perhaps merely because a chisel had been at work, as it had on Eric's face when he was only twenty-three. If Joe knew it at all he did not know its kind; he knew only that

225

her face differed in some moving way from other pretty faces he had seen, and it caused a re-echoing in his brain of all he had known of beauty. She was tall and long-limbed and moved gracefully. He had had something to do with that, he thought—the long hikes they had made together, the stealthy stalking with every muscle under control, their worming their way over snow or tundra until every muscle ached. The good meat and fish of Tekuh village might also have been a factor in her shaping. She looked the way a girl should.

Just now her gray eyes were glistening with excitement. Her friend Lucile had opened the door to him, and was standing there, and when he had turned to Vicky he gently sniffed her cheek, and what complicated impulse caused him to do that, he had no notion. When they had talked only a moment or two, Vicky's gaze flicked briefly to Lucile. Her look had been proud before, defiantly proud; now it showed pure pride. The tall man who stood like young Tecumseh had given Lucile a pleasant flutter. If his dashing uniform had helped start it—Juneau girls along with those elsewhere had become aware that the best-dressed men in America wore uniforms—it had called attention on his black, magnetic eyes and his bony, aristocratic, virile face.

In the following fortnight they were almost inseparable from mid-morning until late in the summer evening. The people of Juneau became used to seeing them together, and although some of them looked embarrassed or away, or shook their heads when they passed on, the larger number realized the two had been childhood friends in a heathen village way upriver and that Joe was going into training soon, and that dusky Indians of another skin, from another continent, were fighting like demons on the western front, black Senegalese led many a charge, refusing to kill except with steel, and Japan had joined the Allies.

They went to the movies, once to the best restaurant for dinner with Lucile and her beau, and the same four attended a public dance where they changed partners but where both girls declined all other invitations. Even so, as Joe and Vicky were returning to their seats, they heard a respected businessman, his voice more resonant than he realized, make comment.

". . . a public dance," he was saying. "If one of the soldiers brought a pretty young half-breed squaw I wouldn't think a thing. But it's t'other way round that makes me . . ."

Neither let the other know that both knew both had heard.

The woods were too wet for pleasant walking without hair-seal pants and mukluks, but southeastern Alaska had been described as a mountainous country with valleys full of water, so there was a world of places to go in Eric's boat, with an auxiliary sail and a built-in gasoline motor. Wearing old clothes, with a brimming lunch basket and a bottle or two of beer, they trolled for king salmon, that noble fish weighing up to fifty pounds; and Vicky squealed with excitement when the churning beauty was brought to gaff.

"I like this better than any fishing or hunting we've ever done," she declared.

"I don't believe you. This is sport fishing, which almost anyone can do. It takes a real sourdough to sneak up to a wild honker in a tundra pool."

"A real Indian, you mean. All I did was follow you and do what you told me. I suppose you'd never be content to live anywhere but up there in the sticks, let alone in the States."

"I might be contented if I made myself to do it, but I'd never be happy."

"They're the same thing."

"No, they're not."

"There's fine hunting and fishing too in some of the mountainous states."

"I know it, but they're not Alaska. Rabbit, do you know what the name means?"

"I don't think you should call me Rabbit any more. I don't any longer draw back my lips when I chew. The nuns taught me better than that."

"You might answer my question—Victoria!"

"No, I don't know what it means and I don't much care."

"I'll tell you, though. It means 'The Great Country.' It must be in one of the languages of the Kamchatka coast, for the Russians heard and recorded it, and that's what made Bering and Chirikof come through the strait. It *is* the great country and think of it being still here, for people like you and me, in the year 1917 still almost as wonderful as when we natives had it to ourselves."

"Sometimes I wish you still had it to yourselves—and I

227

was the only white girl. Let's go back, Joe. We've got enough fish, and I want to read a real sad book and cry. I love you, and you can kiss me if you want to, and then in two days you'll be sailing off on the *Princess Anne*, and the next thing I know you'll get killed. Then we certainly won't go pot-hunting any more, and I'll marry a nice clerk living in Seattle and have a little house and some babies. And Alaska will be like something I dreamed about—in some ways a bad dream."

They made the forlorn journey back to town, and that evening Joe ate with Eric in a Chinese restaurant, then the two men had a drink in the latter's rooms. At ten o'clock the streets were turning shadowy and almost still, and the salt smell came in the window along with the pungent fragrance of the conifers from the outlying islands. When Joe had finished his glass he set it down and declined a second. "I've got something to tell you before I go to bed," he said.

"All right."

"On the last day I was in school Colonel Travis made the battalion a little speech in the assembly hall. The main point was that the war was a bloody business, and this war was the bloodiest of all wars. He said already the number of casualties in the French and English armies would have been unbelievable to the old military authorities, and we'd have our share when we really got started breaking the Hindenburg Line. Then he went on to say that the infantry, the doughboys, were going to bear the brunt. Maybe in future wars the Air Force would take over but in this war the airplanes weren't developed enough and couldn't fly far enough for them to be anything but a damned dangerous side issue. He said when foot soldiers attack a strongly fortified position the slaughter is something awful. Look what happened to the German armies at Verdun."

"God, what a battle!"

"The last thing he told us didn't sound very good, but we had to take it. He said the records show that the casualties among junior officers, men leading companies and platoons, were all out of proportion to casualties in the ranks. The reason was, of course, the German snipers picked them off."

"That's true."

"The whole point I'm making, Mist' Rick, is that I expect to be an infantry officer. That's what I've been trained for. The only other corps I'd like as well would be the Army Air Force and I've heard that's going to be an elite outfit

228

which probably wouldn't welcome an Indian; anyway I doubt if I could shoot well with a gun on a swivel. The chances are I'll come back, but I may not. A lot of infantry officers and men won't come back, unless the job's a lot quicker than we think, and there's not much but chance who gets it and who doesn't. And that's why I wanted to come up and talk to you tonight."

"What's on your mind, Joe? The sooner you can get it off, the better."

"I was raised to believe that my father was a drunken doctor who left the squaw he was living with to hump another. His name was Scott Harris, and he's alive somewhere in Alaska. Well, if I thought it was true —that he was my father—I'd make the best of it. But I don't think he is. No one has ever told me he's not, still I think that my mother and Father Pavlof and H'kah—maybe our teacher and a few more—know he's not. If you ask me for the truth, I believe almost everyone in the village is almost sure he's not, although they don't say a word, out of loyalty to someone they know is a great sourdough."

He fell silent, and both men heard the metallic tick-tick-tick of the alarm clock on Eric's bed stand. A boat on the bay whistled shrilly. His face deeply lined, Eric started to open a small round can, only to shut it again.

"You say you don't think Dr. Harris is your father?" Eric said, his voice very low and deep. "Who do you think is?"

"I think you are."

"Joe, when you were born I was married to the loveliest woman I ever saw or hope to see. My only visit to your village about nine months before then was when I went to get Pavlof to deliver her baby, with which she was already in labor. If I was your father, I must have begotten you on that very visit. That wouldn't be a very pleasant thing for you to live with, would it?"

"I could live with it. I'm a man; you made me become one pretty young. I wouldn't know what the circumstances were, but I do know you're a man too, a greater man than I can ever be, and if you committed adultery that night, you were under great temptation that at the moment you weren't able to withstand."

"Why, then, with Sophia gone, haven't I acknowledged you—why would I have gone to a great deal of trouble to keep the secret?"

"I think I understand that too. You see, I've thought a
229

lot about it. Sophia—Vicky told me her name—died on the night Sant brought me to your house. I think she went out and lay down in the snow and died. She was a great lady, Vicky said—maybe she married a sourdough, the son of an immigrant, against a lot of people's advice and perhaps opposition. She wouldn't ever want them to know that you'd been untrue to her. All your life since, you've acted according to the way she'd want you to act. I don't know how I know that, but I do know it. She's your guiding star."

"She's my northern light," Eric answered.

"Why did you run for Representative to U. S. Congress, when you knew you'd be defeated? Why did you go into public life, knowing it would make you leave the upper river that you love, your home where she had lived with you? It was all for her sake."

"In spite of all that, you still want me to acknowledge you as my son?"

Joe shot to his feet and began to walk about the room, his face like a wooden mask.

"Not acknowledge me publicly, only to me, myself. That's all I want. I'll live and die Joe Harris, perfectly happy, if you can do that much. But I want a real father, not a shadow. I want one who loves me, not one who's scattered his bastards all over Alaska and doesn't give a damn for any of them. I would be proud of you if you were just a sourdough who'd done what he could for me, let alone what you are. I don't need to tell anyone ever, except maybe my wife and children, if I live to have them. If I die in France, I want it to be in my soul when it takes off. Is that too much to ask?"

"By Yesus, it's not. You are my son. You've taken the place of the little son I lost. I'll tell you one more t'ing, that maybe you'll like to hear, then I've got to get off by myself a little while. I had sworn I would tell you before you sailed. I kept putting it off—it was a hard chore—but I would have told you, I swear to God. And now t'ank God, it's behind me."

With a twisted face, Eric sped into the next room. Joe went out the other door, downstairs, into the balmy moist night, and walked to the waterfront. No one saw him there, this half-breed; he was alone; and he wept a long time in silence, the awful pride which his fate enforced at last granting mercy.

8. The Dark Falcon

On the almost endless eve of his departure for Camp Lewis, that of August twentieth, Joe went with Vicky on a long walk up the road toward the village of Amalga. Both were dressed for hiking, and at length they found a log not too rotted by the rains to afford a pleasant seat offering a good view of Lynn Canal. This hundred-mile-long inlet was oddly named, since it was no work of man, and instead one of the noblest of the Alaskan fiords, with rugged shores and many wooded islands. At its head lies the town of Skagway, which is the foot of the White Pass leading to Lake Bennett, whence flows the Lewes River to meet the Pelly and form the Yukon.

"Think of a river rising within fifteen miles of tidewater, flowing two thousand miles in a great loop, and finding the sea again," Joe remarked. "It's just wonderful."

"In your opinion anything that is Alaskan is wonderful," Vicky answered.

"You're wrong about that. Black flies? More mosquitoes than the delta of the Mississippi? Devil-club? What about pack rats and wolverines? I guess I don't dislike either of those; Mist' Rick admires their spunk. There are a lot of things I do like, you the best."

"Yes, I'm an Alaskan. I can't get out of being one till I move away. How do you like going away?"

"I wouldn't like it one bit unless I was going to war."

"You *want* to go to war? To kill people, or to get killed?"

"The right and wrong of it is not my business. I don't even think about it. We're in the war and I'm in a hurry to go with the other fellows."

"You're a savage, Joe."

"I suppose so. Come to think of it, the Athabaska Indians are a warrior people. We've calmed down some up here, the country gives us enough fighting, but we used to raise hell with the coast tribes, and did you know that the Apaches are Athabaska too?"

"Do you realize we may never see each other after tonight? I'm not going to the ship."

"No, I can't realize it, but that doesn't mean it can't happen."

"If you're killed, you won't see me again, unless at some place Indians won't want to go, and you won't see Alaska. Leave me out of it. Just leave in Alaska. Isn't that enough so that when you get to war you won't try to win it all by yourself? Of course you've got to obey orders and do your part, but you don't have to go sneaking up on the German snipers. You needn't lead night raids through the barbed wire just for the hell of it. 'I'll get me a king and a kaiser, too'—that's the new song. I wish I had never laid eyes on you."

"Rabbit, that's pretty rough."

"You won't do what I ask. If you'd promise certain things, I'd do anything you ask—tonight. I'd marry you tonight, or stay all night with you without our being married."

"What kind of things?"

"Not to try to win medals. Not try to be a hero. Not do anything 'beyond the call of duty'—aren't those the words we see in the papers? Eric taught you that because you're an Indian you have to beat everybody. That's all right after the war's over, beat everybody shooting, trapping, or whatever your job is, but why beat everybody in getting killed? Who would you be doing it for? You know how lots of the white people up here treat Indians—like dirt! What has the government ever done for you—a little school here, a hospital there—that you'd give your life getting it out of trouble with the Germans? After the war there's going to be big development up here. Lucile's father says so. He says airplanes will be improved and be the main transportation. A lot of good that will do you, with your head blown off by a German shell. If you live you might have an airplane of your own to go to places no one has ever seen, a two-seater. What do you get when you're dead?"

Joe thought hard about this last, to save him from thinking just now of the offer she had made. His pulse throbbed slow and strong in his finger tips. Yes, Alaska was the perfect country to utilize airplanes.

"What more would I have to promise?" he asked.

"I was going to say something else, but I won't say it now. Maybe when you come back Alaska will be changed and I won't have to say it. Just promise the other."

"There's not much to ask, not to volunteer for dangerous missions or take more chances than the other fellows. Of course I'll promise." He seized both her hands and she felt their hard strength and tension, a vitality that she never

232

perceived in anyone but him, changing and quickening her inner life and seeming to change her outer world so that it appeared sharper, more vivid, more real. There was something she should think of now, something that she should remember. It was not his Indian blood, which she had come to accept as his very self, whom she loved. And now its outcropping in his jet-black eyes and his hawk look caused delicious tingling to cross her skin.

He was whispering, "Break ice . . . Indian fashion . . . here in the woods . . ."

"No, we'll hike into town. I'll give you that long to cool down and think it over. Let's start."

They paced rapidly about a mile. They were within sight of the harbor, its little boats to be dwarfed tomorrow by the big boat, when Vicky suddenly stopped.

"I won't be over there to make you keep your promise," she said.

"I have never broken a promise to you."

"That was your Indian blood. Indians do keep their promises to people they care for. I remember now what I couldn't think of before—your white blood. What does a white man care about a broken promise or a lie when he wants something real bad? Maybe Eric is different——"

"I don't know that he's different. He's bigger than the most, that's all."

"Well, we'll go on into town and you leave me at Lucile's house. Tomorrow I will go to the ship to see you off. I won't say anything more till then."

"Then" came soon. About ten young men, enlisted at the recruiting offices in Juneau, were sailing today to report to various camps, and they stayed close to one another even when they talked to their families and sweethearts, and Joe was one of them, in a swiftly forging bond with them that not one of the others questioned. It was the biggest crowd that old-timers could remember assembled on this dock. Its excitement and emotion rose like static electricity in a thundercloud. When the next-to-the-last bell sounded Vicky took Joe's hand and led him a short distance from the thickest part and began to speak rapidly in the village tongue.

"I've got something to tell you, Joe. It's only a dream I had last night, but it was a bad dream. Do you remember, long ago, we were coming back from hunting and we stopped to watch a hawk hunting fool hens? That part— not the rest that happened—came back as clear as though it

233

was before my eyes. I saw that very tree, the hawk swooping and darting. Do you remember that it couldn't find the hens until one of them flew, then it pounced and killed? Then, when I was half awake, it seemed that you were the fool hen and the hawk was a German aviator."

Joe did not answer for a long half minute and a very strange expression came into his usually impassive face.

"Rabbit, don't you remember the old people saying that dreams go by opposite? The dream of a marriage means a funeral—things like that. Maybe some German flyer was the fool hen and I the hawk, and he made a mighty bad mistake to take wing when I was around."

She gave him a quick, startled glance and a strangely proud glance; then she said quickly, "It was a dream. It didn't mean anything, because you're going to be an infantry officer. You say you couldn't shoot well with a gun on a swivel. If you join any other corps you should go into the artillery. Wouldn't you love to shoot the big guns?"

"I wouldn't want to take time to figure out the trajectory." He had switched to English. "Was the hawk you saw in the dream a white hawk or a dark-colored one?"

"He was snow white," she said, her eyes fixed on his.

Just then the last whistle blew.

"Joe, I take back what I told you last night," she went on, in low tones. "Do what you have to do, what your nature makes you do, but remember I'm here, so is Eric, and come back to us."

"As Mist' Rick would say, 'I t'ink I'll come back.'"

She held out her arms and he kissed her tear-wet lips, and no one in the throng looked at them, and if any were glancing in that direction they looked away.

A moment later he was waving at her from the rail, and laughing his harsh Indian laugh at her attempts to be heard above the roar of the crowd.

2

Joe packed his cadet uniform in his trunk and reported at Camp Lewis in everyday civilian clothes. There he was treated in the military everyday way, lining up to have his fingerprints taken, lining up to be sworn in, lining up to get his uniform and outfit, lining up for chow. The physical examination had been a lick and a promise. "Hell, you'll do," the doctor had said, after what was called short-arm inspection, making him cough for signs of hernia, and a few

234

thumps on his chest. At first roll call he stood near the head of the line, with the tall fellows, and, since they were marched on the double-quick to the drill field, Joe felt sorry for the short-legged men in the rear.

In the next few days he did kitchen police and latrine duty. Evidently this was for the sake of his morale, because shortly the course of training became so hard that there was simply no time for it between reveille and lights out, and the work was done by an attachment from some other outfit. Evidently the need of shavetails in the swelling Army was very great indeed. It did not help matters that the commissions of more than half of the officers at the training camp were very new. However, the sergeant major, Twiggs, had served in the Army twenty of his forty years, and junior officers could speak to him in private about their problems that they did not dare take to the senior officers.

In the first fortnight Joe had bayonet practice, and the yell he was told to give as he impaled the dummy was so truly an Indian war whoop that his buddies promptly named him Apache Joe. On the day that Twiggs summoned every man in Joe's platoon separately to his office, he had not yet fired his rifle. The purpose was the filling out of some forms.

The top lines caught Twiggs's eye.

"You give your father's name as Scott Harris, M.D.," he remarked.

"Yes, sir."

"Was he an Indian doctor? You don't look like you've got white blood."

"No, sir, he was a white doctor."

"After his name you've written 'presumed.' What does that mean?"

"My mother said he was my father, but it was never proved."

"God almighty! Have we got a bastard in our ranks! How did that get by the board of examiners?"

"Sir, I guess they don't give a damn."

"Well, I don't either. Someone told me that Alexander Hamilton, a pretty good general under Washington, was a bastard."

"Yes, sir, from Nevis in the West Indies."

Twiggs glanced again at the lines covering education. "So you went to one of them military schools? At least they taught you how to look smart and stand at attention. Some-

235

times those graduates want to tell us how to run a war——
Wait just a minute. That school won the national rifle tournament for secondary schools last year. Did you try for that team?"

"Yes, sir, I did."

"Well, how did you come out?"

"I came out captain."

"Could you be that Indian I read about in the papers? He was first in every event and shot like lightning. They gave him a great play on the sporting page and his name was something like Harris."

"Yes, sir."

"Good *God* almighty! Does anybody around this camp know it?"

"Nobody's mentioned it."

"Well, don't tell anybody. The day after tomorrow we're going to have our first go on the range. Most of the men there have had rookie training and some of 'em will be fair shots. Do you think you can beat them all?"

"I think so, and the instructor too."

"That gives me an idea. Don't you fail me, because I'm going to put myself out on a limb. There's a tough old instructor, well-named Blood—a master sergeant and a whale of a good shot himself. He'll give you some rough talk before you shoot, that's his way. You keep your trap shut and I'll stand up for you. Then when your turn comes you get busy with that rifle."

The prospect reminded Joe of his first day at the academy and he intended to shoot as Jim Thorpe had played football at Carlisle College.

When it came the turn of his platoon, Master Sergeant Blood more than lived up to his ferocious name. The sight of an Indian among the trainees excited him to a masterly effort.

"A redskin in our midst," he began. "What's your name —Sitting Bull?"

"No, sir, it's Joe Harris."

"I reckon you can shoot a bow and arrow pretty good?"

"I've had practice in it, sir."

"I've heard that no Indian can savvy the science of the rear sight, and they shoot off the front sight. Is that right? If it is, maybe I'd better warn that company drilling in the next field to move off somewheres. Have you ever had a Springfield in your hands before you joined up?"

"Yes, sir."

"Have you had rookie training?"

"No, sir."

"Just graduated from Carlisle College, I bet you, with a friend in Congress."

At this point Sergeant Major Twiggs raised his voice in mild protest.

"Blood, that's no way to steady the nerves of a green hand."

"I'm running this range, Sergeant Major Twiggs. I take orders from the adjutant. This Indian will have worse than this before he starts shooting up the scenery in France."

"Excuse me, Blood, but you may have picked on the wrong man. Candidate Harris looks to me like a rifleman. I could easily be mistaken but I have a kind of psychic feeling that I'm not. You didn't know I was psychic?"

"No, and I don't give a damn."

"I'll tell you what. The men ought to see you shoot to inspire them. Supposin' you borrow one of the men's rifles and get off a clip. Then see how close Harris can come to tying you."

"If he can come within ten points—no, I'll say five—at any target you set up, I'll eat the target."

"You needn't do that. Just make a little bet."

"To use an old saying, put up or shut up, any amount you name, Sergeant Major!"

"Then I'll say ten dollars."

"What?" And Blood looked at Joe again.

"You said 'any amount I name.' I named ten dollars. Also, I get to set up the targets. I'll tell you what they are when I've talked to the men."

"You better tell 'em to make it easy," Blood said in somewhat faltering bravado as Twiggs borrowed his megaphone.

"Target tenders, attention," he bawled. "When I yell 'Target' stand up all six of the cardboard men at once, and leave 'em twelve seconds, and take 'em down."

"Yes, sir," someone yelled from the safety ditch. "Who have you got, Buffalo Bill?"

"Nobody could hit more than three of 'em in that time," Blood said with ire. "Twiggs, have you gone crazy?"

"Like a fox. Are you ready, Sergeant Blood?"

"I sure am."

Twiggs yelled, "Target." At once six cardboard men shot up from the ditch by a mechanical device, invented in

237

France, and used especially for training machine gunners. Blood fired three times with quite rapid aim, and got off his fourth just as the targets were disappearing in the ditch.

"Mark Blood's hits, and run 'em up again when I yell 'Target,'" Twiggs shouted through the megaphone. "Yell when you're ready."

"We're ready, sir," came a voice from the ditch.

"Are you ready, Harris?" And by now the platoon stood hushed, all the faces intent, and the captain of the company came running up to watch.

"Yes, sir," Joe answered.

Twiggs called, the cardboard men shot up, and Joe got off his first shot at what appeared the same instant. His other five shots followed in such rapid succession that Blood looked relieved, for surely the wooden-faced Indian was shooting wild.

Again Twiggs yelled through the megaphone, with an air of ceremony.

"Give us the score of Sergeant Blood?"

"Three hits, the first in the breast, the second in the belly, and third in the left knee."

"Now the score of Candidate Harris?"

The loud voice shook a little. "Six hits, all in the head."

"You've rung in a professional on me," Blood said after a long silence, meanwhile painfully extracting a ten-dollar bill from his wallet.

"No, I wouldn't do that, Blood, not me, nothing like that. All I did was ring in on you last year's National Rifle Champion of Secondary Schools. You should read the newspapers, Blood, and not so many comic supplements."

The whole platoon looked proud, and Joe's squad grinned at one another with great pleasure.

3

It must have been that the lieutenant and the captain conferred about Joe's shooting, and the latter had discussed it with the adjutant, because from then on he went rarely to the range with his platoon. His style of shooting being completely different from that taught in the Army, perhaps these officers thought that the sight of it, and its almost mathematically certain consequences, might confuse the other candidates, who were patiently taught to take certain aim, for God's sake not to flinch, then to "squeeze off" their triggers. Sergeant Major Twiggs found other jobs for him in the interim. One was to visit the range of a nearby batallion of machine gunners, learn to take down and reassemble the Lewis and other machine guns, and to shoot them from a swivel. The latter he learned to do with no difficulty at all. In some degree the swivel took the place of his free arm movements. He continued to outdo any rifleman his instructors and buddies had ever seen, in quickness and accuracy of aim.

He was instantly badly smitten by the Tommy gun. It was a semiautomatic shoulder piece firing bursts up to forty cartridges; with it he could use his own swing, pick up the targets incredibly fast, and blast several batches of them in the time taken by most shooters to cover one batch.

He soon became something of a celebrity in the regiment, perhaps almost as famous as a youth from vaudeville, who could sing not only "Mandalay" but "I'm Old Enough for a Little Lovin'," with great gusto and many grimaces at rare regimental shows. Since Joe did not know how to act like a celebrity, keeping his usual closed mouth, his prowess soon became an accepted fact of nature, such as Twiggs's unfailing know-how, and Blood's orneriness. He was given his full turn if not more at practice command of his platoon and then of the whole company. His deep voice had a ring to it that would carry far and clear. Oddly enough, someone—he did not know who—sent him some books to read in his "spare" time. Most of these were heavy tomes, written by retired officers, dealing with the science of war.

There remained not the slightest doubt that he would graduate with honors from the three months' course; he could readily hope soon to become a first lieutenant and then a captain, and he might end up the youngest major in the Army except for a few West Pointers, the record of whose birthdays had also become confused.

About two weeks before graduation Lieutenant Colonel Stark, second in command of the training school, sent for Joe to come to Headquarters. An Academy man of about thirty, with temporary rank—his actual rank was captain —he answered Joe's salute with two movements, the upward easy, the downward with a sharp thrust almost unimitable by officers from civilian life. Precisely a soldier, he was almost without front, and his voice was pleasant.

"Mr. Harris, I have a matter to propose to you, for you to think over. First I want to say that the legend that junior officers and enlisted men are merely numbers in times of war, let alone cannon fodder, is a legend only. Their various aptitudes are looked into rather carefully, and a real effort is made to make use of them as far as possible."

He paused, and Joe said, "Yes, sir," in the way he had been taught.

"Snipers are usually chosen from among the good shots in various companies. An idea has been broached—it has not yet been ordered—to organize companies of expert riflemen to be directly under the command of Division Headquarters, who would be in a position to know how to employ them efficiently. Quite a number of these experts are men from the back country—mountaineers, squirrel hunters, intelligent men without much formal education. If such companies should be organized, would you like to serve in one of them as a first lieutenant? Those fellows would want to be led by officers who could shoot at least as well and preferably better than themselves. And they are not easy to find. Also it has been found that on the Western Front, sniping appeals to certain temperaments, not to others. A good many expert shots fail."

"Sir, to answer your question the best I can, I would choose not to be a sniper or to command them."

"I am sure you have a good reason and I'd like to hear it."

"I would prefer open fighting, where the enemy can see me as well as I can see him."

"I suppose that attitude is an anachronism in the year 1917. Chivalry passed out of war with the publication of *Arms and the Man*. Well, there may be a lingering exception—the Air Force. But even in their game you can sneak up behind a plane and shoot it down."

"Yes, sir, but most planes have a rear gunner now, and in single-seaters it's the pilot's business to watch in all directions. Besides in one case the attack is in the air and the other it's from the bushes."

"I don't blame you, Harris, if that's the way you feel. We'll find a good command for you, never fear."

On the following day there occurred a minor event of great bearing on Joe's life. A flock of five huge birds, their still wings almost touching, and giving a thunderous call, swooped low over the field and landed on a short air strip at General Headquarters used at long intervals by visiting aircraft. The occasional ship had come and gone before Joe could get a close look at it, but this landing occurred during midday mess, and by missing the meal he had time for a quick inspection.

These were only two-seated trainers, because no fighter planes had yet been seen in America outside of the testing grounds of the factories. They appeared of flimsy construction, but Joe was thinking that so did a silver gull, one of the most beautiful and accomplished flyers on the river. The five pilots were standing about while their ships were being refueled, and all these were lieutenants in the Army Air Force, and there was something about them that stirred Joe to his depths. Their behavior, and even their dress, was not as militarily correct as those of infantry officers; they had a devil-may-care manner and a jaunty look. They employed expansive gestures; their voices were vibrant as are the voices of men who live under unceasing excitement, which is the thing that all men love. Today was good, tomorrow would bring something better; if the ceiling was too low for flying, by nature the skies and hence their own futures, barring accident, were unlimited.

Joe saluted one of the group and asked, "May I speak to the lieutenant?"

"You sure can."

"I'm Candidate Harris of the Officers' Training Camp. Is it difficult to get into the Air Force?"

The officer looked at him keenly; all these officers had keen eyes.

"Not very, if you can qualify, and really want to get in. The gold braid everywhere is hollering for more flyers. This is the *modus operandi*. When you get your commission, apply to your commandant for transfer to the Air Force of the Signal Corps. We're Signal Corps because that same gold braid thought at first that ships would be useful only for reconnaissance, photography and errand running; someday we'll have a corps of our own. You'd have a little training in America, and if you're at all bright, you'd find yourself in France almost before you know it. There you'd be trained in combat tactics, and bingo, you'd discover yourself in the same air with Bloody Baron Richthofen, and that's one hell of a place to be."

"Sir, I'm going to try for it."

"Reflect a few minutes before you do so, young Hawkeye. The infantry has a rough time, lots of good men gone in the general carnage, and lots of officers picked off. Still, judging from what has already happened in French and

241

British air corps, flyers get the ax in proportion to their numbers a lot more readily than junior infantry officers, let alone those in the cavalry, artillery, engineers, and the famous colonels of Parlez-Vous. This festive war has lasted three years; nobody seems to believe it won't last three years more. It will be a great life if you don't weaken."

"Thank you, sir; my mind's made up."

"I can see that it is. By the merest, casual survey, I would say you'd be a fair-to-middlin' flyer." His voice changed and had a glowing sound. "And, Harris, you won't be flying rattletraps like this—I won't either before you can shake a stick. The British DH-9 makes the Sopwith look like a crate. Now they're making the DH-4 and the Bristol Fighter, both two-seaters, and the newest thing yet, the single-seaters SE-5A and the Sopwith Camel. Man, I've been told they can do everything as well and maybe better than the Boche Albatros and the Halberstadt."

"I'll try to get a Sopwith Camel, sir."

"An ambitious young feller! Well, good luck." The airman made a thumb-and-forefinger ring, shook it in the air.

Joe had astonishing good luck. Lieutenant Colonel Stark granted his request for an interview and listened to him civilly.

"I was afraid of that," he said. "I shouldn't have made the crack about how the air forces of both armies retain vestiges of a chivalric code. Why should that appeal to an Indian? When the Indians raided settlers of our outposts in the old days they butchered women and children. Well, each brave shaved his head except for a scalp lock, so the white man who rolled him over could take a pretty scalp. Also in our early wars of decimation we white men did surely decimate. The fact remains that less than fifty years ago you fellows hacked up Custer's men bloody awful. An old drill sergeant at the Academy had visited the scene of the battle the next day, and he had to gulp when he told about it, he was that sick."

"Sir, my main reason for wanting to be a flyer is so that I can hunt and shoot."

"I know of no more natural reason. Well, I'll instruct the adjutant to take your application at once and rush it off to Washington. He'll recommend it, I feel sure. You might even get pretty fast action on it, for you know the English and French flyers were almost rubbed out of the sky along in February, and it's still touch and go."

Only two days after graduation from the camp, with Joe's new uniform spick-and-span and his gold-plated shoulder bars a-glimmer, his orders came through to transfer to the Air Force under the Signal Corps. From then events happened so swiftly that he was hard put to it not to become confused, as when twenty caribou burst from a thicket when he had expected one. Within two weeks he had crossed the continent and was learning the mechanics of flying on a motorless dummy airplane hoisted from a crane. In two weeks more his prowess at machine-gunnery had caused the chief instructor to complain to the adjutant that "he was ashamed to go with that redskin to the range." Relieved of machine gunnery practice, Joe had that much more time to pick up a little rough navigation by dead reckoning, a smattering of meteorology, and far more flying instruction than was his lawful due. Still he had had only thirty-five hours of solo flight, against fifty or more credited to other candidates, when the day came for their graduation as pilots of the Air Force.

"To hell with it," a bold captain told a master sergeant who was a friend of Joe's. "If I was a Boche ace, I wouldn't want that red nigger shooting at me. I'd try to get out of there fustest with the leastest. Russia's gone, and Italy's on the run, and the Germans are building up for the greatest offensive in the West that this festive world has ever seen since Genghis Khan set out with his horde to darken the complexion of all Europe. It has been recommended by someone awful high up to get Joe strapped in a seat behind a machine gun before he steals a plane and decides to avenge Tippecanoe. The old man's decided to lead with his chin and ship him with our first batch."

4

With these other embryo flyers Joe boarded a big transport, the screws churned the stormy seas, official wheels turned rapidly, and raucous voices called, "You'll like it, oh, you boys will like it," as they were transported in what was called a lorry to a French town behind the lines where the Flying Dodos and three other squadrons had their aerodrome. This squadron also had a proper number, which almost nobody knew outside of a few staff officers, since the insignia of a black dumb-looking dodo in a white circle had caught the fancy of the force. But now Joe's luck slowly petered out.

The major who commanded the air group had taken note that the number of Joe's flying hours was below the minimum prerequisites (except for special cases) for action on the front. Nor did he fail to notice that his proficiency in gunnery had the highest possible rating, underlined at that; and for some months now there had been a steady din in his ears from his superiors for God's sake to get those ships in the air so the extent of the German build-up could be observed. So after a talk with the Dodos' leader, he assigned Joe as observer and rear gunner in a Bristol Fighter, a swift and highly maneuverable ship piloted by a steady, sound flyer, Lieutenant Tommy Meade.

Joe found an immediate fellowship with Tommy. The fact remained that the latter's orders were almost always to observe and hightail home, stay clear of German circuses, and to avoid battle with swift Albatroses or Halberstadts hunting in pairs. But one of these days, Tommy told him, they were going to run up on an L.V.G., with nothing much to choose between the two ships, and then a little mark, of great importance, would be made beside their names, and then like enough both would get Nieuport 28s, Spad XIIIs, or Sopwith Camels.

Tommy Meade made this prediction with a curiously wistful smile and a faraway look in his boyish eyes of western New York blue. When he found the black Indian eyes fixed on him Tommy added, "I don't want to go back to Cattaraugus County until I'm an ace."

Engagements with hostile ships had been prevented as much by Joe's hawk-sharp eyes as by Tommy's orders. Joe had felt duty-bound to tell his pilot of each sighting of the Boche, alone, or flying in pairs or in formation, and Tommy would maneuver to attack the lone hunters, but the Bristol Fighter shooting fore and aft was deeply feared by lone prowlers, and this state of mind plus Tommy's caution caused them to become separated. After three weeks on the front, including several days of dud weather, Joe and his friend had the humiliation of turning tail on an L.V.G., high above them with the sun to his back and beautifully fixed to fire the opening blast.

Still, Joe thought, the Boche might have seen them and come in on a steep dive. He could, if he wanted to very much; he knew that many a Yank flyer, new to the war, was easy game, so Joe quieted and cooled himself and spiritually as well as physically got behind his guns. For rea-

244

sons unknown, the German minded his own business.

In the following week their fortunes of war brought forth a different story, and a rather strange one.

Meade had flown his ship under a filmy-looking cloud that apparently would not conceal a flock of swallows. Suddenly, then, there was a German two-seater above her and on her tail, gaining and blasting at three hundred yards. Joe had never seen this model, had been shown no picture of it, its general type was that of L.V.G., but faster and heavier armed; plainly it was new to the skies of the Western Front. With a great surge of feeling, exultation laced with fright and all the sharper on that account, Joe realized that at last he was in battle.

Swerving down to get behind and a little under the Bristol Fighter, where her rear gunner could not get at her without shooting through his own tail, the German had to pass across Joe's line of fire. As would any good flyer, Tommy began a steep, climbing turn. The German did the same, and they found themselves for an instant directly in line. Then a voice that might be a voice from the past said confidently to Joe, "He's near enough now." He swung his piece and saw the two flyers in his sights and his finger moved of itself. At his first burst the rear gunner dropped out of sight.

Joe's brain had moved to find aim again when the German pilot's two front guns gave forth a furious blast, and the whole battle picture became drastically changed.

Joe had barely seen the rip cut in the fuselage when he felt the ship go out of control. When he turned and glanced toward Meade's head it was not where it ought to be and the ship was rolling over. Joe knew instantly that the same blast of fire that had killed Tommy had cut his safety belt and he had fallen against the stick.

A few seconds remained before the German could again get into position for a sure shot. In that interval the Bristol Fighter turned upside down, and something red toppled out, and it was Tommy's body almost cut in two.

The nose of the plane dropped and she began to plunge earthward as in a split S. Instead of following her down to blast her again, the German swooped above her. No doubt he had seen her pilot's body falling with ever gathering speed until it was a red streak far below him, and now saw the plane in what seemed her last dive. She was done for, he thought, and another kill would be marked up beside his name. He did not want to lose altitude and it must be

245

that he looked away, in search for any other Yank who might be zooming through the film of cloud to get revenge.

But as the diving ship gained speed, her wings gained lift, causing her nose to rise. Close to earth she came out of her shrieking fall and began to climb as if starting a "wing over." Swiftly she lost speed and then, following a pattern of behavior neatly sketched in Joe's brain, which he had seen not as it occurred but in an immeasurable instant earlier, she dropped off on one wing and went into a shallow dive. As again she recovered, there came a little interval in which she flew in almost straight and completely level flight.

Joe was never to tell himself that he had been waiting for that to happen, because it would not have been true. He had been only hoping in cool, quiet hope that the vast forces that had immobilized him would let go their grip. Now they had done so. His hands were free to act, his body to move. Without ever knowing the successive actions, suddenly he was out of his own seat and into the pilot's seat and the careening ship had come under his control.

His gaze darted in all directions as he climbed. Almost instantly he saw his enemy, little and far off, hightailing home. That made good enough sense, Joe thought grimly. Her rear gunner sat slumped in his safety belt. He could no longer stand his watch; she flew unprotected from attack in the rear. Impelled, not by any deliberate intention that Joe realized, only by the remorseless drive of his instincts, he opened his throttle wide.

The distance between the two ships swiftly shortened. Joe came in behind and below the German ship, and she stood sharp and clean in his sights. "He's near enough now."

At his first blast, the pilot made a little forward jump and appeared to fold up slowly. A short burst of flame showed bright in the murky sky, and smoke trailed in a lurid streak. The ship went into a spin. Joe pulled clear to watch it fall in a frame of flame.

It was an easy death, Joe thought, and now he must look to not having one of the same. High up, taking advantage of every cloud, he sped homeward, the ship performing perfectly, perfectly easy to fly. Having watched Tommy's good landings so many times, the Indian was not at all surprised to find himself safe on the field. The only surprise that anybody felt, extreme indeed, was that of the field crews who saw the wrong flyer in the pilot's seat and no sight of the

246

right one. Joe shut off the motor and climbed out in the silence of their astonishment, and without a word went to report to the officer of the day, at that moment hurrying out of one of the hangars.

"Well, what in the hell happened?"

"We got messed up with a two-seater that I've never seen on this front. I missed the pilot but got the tail gunner. Tommy was hit, and we went into a dive, and I guess the Boche thought we were done for. But Tommy pulled out and came up under her and had enough life left in him to blast her and send her down in flames. Then we went out of control and when she rolled over, Tommy's body fell out —it must be that his belt had been cut or the buckle broken by the same blast of fire that wounded him. When she righted herself I squirmed into the seat and brought her in."

The officer looked at him very strangely and the compulsion came upon Joe to speak quickly.

"I'm glad we can mark him down for a kill before he went overboard."

"You go to the wardroom and have a big drink and don't say anything more to anybody, do you hear me, Lieutenant Harris?"

"Yes, sir."

"I'll see you later."

5

In just about an hour Joe was summoned to the big tent used as squadron headquarters. The officer of the day was sitting behind the desk with a thoughtful countenance when Joe entered, came to attention, and saluted.

"You're not really a first-class liar, Lieutenant," the captain began. "There may be something in that old yarn of 'Honest Indian.' Maybe they were honest because their lying wasn't too sharp."

"Yes, sir."

"It's quite true that Tommy's safety belt was cut in two by machine-gun bullets—completely riddled for that matter. And the same happened to Tommy. His body has been found and is being brought here. I talked on the telephone to a French colonel calling from an observation post in that sector. He also gave me an eyewitness report of the fight."

Joe remained at unshaken attention, saying nothing.

"Lieutenant Harris, you were emotionally upset when you first reported to me. That's natural enough, after seeing your buddy killed, and other things happening. It's a very serious offense to lie to a superior officer, especially in regard to military matters. I perceive your motive—I must confess a certain sympathy with it—but it mustn't occur again if you want to fly any more with the Dodos."

"Sir, it won't occur again."

"In that case, I'm going to assume you were sort of out of your mind? You were, weren't you?"

"Yes, sir, somewhat."

"Apache, you didn't have to go to all those lengths. It's rather common for a fighter not to be able to report exactly what happened in the big moment. And what's that red streak over your ear?"

"Sir, I didn't discover it till I went in to wash, although I think I felt a burning sensation when I got it. I think it was made by a Boche bullet in the same blast that killed Tommy."

"Hell, that was enough to jar what brains you have and cause a brief attack of—what's the word?—amnesia. The eyewitness report was in the French colonel's broken English and it needn't go any further. I'll support your lie as far as saying that you were slightly incoherent when you landed, and you'd had a running fight with the Boche. That means the kill will be marked up for your plane, scoring for Tommy and you, both, and Tommy's folks in New York State and his townspeople will be proud of him."

"Thank you, sir."

"The plane is an improved L.V.G., to judge from what's left of her. Perhaps the Boche got her out especially to outfly and outgun the Bristol Fighter, and quite possibly this was her first test in battle, with no good news for Ludendorff. The rear gunner getting into the pilot's seat and bringing the ship in is not unique, it's happened before on both sides, but the instances are rather scarce. Still I'm not going to recommend you for a citation and the *Croix de guerre*—that would mean a much more complete investigation than either of us want made."

"That's a good idea, sir."

"Under any circumstances it was a right quick bit of work. You can go on flying, and I think you'd better fly alone. You'll be out of action for about a week, getting the hang of a single-seater. What do you think you would do best, flying in formation, under a leader, or prowling about alone?"

"I'd rather go it alone."

"That's all for now."

Joe saluted and withdrew; and none of his buddies questioned him after his saying that he was not in a condition to relate the details of the fight. The whole mess was depressed that night and at last stood up and sung the song that the Dodos had adopted for their own, a line or two of which, oddly enough, Eric had heard and had once repeated to Joe. It was a tragic song, yet stirring, of deep appeal to these young men, and the verses concerned young Englishmen in India trapped by a plague. Tonight the Dodos only sang the chorus:

> *So stand to your glasses steady,*
> *This world is a world of lies,*
> *And here's to the dead already,*
> *And here's to the last man who dies.*

Two days later an English DH-9, carrying only the pilot, and a Sopwith Camel, landed on the strip. After the pilot of the latter reported to the officer of the day he got into the tail seat of the two-seater, and the two Englishmen took off, rather grumpily. "Why in the hell don't you bloody Yanks make your own planes in all those factories we've heard so much about, instead of lifting ours?" was about what their faces said.

Joe could not blame them. The Sopwith Camel was a beautiful ship, none better in any Allied aerodrome. He waited in almost unbearable suspense until the officer of the day gave him a sharp glance, then jerked his thumb in her direction. He had kept a wooden face during the wait, and it maybe cracked a little when he got the news, for the hangers-around all glanced at him sharply. Then he walked over to the ship, and, after looking at it from all angles, he got into the seat. She had two .50-caliber machine guns timed to fire between the blades of her whirling prop, and her controls were essentially the same as in the Sopwith Strutter. "I could take her up right now," he thought.

"The Old Man assigned her to you, not because you're the best flyer in our squadron by a long shot," the officer explained. "You're a good flyer, but not a great flyer as yet, not holding a candle to Frank Luke or Eddie Rickenbacker, who took racing cars around the course faster than anybody ever drove, before he had ever fastened a belt in a cockpit. But the Old Man is following Eddie's own doctrine, on

249

which he's sounded off several times. He says that expert gunnery is more important than expert flying when it comes to knocking off Boche ships. Snap shooting and hitting while the old Boche is maneuvering and thinks nobody but Wild Bill Hickok has a dog's chance to hit him is an especially valuable accomplishment, and the word has got around that you've got it. See that you don't get potted as Wild Bill did, sitting with his back to the door playing cards."

Joe's first act was to get a paint pot and paint a very large white rabbit on the side of the cockpit. His mechanics made much of her, grinning like urchins at her 190-horse-power engine.

On the following day he took her up and flew her over the French countryside, well back from the Front. She had the blithe spirit of the Sopwith Pup, with almost twice the power and greater speed. She lacked the swiftness and climbing power and rapid fire of the Fokker D-VIII, the terror of the skies, nor could she fly as well in very high altitudes, but up to nineteen thousand feet she matched her well enough to suit Apache Joe. He had an inkling that her wonderful maneuverability played perfectly into his hands. He had always liked to swing a rifle free in his arms, and in this case the ship herself would be his arms; he could swing her, he thought, and at the end of that sweep the target would appear as if by magic, in his sights.

And he was not as indifferent a flyer as the officer had thought best to infer to keep him humble. The same gifts, even some of the same training, that made Joe a marksman almost without peer in the Allied air forces, were turning him into a far from commonplace flyer. The so-called "vision of the air" seemed inbuilt; he had perfect balance, he thought fast, and his reflex actions were high-powered and instantaneous, as an army medico had discovered when Joe applied to join the Air Force. No good sourdough, wanting to be able to find his way out of the forest or muskeg he had penetrated, fails to observe every landmark. Long a hunter, he had learned to stalk with patience and great skill. It was his way to remain wildly alert every minute he was awake, then sleep deep sleep that restored him like a meal of red meat. "To sleep is to eat," is an old saying among the Alaskan natives.

Especially he liked to prowl on partly cloudy days, when his intense vision stood him in such good stead. When there was a new troop movement on either side, he coursed the sectors like a hound, for the Germans were almost certain to send swift Fokkers for reconnaissance, or to shoot down enemy observers.

At the end of his first week of untrammeled flying he dived on an unwary Albatros D-III, and shot her down in flames. There was a man in that plane, a good fellow likely, who liked the beer gardens and possibly the opera, but Joe did not let himself dwell on that after the plane, with her wings of fire like some giant bird of a lost mythology, tail-spinned earthward. To him the plane itself was the trophy. Nor did he give thought to the abstraction that the kill would help win the war. His thoughts and feelings were almost completely self-contained; he was a hunter first, last, and always, on a mighty hunt. He paid no attention to his score, and the back-thumpings and handshakings of his fellow Dodos were pleasant enough, but had no deep meaning for him.

It was almost inevitable that if the war and he himself lasted three months more, he would become an ace. Perhaps almost all the higher officers he had dealt with on his journey to this aerodrome, these being men of some imagination and good judgment to have obtained their rank, had perceived this inevitability, not only from the way he shot, but from the whole look and way of him, the grace with which he moved, and so sped him on his way—to hell with regulations. His second kill with this new gun, called by others a Sopwith Camel, was a two-seater reconnaissance plane on which he dived through a hole in the overcast. He had to think of this ship as a lesser trophy than the Albatros, not as a mallard duck compared to a wild honker, more like a moose than a woodland caribou, which was more fleet and wary and more wildly alive than the black-belled bull.

Joe's next kill came after a heart-stilling stalk through scattered clouds in chase of another Halberstadt. Again and again he thought he had lost her only to catch a glimpse of her in filmy patches where she looked like the ghost of some ship shot down on her maiden flight over the front, and which must forever wing back and forth in impotence with her heartbroken pilot. Sometimes he saw her in small breaks between the banks, vivid as an eagle, and then he came to the big break, his own break. He was far above her and well behind, but his headlong dive fetched him up on her level, only two hundred yards on her tail. It was the position young airmen dream about, a sweet dream, and before the German could dream of her presence, a most evil dream, the cruel bullets were riddling her body and his own. Perhaps he died in great surprise, knowing only his death and no more, and that would be a negative knowledge, all time and space removed from the positive knowledge of his own life, so sharp until just now.

Down out of the clouds the broken ship careened, and the doughboys yelled when they saw she was a Boche and caught no glimpse of her destroyer. If, reluctantly, Joe had not reported to the officer of the day the exact minute of her fall and the sector into which she fell, he might have had trouble getting official credit, for a dogfight was taking place hardly two miles away, in which several more kills had been claimed by members of an optimistic American squadron than wrecked planes could be found. Joe would not have cared very much if one of these had been given the tuft, because he was not tuft-hunting, but big-game hunting, the biggest game there was.

Not long after this he dived through heavy flak on an observation balloon and set it on fire with incendiary bullets, whereof it collapsed and wobbled to the ground, the observer scrambling out unhurt. These blimps were the favorite game of one of the greatest and most intrepid flyers in any air force, Frank Luke from Arizona, who punctured the big bags in a perfect hell of hurtling steel and lead, flak, machine-gun fire, volleys from Fritz rifles, and even hand grenades; and none had been able to hit the wildly careening plane. Joe wanted no more of it. The risk was ten times too great for the satisfaction.

The fact remained that the balloon was enemy aircraft, and with the kill credited to both himself and Tommy Meade, its destruction gave Joe the rating of an ace. He felt precisely the same; for he knew quite well he did not stand shoulder high with the great aces, Billy Bishop of Canada, Charles Nungesser, Major Lufbery of the Escadrille Lafayette, the great English fighter Major McCudden, and, of course, Baron Richthofen, the incomparable German. Still he was the first of the Dodos to make that score; and the group commander, Major Connelly, came to evening mess in Joe's honor.

He came, and inspired by good French brandy at a dollar a bottle, he recited some lines of poetry. . . .

Ye say that all have passed away—
That noble race and brave . . .

The major forgot the next line, but came forth in good style with two more. . . .

> But their name is on your waters—
> Ye may not wash it out.

"Gentlemen, not all the Indians have passed away," the major said with feeling. "And not all the good Indians are dead Indians, as someone—it might have been Mark Twain but I guess it wasn't—was heard to remark. This squadron has a real live Indian and a good Indian, and his name, Apache Joe, is being written on the blackboards in many a Boche ready room, and it will take an eraser better than he's met yet to rub it out."

The major sat down amid thunderous applause. Joe sat staring at his plate and for once he could truly be called a red man, he was so red in the face.

He had his due number of close calls and wild-goose chases and bullet holes in his ship. One of his hardest and longest fights against a prowler like himself, the most agile airman he had ever seen function, ended with ripped fuselage, empty belts, and both flyers scudding homeward dipping their wings in salute. It gave him the same kind of satisfaction, multiplied and finely sharpened, as when an old bull caribou had outsmarted him in the woods at home. He was grounded for a week while his ship was busily repaired, and on his very first prowl thereafter he came suddenly upon a dogfight, two miles behind cloud; then suddenly the open sky was full of darting shapes in splendid silhouette.

It was between a flight of ten French Spads and about twenty Halberstadts; and the German flyers were confident of killing out, and their blood was up and they forgot to watch all the skies and Joe came in high, unseen. It was the finest dogfight he had ever seen or hoped to see, but he did not tarry to admire and instead dived on two airmen who, after steep climbing turns to escape Spad fire from the rear, now were themselves diving on the hapless ships that had missed their chance. Joe shot down one of them almost before he knew it, with no conscious act that he could remember, and, after a little swerve, shot up the other so badly that she made off. The Germans had already lost four ships to French fire, and the sight of another suddenly set ablaze and a second turning tail caused them to arrest their maneuvers and look up, perhaps expecting a formation of Yank

253

ships coming to the rescue of the outnumbered Frogs. All they saw was one Sopwith Camel climbing to swoop again, but that little break in the fight let the agile Spads get out of the line of the fire and hightail for safety.

The Boche did not pursue and turned back to nurse his wounds, and Joe gained his eminence and fled.

It was this last kill, soon verified by ground observers, that bid fair to make Joe famous. A French correspondent was permitted to talk to him a few minutes—good public relations, the group commander said—and although Joe's part in the interview was almost wholly confined to saying yes or no, a long and learned article appeared in a French journal, dealing mostly with the psychology of the *sauvage Americain,* who now had won six victories, and who made no more of them than his equestrian ancestors had made of stalking and scalping plainsmen in the Old West.

But Joe grinned when it was read to him by an interpreter, because he had no equestrian ancestors in the West or anywhere; although some of his footslogging forebears, laying for caribou, might have been ancestors of the Navahos and Apaches.

An American journalist also talked to him and took his picture while Joe was inspecting his plane before a takeoff. The story that the reporter wrote for a sensational New York newspaper was clipped and pasted on the bulletin board, for the vast amusement of all comers.

Joe was reported as always saying "Um," when he meant yes, and making such remarks as, "Me take off, me see heap big tribe of Germans fighting heap small tribe Frenchmen, French our friend, Great White Father say so, so me get in fight, shoot down German, maybe shoot heap more, then me go home."

A much more remarkable aftermath of the dogfight occurred in Paris, where Joe and about six of his fellow Dodos had flown on a weekend. They had wandered into the Ritz Hotel and were gazing at its splendors when a tall, fair-haired, beautiful woman, not more than thirty, came shyly from a lounge table and spoke to Joe.

"Isn't this Lieutenant Harris?"

"Yes, ma'am."

"I couldn't refrain from speaking to you. I am Cynthia Dickenson, and my husband is Captain Dickenson of the Royal Air Force."

"I've heard of him, ma'am. He's a great flyer."

"He'd like very much to meet you, and he's coming in late this afternoon. Have you made any plans for this evening?"

Joe thought quickly. His friends had planned to eat at the Crillon, then go to the Folies-Bergères, which Joe had visited on a previous weekend and where he had been made uncomfortable not in the least by the expanse of naked female flesh, which he liked to gaze upon, but by the noise, the crowds, and especially the mingling of heavy perfumes with other smells assaulting his sensitive nose. Captain Dickenson had invented the Dickenson Roll, one of the swiftest known means of abruptly reversing direction. Also he felt attracted to this beautifully dressed, beautiful young woman with a child's shyness and yet the boldness to speak to a stranger.

Just then a bearded man came by, lifted his hat, and said, "Good afternoon, Lady Dickenson." She replied in an absent-minded way. Joe thought again of what he was about to say, then asked, "Ma'am, are you a noblewoman?"

"By no means. The daughters of an earl have the courtesy title of Lady. We're not peeresses and the title is not hereditary. My father is the Earl of Lockstone."

"I never heard of your husband being called 'lord.' "

"No, because he isn't one. He had no title except Lieutenant until he won the splendid one of Captain."

"I asked because I've never been among the nobility and wouldn't know how to address them. No, ma'am, I have no plans I can't change."

"Then will you come to an informal supper at our flat? It's small, and so I can't invite any of your friends. There will be my husband and me, and my younger sister, Edith, who visited western Canada last summer. It happens she is thinking of marrying a mining engineer living in the Yukon Territory, and that's close to your home on the upper Yukon River."

"Yes, ma'am, it is. I know parts of the Yukon Territory real well."

"She'd love to talk to you and, if I may say so, she's an enchanting girl. I'll write my address on this card and you can take a cab; it's only a few minutes from here. May I expect you at seven; because all four of us would be so pleased to have you come?"

"Yes, ma'am, I'll be there."

Lady Dickenson's flat, in a fashionable neighborhood,

was certainly not large, and the right name for it, Joe thought, was elegant. He wished he knew enough about elegance to appreciate the delicately made furniture, the pictures on the walls, the warm thick rugs, the beautiful lamps. A rather hard-faced woman in a maid's costume had admitted him and showed him a chair. Lady Dickenson came in shortly, wearing very faint and pleasant scent and a striking dress. Several of the Dodos had become worldly-wise since their arrival on foreign shores, and one of their dicta was that while American girls showed little bosom and a lot of leg, French girls were chary of showing either until the right moment, and English girls showed little or no leg but a good deal of bosom. The bodice of Lady Dickenson's dress had been cut very low, without shoulder straps, and she had a fine bosom, as fine as he had ever seen on a young squaw.

"You can't go on calling me 'ma'am,' you know," she said. "That's the address you'd use to Queen Mary. I'm dying to call you Apache, it's a wonderful name. Since 'Lady Dickenson' is rather a mouthful, couldn't you make it 'Cynthia'?"

"I'd like that just fine."

By pushing a button, she opened the doors of a cabinet, revealing various decanters, bottles, glasses of all shapes and sizes, and a Thermos jug.

"Scotch and soda, or a cocktail?" she asked.

"Scotch and soda, please."

"Please who?"

"Please, Cynthia."

"Ready in a jiffy, Apache."

She mixed the whisky with cold water and poured into a large cocktail glass an almost transparent liquid, with green lights, from a decanter. It must be mighty good, he thought, for when they were seated on a small, high-backed sofa she sipped rather greedily.

She talked gaily now, her shyness no longer evident, and told him some anecdotes of the war that she said her husband had told her. None were at all vulgar but some were what Americans called shady and what a few of the Dodos, who had picked up French gestures and a few French words, termed risqué. Occasionally she stole a glance into his face, after which she caught her breath sharply.

"Edith and my husband are late," she remarked when

the glasses were empty. "It may be we'll have to go it alone. Do you want another whisky?"

Just then the hard-faced maid appeared in the doorway. "Supper is ready on the buffet, Your Ladyship," she announced, and immediately disappeared.

"Well, why let it get cold?" Cynthia asked. "If they're coming at all, they can jolly well catch up with us."

She led the way into a small, elegant dining room, where the lace-covered table was set with four places. The stray thought struck Joe that there was no danger of food getting cold, for under each hot dish was an alcohol burner. "I hope you like what I have," she said, "for it's not exactly what you get in an officers' mess."

She identified the edibles, a cold onion soup, a lobster salad, stuffed woodcock, Brussels sprouts, muffins, and Edam cheese. "All inside ration rules and regulations," she informed him, as she filled two soup bowls from a silver-and-gold ladle with a figured handle. Meanwhile he noticed a bottle of champagne in an ice bucket and two decanters of wine.

"This is Smith's night to leave early," she explained, "or we'd dine with a little more ceremony." Smith must be the butler, Joe thought. "I'm going to seat you where I intended, on my right."

When the soup bowls were empty Cynthia sprang up quickly. As Joe started to rise she gave him a long shake of her head.

"I'll serve you," she said. "You're an Indian brave, the term wonderfully fitting in this case, and I want to be your squaw."

She put a woodcock and some of the vegetables on his plate, and set it before him with a glass of red wine. The fowl was a new one to him, he was thinking, but he had heard of it, and suddenly it struck him that, Alaskan sourdough though he was, he felt better acquainted with the exotic food than with Cynthia herself. He did not know her in the least. Her cheeks had flushed and her blue eyes looked drowsy and she was a little nervous. He could see that much, and that she was an unusually beautiful young woman, but there his vision stopped.

She ate quickly and had to wait for him, although he had not dallied. "Cheese and fruit?" she asked.

"No, thank you."

"Then I'll open the champagne."

She did so skillfully, poured a little into her glass, tasted it, filled his glass, then finished filling her own.

"We won't drink for just a minute. Apache, in the old baronial halls of England, the daughters of the house had a pleasant way of honoring winners of tournaments and other heroes. That's the way I want to honor you."

Her face very grave, almost sorrowful, he thought, she rose, stood beside him, and bent down. Then she gave him a long kiss, her lips drawing slowly across his.

"You didn't respond to that very well," she said quietly.

"It took me by surprise."

"Well, I have a few other surprises for you. I'll give them to you in just a minute." She touched a bell under the table and the maid came in.

"Smith, you may go now."

Their eyes met in a brief, searching gaze.

"Thank you, Your Ladyship."

"Have a nice outing tomorrow."

The hard-faced old bat did not answer, Joe noticed, and the door closed with a decided bang.

"Apache, to win your trophies you use a good deal of guile—so I read in a French journal," Cynthia said, with a faint smile. "Aren't Indians often called 'crafty redmen'? But you're not in the least red. Your skin is a wonderful pale brown, with dark lights in it, if lights can be dark."

"I use what I know of hunting," Joe answered, disregarding all the rest.

"Well, I wanted to win a trophy—a very big one. To that end I told you two lies. My husband is stuck for the weekend in Kent. I haven't any little sister named Edith."

Joe bowed his head a little and waited.

"Aren't you what the Americans call 'hard up'? It's a very apt term, too. I'm rather pretty, am I not? Also you'd never forget this night, if we spend it as I hope. The telephone won't ring. There's no one here but you and me. Instead of going back to that stuffy little parlor—and wasting time on preliminaries—let's go to my bedroom?"

He hesitated too long, then drank a little champagne.

"You'd be a wonderful trophy, if you want to put it that way," he said at last. "A lot of my friends would jump at the chance. But these days I'm hunting other kinds of trophies. It's what American frontiersmen in the old days called the Long Hunt. The trophies are German planes, and the German flyers are hunting me at the same time. That's

258

the whole bent of my mind. You ask if I'm hard up—I'm not. I think that hunting hard enough expels the same kind of energy you're thinking about. For the present I'm not interested in the other. When I daydream it's not of a beautiful woman but of an Albatros or a Halberstadt I might meet in the open sky, one with a hunter pilot crazy to engage. An American newspaper article spoke of me as a falcon. Falcons and I have one thing in common—when they hunt they don't make love, and when they make love they don't hunt."

"I suppose you know that attitude makes you all the more desirable to women—and desirable isn't even the word."

"I didn't know it."

"To keep this conversation on the same plane—you're either lying, or Nietzsche was an awful liar. Probably you haven't read the son of a bitch. His doctrine is, the main business of a man is to make war and the main business of a woman is to let him—well, I'll be ladylike and say fornicate with her. Come, Apache, be a good little Indian. I refuse to believe that you're that deeply dedicated to hunting and killing. Let's go to my room and take the champagne with us and see what happens." She drew a deep breath and said in a low voice, "Wouldn't you like to see my whiteness against your darkness?"

"No."

And then a tall, slim man, very blond, strikingly handsome, wearing the uniform of the Royal Air Force with captain's insignia, stepped quietly into the room. Joe saw him before Cynthia did, perhaps only because his angle of vision was unusually wide, perhaps because he had stayed alert. Looking at him, he did not see Cynthia's face.

"I beg your pardon, Lieutenant Harris," he said quietly.

"You'd better beg mine, too," Cynthia said, her voice cracking. "To telegraph that you wouldn't be home—then come in with your passkey without ringing——"

"I beg your pardon, Cynthia, for interrupting you at dinner. Actually I didn't expect to find you and your guest in this room—I thought you'd be in another room. Your actions were more deliberate than usual; you were after bigger game. Judging from what I heard just now, standing in the parlor, the game proved too big."

"Well, if so, it's the only thing I'm ashamed of."

"I, too, have something to be ashamed of—the pistol in

my pocket. I'd been brooding a little these past weeks—it's made me a little nervy when leading my squadron—it might cause an accident—so I decided to shoot you right between the boobies. But, Cynthia, it's not worth the powder and lead. I'll save it for the Boche."

"That's a fine speech, Captain."

"Lieutenant Harris, I'm sorry to foist these domestic matters on your attention. I'll be going now. Good hunting!"

Joe waited until the outer door closed. Then he spoke.

"I'm going too. Thanks for the good dinner."

"Are you sure you haven't changed your mind? He won't return—he never will return."

"No, thank you, Lady Dickenson."

"You understand, Lieutenant, that I can't help it. I've never been able to help it, beginning with the gardener. My father's earldom is an ancient one, and the seed may be turning bad from overselection. I may be driven by an authentic urge of nature to have planted some good seed."

He glanced at her, then started. The almost childish shyness he had seen at the hotel had come back to her. But sometimes, when he had felt a sudden impulse to engage the enemy he had found himself veering off. Quickly he made for the door.

6

Joe's list of kills lengthened slowly in proportion to the number of hours he hunted, very rapidly in comparison to most fighter pilots. His fame increased prodigiously in all the armed forces in Europe and wherever correspondents and photographers, covering the Western Front, printed their stories and pictures. Apache Joe became almost a household word throughout America, the British and French empires, and in the great cities of the Triple Alliance, where the people watched the vast darkening shadow of impending defeat. It was an easy name to remember, a picturesque name. In one way he was the perfect hero, simply because he could not realize he was any kind of hero: his mind would not turn in that direction. He could not help but see such headlines as JOE DOWNS ANOTHER, or ANOTHER SCALP FOR APACHE, or REDSKIN PROWLER PICKS OFF GERMAN ACE, but he never read the stories in the American papers sent daily to the wardroom, and flushed when they were mentioned in his presence.

He did not open the sack full of mail arriving almost every day; and since someone had to read the letters and answer most of them—a public-relations chief had decreed as much—a disabled officer was assigned the duty, with the help of an Armenian and a Swiss typist, whose neatly combined talents could deal with nine out of ten civilized languages, and an old top sergeant with one leg who made a good thing of selling mash notes with good addresses at five francs each to homesick soldiers of corresponding nationality. There remained an occasional letter in Finnish, Lappish, Hungarian, and Pashto, at which the interpreters dropped their hands.

They had instructions to put aside unopened all letters from Alaska and the Yukon Territory, and these Joe read in privacy, sometimes with great joy. Also there was delivered to him personally and somewhat furtively by the officer in charge an opened letter from Fort George, British Columbia.

"We thought you ought to see this, Apache," the officer said.

The letter, in shaky handwriting, read:

Dear Lieutenant Harris;
There is only one half-breed Indian from the upper Yukon with your cognomen of whom I know. There is a Jim Harris from the Flats, a Joseph P. Harris from Nome, and a John Harris from the Kuskokwim, and finally (I say finally without being sure) a Henry Harris from the Tanana, but I repeat without fear of contradiction, you are the only Joe.

A good many years ago I entered into a financial transaction with someone in regard to his adoption of a papoose of that name. It may be that one of the terms was, I was not to pursue your acquaintance, but a letter of congratulations could hardly be construed as coming under that head.

The sums received seemed absurdly high at the time, but I fear I made a bad bargain. I should have known that, in living up as staunchly as possible to my ideal of improving the human species, one of the improvements would be astonishing. I am sorry I have no clear memory of the original event, but I must have been at my best that night, the so-

261

called genes in a singular and superior pattern, and the ensuing race as thrilling as the Grand National. You, Joe, as did I, in a previous race of all-importance to you, won the Grand Prize, which was an egg.

Quite seriously, I am quite overcome by humility at these consequences. I came perilously close to abjuring the bottle. Now I lift a glass to you, rejoice that my original success has been crowned with a greater one, and wish you a happy return to the beautiful North that each of us, in his own way, loves.

I assure you I do not intend that we shall ever meet.

Sincerely
Scott Harris, M.D.

"I hope the old fellow never learns the truth," Joe thought.

Once Joe received serious advice to paint out the big white rabbit on his fuselage, for the good reason that it was too easily seen from afar and too well known in the aerodromes of the enemy, where many good flyers sought sudden fame. He did not follow it for two reasons: one that he believed the emblem brought him luck, and for another reason that he did not attempt to explain, although it made perfectly good sense in Athabaskan. The hunger being remorselessly hunted added to the excitement of all parties concerned, and he did not want any of his friends among the Dodos killed in a grim case of mistaken identity.

In mid-September Joe's record stood at eleven enemy ships shot down, and four listed as "doubtful," although Joe himself had no doubt whatever of the deadly outcome because the planes had stood in his sights when he had touched trigger; and the .50-caliber machine gun functioned as a precision rifle. This score put him among the very top few American aces who had not flown with the French or English or been members of the Escadrille Lafayette. The great Rickenbacker would have beaten him soundly if, after becoming an ace, he had continued to hunt alone instead of flying in formation, subjecting his own will to the welfare of American arms. Rickenbacker was a great man, as Joe knew quite well; he himself was only a great hunter. And in the final reckoning Eddie would likely beat him two for one, for he was a steady sure shot as well as one of the great flyers of all time, and this month he had begun ranging on his own, and this month something was going to happen to

Joe, signs of which appeared in his dreams, which he felt in the air and saw in the faces of his superior officers.

Joe's hours in the air were long past counting. The leaders of formations ordered their takings-off and landings, but it was the easygoing way in many squadrons to let successful prowlers come and go when they pleased. They would look at the weather reports, go out and squint at the sky, and then climb into their ships or return, cursing, to the wardroom. Joe rarely went back. He observed no holidays, took almost no leave, and preferred dark days as long as he could see to set down his ship. He had received the *Croix de guerre* and a buss on each cheek from a French general. He had not been promoted because he had no command but his own plane.

He had once said that after fifty rifle shots in fairly close succession he could not group the hits. After his eleventh victory he noticed that his power of concentration, the essence of good shooting, had deteriorated slightly, his reflexes had slowed down a little, and he was no longer quite so accurate in judging speed and distance. In his next fight four Halberstadts came out of the sun and took him by surprise, and their first blast at five hundred yards ripped his fuselage and dealt him a hard thump in the calf of his right leg. Only the Dickenson Roll and a wild climb into the sun saved him from going down in flames.

The wound was superficial, the army doctor told him. The steel bullet had pierced the muscle and gone on its way without injuring the bone or a big tendon, but both holes had to be kept clean and he had better not do any fancy footwork for at least two weeks. Flying a Sopwith Camel well took extra fancy footwork.

"Look, Apache," the squadron leader said, when he had read and digested the reports. "This 'Long Hunt,' as you call it, has lasted too damned long without diversions, and besides, you're a wounded man. Anyway this festive war is folding up fast. Half a million Yanks and a hundred thousand Frogs have got the St. Michael salient, and are ready to hit the Meuse-Argonne. Bulgaria is out of the war and Allenby smashed Turkey no later than yesterday. I'm going to recommend to the Old Man that you be given three months' sick leave. That's what I said—three months. And you are grounded until I tell you what the Old Man says."

The Old Man spoke in no uncertain terms, as the American newspapers were fond of saying about almost any utterance without a "but." It was to the effect that Joe should take that leave, whether he liked it or not, and that he would be recommended for first lieutenant, temporary rank; and on his return—if there was any need to return—he could damned well become a shooting instructor. That would hold the son of a bitch for a while.

These orders were transmitted the next day by telephone, to be followed by a runner, for the very name of Apache Joe quickened the turning of military wheels. On the following day Joe was called forth from the jaunty line of Dodos, his gold-plated shoulder bars removed, and silver-plated bars fastened in their stead. Even when the ceremony was over, his buddies behaved somewhat quietly. The mess would not be the same without Apache Joe keeping his mouth shut. Joe himself went to the hangar where his battered Camel stood, painted out the big white rabbit on her fuselage, and painted in a wild Canadian goose, sure to bring good luck to any flyer behind her stick, for no fowl of Joe's acquaintance was so wary and so wise.

Suddenly sick for the Alaskan autumn, wild geese circling and honking, the woods draped in new snow, the caribou and the moose in good horn, and sick for much else he could not precisely identify without great strainings of heart, he caught the train for Havre and went aboard a quarter-empty troopship that had discharged its sardine-packed doughboys only two days before. A converted passenger liner, she afforded Joe a stateroom to himself and even a private bath, which he used once soon after boarding, and once more off Sandy Hook, this time noticing no discoloration of the bath water to justify the adventure. Now he came to think of it, he had downed more planes on the Western Front than he had taken baths. He wondered if he still carried with him a faint aroma of fish. After all, it was bred in his bone.

The ship was met by some dignitaries, including the mayor, and quite a crowd of newsmen. A returning major general received attention from them first, but many an eye cocked in Joe's direction during the ceremonies, and the instant these were over, the reporters came on the run. Some of them took his picture, but none got any story except what he could invent. Joe said, yes, it felt good to be back in the U.S.A., but that the giving out of military information was for appointed officials. Then he went into his stateroom to read quite a large stack of telegrams, most of them heart-warming congratulations. A good many requested his presence at affairs to raise money for the Red Cross, the Y.M.C.A. and other good works, and rallies to sell Liberty Bonds. The most attractive was from an old Indian in Pierre, South Dakota, inviting him to become a chief of the Sioux. The nearest to his heart were two from Juneau, one of which read,

COME HOME QUICK JOE BEFORE RABBIT TURNS WHITE IN WINTER

VICKY

The other read,

MUST START UP RIVER OCTOBER FIFTH SO WILL MISS YOUR ARRIVAL IN JUNEAU THEN MUST TAKE SHIP FROM SKAGWAY. ABOUT TWENTIETH GO OUTSIDE SO TRY MEET ME THERE ABOUT EIGHTEENTH. HAVE MOMENTOUS DECISION TO MAKE AFFECTING YOU. LOVE.

ERIC

Joe had only an inkling of what Vicky's telegram might mean, he could make no guess as to what decision confronted Eric, and all he could do about either was hasten on his way.

7

Eric's dilemma rose from the contents of a registered letter which he had opened in his hotel room, and which took a little tug of his will to open at all, since the envelope bore the engraving, The White House, Washington, D.C. It arrived on October first. Since it was postmarked September twenty-fifth, his reason told him it could not contain condolences from the nation's head over a national loss in battle, for that would have been sent by wire. Some weeks before, the President himself had written him congratulating him on his adopted son's service to the Allied cause, and thanking Eric for his own service in connection with government-sponsored fund raising in Alaska. This was something far more important.

It was from the President and it read:

There has been called to my attention, in addition to your patriotic service for the Red Cross, your outstanding service to the Territory of Alaska and hence to the nation in your eight years of leadership as representative and senator in the Territorial Legislature.

265

Your stand on labor disputes and on various projects for development of Alaskan resources, strong backing of good Territorial schools, and finally your support of the plan to establish the University of Alaska in the next few years, meet with my high approval.

I know of no one who seems to me better fitted for the office of Governor of the Territory of Alaska, soon, I believe, to be vacated by its present incumbent. If you are agreeable to accepting the responsibilities of this high office, I wish to invite you to meet me at the White House on November 3, to discuss the matter with me. Vouchers will be sent you for your transportation both ways.

Eric sat down and took a little snooze. The letter had not mentioned, he had noticed, his long being a thorn in the Administration's side in regard to a greater extension of the government schools and hospitals for Indians and Eskimos. But others had commented on it and lately a political adversary had wondered about it out loud, in the most guarded and courteous terms, hinting that Eric's solicitude for the native population might have some kind of emotional bias. Before then, Eric had known that his fathering a half-breed was no longer an ironclad secret. No hint of it had ever appeared in the Alaskan press, it had never been spoken of publicly as far as he knew, but now a new generation of Tekuh villagers had grown up, some of them easily debauched by firewater; and Eric, spending part of every year in Juneau and almost all of the last two years in activities related to the war, did not have their loyalty in the same degree as their elders'.

If Eric became governor of Alaska, Sophia's prophecy would come true. But if she had lived, would she want it to come true at any cost to that high pride that had somehow become his northern lights? And his first "if" was a big "if," because he perceived instantly that he could not accept the appointment without full confession to the President, nor would he be able to promise that the secret would be kept.

Light was thrown on this latter point two evenings after the arrival of the letter. While he was walking on Willoughby Avenue a small man with a look of anonymity paced quickly and overtook him. His wool cap and pants, flannel shirt, and heavy Mackinaw coat were common on

266

the streets of Juneau, often worn by commercial fishermen and other seafarers, but to these their weathered faces lent attractiveness, the individuality that is so marked among almost all Alaskans, while this man's clothes seemed a disguise. His face was unmemorable. Perhaps his eyes would stamp him in better light; Eric thought they had a troubled expression. His voice had no vibrance.

"Can I walk along with you a little way, Mr. Andersen?" he asked humbly. "I've got a message for you."

"You sure can."

"Of all the jobs the boss ever put on me I hate this one the worst. I'd of got out of it if I could, but nothin' doin'."

"You go ahead and give me the message. I won't blame you."

"I'd sure thank you if you don't. It's a dirty business. Well, some of the knowing ones say the governor is going to resign and you'll be appointed in his place. They say you were strongly recommended to the President. The word of my boss and his friends is this. If you take the job, they're going to let it out that the famous half-breed aviator, Apache Joe, is your son by an upriver squaw. They say they can prove it. And everybody will know that you laid up with her the night you went for a doctor to deliver your wife's baby. They said to tell you that would be a fine recommendation for a new governor of Alaska."

"Is that all?"

"Yes, sir, that's all, and I hope you'll excuse me."

The man turned into an alley and disappeared.

Eric walked on, wondering if his political career had been summarily closed.

On the following day he caught the *Princess Alice* for Skagway and on the following morning took the White Pass Railroad to Whitehorse. He was not bound for Tekuh village; nothing could be done or decided there; by instinct he was heading home. Before he disembarked at Gertrude Creek he asked the mail-boat captain if he would wait ten minutes for a passenger to Circle City.

"Sure, I'll do that for an old customer like you," the Captain answered. "What the hell is time for? All the boys are betting that the freeze-up will be late this year, maybe about the twentieth, the fall has been so warm, and even the river ducks haven't taken off. Anyway ten minutes isn't likely to make much difference."

At the landing Eric was met by his friend, Fritz, who

operated the Gertrude Mine on shares, and had seen the boat change her course a long way upriver.

"Fritz, can you get aboard this boat within ten minutes?"

"By damn, I could do it in five. What's up?"

"I yust want you to go to Circle City for a little vacation. If necessary you can come back by dog team. I want a few days here by myself. I've got somet'ing to t'ink over."

Fritz understood perfectly. Many sourdoughs who had left the solitudes had not broken with the occasional need of solitariness, and returned to it from time to time for their souls' repose. He ran to his cabin, hurled a few toilet articles in a handbag, put his poke in his pants pocket, and ran back.

"I may use some of your grub," Eric called, as Fritz was boarding the mail boat.

"Help yourself," Fritz bawled, "and lock out them wolverines when you take off."

Eric glanced again at his watch; the whole transaction had taken eight minutes. Sourdoughs could stay happily in one place for a long time, he thought, but they could also leave in a hurry.

Eric walked to his own house, unlocked the door, and went in. On his returns here he was always thinking he would find it changed, at least in some subtle way, by the slow, soft, remorseless hand of time, but he never did. By Yiminy, it had been well built, to keep out pack rats as well as wolverines! The caribou-skin rug lay unfaded and ungnawed; the pretty chintz curtains on the boarded-up windows were as clean of dust as though just hung. Kindling had been set in the cooking and heating stove; matches lay nearby; on the bed were folded blankets to warm a freezing wanderer. He went into the other two rooms, then the bathroom. He took a book of poetry from the shelves, one that Sophia had ordered from Seattle—her favorite book, he thought—let it fall open where hands had once made a habit of opening it, and read one verse:

St. Agnes Eve—Ah, bitter chill it was!
The owl, for all his feathers, was a-cold;
The hare limp'd trembling through the frozen grass . . .

He put back the book and took one of the big chairs. Here he sat until sundown, lost in a maze of memories; then walked to Fritz's cabin to find edibles for supper. There was plenty of rice, dried apples, canned milk, and a freshly killed grouse, which made better gravy than any chicken that ever walked a barnyard, hung in the shed. Returning, he cooked a delicious and filling dinner on his own stove, ate it with pleasure, mixed a long drink of whisky with water from the ice-caked rain barrel, drank it slowly, washed, and went to bed.

Beyond the middle of the night he dreamed that some-one had called his name. That wraith of sound wakened him, and as he lay, strangely alert, his neck prickling, an idea hit him with great force. People would say that only a madman would think of such a thing. Well, all squareheads were a little crazy; in fact "crazy squarehead," was one of the most common of Alaskan expressions; and many sour-doughs, especially old sourdoughs, appeared more than a little crazy. Eric remembered hearing that as long as people perceived that to believe themselves Napoleon or the President or Jim Jeffries' dog was, of course, ridiculous, they need not fear commitment for life; it was when they re-garded everybody else as crazy that the keepers shook their heads. Well, that looked bad, for he could see nothing in-sane about the idea which so far he was trying to see from other people's viewpoint. Rather than that, it seemed a glimpse of almost sublime truth.

He had had a hard time thinking those cool thoughts, because he was so excited. He got up in his warm under-wear, lit a lantern, and then opened the front door. He knew well the vista that the open door disclosed—he had stood here a little while on a thousand nights—and tonight it lay immersed in moonlight; and the old spruce trees and the young ones that had seeded in the last twenty years standing soldier-straight touched his heart with beauty.

He glanced at his watch. To his surprise it read past three. Instead of going back to bed, he dressed slowly, then lighted a small fire. Long before the chill had been driven from the room his mind was made up as to the projected undertaking. Who was there to make it up but himself? He need answer only to his own troth, with which were in-terbound Sophia's memory and his attitude, whatever its source, toward himself as a man. He gave brief thought to the risk involved. It was very slight, and indeed he need not run it, for before the undertaking was half completed he would know whether or not to proceed with it or to give it up.

The equinox was hardly two weeks gone, but the nights

were lengthening swiftly, and he could not wait till dawn. So with his lantern he made for Fritz's shed and got what he needed in the way of equipment: a pick, shovel, drills, claw hammer, dynamite, caps, and fuses. Then he returned to a little shelf on the hillside, and counted four white stones.

He cut wood nearby and built a big fire to give light. Far out on the river he saw its reflection as a shimmering inverted wedge of sunrise colors. Carefully uprooting one small spruce tree growing between the stones, he cleared away a little undergrowth and began to shovel out frost-seamed earth. A little over two feet below the surface he came to the permafrost, solid and unmoved except for the congealing of the fragments he had placed there. Now came a glimmer in the east, so he went to the house and warmed up his leavings of last night's supper for his breakfast.

Before he returned to his labor he glanced at the thermometer, a good one to start with and sturdy as ever at recording the extremes of heat and cold. It stood at twenty degrees above zero. A chill north wind was blowing, clouds hung gray, shallow pools no longer glassed the sky but had turned gray with ice, which sometimes fooled flying ducks and caused them to skid, squawking, when they had volplaned down against the wind to light; and the noise of little waters, which people hardly noticed in summer season, background music to the drama of Northern life and growth, had now ceased, leaving the land to silence, although the great river flowed with imperial power. The temperature might reach thirty in the shade of midday but not more.

Now he could see to drill with great care, not more than four feet deep. In the holes he placed light charges of dynamite and laid his fuses. When he had lighted them and run a short distance, ducks on the river took wing at a muffled roar.

Until nearly noon he worked with pick and shovel, and no boat passed from whose crew he must conceal his occupation, and the only spectators were a family of chipmunks in beautiful autumn fur, and a Canada jay that perched nearby turned her head this way and that to watch him with beady eyes, then uttered her raucous cry and flew away. He had felt an all-pervading loneliness when he had worked by firelight, an old familiar visitor, but it passed off as his task neared its close. Toward the very end, he handled his pick with great care. The last pieces of frozen ground he removed rapidly with his hands. Not a board in the box had rotted, no water had seeped down through the implacable ice-locked ground. He had made room to sit down by it, and after a few minutes of stillness, his hands stopped shaking, and with the claw hammer he drew the nails from the lid and lifted it off.

The body of Sophia lay utterly unchanged since he had lain it here that midwinter day not quite eighteen years ago.

Time had stood still, powerless in this frozen vault. Beauty endured, as with the Grecian Urn of which once she had read to him beside their fire.

"I was going to ask you something, Sophia," he said, "but there is no need."

Quickly he nailed back the lid and re-covered it with pieces of rock-hard frozen ground. In five minutes it lay two feet deep, the abysmal cold imprisoned, then with his shovel he refinished filling the grave. He replaced the little spruce tree and spread the summer growth already snarled by the fall frosts. At last he replaced four small white stones, picked up the tools, and returned them to Fritz's shed.

For the rest of the time before the last mail boat came up from Fairbanks to winter in Dawson, he thought he would hunt moose and caribou for the Tekuh villagers, increase their store of fish, attend to the mine, rejoice in his happy memories, and declare truce with his bitter ones, and muse on what fate might bring. •

8

Rushing from the Seattle station to the Canadian Pacific dock, Joe arrived only in time to see the passengers of the *Princess Sophia*, with her usual thick-as-thieves assemblage of sourdoughs, waving from the rail, and hear their shouts and her whistle's boastful blast as the strip of water between her and the dock widened to cable's length. No fast power boat was nearby that he could hire to overtake her; anyway Captain Locke would not want the bother of picking up a passenger with a Jacob's ladder, Joe thought, although in this case he thought wrong. This dour skipper, who said so little, harbored thoughts that no one knew, and in the solitude of his cabin or alone on his bridge he sometimes daydreamed of possible pleasant happenings and of triumphs reasonably within his reach and of how he would behave; and he had followed with great joy the newspaper accounts of the career of Apache Joe, who was Eric Andersen's adopted son and an Alaskan. He would have hauled the *Sophia* back full speed astern, upsetting some dishes and drinks and possibly some sourdoughs whose balance was precarious just now, to garner in the great ace and carry him proudly where he wanted to go.

Luckily Joe had to wait only two days for the *Princess Mary*, almost a sister to the *Sophia* in outward form but having a different soul, making for the Panhandle towns to pick up draftees on her last Alaskan voyage of the year. Joe had never mounted her plank before, knew no one in the crew. Her passengers were mostly war-rich tourists not allowed on the Atlantic or even in the warm Caribbean, who had few places to go other than the beautiful Inside Passage, where raw weather was setting in and much rain fell but where at least they would be safe from submarines, and among whom Joe thought he could pass almost unnoticed. There were quite a few other soldiers on the ship, some bound for Chilkoot Barracks, some invalided home or on two weeks' leave or furlough from Camp Lewis, lieutenants or enlisted men including three who looked part Indian, and surely few civilians noticed insignia or a ribbon or two on a tunic. Joe had signed as Joseph Harris, a common enough name, even a good alias for a shady character, and given U. S. Army as his address.

Joe's prognostications went awry. He gained his stateroom without attracting attention, but on his first entering the social hall a big man in a sport coat, wearing horn-rimmed glasses, gazed at him fixedly, glanced quickly about as does one who sees a purse lying on the sidewalk, then hurried toward him.

"I've seen your picture, Lieutenant, in the papers," he said in a low, excited voice.

"I dare say." This was an expression which the Dodos had picked up from the English flyers, and which Joe had not known he ever used.

"I'll make one guess and if it's not the right one, I'll buy you a case of scotch."

"Thank you, sir, but I don't need a case of scotch."

"You're Apache Joe, just as sure as I'm W. P. Trenton from San Francisco."

"Yes, sir, I am, but the less notice that's taken of it, the better I like it."

"That's natural enough. You're tired of fuss being made over you, but my wife and I and our friends won't make any, you'll just be one of our gang. Can I speak to the captain about having you sit at our table in the dining saloon? How about a small cocktail party before supper tonight in our stateroom? My wife and I have the so-called bridal suite."

"If you please, I'd rather you wouldn't speak to the captain—he'll have his own ideas as to seating. I'll drop in for a drink before supper, but I'd rather the gathering not be in my honor. You understand there are soldiers aboard who deserve honors more than I do—doughboys seriously wounded in battle. I wouldn't feel right about it."

"It will be just as you stipulate. I won't even tell anyone you're aboard—even my guests tonight can find out for themselves. It's Cabin Number One, and let's say half-past five."

Joe agreed, and Mr. Trenton walked away in a glowing daze. Joe hurried off to find the chief steward.

"Look, Chief," he said to that worthy, "I'd like to make a request about my table seat."

"I haven't got around to that yet," the chief answered, rather coldly because he was raised in Petersburg, a Panhandle town, and he had never become quite reconciled himself to Indians, even if lieutenants in the Army, eating with white people.

"I think very likely the captain will consider himself obligated to invite me to eat at his table, and I'd rather not. I'm Apache Joe Harris."

"Good God!"

"I want to eat with the soldiers, preferably enlisted men. Is that all right?"

"Well, it's all right with me, if the cap'n says okay. I'll have to tell him you're on the ship—it's one of the chief's jobs to know who's aboard, especially who's who aboard. Well, I ought to have known it was you. I heard you were heading west; how did you dodge the reporters at the station?"

Joe had dodged the reporters by a simple lie, told in New York, that he was heading for San Francisco, and gave no thought to newsmen there making disgusted trips to meet one train after another. In Seattle he had passed his time of waiting at an obscure hotel where no guest could dream of a celebrity showing up, and where the sight of an Indian first lieutenant, no doubt short of cash, had caused a little glowing in humble hearts. Joe had not seen the headline in yesterday's San Francisco *Examiner*, which read APACHE JOE HIDES OUT.

The chief steward had seen it and read the story. It had been cleverly written, a top-hole alibi story for the real story, to the effect that Joe was no doubt using the same tactics with which he had taken many a Boche flyer by surprise—concealing himself in a cloud and possibly in the sun.

"Well, I've got a good joke on the purser. He'll never hear the last of it if I have my way."

When, at half-past five—for punctuality had long been drummed into his head—Joe knocked on the door of Cabin Number One the babel within suddenly ceased. When the door opened Mr. Trenton had a little speech prepared.

"Oh yes. The young lieutenant I met on deck. So happy to have you join us." Then, in a husky whisper, "What did you say your name was?"

"Harris."

"My friends, Lieutenant Harris."

Trenton's guests looked at him politely, then a young woman shrieked, screamed almost, rushed forward, threw her arms about Joe's neck, and kissed him. At once she broke into wild laughter.

"Apache Joe!" she yelled. "I was the first to recognize you! Trent, you old slicker, you lion tamer you! We all knew you had something up your sleeve but we never dreamed——"

"I promised him no one would make a fuss over him, and don't do it or I'll put rat poison in your drinks. Apache, we're mighty proud to have you here, and we'll let it go at that. I've got some Round-the-World Scotch. Will that do?"

This party set a pattern, rough replicas of which marked his social activities for the rest of the voyage. Quite a few tourists invited him to affairs which he either attended or declined, and some who had no opportunity to do so came up and condoned with him over his lionizing, because they themselves knew some lions whose dearest wish was to be treated like anyone else, yet they had to be polite and stand it. One gentleman remarked to him that he hoped the rushers would be as appreciative of his career a year from now, since no glory faded as quickly as military glory. His words confused Joe a little, because his whole realization of glory was somewhat dim.

Joe had hoped feebly that no wireless message had been sent to Juneau of his coming. That hope was exploded at distant view of the dock, where there appeared a flat cluster of bees. When the ship was sidling in a roar went up, and two soldiers, themselves wearing decorations for bravery, although already disillusioned about their own chance for a noisy welcome, caught Joe by the arms as he was ducking toward his cabin and marched him firmly to the rail. At once the town band led by Hans Gobel, who owned a butcher shop and beat the bass drum, struck up "The Conquering Hero." By the time the gangplank was run out the band was playing the hit piece, "My Totem Pole," from an almost forgotten comic opera named *The Alaskan*.

The governor stood there, although not wearing a silk hat as had the New York mayor, let alone a cutaway coat and striped pants, for such apparel would inspire salty jokes among the squarehead fishermen; and anyway everyday custom was *de rigueur* in the Territory. The mayor was present also, giving orders to everybody, and Joe caught sight of Vicky—knowing her by the way she moved as much as by her sunrise coloring—trying in vain to melt into the throng. There was no sign of Eric, as his telegram had foretold, and no doubt he was hurrying upriver to catch the train to Skagway, to meet Joe there on October twenty-first.

Even to the last Joe had stubbornly dared to believe that no ceremonies would be performed. Now he saw their preparations as in a bleak and only too credible dream—the crowd drawing back from the gangplank to leave a wide aisle. The governor, the secretary of Alaska, the mayor of Juneau, and a few other dignitaries walked up the aisle. The band stopped playing, the crowd stopped yelling, and presently Joe, very red, was confronting the governor, who was making a speech of welcome. At the end of the speech, which was happily brief, Joe was presented with a plaque bearing an etching of an airplane marked with a white rabbit and an inscription.

Joe spoke his thanks and accepted the plaque, then stood holding it as awkwardly as was possible for him.

"Now I think you want to greet first your old playmate from the upper river," the governor said pleasantly, at which the mayor walked to one of the side lines and brought Vicky front and center. She was not in the least awkward, feeling a dignity that she could not have expressed except in grace, all the deeper because of the com-

275

plexity of the situation. She came up and smiled and kissed Joe on the lips.

The crowd yelled its approval. It was now a real crowd, not a conglomeration of people, with shared emotion, and the prejudices of the few were washed away by the strong surge, and the human feelings of the many predominated. The governor, a man of true eminence about to take a post high in government councils, had struck the right note when he had called Vicky Joe's childhood friend.

Then, for a few minutes, as the *Alaskan Empire* put it, chaos reigned. Joe was half carried, half thrust into the top of the back seat of an open Packard automobile. With the governor beside him, the secretary of Alaska in the right front seat, and the governor's chauffeur behind the wheel, the parade began, led by the band. It moved up one street and down another—there were not very many—and no confetti was thrown, and no motor policeman rode in escort. But the people stood in the doorways and on the sidewalks; the sporting girls, as they were called in Juneau, came forth from the row houses in their finery, showing off as always, something they could not help, intrinsic to their profession; and the best of all were the Indians by the streets of native town, watching quietly with shiny black eyes.

The ship had docked at five, close on suppertime, so the parade ended at the Oddfellows' Hall, where the ladies had prepared a spread. About two hundred people had bought tickets, the funds going to the Red Cross, and by all indications it would be over when the paper plates were empty, and Joe could take Vicky home. A little thing went wrong. A lady started to play the piano, and instead of singable music, which the Alaskans love and during the hearty harmonizing of which Joe and Vicky could sneak off, she played dance tunes. At once some young people began to fold up the card tables that had held the supper and put them out of the way, and to line the folding chairs against the wall. Almost before anyone knew it, several couples were dancing.

Joe and Vicky danced through most of one piece, meanwhile edging toward the door, and were furtively making for it when someone called Vicky's name.

She turned and said one word. "Kate."

The girl was tall, like most Alaskan girls, well dressed, not as pretty as the most. Joe had heard of Kate in some connection with Vicky, although he could not immediately recall when or where. She had two escorts, one a cheechako

276

civilian, and the other an infantry officer, and the two girls had barely spoken to each other in rather strained voices when the civilian escort, in what he fancied was the robust Alaskan way, whirled Vicky away to dance. Joe did what he had been taught to do at military-school dances. He bowed his head to Kate and said, "Miss, would you like to dance?"

Too late, then, the words out of his mouth, a swift memory flashed to Joe and he recalled perfectly clearly his hearing about Kate. Actually it was Eric who had told him. Fannie had visited Kate's mother in St. Michael when Vicky was a little girl, and Kate had used all the dirty words her tongue could find to give her opinion of Indians. She had been prettier than Vicky then, as well as better dressed, and hence she had impressed Vicky greatly. She was still better dressed but not nearly as pretty, because her meanness had found its way into her face.

A shocking scene followed, which Kate thought was a very effective scene for the benefit of the spectators.

"No, no, I can't!" Kate cried, as though close to hysteria. Then, clasping the lieutenant's arm, "Don't let him dance with me, Kenneth, please don't! I couldn't stand to dance with an Indian."

Joe could not speak; he did not know how to meet such a situation, but the officer spoke.

"Kate, your behavior is vulgar and inexcusable. I'm ashamed I came with you."

"Then take me home at once. I don't want to stay at a dance with an Indian."

"Only too gladly."

As they were leaving, Vicky and her partner hurried up to Joe, the man said a hasty thank-you and sped after his companions. She was white as the snow that was once her element.

"Shall we leave now?" Joe asked.

"No. Everybody heard what she said, and you can't run. Apache Joe can't run, and you've got to stick it out awhile. Let's just stand over by the wall. We'll talk of old times."

They did so, although their talk was jerky and not very coherent. They waited while four pieces were played, then Vicky said, "We can go now."

"I've got to speak to the governor."

They walked together to where he was sitting with his wife, his sprightly daughter of about twenty, and a young

277

assistant. Joe was presented to the ladies, giving them his best military-school bow, and shook hands with both men, then introduced Vicky. Joe expressed his thanks simply and well, for although many Indians are rather closemouthed, Joe one of the most, they are far from an inarticulate people and on occasion are capable of true eloquence, of which American history gives many instances.

"Why don't you young people dance?" the First Lady of Alaska suggested.

"That's a good idea," the young assistant answered. "Miss Ford, will you dance with me?"

Without a glance at Joe, Vicky answered, "I'd love to."

The couple went out onto the floor and Joe became as taut as in battle.

"Miss," he said, looking at the governor's daughter, "may I have this dance?"

"You certainly may, and it's high time you asked me."

He offered his arm, again military-school training, and since they were both good dancers—Joe because of superior co-ordination and a feeling of rhythm that marks almost all excellent athletes as well as every good musician, his partner because of native grace and a belle's experience—they had not much need of talk, to which Joe did not feel inclined. Only two couples moved off the floor, and it was not a popular move, since the sitters and other dancers looked studiously in another direction. When the music stopped, Joe escorted his partner to her seat, Vicky and the assistant came up, good nights were said, and now there seemed no obstacle between the two upriver sourdoughs and the door.

They had reckoned wrongly. When they were full in the middle of the floor a burly young man with a florid face, wearing civilian clothes, came forth and spoke to them.

"Vicky, will you sit down a minute?" he asked in a loud voice. "I wish to speak to Joe Harris alone."

Vicky gave Joe one glance of pitiful entreaty.

"Wait for me at the door, Rabbit." Then, when she had sped away, clutching her handkerchief, "I don't know you."

"You will in a moment. My name is Matt Harkins; I'm Kate Harkins' brother. I approve of what she did; it was the duty of any white girl. I was out in the hall at the time or I would have had an account to settle with that lieutenant. I waited around to see if you'd ask any other white girl to dance. If you didn't, I would have let well enough alone.

But you did, the daughter of the governor, who you knew couldn't refuse you."

"Do you want to do anything about it?"

"Yes, I'm going to. I'm going to teach you a lesson you won't forget. My hat's off to you for the fighting you did in France, but in a dance hall in Juneau you're just another half-breed siwash. And now——"

His arm started to swing. Joe was watching his eyes instead of his hands, and they signaled the coming effort. Joe was well rested from flying, all his springs had coiled, and it was doubtful if more than a dozen people saw his sudden and deadly swift upthrust. His fist struck where he had aimed it, on the side of Matt Harkins' jaw. Matt did not crumple down, as men do when blasted with machine-gun fire, but he crashed down, the knock of his head heard all over the hall.

At once a great yell of purest joy rose from the crowd. But a bellow from an old sourdough, who had nothing to say until now, resounded above it.

"Chalk up one more Hun for Apache Joe!"

Joe glanced at the fallen, observed that his eyes had rolled up, and the idle thought struck him that he might have suffered a concussion of the brain. If so, that was all right. It would be quite all right with Joe if the skull had cracked and he died. In hunting Boche ships, he had had to kill many men against whom he had felt no enmity and with whom he had shared the joy of battle and risked the fortunes of war.

He caught up with Vicky and they walked through the quiet streets to the boardinghouse where she lived. On its porch she stopped, took both his hands, and spoke with great earnestness, as often they used to speak to each other in the woods at the broaching of some serious matter involving each other rather than their quarry.

"I love you, Joe. I'll never love anyone else. And if you want me to, I'll marry you—on one condition. That we go to Skagway together, meet Eric, and take the *Sophia* Outside. I don't want to stay here any more."

9

The latest news was that the *Sophia* would sail about noon of October twenty-third. Already no whole staterooms were available, only a third berth, to be used when the vessel was pack-jammed, could be had in various staterooms already engaged. The interior was closing up, the upper river had frozen over on October twentieth, and passengers were pouring into Skagway via the White Pass Railroad from the upper Yukon and the Tanana and Yukon Territory, from Anchorage, Seward, Valdez, and Cordova, no few from Nome, some from the west, and a few scattering from further afield. The word had gotten out that *Sophia*'s company on this voyage would comprise the greatest assembly of old sourdoughs since she began her Alaskan run in 1912. Passengers from long exile in the solitudes who could have more handily caught the ship at Juneau went out of their way to Skagway, so they could be present at the reunion and ride her all the way. Many were going Outside for the winter, most had business of a sort, a few were on holiday. It was a fine time to visit Seattle. Everyone knew that the German armies were in retreat, almost in a rout, and there would be great doings in the city when the glorious news was told.

Eric arrived in Skagway on October twenty-first. He said very little to Joe at their first meeting—mainly the purpose of his intended visit to the White House—and Joe said even less, waiting for a long evening alone with Eric, although his face reflected, as far as an Indian face can, the joy in the lean Norse face at his safe return; and there came with it—changing it a little, a change not readily discernible except to a sourdough who knew Indian faces well—a great joy that Eric was here to return to, and in due course to listen to all he had to say and make straight reply.

As Joe and Vicky were entering the offices of the Canadian Pacific, the most imposing in the town of Skagway, Joe called her aside and they stood on the busy sidewalk and spoke in low terms.

"Before I buy my ticket I want to tell you something," Joe said. "I'll go with you to Seattle and stay at least a month. If by then I find I can't get along without Alaska, if I can't live there in happiness and according to my own idea of success, I'm coming home."

"That's perfectly fair," Vicky answered. "It just means that we won't be married until then; we'll just go together as in the past. Maybe you'd be willing to go to some other frontier, say Montana, the Jackson Hole country in Wyoming, perhaps to the Amazon that's wilder than Alaska or even to East Africa. If you still want to take me, I'll go with you. You could adapt yourself to any wild country where you can do what you love to do. It's not the wilderness of

280

Alaska that I can't stand any longer; I love the wilderness. It's the towns that are growing and new towns being founded, towns that I couldn't stay out of, no matter how hard I'd try."

But the *Sophia* did not sail, as she had originally planned, at noon of the twenty-third; a bulletin had been posted that she would be delayed at least until six in the evening. Vicky had gone aboard when she heard the news and was waiting for Eric and Joe, so she got off with her handbag and went back to the hotel. Here she found Eric quickly but no sign of Joe.

"He hasn't gone far, you can be sure of that," Eric said.

"I'm not a bit sure. He could have very easily taken the railroad to Whitehorse and is going to mush to Tekuh village. I never know what he's going to do. Who knows anything about Indians? Well, if he doesn't show up before the gangplank's taken in, I'm going Outside without him, and then I'll never speak to him again."

Actually Joe had not gone far at the moment Eric and Vicky were talking—only to the office of Dr. Rogers, where he had been hurriedly called. Rogers was a middle-aged man held in great esteem; he had gone all the way to Tekuh village the previous spring to help Pavlof and Fannie combat a sudden outbreak of smallpox. He minced no words on what he wanted of Joe.

"There's a half-breed Indian and his family living in the village of Atlin at the big lake. Do you know where it is?"

"Yes, sir."

"Well, they visited Carcross and when they got home one of the two children came down with what was obviously diphtheria. The child died and an Indian slogged it to Whitehorse to say that the other child's throat is sore, and could he get any medicine? A government man guessed what was up—there's been scattering diphtheria through that region —and told him there was no medicine—he meant antitoxin —either in Dawson or Whitehorse—they'd had some but have used it all and waiting for more to be sent—so the Indian caught the train down here. But if her throat was sore three days ago, she needs that antitoxin mighty bad by now."

"Well?"

"I was going to send it by the only plane in Skagway. The Indians had anticipated this, not being fools, and they've

281

cleared off the snow from the new bay ice to make a landing. Archie Miller owns the plane, a Curtiss trainer; also he's the only flyer who lives here and he's down with flu. I reckon you can guess the rest."

"Yes, I can."

"I'd come with you if it would do any good, but Archie said you've a better chance of getting over the pass if you went alone."

Joe noticed that Dr. Rogers' language indicated no doubt of the young war bird's accepting the mission if the plane would fly. Well, that was all right, Dr. Rogers was an old sourdough. In the back country of Alaska and the Yukon Territory people went a week's journey out of their way to help someone who was down sick. It was an old custom there, as inviolable as that of leaving kindling in the stove or of not stealing from a cache. Such customs had been imposed by mutual dependence on one another in a vast, sparsely peopled country. Joe thought of mentioning that he had been due to sail on the *Sophia*, but thought better of it.

"Are there runners on the plane?"

"Sure."

"You'll have to tell me how to inject the antitoxin."

"I'll send it ready in the needle in a cotton pad soaked with alcohol in a cardboard box. Carry it in the inside pocket of your coat that you wear under your flying suit, to keep it from freezing.

"Wipe off the top of one cheek of the child's butt with some of the cotton and stick in the needle and draw back the plunger to see if you've hit a blood vessel. If you have, pick another spot nearby, and push in the plunger all the way. That's all there is to it. Of course, the child may be dead. In that case, I've given you a trip for nothing."

"Have you heard when the *Sophia*'s sailing?"

"Not until six o'clock."

"Well, I might make it back in time to catch her, so I'd like to start at once. And please give me a pencil and paper; I want to write a note to Vicky Ford."

Joe wrote swiftly, sealed and addressed the note, and then asked the whereabouts of the plane.

"It's in what Archie Miller calls his hangar, close by his house at the south edge of town. Anyone will show you. Since the big snow, he's got a good take-off. He'd just flown to Bennett when he came down with the flu."

Dr. Rogers carefully prepared the needle. Joe sped to

the hotel and was somewhat relieved not to find Vicky there, since his note would explain the situation better than any speech he would be able to invent. Since Eric, too, had gone out—apparently with Vicky—Joe left the note with the Filipino bellboy, who promised its safe delivery as soon as Missy returned. Taking his teddy-bear suit, helmet, and goggles from his trunk, Joe stuffed them into a handbag that would not be conspicuous on Skagway streets. Telling no one where he was going, with the same closed mouth he had kept at the Dodos' aerodrome, he made for the "hangar" of Archie Miller.

A neighbor, who regularly helped Archie take off, was waiting for Joe and helped him slide the ship onto the well-packed snow of the runway. Joe put on his flying togs and strapped himself in the seat.

It was a perfectly good ship, he was thinking. He thought even better of her when he had yelled, "Contact!" and the engine started with a robust roar. This was the first time he had ever flown a ship with runners instead of wheels, but she behaved herself well, and after a somewhat thrilling glide down the runway, she took off cleanly. Well above the trees, he had a good view of the *Sophia*, beautiful, black and white, to all Alaskans the most beautiful vessel in the world including the *Leviathan* lying, commandeered, in New York Harbor. He gave her a little salute, pulled back his stick, and made for White Pass.

It was truly white today, every way he gazed, and this was his first view of the Coast Range from the air, and he wished that some of the Dodos, who on convivial occasions spoke of the scenery of their various countrysides, could look upon it. He climbed steeply, all his bus would take, to clear the peaks, and then he flew in the clear dry air a thousand feet above their whitest, loneliest summit, perhaps as might an archangel who had received permission to visit Creation on the fourth day, before the people and the beasts and the birds had been given life, and no other eyes had seen it except God's own.

His mind dwelt very little on the failure of his assignation with Vicky. Old Indians had taught him, by example, not to worry about what he could not help. After a while he got out Archie Miller's chart of the Lake Atlin region, not a very exact chart, and since the stick needed no attention, the plane keeping this course until something happened to change it, he searched carefully, estimated his position by dead reckoning, veered slightly east by north, and began to lose altitude. This was a slow ship compared to a Bristol Fighter or a Sopwith Camel, yet he had been air-borne less than an hour.

Now he could identify the long narrow lake by its smooth look as opposed to the fuzzy look of snowy forests. Dropping lower, he scanned its shores about midway its length until he saw a cluster of tiny white squares, most certainly the village of Atlin. At his second swoop over the roofs about half a dozen tiny, lively figures scuttled about, all of them pointing to what looked like a strip of open water, a hundred feet wide, five hundred feet long, and perfectly straight. It could fool a flock of ducks, Joe thought, as he carefully set down his runners and began a delightful glide toward the snowy lake shore.

Joe had not known how a plane behaved on glass-smooth runners on glass-smooth ice, and of course the Indians had had only the vaguest notion, having seen Archie Miller put down his ship on well-crusted snow at Carcross. Almost immediately Joe perceived that the friction was a great deal less than that of rubber tires on a good airstrip, and his landing field was not long enough, and he had no brakes. Still traveling twenty miles an hour, he plowed into a foot-high bank of snow. The ship did not nose over, and one of the runners stood the gaff; the other broke in two. "I'll miss the *Sophia*," he told himself, as he clambered out.

The Indians came on the run. "*Sohteentuk?*" Joe asked in Athabaskan.

The Indians shook their heads. No, the child, Chihtsul, was not dead yet, she was still alive. Joe knew by the way they hurried him toward one of the cabins he had not come long too soon. She was lying on a bed of skins, flushed with fever and breathing with great difficulty. And suddenly Joe did not give a whoop in hell about having missed the *Sophia*. If the right medicine had been made in some great medicine house on high, he would in due course have Vicky for his own, his companion in all the lonelinesses of his life, but if the wrong medicine had been made, she was lost to him forever, and he must take what comfort he could in a pretty young squaw. He would not grieve. Only old squaws, whose fortitude had been proven, let themselves grieve over what could not be helped. He would turn his face into a piece of carved wood and his heart to a lump of stone.

He got out the needle, wiped its long point with the inside of the alcohol-soaked cotton, which was still damp, and still smelled like firewater. Then he stuck it into the top of one side of the child's small, round, brown butt, just as he had been told, looked in vain for blood, then pushed the plunger. Thereby he might save her life. Although he had never had a moment's remorse about the lives he had taken in the last year, their taking being intrinsic to the Long Hunt on which he had gone, yet he felt sharp pleasure as he withdrew the needle. He would tell Eric about it when he saw him, and Vicky, too, if he ever saw her; no one else.

At once he gathered the men, had them get their axes and their knives, and get to work to replace the broken sled runner. Suitable wood was found with great difficulty, shaped out and hand-hewn, then polished as smooth as the lake ice itself, and then laboriously fixed in place. The sun had set and shadows were gathering too fast to attempt the flight over the pass tonight. So he ate a huge meal of half-cooked caribou meat and spread skins on the cabin floor for his bed.

Just before he lay down he crouched by the bed of little Chihtsul, looked into her face, felt her hand, listened to her breathing.

"*Skookem!*" he muttered, deep in his throat.

9. The Beautiful Ship

By midafternoon of October twenty-third Eric alone and Vicky alone had begun to feel a distinct anxiety over Joe's mysterious absence. This they did not share with each other, because neither cared to confess it; such a confession would imply that it was not wholly an unreasonable anxiety. Mixed with it in Vicky's mind, occasionally blotting it out, was a good stock of exasperation, injured vanity, and plain anger. If Joe had decided to quit her, because of her demands, because he had never really loved her anyway, because of any one of a dozen reasons she need not attempt to guess, at least the brown-skinned bastard should have had the decency to tell her so, although she had not a shadow of reason to believe that he would have told her. For him to get the hell out without telling anybody was only too believable.

The thought crossed Eric's mind that Joe had been murdered by someone insane. He knew well that insane people often hear voices instructing them to kill such and such a person, quite often a person prominent in the news, and that news can be the Associated Press, or it can be the columns of a country weekly, without diminishing or increasing the urgency of the voices. Juneau had more than its share of eccentrics, one of whom, perhaps, if the whole truth were known, should be committed to the wards for homicidal maniacs. He might be wholly or partly of German descent. He would believe that the voice commanding Joe's destruction came from God. For Eric, the whole picture was a morbid fancy only. His common sense denied that anything serious had happened other than the widening rift between Joe and Vicky.

From the hotel clerk Eric obtained a duplicate key to Joe's room and gave it a quick search. Joe had not taken his toilet articles or put on any clean clothes; however his handbag was nowhere to be seen. Since his trunk had been locked, Eric could not tell if any of Joe's other belongings were missing; as far as could be seen he had taken himself off hurriedly on an excursion of a few hours or few days, and had every intention of returning. Eric asked for the bellboy who had been on duty about eleven o'clock. This Filipino had been spelled at noon, and his speller believed he had mentioned going to Douglas Island, where some of his kinfolk stayed. No one knew who the kinfolk were or where they could be found, hence that possible avenue of information was temporarily closed.

What no one in Eric's reach could know was that a domestic situation arising in the family of the bellboy's sister-in-law had so upset him that he had quite forgotten to give Missy Vicky her letter, and that he still had it, somewhat crumpled by nervous movements of his hands, in the inside pocket of his coat.

Eric thought of questioning Archie Miller, the only other airman in town, and inquired of an acquaintance as to Archie's residence, only to be told that he was "away, somewheres, as usual," and had in fact been seen taking off alone in his ship a little before noon, heading eastward.

Eric reported these findings to Vicky. "I can wire Carcross to find out if he was on the train, and get an immediate answer," Eric said.

"Do it if you like, but don't bring me into it," Vicky answered. "I wouldn't want the louse to know that I'm that much interested."

Eric decided against sending the telegram. Apparently it was in respect to Joe's maturity, grown upon him in three years' attendance of a tough school, more than a year in the U. S. Army, including half a year of making split-second decisions of great import to himself and others, when he flew and fought alone. What Joe was up to just now was really none of Eric's business. If he returned in time to catch the ship, presumably well and good. If not, Eric would likely find out the truth when, the President's verdict known, he returned to Alaska.

A notice had been posted in the hotel lobby that all passengers southward bound on the *Princess Sophia* must be aboard by 8 P.M. Well before then Vicky had gone aboard, her trunk in the baggage rooms, two handbags in her stateroom, and her dress, face, and hair as prettily gotten up as she knew how. The throng gathering on the deck about the gangplank was excited by itself. "Old home week," someone said, and the thought was repeated in various wording a thousand times in the next hour. No one could remember a gathering of more old friends. The ticket holders felt triumphant, for at least twenty people, some said as many as fifty, had been unable to get tickets for love or money. The visitors wished they were going along. She had two hundred and sixty-eight passengers, chockablock, and her crew of seventy-five made a grand total of three hundred and forty-three; except in the wildest days of the gold rush, that many people had never shipped together on Alaskan waters.

The sight of so many sourdoughs Vicky knew, or knew of, or had seen before, took her out of herself in a large degree, even though a small dark spot of self-awareness, and hence of loneliness, refused to fade away. Their happiness and jokes and laughter raised her spirits so that she could think forcibly, To hell with the half-breed buck, and even at times tell herself that his characteristic take-off was a good riddance. Was it characteristic? Perhaps not, but that caused the riddance to be even better, since it was deliberate, meaning that he did not love her enough to leave Alaska, that he couldn't love anyone that much, or anything except hunting and battle. If he had come with her, in a month he would be trekking back to his own true love. She could never tame that hawk; always he had to fly, scream, and kill. As for herself, she would make a good life in Seattle. She would become the secretary of someone important —she was pretty enough and could type and write shorthand—and before long she would marry, someone to take her fishing and to parties, someone to make babies with no eagle beak and close-set killers' eyes, fair-haired babies to learn English, and then Alaska would be only a dream in the night, the dark forests, far-flung dreary muskeg, interminable snows, and awful lonesomeness.

These thoughts crossed her mind in snatches, because she was so busy shaking hands and talking excitedly with fellow passengers. The excitement took hold of the children, so that they ran wildly about, fought, showed off, and would not mind their mothers. It seemed all the more marked because of the weather, only fair for late October, if even that: a wet snow sifting down and a chill breeze, that cheechakos would call wind, out of the northeast. At ten o'clock, with not a line loosened yet, visitors still aboard, old Pike, spry as ever, ordered the serving of hot coffee and cookies. As his stewards were busy, Pike himself was called to the head of the gangplank. Vicky, standing near that plank against her will, somehow sidling up to it whenever she forgot what she was doing, heard the conversation clearly.

"Mr. Pike, a passenger named Joe Harris has not picked up his tickets."

"Yes, sir."

"At the office they told me they couldn't wait for him any longer and since I'm number one on the waiting list, they sold me his reservation."

"If that's the way it is, that's the way it is. The purser will assign you a berth."

That's the way it was, Vicky thought. She was relieved, honestly she was, to hear the news; now she could stay away from that damned gangplank and stop looking at the snow-wet dimly lighted wharf, abandoned except for dock hands. She fell into spirited conversation with a middle-aged drummer of mining machinery, Mr. Ralston, to whom she had just been introduced.

"There was a young lady named Ford aboard ship my first trip to Alaska," the man confided. "I wasn't very popular on that trip, for when almost everybody else was seasick I went around and tried to cheer them up. For a landlubber, I'm a disgustingly good sailor. The ship was the old *Victoria*."

"Ford is not an uncommon name," Vicky answered, "but the lady you speak of might have been my mother. Her first trip to Alaska was on the *Vic*."

"Mrs. Fannie Ford?"

"That's right."

"Think of that. And now I've met her daughter—it doesn't seem that long ago—twenty bloody years. The world's a small place after all."

"Alaska's a big place with a small number of people."

"What have I done with those years? Not what I hoped —but I guess as well as most. Well, my first trip was with Mrs. Ford, maybe my last is with Miss Ford. That's rounding out the story."

"Why your last trip, Mr. Ralston?"

"Because I've been offered a better territory—all of Central America. Well, I'm ready to take off. I wonder what we're waiting for?"

"I'm ready to take off too."

The crowd about her seemed the same, a short while later; actually it only looked the same and made the same noise, for it was in motion and was being divided as sheep from goats. The reason was a warning whistle—all visitors ashore.

Tall Eric came through the crowd and stood beside Vicky and spoke to her in low tones.

"Why don't you get off, Vicky?" he asked. "This is your last chance."

"If I get off, it's because I'm thrown off, bound hand and foot."

"Well, I was yust t'inking that maybe you were letting nonessentials get in the way of essentials—unimportant things interfere with important things. My son Joe—that's confidential for the present——"

"I've kept it confidential about half my life. Before I was ten years old I knew you were his father. No one could live in that village and not know it."

"I started to say that Joe can never be controlled by a woman or by anybody. He'll come and go when he pleases, when he hears some kind of call, and nobody can stop him without killing him. Maybe that's the Indian, maybe it's just the hunter. But he'd give you a good life, yust the same. It would never get stale. It would always be exciting."

"Just the same I'm not going to get off and hang around the hotel waiting for him. To hell with him."

Eric looked sorrowful and walked away. Vicky noticed the visitors saying hurried good-byes and hastening down the gangplank. Dock hands stood at the snubbing blocks ready to loosen the lines. Deck hands were waiting for Captain Locke's command to take in the plank. Vicky looked at the little French watch that Joe had sent her on her birthday. It said five minutes until 11 P.M. and the day was October 23, 1918. The sailing was quite late, but how early the hour was, really! How many more hours to pass, how many more days, how many more years?

She ran after Eric and caught him.

"Quick, get my bags out of my stateroom. If you've no time to pass them to me, send them to me?"

"You bet you, Vicky!" Eric called back over his shoulder as he ran.

The hands had hold of the gangplank as she ran down. A tall man, waiting on the dock on a long chance saw her and started up. As they squeezed past each other, she recognized the finely chiseled face as one she had seen in St. Michael once, the face of Arthur Dudley.

"Hello and good-bye," she called.

She waited a moment at the edge of the dock, her heart thrilling, and presently Eric came to the side hatch and dropped her two bags, one at a time, into the powerful arms of a Swedish halibut fisherman who had lately returned from winter fishing far down Lynn Canal and who had wandered by to see the *Sophia* sail. Vicky was thinking that her prettiest clothes, as well as her toilet things, were in the bags, so now she could dress becomingly for any enterprise she must undertake. Not that the son of a bitch didn't like her better in hair-seal shirt and pants.

She thanked the Swede and, sure of his occupation by his wind tan, his clothes, and the fine full flavor of halibut and cod he had just finished dressing, she thought to be sociable in the Alaskan fashion.

"Did you make a good catch?" she asked.

"Lots of bleatin' but little wool," the fisherman answered in that bland, humorous, wonderfully pleasant singsong of Alaskan Swedes.

Together they watched the *Sophia* stand to sea. The Swede spoke again.

"By Yiminy, she's a fine ship! She's a beautiful ship. . . . The *Princess Sophia* is a good name for her."

All this was true, Vicky thought. It was wonderfully true, even that part about the name. She knew it from something her mother had said, a long time ago, but she could not remember what it was.

Quiet came over the passengers when only scattered lights, swiftly dimming in the light snowfall, remained of Skagway. A few men, associates in his public affairs, came up to speak to Eric; and presently he went in search of two fellow passengers whom he wished to greet before going to bed, and of whom he had only caught glimpses in the crowd. The fact that both of these men, so close in his life, should be his shipmates on this voyage aroused his wonder as though it were an oddity of fate, although he knew well it was nothing of the kind, since Alaskans were forever encountering old intimates on their journeys back and forth Outside, especially when they traveled on the sourdoughs' love, the *Princess Sophia*.

One of the two was Arthur Dudley, who had come up the gangplank as Vicky was going down. Eric found him just leaving the purser's office, where his late arrival to claim a reservation of a female passenger naturally caused a little head scratching by that official, who nevertheless solved the difficulty by moving Vicky's appointed roommates to a two-berth cabin previously assigned to two miners, and switching these to the former's three-berth cabin, which Arthur could share. All were still up, of course, perfectly agreeable to the change, and the lugging of bags between the rooms was now being looked after by two stewards.

"How did you leave Ermine?" Eric asked his friend, after a cordial handshake. And Eric need not ask about Arthur's own well-being, it was so evident in his youthful face, graceful stride, and vibrant voice.

"Lovely as ever," Arthur answered quietly. "And happier than ever, I think, because of some good luck. You know we lost a baby in the second year of our marriage. A traveler brought in tonsillitis, the baby caught it, and it developed into pneumonia. Now she's five months along with another. It's begun to kick and will be good company for her while I'm away. The old Eskimo women say it's a boy. They felt her belly, asked some questions of a downright nature in regard to its conception—and spoke their decree without a dissenting vote. Having had enough formal education to set much store on informal education, of course I believe them."

"That's yust fine. Are all your villagers all right?"

"Getting along wonderfully well. And, Eric, of course you know that Stanley Hill is aboard."

"I've seen him but haven't had a chance to do more than say hello to him. He went straight to his stateroom to finish some reports he wants to deliver to the governor at Juneau."

"It was Stanley who had me make this trip. He has a project for extension of native schools clean to Demarcation Point, and we've got to go into a song and dance not only to some chiefs of government but to some big guns in Congress."

"Maybe that means we can all three travel together all the way to Washington."

"I suspected you were headed for Washington, Eric. We'll do it if we can. We've traveled together, in a way of speaking, ever since we sailed together on the old *Vic*. How many more of that memorable company are aboard?"

"I'm sure of at least one more, not counting Pike and Captain Locke. He's a representative of a mining-machinery firm: Mr. Ralston."

"Heavens, I remember him well. The fellow who wanted to play quoits when we were rolling about in the big storm on the run to Kodiak."

"I've got some other good news. Do you remember Terence O'Hara, known as Windy Willie? He wasn't our fellow passenger, but we met him at Dutch Harbor and he told us about killing a bear."

"As if I could ever forget! How many bear killings and other adventures he must have had in the last twenty years! I want to hear about every one."

"You'll hear a good many, I t'ink. He's been over to Dawson on a trading venture, and now he's bound for Seattle, and he's the same old Windy."

"Delightful!"

"Now I'm going to walk by Stanley Hill's cabin and see if there's light still under his door. I wouldn't want to turn in without a word with him."

The light was still burning, so Eric knocked. Stanley let him in, and this was the first good light in which Eric had seen him in two years, and he found him more white of poll, otherwise very little changed, and the darkness that Eric had seen in his eyes that awful night in St. Michael had never faded and could never fade as long as he lived.

"I dreamed about you, just last night," Stanley told him, after their quiet greeting. "Sophia came into the dream, and seemed to be trying to tell you something, but she couldn't make you hear. That part was confused, but later she came and took my hand and called me Dear Papa, and when I was having a hard time getting on this ship I dreamed that she helped me with my baggage. 'It's a beautiful ship,' she told me, 'and black and white.' I woke up with a very strange sensation, not knowing where I was, and I had a hard time getting back to sleep."

They parted shortly, agreeing to have breakfast together, and Eric turned in.

On the bridge Captain Locke stood quiet and alert beside Second Officer Murphy, who had the watch. He had ordered the whistle to sound at intervals, since the snowfall was somewhat heavier than at first, dimming his running lights, and he did not want to run down a fishing smack making into Skagway. He had noted that the barometer was holding steady, a pleasant fact this time of year, and the wind out of the northeast did not seem to increase. He hoped that the currents off Berner's Bay would not be heavy; sailing by dead reckoning was tricky enough in these latitudes, with the compass needle swinging far from the North Star toward the Magnetic Pole. He took bearings on Battery Point and ● thought to turn in at eight bells, then decided, without any good reason, to stick it out awhile.

He was feeling his way, at quarter speed,* into the snowy night, when a great shudder ran through the ship, her iron bones groaned, there was a grating noise that loudened for several seconds. At the first tremor his heart had sunk almost before his brain could move, and he knew he had run into something solid. Then he felt the bow rise, the ship's swift loss of headway, then its complete and stunning stillness of either sound or motion. The only sound was wave noise against her stern, the swish of the low wind, and his own muttered voice.

"Good God, I've run up on Vanderbilt Reef!"

The second mate looked at him and he looked at the mate. The silence between them seemed long; actually it hardly lasted a second before Captain Locke spoke, and truly he had hardly need to speak, so well Mate Murphy knew what his first command would be.

"Listen at the cargo ventilators one and two hatch, and see if water is coming in."

"Aye, sir."

* Note 1.

The mate departed on the run while Locke waited, a feeling of great loneliness rather than sorrow upon him. There was no use telephoning the wireless room until he knew what message he should send, an SOS, or one of not nearly such awful urgency. In a moment the mate returned.

"I can't hear any water, sir."

"Tell the carpenter to sound every bilge, starting forward."

"Aye, aye, sir."

This investigation took a little longer and still the news was good.

"No rise of water in the bilges."

"Have Mr. Goose make a chain of soundings all around the ship, and chart them."

While this was being done, Captain Locke talked to the wireless operator. It was fifteen minutes after two when the latter made contact with Carey Stubbs, night operator in Juneau. Much could happen before Juneau boats could put out and reach the scene, so the operator was told to call Chilkoot Barracks, less than thirty miles on the *Sophia*'s starboard stern, and ask the commandant to send the *Peterson*, the barracks tender under command of Captain Tidham. Locke did not use the term "scene of the wreck." There was no wreck that he knew of, only a running aground.

The Juneau operator called in vain for more than half an hour. The barracks operator was off duty, but finally a soldier passing through the hall heard the click of the instrument and aroused him. Shortly after three Locke received the message that the *Peterson* would stand to sea within forty-five minutes. Sped along by a tail wind and her powerful engine she should be in hailing distance two hours thereafter.

Well, nothing bad was going to happen within two hours, Locke consoled himself. He had never seen a ship more stanchly grounded, she did not even tremble now, the wind was no higher, the barometer did not move a point. But nothing very good would happen either. Locke would not dare reverse his engines and try to haul her off until many ships stood by.

Locke thought of other vessels he had known who had run aground. In 1910 the *Princess Mary* under veteran Captain McLeod had grounded on Sentinel Island in these very waters and stuck there thirty days, with no harm done, until tugs pulled her off. In 1914, when Captain Charles Campbell had been briefly in command, the *Sophia* herself had twice run ashore in thick weather, once on Sentinel Island, where her bow was damaged, and the second time in Johnstone Strait, when she had lost her propeller. Her crew remained aboard, warm, comfortable, and safe, while her passengers were taken off, chilled, discomfited, and seasick, subject to accidents, without need.

He did not let himself think of the *Clara Nevada* or the *Islander*, since he had a strong mind that kept reminding him that conditions had been completely different. In 1898 the first of these had slid up on Eldred Rock, slid back and went down with all hands lost. The second struck an iceberg in 1901 and sank in five minutes. The *Sophia* lay with half her length wedged in a crevice in the rock, with practically no list* and only a slight forward incline of her decks.

So he found himself writing two wireless messages, one to the Canadian Pacific agent in Juneau, to be given to the press. It read:

Ran up on Vanderbilt Reef in heavy snowstorm hour 2 October 24. Ship secure, passengers comfortable, will keep public informed.

The other message was to be forwarded to the general manager of the Canadian Pacific Company in Vancouver, B.C.

After passing Haines got off course to starboard from misjudging speed of tail wind, magnetic disturbance at Battery Point, and possible tidal currents. At quarter speed ran up on Vanderbilt Reef, ship undamaged, tightly wedged, no present danger. Please inform when can expect help.

Telephones must have been busy in Vancouver, officials wakened and speaking into them in pajamas and dressing gowns, because within an hour Carey Stubbs transmitted a reply.

Sending Princess Alice *to take off passengers. She will arrive Saturday morning, October 26. Meanwhile do what you think necessary for ship and her company, employing emergency measures if see fit.*

This was already Thursday morning, Captain Locke was thinking. Two days would pass swiftly. Alaskans were hard

* Note 2.

to scare, many of them had had previous journeys inter-
rupted by accidents more serious than this; they would eat
heartily and drink a little more than usual and have a good
time. He himself would do exactly as proposed in the wireless message—what he deemed necessary. The fact remained that he had a feeling, almost a presentiment, that a
mistake in navigation, which he had not yet confronted and
accounted for, would end his captaincy of his beautiful *Princess Sophia*. Perhaps the company would merely switch him
to another Princess ship, this as a matter of good relations
with the public, one might almost say good form. If his mis-
calculation proved a flagrant one, reflecting on his good
judgment, he might be exiled to an old hooker rounding the
Horn. In either case it would be like commanding a ghost
ship after he had died.

3

Eric had been wakened from sound sleep by the long and
violent shudder that had passed through the ironclad hull,
and by the scraping noise. It seemed that between sleep and
waking he had dreamed a long dream about Sophia and
snow; then a sponge had wiped his mind and no further
memory of it remained. He soon perceived the motionless-
ness of the vessel, the ceasing of the engines' throb, and the
deepening silence. Bells rang, but there was no hurrying of
feet, no whistle of alarm.

He got out of bed, dressed, and found his way to the
social hall. A few sourdoughs had already assembled there,
fast dressers who slept in their underwear, as Eric himself
did. They were neither jovial nor long-faced; they talked
quietly about the accident.

One man told how he had regaled himself pleasantly the
night before, gone to sleep in his far-forward stateroom, and
was only wakened by impaired circulation in his feet, these
being slightly higher than his head.

There was nothing to do, not much to be seen, until the
light cleared. A scout went out on the promenade deck and
on his return reported that the northeast wind had picked
up some and bit like a snapping turtle.

"That don't surprise me none," someone answered.
"Doesn't Skagway mean in Indian 'the cradle of the winds'?
Some such fancy title. On Lynn Canal the wind is either
blowing, has just stopped blowing, or is fixing to blow. Whoever named it a canal was weak in the head."

"October twenty-fourth," mused the gray-haired old sourdough who had been wakened by cold feet. "That's Indian summer Outside, but it's right late in the year up here in Alaska. Well, I guess Cap'n Locke knows what he's doing. I'm glad he's not one of them new skippers, with the gold braid on his sleeves stitched on last week. Cap'n Locke's gold braid is beginning to look like my old hat."

About half-past five Arthur Dudley joined the company, the men pulling aside their chairs to give him room, and at six o'clock Dr. Hill came in quietly and sat down. Neither newcomer had anything to say or questions to ask; both seemed to be studying the faces about them, faces of men better acquainted with southeastern Alaska weather than themselves. When Captain Locke entered carrying a lantern all eyes fixed on him, although unable to read anything in his grave face.

"I'll tell you gentlemen the present situation. We're stuck tight and we're not going to get off until we get some tugs. I'm hoping that the passengers needn't be taken off until the morning of the twenty-sixth, when the *Alice* is due to get here. But if I do have to take drastic measures—and that would mean a lot of getting knocked about and seasickness and the chance of accidents—there will be plenty of boats."

"That's good," Eric said, after he had waited a few seconds for someone else to speak.

"The *Peterson* from Chilkoot Barracks is already standing by. The *Elspeth*, Cap'n Jim Davis, the mail boat on the Juneau-Sitka-Skagway run, left Juneau at three forty-five, and so did the *Amy*, Captain Ed McDougal, the mine-company tender. The *Lone Fisherman*, Captain Charlie Gilbert, of the Juneau-Douglas Ferry and Navigation Company, will put to sea before seven. The *King and Winge*, Captain J. C. Readham, will leave at eleven and arrive about six this evening. The *Elsinore*, Captain Jack Harrington, and the *Elinor*—I don't know who's got her—both cannery tenders, will get away by half-past eleven. The *Cedar*, Captain John Leadbetter, is somewhere between Juneau and Ketchikan tending lights, and although she's got wireless, the Juneau operator hasn't been able to make contact. He will, though, and she's big and powerful and can buck these seas in a hurry."

"I call that rallying around," an old-timer said proudly.

"I don't think we're going to have to take off passengers," Locke went on. "But the whole crew will stand duty until this wind lets up, and I've decided to appoint a passengers' committee for seeing to the passengers' welfare, to keep them informed of developments, plan entertainments, and set good examples. I've got the list written down—Mr. Andersen, Reverend Dudley, and Dr. Hill are on it. Eric, will you be chairman?"

"Yes, sir," Eric answered, long used to accepting responsibility.

"First Officer Goose is going to take you, and any of you others who feel like climbing ladders, below to examine the hull. We've already examined it, but I'd like to have you see for yourselves."

About five of the other men went along and they had never seen a more solid-looking structure. The outer hull, called the skin, had been punctured, Goose said, but not a drop of water had come into the hold.

After this inspection Eric and Stanley Hill met on the weather-boarded deck for a private talk.

"What do you think, Eric?" Stanley asked.

"What I think won't cut any ice," Eric answered. "You see, as head of the committee I can confer with passengers but I can't confer with Cap'n Locke. I mean, I can't give him any suggestions as to what he should do. He's the captain. I'm a landlubber. He'll talk with his officers, who are sea dogs too. Whatever he decides, I'll go along and advise the passengers to do the same. At present it's purely an honorary position, without a shadow of authority."

"I hope it stays that way. Why did he appoint a committee?"

"He's an odd man, Locke, and a hardheaded man, like so many Scots. He likes to have everybody support his decisions, and when they don't he goes ahead anyway."

"Now, will you tell me what you really think is going to happen?"

"I t'ink we'll sit here till the morning of the twenty-sixth and then the passengers will be taken off by the *Alice* and proceed to Vancouver. That's the natural t'ing to t'ink. It's only two days, and while we'll probably have squalls this time of year, anything like a real gale is highly unlikely. I would say it would have to be out of the northwest to raise a really heavy sea and put this tightly wedged ship in danger. She's the pride of the company and built mighty strong."

"If a vote were taken—of course that's beyond imagination—would the passengers vote to stay with the ship or get off?"

"They'd vote overwhelmingly to leave it to the captain. If he'd put it up to them to decide—which of course he won't—I t'ink they'd vote to stay on. They love this ship. They trust her completely."

"People trusted the *Titanic* too," Stanley broke in.

"The *Titanic* had a hole torn in her side that an express train could get through. Even so, if one or two more water compartments had remained intact, she would have stayed afloat. Our inner hull is uncracked, as we saw. All she does is tremble when the seas pound against her stern. The Alaskans are used to expecting good luck—that's their state of mind—they're forever optimists, for if they were pessimists they couldn't stand it up here. They love being together and don't want to get separated in various boats and get wet and cold and sick and spend the night in some cannery bunkhouse. They all admit the possibility of us being twisted off that reef and good-bye everybody. Still, they don't think it will happen, and in that they agree with Captain Locke and with me, so they'd stick it out."

"I've got only one more question, Eric. If that unimaginable ballot were taken, would you, personally, vote to stay on or get off?"

Eric did not answer for a moment. His lips curled sorrowfully, and his curiously green eyes gazed at the blowing snow.

"For two reasons," he said, "I'd vote for all passengers, and the crew if they wished, to get off."

"What are they, if you'll tell me?"

"One is because we've children aboard. Children see life differently than we grownups. It's a terribly precious possession. They haven't found out yet what it's going to do to them, if they live long enough. I'm not t'inking about the ladies or the grown men. They can stand the gaff. But I don't want children to have to stand any gaff."

"What's the other reason?" Stanley asked quietly.

"To tell it, I'll tell you what perhaps you already know. I'm on my way to see President Wilson, with the possible outcome that I'll be appointed governor."

"Yes, I did know it. And I know what you intend to tell him—the proper, the only thing—and I don't think it will change the outcome. The accident occurred nineteen years ago. I've come to think of it as an accident that could hap-

299

pen to almost any man: there is no more precise word as far as I know, considering the frailty that God almighty saw fit to make part of us all. The President is an idealist and a practical man in one, and he is a fearless man. He'll do what he thinks is best for Alaska. Now go on and tell me the second reason you would vote to debark the passengers."

"It isn't a reason, really; there's no reasoning in it; it could be called an inkling, or superstition. Sophia told me about a dream she had. She was visited by many strange dreams, and some of them seemed to have been prophetic. Perhaps she had many when she was a little girl; perhaps they came more often up here and ran deeper. Perhaps you find yourself dreaming more than when you lived Outside. I guess it's the loneliness of the country, the soul beginning to search as soon as we fall asleep, searching for something —for someone—that will ease that loneliness. Perhaps it's only up here, in this lonely land, that the soul discovers its aloneness; maybe it fools itself in the cities and towns Outside. Stanley, I think I'm saying all this, yust now, partly to delay telling you her dream, which I'd dread telling anyone on this ship, but now I'm going to cut it out and tell you. She dreamed that I was about to be made governor, but something black and white—she couldn't see it plain—got in the way. The object disappeared and then the dream ended."

"I don't like the idea of it too well, either. Sophia was fey —meaning that she lived half in another world."

"And maybe there are three reasons, Stanley. The other involves me very deeply—to judge by what you told me that night in St. Michael, it may involve you too. This ship was named for Sophia. Captain Locke picked out the name from the names of three or four English princesses—but Sophia, our Sophia, is her real namesake. Captain Locke had never thought of this ship in any other way; it accounts mainly for his feelings about her, that whole, strong, fanatical Scotch heart given to her."

"I sensed that, when he was talking to us a while ago. That heart has received an awful blow—perhaps a mortal blow. I hope it doesn't affect his judgment."

4

Terence O'Hara, affectionately known as Windy Willie, slept until seven, ate a hearty breakfast, then joined a group of men sitting in the social hall, quiet now because everything that seemed worth saying had been said. Actually there was very little to talk about this early on Thursday morning, except that the snow had quit, and that the northeast wind had risen a little. Their faces turned to Windy expectantly and their eyes had a pleasant shine.

"You're all dressed up as though you was going to the annual ball of the Arctic Brotherhood," one of the sourdoughs remarked.

"When I got into Skagway from off the westward I had to buy a whole new outfit," Windy answered, in an absent-minded way.

"It's mighty fine." And then, after a long pause, "How did that happen, Mr. O'Hara?"

"I went to Kodiak on one of the cannery tenders out of False Pass," Windy Bill explained. "From then on I had to take the *Chelsea*, a halibut boat berthed at Ketchikan. But she had some ice left, some bait, and some room in her hold, and the signs looked good, so her cap'n asked me if I was in a hurry, and if I wasn't he thought he'd set out his lines a little eastward of Afognak village. I said sure, so the men baited the skates—those are lines coiled in piles each nearly a half a mile long, with big halibut hooks on leaders bent to the line every thirteen feet. You know how halibut boats make their sets. They bend an anchor to the end of the line, then go like hell, letting the skate uncoil and run out. Sometimes gulls dive at the bait and are caught on the hooks and are carried to the bottom."

"That's right, Willie," a former halibut fisherman remarked when the speaker paused.

"I was standing too near the chute, watching a flock of gulls. Dinged if one of those leaders didn't fly my way and catch the sleeve of my Mackinaw. Before I knew it I was jerked off the stern and on the way to Davy Jones's locker."

"Well, I'll be damned," someone said in an admiring tone.

"You wouldn't believe it but I couldn't get shed of that Mackinaw. I'm right-handed and it was my right sleeve that was caught and my arm was held out stiff by the pressure. I'd gulped in air before I hit the water, but I was going down fast, and the water was turning a queer, green color, and a shark went by me, zippo! My knife was in my right-hand pants pocket; anyway I don't think I would have had time to get it out and cut the line. I did the only thing I could do, I guess, bent my head and got the leader in my mouth and bit it like it was a piece of gristle. I've good teeth and I bit through the leader and went shooting up like a skyrocket. But dinged if I didn't break off a little piece of one tooth. Look here."

Windy drew back his lips and stuck the end of his finger in his mouth. A few close by saw that a little piece was missing from the bicuspid. Others sitting further off could not tell it but they did not come up for closer examination, for, from knowing Windy, they knew it would be needless.

"The cap'n had reversed his engine and soon picked me up," he went on. "I was awful cold, and glad to get into that warm galley. I'd put on an old shirt and pair of pants for the halibut-boat trip, and I dropped 'em overside, but my Mackinaw was new and I thought if the salt could be got out of it—washed in barely tepid water and dried in a barely warm room—it wouldn't shrink and I could wear it some more. Well, a halibut galley is hot as hell, as you all know. The deck is cold as hell. So I let it dry the best I could and brought it along. You fellows take a look at it and see if it's worth saving."

Bill headed out the door. No one spoke in his absence; everyone waited in pleasant, even excited expectation, as people wait for a rising curtain on the next act of a good play. Bill returned with the garment on his arm.

It was shapeless from having been dunked in salt water, a strand of seaweed had been wound around one button, and caught in the sleeve was a steel halibut hook, to which was fastened about twelve inches of line with a frayed end.

An old sourdough of thirty years' residence on the Kuskokwim finally broke the silence. "Bill, I guess you can fix it fit to wear again," he remarked gravely. "But I think it ought to be hung up, just as it is, in the Territorial Museum at Juneau."

"Oh, it wasn't anything. It just taught me to stay clear of those flying hooks. By the way, the captain's set made a good haul. The gurdy brought up a lot of seventy-five-pounders and one hundred-pounder, as well as a big devilfish and two dead sea gulls. I wouldn't wonder but what those extra fish will make her lead boat of the season at Ketchikan, maybe the whole fleet. And I was mighty lucky that the gurdy didn't bring up me."

"We're all lucky," said First Officer Goose, who had paused to listen to Willie's story, "to have you aboard this ship. It's luckier than if we'd all bought life insurance. With you aboard, we'll sure come through okay."

302

5

The wind was blowing hard from the northeast, but at nine that morning there came a lull noticeable to everyone. Men busied themselves on the boat deck and a lifeboat was swung out on the davits and began to lower, the passengers watching quietly, with no other sign of profound suspense unless it was written in the lines of their faces and showed in the intentness of their gaze. The action looked like the first move to take off the passengers. Perhaps Captain Locke was going to have members of his crew make other soundings. But no one entered the boat; maybe he was thinking there was no use to start debarkation until other vessels arrived, which would be soon. At ten o'clock the wind shifted to the northwest and blew harder than before. The clouds indicated it was a passing squall.

Many passengers went to the deck windows to see the *Elspeth,* the Sitka mail boat captained by Jim Davis, come up and moor at the buoy almost in stone's throw of the ship. No one cheered or waved a hand, yet the presence of the stout vessel counteracted a feeling not so much of disappointment as of letdown after the excitement of seeing the boat swing out, and was a kind of compensation for the shift and increase of the wind. Another vessel soon recognized as the *Amy,* a mine tender captained by Ed McDougal, steamed in and dropped her iron.

Shortly after noon the northwest squall passed by, the wind again shifted northeast, and Captain Davis of the *Elspeth* was seen to be lowering one of his boats. He piled into it with members of the crew and began rowing stanchly against the wind to bring him up to speak to Captain Locke. The passengers heard his voice wind-caught and streaming off and thin, yet they could catch the words.

"Are you all right, Cap'n? Do you need help?"

"We're all right," Captain Locke answered. "I see no present danger, and the wind seems to be going down. Please continue to stand by."

Jim Davis returned to his ship. Another northwest squall, no heavier than the first, broke soon afterward; yet there was good news, too—the *Anita Phillips,* a halibut-type vessel under veteran captain Jack Rowe, came up by way of Fort Retreat; the *Electo* and the *Elinor,* built to weather rough Alaskan waters, stood by; the *Elsinore* hove to and lay jogging. These waters roughened still more as the squall reached its height. Captain Baers of the *Electo* drove in close and yelled to Captain Locke. His words were few, with no unnecessary adjectives, as in a telegram; but the meaning perfectly plain.

"Can't lie here. If you want to, put passengers in life-boats, drift down-wind. We'll pick 'em up, no fear!"

"Too rough," Captain Locke bawled back. "We're all right here. Isn't the wind abating?"

"Can't tell it," Baers shouted, then he ran for shelter behind Mab Island.

There came no abatement of the wind that the passengers could note, but a splendid thing occurred before their eyes to make a splendid story. It was what Arthur Dudley would call a tragicomedy. The passengers knew it was a tragic scene, at the same time having almost unbearably comic relief introduced by Windy Willie, not in his usual role as Baron Munchausen, but in an entirely different role, somehow akin to the heartbreaking postures of Don Quixote.

On board was a Mrs. Griffin, with a babe in arms. Her eyes were dark pools of sorrow and she could not follow a conversation very well. She had had a nervous breakdown before going to Skagway to stay three months with her sister there; by some compulsion she had terminated the visit a month early and sailed on the *Sophia*.

No one knew or would ever know why the sight of the retreating vessels threw her into sudden and utter despair. Far aft on the promenade deck, almost at the stern, she rushed wailing to the rail, dropped her baby overboard, and started to leap over herself. One man caught her, another rushed to his help; together they confined her. Meanwhile the hard tail wind was sweeping along a little object wrapped in the soft, clinging comforters given to babies by doting elders, its quilted pads not yet fully water-soaked. Far forward, almost where the waves broke against the rock, Terence O'Hara, known as Windy Willie, saw the baby hurled overboard, and saw it coming his way.

He had time to straddle the rail and press his palms together in front of his face in the attitude of a fancy diver. He was a fool and he knew it; he could not swim, he had never taken a high dive in his life before. More serious than being a fool, he was out of his mind. Yet he leaped down, and the baby floated against his chest almost the same instant that a life buoy, attached to the rail by a long line, struck the water beside him. It had been thrown by a quick-moving sailor who had happened by.

With the baby tucked under his arm, Windy Willie put one arm through the life buoy, linked his hands, and was immediately hauled back to the deck, with a hearty heave ho by half a dozen enthusiastic bystanders. He was as soaking wet as though he had been hauled down to the green depths by a halibut line, but had swallowed no water, and the little that the baby had gulped was immediately expelled when it was held head downward and its back slapped. It began to bawl. Its mother, her sanity restored, came on the run and gathered it in her arms. In a moment she, her charge, and Windy were being led to warm cabins where drenched clothes could be changed for dry.

"A sadder and a wiser man" is a stock phrase in the English language, employed by millions of people who have never heard of Coleridge. It applied only too well to Terence O'Hara when finally he joined a group of old acquaintances in the social hall.

"Don't say anything about what I did, if you please," he said solemnly. "I'm glad I saved the baby, but it's changed my whole life—taken all the fun out of it. I can't make up any more stories. One true story has put them all to shame. You see, I'm Irish—we Irishmen have got to have phantasy to brighten up our lives: fairies and elves, banshees, the O'Neil, cattle stealing, landlord hating, Cuchulainn and his phantom chariot, anything that's illogical enough to fight for. We Irish starve to death on logic. Well, my phantasy has been drowned in that ice-cold water."

No one laughed at him. Eric himself brought him a drink, and he sat brooding.

Then at a nearby table Arthur Dudley spoke in low tones to Eric. He did not quite succeed in keeping tension out of his voice.

"You heard what Mate Goose said to Windy Willie this morning when Bill told us the adventure of the halibut boat. He said we were lucky to have him aboard—that Willie's luck would bring us all through all right. Well, we've lost that luck."

"I don't follow your thinking."

"It isn't thinking. It's just feeling—Eskimo at that, I'm afraid. Windy Willie isn't with us any more. He's ceased to exist. There remains a brooding Irishman named Terence O'Hara. You see, he survived his other adventures because

305

they were fictitious. Now he's had his turn at surviving a real adventure—not the *Sophia* going on the reef but fishing a baby out of those rushing seas. He was entitled to survive one real adventure, after all those he invented for the delight of his fellow humans. Now he's rounded out his life and the book's closed."

"Arthur, I didn't know you had that streak of mysticism. I have it—all of us squareheads do—otherwise we couldn't have invented Odin, god of war and wisdom, lord of Valhalla until *Götterdämmerung*. But I considered you the most completely sane man I ever met."

Arthur laughed, his eyes shiny bright with mirth.

6

The mettle of the passengers was proved about half-past nine, when all the lights aboard suddenly went out. No water had seeped in to drown a cable; merely one of the two generators had blown a gasket. But the electricians had to wait until steam cleared out of the room before they could turn on the other generator. All eyes were darkened as with a foretaste of death until lanterns were brought to the social hall, and in this period the people sat quietly, talked calmly to one another, and sometimes laughter rose from some dim group. In less than an hour the lights flashed on as suddenly as they had vanished, as life flashes on again in the mind of someone who, lying stricken and unconscious, revives and knows himself. The still-lighted lanterns looked queer and dim.

Mothers traveling with their children went to their staterooms, but almost all the men and unencumbered women and the few youths obeyed an instinct to hang together in the social hall. So it happened that by far the greater part of the ship's company heard the good news announced by Mate Goose and passed by word of mouth among the stewards, deck hands, and black gang—that the U.S. lighthouse tender *Cedar*, whose master was John Leadbetter, had reached the scene. She was equipped with wireless, and although the wind was too heavy for her to stand by, she would lie behind Lincoln Island and be in constant communication with the *Sophia*. Thus she, the *Peterson*, the *King and Winge*, the *Lone Fisherman*, the *Elinor*, the *Elsinore*, the *Elspeth*, the *Anita Phillips*, and the *Electo* lay close at hand. The *Amy*, knowing of this assembly, was heading back to Juneau.

Another who did not seek sleep was Captain Locke. He found that his mind would move in only one channel. When it came to that channel's end it would dart back to the beginning and repeat the journey. It covered every command that Captain Locke had given in the time between his ship's departure from Skagway and its grounding on Vanderbilt Reef.

Two facts were indisputable—that the *Sophia* was his ship, his alone in a way that many other captains could not understand, that he himself could hardly understand, and that he had taken her off her course. This last was the only mistake that he would recognize, all his decisions since were its logical consequence, but that mistake had been a terrible one. He was a terribly proud and solitary man. Since he had won his captaincy he had listened to the opinions of his first mate and his chief engineer, and his mind had almost always been made up before he talked to them, and always he had obeyed its dicta. With the stiff wind and running sea behind him he had known he was a little ahead of his normal running time when he passed Haines; he had been long aware of compass disturbance at Battery Point; but he had thought he had compensated for both of those conditions. His falling away to starboard must have occurred when the wind was on her port quarter while she was crossing the entrance to Berners Bay. He wondered if any of his officers had suspected the deflection—or even one of the old sea dogs, well acquainted with Lynn Canal, among his passengers. If so, they had not said a word of warning. They knew him too well, he thought. But in truth they did not know him at all. No one did.

He made a halfhearted attempt to review his decision not to debark the passengers when the chance had offered early this morning, and again shortly after noon, only to cling stubbornly to his belief in its rightness. His beautiful, proud ship was in no real danger. She had weathered every squall without a shudder. Her passengers remained warm and comfortable, many of them having a fine time in the social hall; they were not spread about in rolling, pitching halibut boats or spending a dreary night at Tee Harbor cannery. His mistake was bad enough already without multiplying its consequences by debarking passengers on this rough, cold sea. He did not give a damn about pleasing her owners in Vancouver; it was not for their sake that he had acted as he did;

307

as always before, he had moved by his own mind. What captain worth his stripes did otherwise?

He read a wireless message from the *Princess Alice*. She was well on her way now, with a full head of steam, and would be standing by to pick up the boatloads of passengers early on the morning of the twenty-sixth. They would be in Vancouver forty-eight hours later, having had an experience of which to write home—and able to say that there was no ship on the Seven Seas, regardless of tonnage, to beat the *Princess Sophia*. He and the crew would remain comfortably aboard until tugs hauled her off the reef on the full-moon tide, and then, practically undamaged, she could sail for Vancouver under her own steam. He could make a good guess at what would happen thereafter. Among the various likelihoods he had no favorite.

He left instructions with the wireless operator and the watch, then went to bed and to sleep. When he was called at six he hardly heard the steward's voice, he was listening so intently to the sound of the wind. Blowing through his dreams, it had seemed to decrease. Still high, it was not as tempestuous as when he had gone to bed. Surely the storm was passing.

When the dim dawn spread, just before eight, the wind and seas had abated sharply. The passengers knew it as well as he; some of them were thinking he might begin launching lifeboats, turning their eyes frequently to the bridge, but they did not know their man. Another squall might break between now and the arrival of the *Alice;* if so, she—beautiful she—would weather it as she had weathered the others. Anyway he expected an end to the nasty weather; he felt it in his bones. Although the glass had not risen, it had not fallen either. The wind was back in the northeast where it belonged. The gulls shrieking about the stern, waiting for breakfast scraps, soaring and gliding, made a pretty sight. The *Sophia* remained queen of the waves.

Just before noon the gulls gathered in a close flock and climbed very high, uttering a different cry than before, until they were invisible in suddenly lowering cloud. Almost before Captain Locke could believe his eyes the noonday light grew dim. He glanced at the glass, then stared at it, and only Mate Goose saw receding color in his dour face. In a matter of minutes it had dropped from 29.90 to 29.70. The sea seethed, and a long wolf howl of wind sounded, not in the northeast but the northwest. A moment later it was picking up the crests of the waves and hurling them down its blast.

From his bridge Captain Locke saw ships emerging from behind Lincoln Island; many of the passengers saw them, too, and perhaps thought they were coming alongside. Locke was not deceived for a moment. They could no longer lay behind Lincoln Island and were making for the lee of Mab Island. He could call them now until he was hoarse, but they could not come.

He stopped and put his hand on a brass rail. It seemed that his heart stopped beating as he turned himself into a kind of instrument as delicate as a seismograph or a splinter of whalebone that an Eskimo sticks into sea ice to see if it is breaking up far off. The metal thrilled slightly as the waves struck. There was not a tremor. The *Sophia* stood like the rock itself." *

7

Standing at a window, Eric watched the running seas. The waves rose higher with every surge, for this was the time of their most rapid rise, immediately following the breaking of a gale. Old sailors would say they were "hurrying to catch up." In due time, unless the gale itself increased, they would vary in height in a kind of rhythm with no known law; the old belief that the highest wave in the range was the seventh had been long dismissed as superstition. Actually those driven by violent gusts rolled highest, except for so-called "freak waves" with no known cause, and a steady wind drove surges of almost the same height. Those that smote the stern of the *Sophia* broke and dashed high. On both sides they rushed to break on the reef. Eric watched their rise and fall, the billows and their hollows and the black blown spume, as if gazing down from a rock. The ship did not rise with them in the least degree, did not even stir; otherwise there would be no time for him to watch them in deep thought.

That thinking brought him to certain conclusions—accepted calmly enough, since they did not seem to be open to question—but to only one great realization, which was his own leadership. Among the passengers he was the leader; he knew it as well as they. This leadership had been given him through authorizations and from sources he did not try to understand, and he decided to employ it.

* Note 3.

The thought came to him to speak to Stanley Hill and perhaps to Arthur Dudley before he moved. He dismissed it and went straightway to the bridge.

"Cap'n Locke, I would like to have your permission to call a meeting of the passengers in the social hall."

"Well, I think that's a good idea," Locke answered affably, although his eyes looked like dull glass. "And I don't know anyone who could handle it better."

"I want to do what I can for their morale. I'm not going to tell any lies, although there will be some lying by mothers to their children, but those will be white lies. I would like to help save all of them the worst—according to my opinion of what would be the worst. I would like to help bring out the best that's in them, and there's a mighty lot of that."

Captain Locke's dimmed eyes lighted briefly. "That would meet with my wishes. Except for my direct orders to the contrary—and I have none to give now—you have carte blanche."

Eric thanked him, went to the dining room, and spoke to Pike. The old man stood with his back straight, his head high. A wonderful old man, Eric was thinking, tough, vital, intelligent, brave.

"I don't think it's necessary to ask this, but I will," Eric said. "Have you any weaklings on your staff?"

"No, sir, not one."

"Are there any in the crew that you know of?"

"If there had been, Cap'n would have got shed of 'em long before now."

"All right. What can you do in the way of a bang-up dinner? The best your pantries can afford."

"I was already figuring on that. I hope the old brig will last long enough for the people to eat it. I've got the best Chicago steaks, and plenty of barren-ground caribou shipped in from Whitehorse. I've got canvasback ducks and mallards. Plenty of vegetables, of course, and a good rich soup. For dessert——"

"How about champagne?"

"Plenty for everybody, free."

"If you see that any fellow's getting drunk, please tell the stewards to stop serving him. I don't want the passengers to have to contend with drunks, or the children to see any. Be sure and tell your barman that, too. He'll know the signs and he can take it from me to refuse service, and I've talked to the captain. I don't think the occasion will arise, after we've all met in the social hall. Now please ask the stewards to assemble the people there and have one of them stand at the door and ring a bell."

"Yes, sir."

"One thing more. Be ready to give a children's party immediately after dinner. Games, prizes, ice cream and cake, if they can hold it, anything you can think of. I want this to be a great day to remember—*always*."

Pike's eyes slowly filled with tears. "So do I, Eric. So do I."

People were already gathering in the social hall; the seats filled, many stood about the walls. There was a buzz and murmur of talk, no different than usual, until Eric walked to the head of the room, then it died away. His manner was easy, yet instinct with dignity.

"Shipmates," he began. "I'm going to ask the mothers here to take their children into the dining saloon. Head Steward Pike is planning a party for them this afternoon, and I think he wants their advice as to what to provide for refreshments. Youngsters as old as thirteen will be needed to referee the games and such as that. Those past thirteen are perfectly welcome to remain here with us oldsters, to sit in with us at a discussion."

Eric had chosen thirteen as the age separating childhood from what might be called youth through a brief, positive thought process. He remembered himself at thirteen: he had been eager to cope and had coped with his parents' financial and social problems. He remembered reading of a frontier Indian fighter and captain in the War of 1812 who had refused to enlist any boys under twelve, on the ground that they were a "leetle" too green.

Mothers with younger children moved toward the door. He had been thinking that there were very few aboard; now he was appalled at what a long line they made. Still, his plans had dealt with them as well as his brain could work.

"Will someone shut that door?" he asked, when the file had passed through. He took one long, careful glance at those who remained. The youngest was a grave-faced stripling of fifteen. There were far more men than women; and he did not see a single weak face. The woman who had attempted to kill her baby and herself was not in the audience.

"Now we have to face the music," he said. "We have to face it with the same strength of heart and strength of purpose with which we faced the flag, when at numerous affairs in the last two years the musicians played 'The Star-Spangled Banner' and we all stood up. Everyone here knows the desperateness of our situation. This northwest gale is going to increase in the next few hours, in the way of northwest gales. It's not a passing squall, the barometer is still falling; everyone who knows Alaska weather knows that a gale that started as this one did takes many hours to, blow out. Our bow is wedged in the reef, our stern is afloat. The seas will rise and exert more power. The very solidness with which she is stuck saved her from any damage in those squalls. But if and when the time comes that she can't take any more, it will make for sudden and complete disaster. That's what I t'ink. If any experienced sailor disagrees with this, I ask him to speak up."

A captain of the sea of which there was no stancher kind, a Norwegian ex-skipper of a halibut boat, shook his head at Eric's glance and gazed at the floor. A mate of a cannery tender from the westward folded his arms. A few people gazed about them, hoping, it seemed, for someone to dissent, but no one did.

"Some here, unused to sea, may be asking themselves why those boats don't come to our help," Eric went on. "The reason is this: they can't. They can't possibly get alongside in this weat'er. With all the power of their engines they can't stand against the wind. This is floundering weat'er."

"I wish to ask a question," a young woman said in a steady voice.

"Yes, ma'am."

"Mr. Andersen, how long do you think it will be before —well, I'll put it just as plain as you have. How long have we to live?"

"I t'ink that except for a miracle, all our lives, every one on this ship, will end sometime this afternoon."

"Then why aren't we wearing life belts?" a young man asked.

"You can, if you like. I'm not going to, because they're uncomfortable and if a child asked me what it was for, I couldn't answer, and he'd be frightened. I couldn't tell him the truth either, but I can tell you the truth, and there is no man here who has followed the sea that won't affirm it. No life belt is any good in waters like those, beating against the reef. It might delay the certain end for a few seconds

—terrible seconds that I don't want to endure myself or have any shipmate endure. When the time comes I want it to get over wit' quick and I promise you it will be quick if you don't wear life jackets. The most powerful swimmer in the world could not live one moment in those seas. I predict that the suffering will last only a few seconds, we'll hardly know what hit us. Again I ask any seafarer in this room to refute what I say if it isn't true."

One man rose from a chair that a child had vacated.

"I'll say this, Eric. What you say is perfectly true if this ship breaks in two, as I think it will, the first time the seas raise her off the reef and she hits again. But she might not be wedged as tight as we think, in that case there would be a lot of pounding, which God forbid."

"Henry, are you going to put on a life jacket?"

"Hell, no."

"You speak so calmly, all of you," a woman cried. "Isn't there anything——"

A man from Juneau whom Eric knew slightly, a respected, middle-aged businessman, rose to his feet, braced himself, and spoke.

"Mr. Andersen, you said 'except for a miracle'? Why don't we pray for a miracle? There are two hundred of us here. Surely God will hear our voices. Among us is a minister, Reverend Dudley. I ask him to lead us in prayer."

"Arthur, you heard the gentleman's request," Eric said.

Arthur had been standing against the wall; now he walked forward and posted himself beside Eric.

"I have to make a brief explanation," he began, not in the sonorous voice that had once filled the nave of a small, beautiful church far away, many years ago. It had been roughened by strong Arctic winds and strengthened by deep living. "I am not a regular minister in that I am no longer affiliated with any Church—I guess I'm what you would call a free-lance minister. Instead of that, I call myself a teacher, and whether or not I teach the truth or part of the truth God only—God alone knows. My friend, I don't find it in my conscience to ask for a miracle. God passed no miracle when the *Lusitania* was torpedoed, when Mount Pelée erupted, when the Iroquois Theatre caught fire, when uncounted numbers lay dying this year with flu. Those dead were people just like us, no better or worse, and as important to Him. You may ask for a miracle—any of you. But I cannot lead you in prayer except in one prayer.

313

I do not know what is in your souls, for every soul is solitary, related to God in some way that no one else knows. If you will bow your heads I will obey an injunction and repeat the Lord's Prayer, the wisest, simplest, the most humble and the most proud of any prayer I know."

8

When Arthur returned to his place the throng stayed so still that it seemed they were listening to the storm. Because of the stout construction of the hall, with built-in ports and doors, it was almost as impervious to sound as to wind and cold. The crash of waters and the long howls of the wind came through as a muffled, undulating uproar, and the people could hardly imagine its stunning impact on ship officers and men who ventured on the boat deck. Only sailors know that sound, and can recall its every occasion.

"I haven't much more to say or hardly know how to say it," Eric went on, putting just enough force into his voice to be heard by everyone. "The gist of it is this. Let nobody frighten the children. I ask you not to show them any long faces; I ask you to remember you are Alaskans, from the Great Country, or you have just visited the Great Country and let its bigness take hold of you and make you keep your chins up. Many of us are old friends. Very few are newcomers among us. Pike is going to give us a fine dinner. After that there's going to be a children's party. After that, why not a song fest? Whatever happens to one of us, will happen to us all. We'll be together to the last, and that's a fine t'ing."

He sat down, and someone started clapping, and then everybody clapped, half hysterically perhaps, and the men yelled.

At that moment there came into being a mood that did not pass away. That outburst of emotion struck the key of the melody that did not cease throughout all the affairs of the afternoon, and for all that the people knew—for how could they or anyone know what hereafter means?—might never cease. It was the melody of life being greatly lived over the abyss of death, which position is the law of life. Its essence was fraternity and mirth, the prize that is given the valiant.

Dinner was a prodigious meal, cooked, as Pike remarked with due modesty to Eric, to a queen's taste. Champagne bubbled in the glasses, toasts were drunk; if the laughter

314

was too loud for a proper dinner party—this was a highly improper dinner party from one point of view; there ought to be weeping and wailing and praying, not stuffing and joke cracking—that laughter was still real, far from an empty show. Four men and one woman bolted their food in order to go to their staterooms and get musical instruments. When they returned, with flushed faces, Eric spoke quietly to their leader, asking that at first their orchestra play military and circus pieces, not old songs, for the song fest should not start for a while yet, lest the singers run out of familiar songs and breath. Now and then a long shudder passed through the ship, rattling the dishes. These came at shorter intervals as the meal drew to its close, but no one appeared to notice them. They did not interrupt the buoyant conversation, the musicians never missed a note.

Every woman and child and most of the striplings stayed for the party Pike had planned and now gave in his best manner. The fathers of the children lingered too, to be near them in case of some sudden happening. Unattached men, most of them old sourdoughs, went into the social hall. Here, for one moment, they stood in danger of becoming sober, the champagne they had drunk and their great geniality dying out, but a gold rushee of '98, who had gone up the Kuskokwim and had loved it there and stayed there ever since, saved the day. His name was Jim Parker. He was a somewhat dissolute old man, with a big nose and very bright eyes and distinguished-looking white hair.

Standing forth where his voice would carry well, he drew everyone's attention.

"Do you boys know the definition of a sourdough?" he shouted.

Almost everyone here knew a half-dozen definitions, but in respect to Jim Parker they kept silent or shook their heads.

"Well, I'll tell you. Everyone who can qualify, raise his hand. To be a real sourdough, you've got to kill a b'ar, take a pee in the Yukon River, and hump a squaw."

All except a few cheechakos and one old-timer, Arthur Dudley, raised hands.

"Excuse me, Reverend," Jim Parker said, in quite real apology. "I just didn't notice you standing there. I hadn't ought to have said that."

"That's all right," Arthur answered. "I couldn't hold up my hand because I've never killed a b'ar."

The men roared, a few clapped him on the back, three took turns in shaking his hand. They began to tell stories, not the smoking-room kind, but true stories or great myths of the North such as Eric had told Sophia on the deck of the old *Vic*. None were too long-drawn-out; their narrators wanted others with good stories to have their turn. Shortly before four the party attenders returned from the dining hall and the musicians drew chairs together close to the piano. Their leader looked at Eric. He nodded in reply.

The first of the songs was "Over There," which everybody knew, one of the most singable of all the songs that triumphed over war. The next was, "It's a Long Way to Tipperary," and before it was done the whole throng was singing, and stewards and deck hands who had nothing to do rushed to join them. "K-k-k-katy, Beautiful Katy," proved a great hit, and so did "Show Me the Way to Go Home," far from a war song, almost a folk song now, and there was a terrific emphasis put on the line "Over land or sea or foam." Various passengers started favorites, to which the orchestra caught on.

"Oh, How I Hate To Get Up in the Morning," was sung with great vim, and the bugler would surely be murdered if the roaring forth of that line was an augury. No one, Dr. Hill noted with relief, started "A Baby's Prayer at Twilight," and the sourdoughs eschewed "Mademoiselle from Armentières" because of the ladies present. They did extremely well with the easy tune and hard words of "Madelon."

The singers had begun on Irving Berlin's great hits when Eric signaled to Arthur and Dr. Hill, and led the way around the throng and through the entry to the foredeck. He knew by the feel of the ship that her stern compartments were flooding and putting a great strain on her hull. Probably the horses stowed in the hold amidships plunged and screamed unheard, and perhaps had fallen and drowned. The wireless operator would be still sitting at his key, tapping out such messages as the old man ordered. Eric led his two friends to the enclosed deck.

Gazing through storm windows, they beheld the sea in wildest turmoil, beating against the reef. Arthur, who dearly loved the Bible, thought upon the division of the land from the water as told in Scripture, and of how also the water must have been divided from the air, but this last division did not hold this day of tempest, and the sea and the air seemed one. The uproar was appalling. Arthur had never heard its like, the experience coming late in his life—late indeed, he thought—yet he was glad he had listened to it for some good of his soul that he did not know and that he wondered if he would ever know.

The three men returned to the entry. Now they could hear through the thick door the louder outbursts of song, which dimmed away when the wind screamed.

"Aren't you COMING back to old New HAMPSHIRE,
Molly?
Aren't you COMING back to see us all AGAIN?
The folks say you won't come back and you
won't come back, and you won't come back,
But SOMETHING seems to TELL me that you LOVE
me . . ."

Then Eric was shouting to his two friends, employing an economy of words to save his breath.

"Seas still rising."

"How soon?" Stanley Hill shouted in reply.

"Real soon. She's leaking bad. Do you feel her slip?"

"Yes."

"Listen to the singing," Arthur shouted.

"I was only dreaming, dreaming,
Blow the smoke away . . ."

Just then a great light broke in Arthur's mind, for he was a man of great heart and spirit, and he shouted something that astonished himself as much as the others.

"They're not lonely!"

"By God, they're not!" Eric answered.

"The loneliness all gone, never to return."

"The last communion," Stanley yelled. "The great communion. Perhaps the only real communion."

"I don't know," Eric answered.

"Will you be glad to go, Eric?" Stanley asked, feeling queer over putting so much breath in such an intimate question.

"Yes, I want to be with Sophia. You, Stanley?"

"Ever since that day."

"You, Arthur?"

"I love life. I can laugh and weep, not bottle it up. Wanted to see baby. Maybe another Apache Joe. But I'll go

317

with you fellows." And Arthur laughed over the certainty of that last.

> "There's a LONG, LONG TRAIL a-winding,
> Into the land of my DREAMS,
> Where the nightingale is singing,
> And a white moon beams . . ."

"Most of them have never heard a nightingale," Arthur yelled.

"Have you, Arthur?"

"In England."

"I listened to mockingbirds," Stanley bawled. "Almost as sweet."

"Eric, did you ever hear one?" Arthur shouted.

"No. Heard trumpeter swans."

> "The SUN SHINES BRIGHT on my old Kentucky home,
> 'Tis summer, the darkies are gay . . ."

"That's a long gust, the hardest yet," Stanley roared, after a long silence, trying to be heard above the blast.

> "'Way down . . . Swanee Ribber,
> Far, far away,
> Dere's where . . . turning ebber:
> Dere's where de old folks stay."

"She's lifting, isn't she?" Stanley cried.

"Yes. She'll hit now," Eric shouted in answer.

> "All the world . . . sad and dreary
> EVERYWHERE I ROAM!
> Oh, darkies . . . grows weary,
> Far from de old folks . . ."

The great wave receded and the ship struck. That single blow was her deathblow. There followed prodigious sound, some of its components Eric knew, cool and deep within his brain—the tearing of steel housing, decks ripping wide open, bulkheads parting, rivets sheering off. Amid the cataclysm, when sound seemed to cease because the brain could no longer register it, Eric saw a forward mast tilt sideways. The ship was literally breaking in two parts between the reef and the sea, but the keel and what remained of her double bottom held them both in what seemed a last, desperate clutch. In the few seconds more that Eric's brain lived, her bow remained on the rock, listing and elevated only slightly, while her stern hung steeply down, like the end of a broken stick. This part was swinging wide.

Then, with merciful swiftness as time is measured, yet with what might seem brutal leisure to the human souls still suspended in that interval between life and death, the sea completed the destruction of its once proud mistress, who perhaps had never been more than its toy, to be admired, then torn to pieces in one frantic tantrum. It rushed into her thousand rents, flooded her smashed rooms. What had been her stern rolled over and went down, her bow toppled off the reef, and then nothing was left but the gale-driven sea breaking against the rock, its wild sound that no one heard, the blown spume that no one saw, its fury and its violence that found nothing to vent themselves on except a part of a mast thrusting up as though to mark a grave.

Thus passed away the *Princess Sophia*, pride of the fleet, with all her company of three hundred and forty-three, a tragic portion of the brain and sinew of the Northland. The entry to be written in the logs of a hundred big and little vessels gave the time as hour 17 of Friday, October 25, 1918. At hour 8 of the twenty-sixth, at daybreak, when the worst of the gale had subsided, the *Cedar*, the *Elspeth*, the *Anita Phillips*, and the *Electo* were able to emerge from the shelter of Mab Island and steam to the scene of the wreck, and from there the *Cedar* sent wireless messages which made no lasting impression on a world whose eyes were fixed on the accelerating vast event of a crumbling war. But the last four words of her final message stopped every Alaskan heart:

"There are no survivors."

In the crowd about the wireless office that had waited for those last words, the implacable verdict, stood a young woman whose coloring had been caught from the sunrise hues of the upper river, and a young man of Indian darkness. He had been taught to reveal no emotion, and his face looked like stone; her face was wet with tears. But this difference was not a barrier any longer, there were no barriers that the gale had not blown down, and they stood close. Their hands met and clasped and pressed hard.

NOTES REGARDING THE *PRINCESS SOPHIA*

NOTE 1 (page 293). In a letter that was found written by a passenger and later published, the writer stated that the *Sophia* was at full speed when she struck the reef. It is unlikely that a passenger would be informed on this matter. Various mariners have said that had she struck at full speed, her bottom would have been torn out and she would have floundered at once.

NOTE 2 (page 295). Newspaper accounts speak of a heavy list of the vessel, but a clear photograph of the ship on the reef, taken on one of the boats standing by, shows the bow raised but practically no list.

NOTE 3 (page 309). One of Captain Locke's wireless messages reads, "Ship pounded." This is the mariner's expression meaning pounded by waves. About midnight of October 24, what seems a strangely contradictory message was received from him. The first sentence reads, "Ship sitting firmly on reef." Later in the message is the wording, "Ship pounding heavily." The latter expression would mean that the vessel was rising with the waves and pounding the reef. If so, Captain Locke would have disembarked his passengers the following morning at whatever risk; actually the vessel would not have lived that long. Thus this downright contradiction can only be explained as a slight error in the transmittal of the message. Captain Locke meant to say, "Ship pounded heavily," not, "Ship pounding heavily." In a later message he wirelessed, "Passengers normal." This would be unthinkable if the ship had been pounding. Every skipper knows that there is only one command to be given when his vessel is caught on a reef and pounding. That command is, "Abandon ship."